Wild Card

A SPICY SPORTS ROM COM

STACI HART

Wild Card

A SPICY SPORTS ROM COM

STACI HART

*To those who thought
their dreams were lost:*

*It's never too late
for a comeback.*

1
good luck

JESSA

I WAS PROBABLY ABOUT to get murdered.

When I stepped out of the taxi and into the soupy humidity, I looked down the gravel lane and confirmed my suspicion that murder was imminent. Or at the very least, abduction. Beyond the metal bar blocking the way, the dusty drive disappeared into a thick and endless forest, and as the driver removed my bags from the trunk, I stared into the dense tree line, wondering if anyone lived close enough to hear me if I screamed.

I'd certainly need different shoes if I was to run from a serial killer.

"You're absolutely certain you can't take me up the drive?" I asked, still eyeing the mouth of the forest.

"Sign says no tresspassin', and you don't happen to have a key to that gate, do you?" he asked in a big-voweled Tennessee accent. When I shook my head, he added, "Well, I reckon you're all right, since you're invited and all. I'd just rather not get shot at today if it's all right by you."

"Shot?"

He snorted a laugh. "Well, yeah. Everybody 'round here

1

has a shotgun by the door for such occasions. Guess they don't have a lot of that in jolly old England, do they?"

"They do not," I answered. My words were flat and stuffy next to his melodic lilt. "You're not giving me much confidence, I'm afraid."

"Don't worry. They'll give you a chance to tell 'em who you are before they shoot."

My head whipped around to find him stifling a smile.

I gave him a look. "I believed you, you know."

"If you hadn't, it wouldna been funny." When I sighed, he patted my shoulder. "Don't worry, ma'am. Just head on down there—I'm sure it's not too far."

I took a breath and starched my spine, gripping my suitcase and overnight bag. "All right, then. Off I go."

"Want me to wait a minute? Just in case?"

Another sigh, this one melting into relief. "Would you?"

"Sure. I'll listen out for gunshots," he said, leaning against the side of his taxi with a sardonic smile on his face.

"A true gentleman."

"Good luck."

I offered him a tilted smile of my own. "Thank you. I'll take all the luck I can get."

And up the path to homicide I went.

When I say I'd been anticipating my best friend's wedding for a decade, it was no exaggeration. They'd met when we were all at Oxford, and within two dates, Cass had declared she would marry Davis, and we'd been waiting ten years for it to come to fruition. It was a knack of hers, telling the future. She followed her gut, which was decidedly psychic, and could be trusted under any circumstance.

You see, Cass was my roommate, and Davis I knew through my childhood crush, Henry—they'd gone to Eton together. My family and Henry's were the best of friends, and as such, we'd spent nearly every holiday together since we were born.

As Cass predicted, here we were in her hometown for their wedding where I was the maid of honor, Henry was the best man, and we were both single.

Everyone knew what *that* meant.

My childhood crush and I were finally going to happen.

That thought fueled my cheerful smile, even though the probability of breaking an ankle on the uneven road was astronomic. To get around the gate, I had to venture into a ditch of knee-high grass. By the time I rounded the other side, I was in a full sweat and regretting my decision to wear heels and trousers. Cass had told me about Tennessee loads of times, but it'd become clear the information I possessed wasn't enough to prepare me for the oppressive heat or wild nature walling me in as I hobbled up the drive like a newborn giraffe.

I was a mess, really. Sweat rolled down the valley of my spine and raced down the length of my legs. Slid down my neck and into my hair, which was regrettably loose and draped over my shoulders, sticking to my skin in branches. If I hadn't been exerting all my energy wrestling my suitcase, I'd have been worried about my appearance, which must have edged monstrous. But as it stood—or rolled—all I wanted was to reach the end of the never-ending lane where I could abandon the fight.

But then I rounded another bend and stopped to appreciate the view.

The woods opened up to a lush, green meadow surrounded by ancient trees, and in the center stood a little white cottage with black shutters. It had all the charm of a quintessential Southern home, with a wrap-around porch, a peaked roof, and a little room up top that I imagined had slanted walls to match.

If that wasn't enough to gaze upon, parked in front of the house was a vintage truck with the bonnet up and a man half inside.

3

Man. The word wasn't enough to describe the shirtless beast hinged over the truck's engine. He was mounds of hard flesh, muscles bunching and coiling as he twisted something inside. His tan skin was smudged with grease where he'd fought off mosquitoes, keeping them from a feast.

I couldn't say that I blamed them.

On his narrow waist hung a pair of worn jeans, his shirt tucked in the back pocket. In profile, I assessed the back of him with appreciation, the lines of his powerful backside and thighs telling a tale of strength swathed in denim. A lock of thick, dark hair slipped into his face, and with a gargantuan, greasy hand, he raked the wayward thatch of hair back into place only for it to slip loose again.

A beast if I ever saw one, shining with sweat and streaked with filth. They didn't make men like this where I came from. In fact, I couldn't recall ever seeing someone so utterly masculine in my life. The men I knew wouldn't—and thus *couldn't*—fix a broken lightbulb, never mind a motor. *What else can his hands do?* I wondered absently, so distracted by the thought, I failed to notice him notice me.

"You lost?" he asked, straightening up and turning to face me as he wiped off his hands.

The view from the front was even better than the profile. The discs of his pecs shifted as he wiped his hands on a red rag, the rolling curves of his shoulders and arms bunching and hardening with the motion. My gaze caught on that deep, inviting valley that angled down from his hips and disappeared into his jeans, and a fat bead of sweat snaked its way down my chest at the sight. But his face was the best part of all, touched with mischief and promises. His jaw was sharp and square, the line hardened by the shadow of a short, unkempt beard. And in the middle was a crooked smile that I was positive could inspire an immaculate conception on sight.

I snapped to, putting on a smile and blaming my momentary madness on jet lag and the heat.

"I might be," I said, dragging my suitcase noisily beside me. "Lost, that is."

"With shoes like that, you've gotta be." He strode to meet me, his long legs eating up the space between us. "Here, lemme get that for you."

"Thank you. But I think there might have been some mistake—I'm in Cass Winfield's wedding. Do you know her?"

"I oughtta. She's my cousin." That smile of his again, his eyes bottle green. "Remy Winfield. I'd shake your hand, but . . ." He held up a huge hand and wiggled his dirty fingers.

"It's a pleasure to meet you. I'm Jessa."

"So polite. Don't y'all say, *How do you do*?"

"Sometimes. Perhaps I should have opted for *Howdy* instead?"

A chuckle as we approached the house. The closer we got, the more I noticed disrepair. Peeling paint and cracked wood, a sagging roof over the patio, and poorly installed windows. The sudden and inexplicable urge to take care of it flared in my chest.

"Hang on," he said, setting my bag on the porch with a thunk. "You're that princess, aren't you?"

My brow quirked. "Princess?"

Remy snapped his fingers. "That's right. You're Cass's bestie, the English princess."

"I'm no princess, I'm afraid."

He leaned against the porch rail, folding his arms across his chest. "Hang on—what's the next one down? A duchess?"

"I'm not a—"

"I like duchess. Makes me think of those fancy white cats in the cat food commercials, eatin' dinner from a crystal bowl. Suits you."

I tried not to huff. I truly did. "I'm not royalty, and my father is a marquess, not a duke."

"So what does that make you?"

My cheeks flushed in revolt. I paused, not wanting to say —a joke at my expense seemed inevitable—but I had no choice in the matter. "A lady."

He laughed, flashing movie star teeth. "Lady Jessa. Doesn't quite sound right. Too . . ." He waved his hand in a circle. "Common?"

"It's actually Lady *Jessamine*, but only my parents call me by my full name."

He considered it for a moment. "Nah. Think I'll call you Duchess."

"But I'm not a—"

"So what I don't understand is what you're doin' at my place. Some guy named Jeremy is supposed to stay with me."

Another huff that I schooled into a sigh, and I gave up my argument for the sake of moving on. "I'm not sure. I was given this address by the aunt who assigned everyone rooms."

"Julie."

"Yes, that's right. But I thought I was staying with Cass's aunt Linda, not . . ." *A bull rider.*

One of his brows arched when I didn't finish, but he didn't comment. "Linda's my mom, but she doesn't live here. Must have been a mix-up. Don't worry—we'll get it sorted out. I mean, unless you *want* to stay here." He gave me a smirk so salacious, something shivered deep in my belly at the sight. "I think I could be accommodating. Never hooked up with a duchess before."

The shiver turned to ash. *What an unmitigated arse. A very hot, unmitigated arse.* "As lovely as that sounds, I think I'll pass."

He shrugged his massive shoulders and pushed off the rail. "Suit yourself. Come on in. Just need to shower off.

6

Mama'd never let me hear the end of it if I showed up like this. 'Specially with a duchess present." Remy pulled open the screen door and let it close behind him with a crack of wood against the threshold. "Make yourself at home," he said over his shoulder.

I blinked at the screen, unsure what to do. He'd invited me to follow him—barely—but I found myself concerned with what I'd find inside. Furniture made out of antlers, perhaps. Dead animals with lifeless eyes on the walls. Or a different sort of animal—the half-naked male who'd just propositioned me.

None of it sounded enticing, not by admittance, at least. But I needed to change my shoes to something more appropriate, and getting on my knees to rummage in my suitcase here on the dirty patio wasn't an option. So I rolled my bags inside, stopping just inside the door to take a moment and battle the impulse to walk right back out.

2
that arsehole

JESSA

THE PATIO WAS CLEANER.

I wasn't sure where to look first. Clothes had been discarded on nearly every article of furniture, all of which had seen better days, and those days were decades gone. The layer of dust on every surface was so thick, it could have supported weight. On assessment, the sofa was my best option, but when I moved to take a step in that direction, I nearly took a tumble over one of three pairs of work boots scattered haphazardly on the hardwood.

Gingerly, I made my way to the sofa, nudging boots out of the way with the toe of my shoe. A rogue pair stuck out from under the coffee table, leaving me wondering how many pairs of the same boots one man could need as I kicked them farther under so I wouldn't trip again.

As I opened my suitcase in search of flats, I listened to the shower run, the slaps and sounds of runoff as he washed his hair maybe or lowered his arm. His voice startled me, floating out from the loo as he sang a song about a whiskey river in a husky baritone. I stilled.

What the blazes is *he?*

8

He kept on singing while I found my shoes and slipped them on, careful not to let my bare feet touch the ground. And I realized I had a second problem. These trousers were too long for flats, which meant I either needed to change or put my heels back on.

I glanced at the door that separated us, weighing my options. I could be quick, wouldn't even have to take off my shoes again. A pair of tailored shorts sat on top of my other clothes, and I took it as a sign.

With my eyes locked on the bathroom door and ears sharp, my hands flew, unzipping and dropping my trousers, shorts in hand before they hit the ground. One leg in. The shower squeaked.

"*Shit*." I hissed, stuffing the other leg in and tugging them over my bum, my heart slowing as I zipped them.

Proudly and with great relief, I packed up again, fitting my heels in without trouble. But just as I reached to close my suitcase, I heard a flap of plastic followed by a quartet of nails clattering on the hardwood. My eyes snapped to the hallway, and out shot a massive, slobbering, very enthusiastic boxer. And it was heading straight for me.

Without thinking, I backed away as the beast hopped onto the sofa, somehow finding the space to run in wild circles with mad eyes and a dribbling mouth. But there was no escape—the coffee table hit me in the backs of my knees, and I went down like a stone.

With that, my defenses were gone.

I hit the ground with a thud, and the beast climbed into my lap, its sopping tongue seeking skin to bathe. Hands in front of me, I squeaked and laughed through the slight fear of being mauled. But I couldn't push the animal off with the two of us wedged between the sofa and the table.

"*Beau!*" Remy yelled. "Goddammit, Beau—*comere*, you dumb sonofabitch."

Just like that, the dog disappeared. I cracked an eyelid to catch Remy dragging Beau away by the collar with one hand, attempting to hang on to his towel with the other. Unsuccessfully, I might add—his bare backside was on full display. My head cocked like a bird. How could a backside be both round and square? It made no logical sense, and yet there it was, simultaneously ridiculous and fundamentally perfect.

Beau twisted like a fish on a hook, but Remy couldn't hang onto him.

Or his towel.

What was likely only a second or two stretched into minutes inside my mind. The towel falling. Remy turning with both hands reaching for the dog. Disappointment over losing the view of his backside, only to be shocked mute by the sight of his cock, rooted in a thatch of dark hair and hanging low enough to leave me breathless.

It couldn't be real, a cock of that size and stature. My brain tried to math an equivalent length on my body. My forearm perhaps? Certainly not my vagina. She'd not seen something so impractical, but it was impossible not to imagine what that sort of steel would do to a woman.

Said vagina ached at the thought.

Remy grabbed the dog by the collar with both hands this time, unaware of his swinging spare appendage as he dragged Beau out of sight. A door opened and slammed as I collected myself off the ground, rolled up my tongue, and did my best to cool the roiling heat he'd inspired. And around the corner came Remy, with a dishtowel over his cock, still largely unbothered by his nakedness.

He snatched the towel off the ground and wrapped it around his waist with his face pinched in concern.

"You okay?" he asked.

"Yes, thank you," I said, a little shaky.

"Sorry about the—" he motioned at his waist. But then his eyes flicked to my suitcase and softened with guilt. "Goddamn that dog," he huffed, scratching at the back of his neck. "I'm real sorry about your clothes."

I glanced at my things with mounting horror. The contents had been tossed with Beau's trampling, but that was fixable. What didn't appear to be fixable, however, was the fact that he'd been busy digging his way to the center of the earth prior to galloping through the door.

My throat constricted as I rifled through my muddy clothes, holding them up for inspection one by one. I wouldn't know if they were ruined until a dry cleaner got a good look at them, and I held onto the small hope they could be saved. Propriety dictated my action and reaction—I heard the stiff voice of my father in my mind say, *Master yourself or they will master you.*

With a hard swallow and nothing else to be done, I began folding them to pack away.

"It's not your fault," I said, afraid I'd cry if I looked at him.

A pause. He secured the tail of his towel and stepped next to me smelling of soap. "Here, lemme help."

"I'm all right, thank you."

Remy reached into my suitcase anyway, the heat of his body distracting and alarming and delectable. He smelled incredible, his skin damp, a droplet of water falling from his hair onto his broad forearm. His big hands fished around for an article of clothing, emerging with a very small pair of underpants twisted in his thick fingers.

I groaned, snatching my knickers. "Would you *please* just go put your bloody clothes on?"

He raised his hands in surrender and backed toward what I imagined were the bedrooms. "'Scuse me."

I pointed. "Go!"

"I'm goin', I'm goin'."

11

He gave me his back, and I charted its topography shamelessly and furiously and a thousand percent ready to get to a clean house—preferably with air conditioning, my best friend, and a well-stocked drink cabinet.

And *without* the bedlam of Remy Winfield and his rogue cock.

3
slings and arrows

REMY

THE DUCHESS sure was cute when she was angry.

Her button nose wrinkled up, her creamy skin flushed, her pretty lips flattened and her jaw set. Her nipples were hard even in the heat, and I absently wondered if my loose cock had anything to do with it. Either way, I swore I'd seen a flicker of actual fire in her eyes when she'd pointed to my room and commanded me to get dressed.

Wasn't often a woman hurried me to put my clothes *on*.

I tossed my towel on the chair in the corner and grabbed a pair of clean jeans, considering the turn she'd just put on my day. Here I thought I was housing one of Cass's fiancé's buddies, and up walked a duchess instead.

I'd never seen anything so out of place in my yard as Jessa in her fancy outfit and heels too high for a gravel road. I figured when her golden hair wasn't subject to the weather it was probably all shiny and smooth and perfect. As it stood, she looked a little like a Muppet.

Beau probably hadn't helped matters much.

She didn't seem to care for me either, but I didn't take her general disdain personal—wasn't the first time a rich girl wouldn't give me the time. She was probably used to five-star accommodations, and my place would have had negative stars if they were awarded, seeing as how I couldn't remember the last time I'd cleaned. Granted, she might be hard pressed to find anything up to her standards in Roseville. But any way you cut it, my house held a firm spot at the bottom of that particular list.

Still, I wouldn't have been mad about keeping her here and the potential that particular possibility held—I could think of a great number of things to occupy her time while I had her. I might have even dusted, which was an admission that'd probably knock my mother over dead. But to have a chance at *that*? I'd dust. Hell, I'd even scrub a toilet.

But a good time was all it'd ever be. I'd been with princess types before and had learned that lesson well: girls like that didn't go for guys like me. And it was just as well. Ducks didn't end up with geese, and British Ladies didn't end up with bartenders from Tennessee.

I punched my arms into a plaid shirt and headed back to the living room, fastening the pearl snaps as I walked. She'd done up her suitcase and rolled it onto the patio where she sat on the top, staring down the drive with a far-off look on her face that left me curious as to what she was thinking about. I hooked a pair of boots on my fingers and pushed open the screen.

She looked up with a weary smile on her face. "Well, don't you look smart."

I smoothed a hand down my shirtfront. "This old thing?"

Jessa chuckled and stood while I pulled on my boots. "Why do you have so many of those?" She nodded at my shoes.

I inspected them. "Well, these are my everyday boots. I've got a work pair, a huntin' pair, a Sunday best pair, and a trash pair for the dirty work."

"I see. Wouldn't want to get your Sunday best covered in muck."

"Exactly." I grabbed her suitcase and trotted down the stairs, past the truck I'd been working on, past my old Camaro, and to my Scout.

Besides my mama and baseball, I'd never loved anything as much as I loved that baby blue hunk of metal. I'd rescued her from the impound, restored her nearly from scratch. She was almost always topless—as it should be—especially in the summertime, and I realized a little too late that I hadn't parked under the big oak next to the house like I usually did. The seats were probably a thousand degrees, but with the truck half gutted and the inside of the Camaro covered in dog hair, her ladyship didn't have much of an option.

Her ladyship. Inwardly, I chuckled. That irritated, pink look on her face was too good not to summon at every opportunity. *Woulda gone with princess over duchess if I didn't suspect she'd have an aneurism.*

I reached over the side of the Scout to put Jessa's suitcase and overnight bag in the trunk, snagging a T-shirt from the back seat. But then I caught sight of her, and it took just about all I had in me not to laugh.

She'd opened the door with a squeak of the hinge, but then she just stood there, looking around for a clue as to how the hell to get in. Might as well have been advanced calculus for the figuring that went on behind her eyes. The floorboard hit her mid-thigh, and I wondered if she'd ever endured the unladylike spread of her legs it would take to get her in.

I wondered a lot about the unladylike spread of her legs and what had and hadn't been done there.

"'Scuse me," I said as I reached her, and she moved out of the way so I could lay the shirt down on the seat.

"I'm not sure how to . . . that is, should I just—"

"Come here," was my only warning.

I grabbed her by the waist and hoisted her in to the sweetest little gasp of surprise. She leaned back into me for balance, and I took a moment to enjoy the feel of her ass against my stomach as I lifted, her hands gripping my forearms, the sweet smell of her in my nose.

Her face was red as a firetruck as she found her feet and sat. "Surely there's an easier way."

I closed her door and shot her a smile. "Probably, but that was more fun."

She didn't say anything, but her face was a mixture of disdain and a flustered sort of awareness. Or maybe disdain *because* of the flustered sort of awareness, which amused me endlessly. Spinning my keys around my index finger, I made my way around the truck to get in. But the second I opened the door, Beau shot in like a goddamn cannon, running around and slobbering all over the place.

"Beau, you asshole," I grumbled through my teeth, reaching in to try to get ahold of his collar. But, seeming to know what I was after, he jumped in the back seat, sat up straight as a soldier, and panted so hard, he was smiling.

I sighed. "You okay with him back there?"

"If he stays put," she said, brushing copper dog hair off her shorts.

"Can't promise you that."

A sigh and a resigned smile. "It's fine."

"Well, aren't you a good sport."

I hopped in, and a satisfied shiver worked through me at the rumbling sound the Scout made when I turned the engine over and threw her into gear. We bumped and bounced our way out of the yard and to the drive, and I wasn't ashamed about hitting every hole so she'd bounce on the squeaky seat with that terrified look on her face. When I stopped to unlock the gate, I pulled a hair tie off the stack hanging on my gear shaft and tossed it into her lap.

"You're probably gonna need that."

And she did.

Couldn't talk much with the top off, so when we hit the road, I cranked up the radio and hummed along to the old honky-tonk cassette tape that'd been in the deck since I'd rescued her. Beau hung out the back fearlessly, snapping his jaws at the wind. And all the while, Jessa struggled with her hair, hands alternating between keeping her ponytail from whipping her in the face and hanging on to the jutting dashboard for dear life. When we finally hit town and slowed down, she let out a relieved sigh and sat back in her seat. A smile brushed her lips as she took in the town, and I found myself smiling too, seeing it through her eyes.

The duchess was impressed.

Roseville was a little gem nestled in the Smoky Mountains, untouched by the big box stores and city-goers moving in search of a small-town escape. Our Main Street was straight out of a Norman Rockwell painting, lined with shops—most of which had been in place for seventy-five years or more—with an emerald green park right in the middle of town. Many an engagement had been proposed at the gazebo standing proud in the center. Even my own, once upon a time.

Didn't matter how long it'd been since my future rode off into the sunset without me—every time I drove down Main Street, a tiny little piece of me ached, that deep, invisible bruise pressed. There'd been a time when I didn't think I'd be back here for anything other than holidays or the occasional vacation.

It seemed like a million years ago that Mama got sick, back when the future was nothing but a golden road of yeses running all the way to the horizon. College baseball had been so good, I'd been drafted to the Majors. Hadn't signed my contract yet when we found out about her cancer. She didn't want me to come home for her, told me to go. But there wasn't a choice to make, not really. So I came home and gave up my spot. Took a job at The Horseshoe slinging beer. Cared for Mama through two rounds of chemo and a double mastectomy. And when she was out of the woods and told me to try to walk on to a pro team, I just . . . couldn't. That door wasn't just closed—it was painted over, the cracks cemented, and the lock didn't have a key. And now at nearly thirty, it wasn't even an option. The door had disappeared from everything but the list of regrets I kept tucked away where no one could see.

"Oh, it's gorgeous," Jessa said around a smile, her hungry eyes scanning the street.

"Not too bad, huh?" From the steering wheel, I flicked a two-fingered salute to old Pete and Curly where they sat at their usual spots outside the barbershop. Some of the pedestrians waved too, and Jessa grinned ear to ear, waving back.

"They're all quite friendly."

I snorted a laugh. "Stay away from old Curly or that opinion'll change real quick."

"Why?"

"Oh, he's just a grumpy old codger who likes to tell everybody they're wrong and educate them on how they could do things right."

"Sounds charming."

"Oh, yeah. Eugene's just a regular bucket of sunshine. We're almost there—Mom's right around the corner. You get ahold of Cass?"

"We're meeting at your mother's."

She sounded proper without trying, the gentle rise and fall of her accent next to mine making me sound like a hillbilly.

"Good. Sorry for the mix-up, Your Highness."

"I'm not—" A sigh. "Oh, it's quite all right," she said, and I actually believed it. "Wasn't your fault, was it?"

"Aunt Julie's roof ain't nailed on tight, if you know what I mean. A steady breeze, and—" I blew air through my lips and pantomimed the top of my head coming off. "I can't imagine how she got you so mixed up, even though it's one of her special skills. But she makes a strawberry pie that'll make you see Jesus, so we try not to give her too hard a time. How she ended up with this particular task is beyond me."

"I have an aunt like that. But rather than causing mayhem, she wanders around the estate picking things up and moving them without purpose, then forgetting and accusing her staff of stealing."

One of my brows jacked up as I turned onto Mom's street. "Guess I can be thankful old Jules has never landed anybody in jail then."

"Never say never," she warned with a sass look on her face.

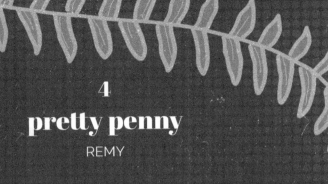

4
pretty penny

REMY

I **PULLED** up to the curb, chuckling first at the thought of Aunt Julie getting one of us put in jail, then at how much I enjoyed being around Jessa. When I cut the engine, I shifted to rest my hand on the shoulder of her bucket seat and gave her my most persuasive smile. "You sure you don't want to stay at my place? I think you and me could get along."

Instantly, she was irritated again, her little nose all crinkled up. "Is that some sort of slang for sex?"

"In this context, yes."

Bang, there went the angry flush. Her blue eyes darkened a shade when she was pissed and fighting to keep it bottled up, a little frown line dissecting her eyebrows. Those rosebud lips of hers flattened, though they were still very much kissable, her alabaster skin flushing from collarbone to cheeks. Even with her hair wild from the weather, she was a stunner—untouchable and pristine. I'd have given my left arm to dirty her up.

Needed the right one to do the dirtying.

"Are you always this shameless?" she snapped.

"Always. It's been said that's part of my charm."

"Were the speakers lucid?" She brushed Beau off when he tried to lick her face.

"Pretty sure, but Marty might not have been. We'd just gone mud doggin', and he hit his head pretty hard on the—"

She opened her door and climbed out.

"So that's a no, then?" I called after her as she stormed up the steps without stopping. "Guess so." I pulled my keys out of the ignition and got out, grabbing her suitcase and bag on the way. Beau hopped out and trotted up to the door with me.

When I reached her, she'd already knocked, and before I could open my mouth, the door opened. Cass lunged out like a wolf spider, grabbing onto Jessa with all eight legs.

"You're here!" Cass squealed. "You're really here!"

Jessa laughed, "Hello, darling."

"God, I love it when you speak British to me." Cass leaned back to take a look at Jessa. "You look terrible."

"Your cousin's work," she said snidely. "He's quite . . ." she turned to assess me. "Well, I actually don't know what he is. I've been trying to sort it out since I met him."

"I think the word you're looking for is *dashing*," I offered. "I'll also accept delightful, ravishing, and/or irresistible."

Jessa and Cass shared a look before bursting into laughter. I mean that side stitching, hysterical laughter where just as soon as it died down, one more look would have them off again.

I gave them a bored look and walked inside around them. "Pardon me, wouldn't want to disturb you two maniacs."

"Oh, I'm so tired," Jessa said around laughter. "And I have missed you."

"We have two whole weeks to spend together," Cass said from behind me, shutting the door. "You're going to be sick of me."

"Never. Has Henry arrived?"

Something in her voice set my hackles tingling. I pretended not to listen.

"He has," Cass said conspiratorially. "And he's dying to see you."

They giggled like little girls, and I decided I didn't like Henry, whoever he was.

"Once I've washed this day off me and had a nap, we have to meet for dinner."

"Already planned for it."

I cleared my throat and set down her luggage. "So where's Mama?"

"Right here," I heard from behind me. When I turned, she was almost on me, her arms open and cheek poised for a kiss, which I granted. "Hi, honey. And who's this?"

Cass took Jessa's arm. "Aunt Linda, this is Jessa Hastings."

"How do you do?" Jessa said, extending her hand for a shake. I half expected her to offer her knuckles for a kiss.

But Mama bypassed her hand for a hug. "I'm sorry, I'm a hugger."

Again, Jessa chuckled, hugging her back. "It's lovely to meet you."

"My God, if you aren't the cutest thing," Mama said, leaning back. "If my son wasn't such a mess, I'd nudge you in his direction."

"Believe me, I know. I've been inside his house," Jessa answered.

Mama took her by the shoulders and faced me. "I told you never to bring a girl to that barn."

"Never had any complaints," I snarked.

"Well, Jessa, it's nothing a hot bath won't fix."

Jessa's eyes practically rolled back in her head. "Could I?"

"Yes, of course, but . . . well, I have bad news, honey. See, we only have the bed-and-breakfast here in town and a few vacation rentals, and the closest hotel is thirty miles from here. You can stay here tonight, but with half the family coming in for the strawberry festival tomorrow, well, I'm afraid there's nowhere left but Remy's."

Jessa's head swiveled back and forth like a perpetual motion machine. "What about the man who was set to stay with Remy?"

"He's at a house with ten other boys, all of them sleeping on couches and air mattresses. You don't want to stay there, sweetie. At Remy's, you'll have your own room, and that house is so peaceful and quiet, not like in town."

I salivated at the thought of getting to hang onto her. And even if I couldn't bring her around, messing with her was too much fun to pass up. But my amusement slithered away when I realized Jessa was about to cry.

Cass and Mama swarmed, flanking her.

"Oh, now don't cry, honey," Mama said, stroking her hair. "I promise we'll clean it up real nice. Put on fresh sheets. We'll even clean the bathroom, won't we, Cassidy?"

Cass's nose twitched. "Of course we will."

"It'll be just fine—you wait and see. And Remy will be on his very best behavior. Won't you, son?"

It wasn't a question. It was a warning.

"When am I not on my best behavior?"

Mama's eyes swept the ceiling. "Here's what we'll do, Jessa. You go take yourself a nice long bath, and we're gonna go start on that mess. You can take a nap if you want, and when you're all fresh, you text Cass."

Jessa managed to look both devastated and grateful. "I'm terribly sorry to be such trouble."

"None of that," Mama chided. "I'm sorry to ask you to stay with Remy, but if he doesn't behave, you tell me, and I'll handle him."

"I'm standin' right here, you know."

"Take her suitcase upstairs, Remy. Do you want tea, Jessa?"

"Perhaps after my bath? Beau and I have been acquainted, and I'd like to wash off my welcome."

Cass eyed Beau, who was stretched out on Mama's couch, and gave me a look. "Really?"

I shrugged and picked up her suitcase, heading for the stairs.

"Well, I'll leave the tea bags out. Kettle's on the stove, sugar's on the counter, cream is in the fridge. If you need anything, just text Cass."

"Thank you again," Jessa said before following me up the stairs. I turned for Mama's room and set her things down.

She reached for her overnight bag and unzipped it as I stood there, watching. Her eyes flicked to mine.

"Did you need something?" she asked.

I rubbed the back of my neck, feeling sheepish. Maybe I'd pushed her too far.

The thought made me feel like scum.

"Sorry you've gotta stay with me."

Jessa gave me the fakest smile ever smiled. "Good manners are made of small sacrifices. And if you consider putting your hands where they don't belong, know that I took six years of judo and am fairly certain I can break your nose without much effort."

"Understood. But I'm not responsible if *you* can't keep your hands to yourself," I said, unable to help myself as I backed toward the door with an involuntary uptick of my lips. "We'll get you all set up. It won't be so bad—I'll even close off the dog door and make Beau sleep in his doghouse. He oughtta be in it anyway after what he did to your clothes."

"I'll be sure to send him my dry cleaning bill."

"Deal. He can work it off with me."

That earned me a little smile, enough to hope this wouldn't just be a cycle of the two of us driving each other crazy. At least not without results. So as not to press my luck, I headed downstairs.

Cass and my mother were nose to nose, whispering about something or other.

My eyes narrowed. "What are you two talking about?"

"How you're going to pay us for our cleaning services," Cass answered.

"She's gonna end up costing me, isn't she?"

"Yeah, but she's worth it," Cass said as she walked to the door, shooting me a wink.

5
petite fille

JESSA

I ROSE from my nap still tired, but no longer angry. Remy had been all but forgotten.

I was about to have dinner with Henry Howard.

An unstoppable smile played on my lips as I strode toward the restaurant, smoothing the skirt of my dress before reaching for the door. Fortunately, the clothes at the bottom of my suitcase had remained untouched, and I counted myself lucky to find something clean and suitable to wear to a restaurant named after a horse.

The Filly was apparently the nicest place in town, though my expectations had been schooled by Cass as to what that meant. When she mentioned pressed jeans as locally preferred attire, her point was made. So I opted for a black-and-white striped tailored dress and flats. The bodice panels were cut so the stripes ran at different angles, cinching my waist and accentuating the curve in a way I appreciated.

As I'd walked the two blocks from Linda's, I came to find that everything about Roseville was charming—that was the only word for it. Linda's home was another perfect cottage on a patch of green land a few blocks from Main Street. Inside was clean and white with touches of dusty pink and navy blue. One of the walls had been treated with boards Cass had called . . . boatlap? No, that wasn't it. Shiplap, I remembered. And it only added to that undeniable appeal that touched everything in this town.

Other than Remy, of course.

I was sure *someone* found him appealing—men that confident didn't just happen upon it. If the hair ties on his gear stick were any indication, *quite* a few women found him appealing, and I saw the draw. He was indescribably masculine, a man who made things with strong hands, who would hold a woman with arms like burnished steel. He'd picked me up and deposited me into his truck without even bending his knees, and I wasn't sure what he could have possibly done to form a backside of that size and strength, but it must have been serious business. Remy Winfield was a genetic marvel—his cock being the most marvelous of all— and I'd have been lying if I said it didn't trigger some deep, instinctive attraction in me. It was part of my code, I supposed. Out of my control.

The rest of him was the equivalent of a cold shower.

On walking through the door of the establishment, I caught sight of Cass, who raised her hand, smiling from Davis's elbow. And across from Davis sat the one and only Lord Henry Howard.

I'd known Henry all my life. Our parents were the best of friends, our families a comfortable constant of every summer holiday and in between. His father was a Duke, and as the only child, the immense pressure on him had always been a source of contention, particularly with his father. Under that sort of strain, things go one of three ways: either you go all in, you become a louse, or you reject the mantle altogether.

Henry had chosen the latter, running away to spend his days covered in dirt and dust in remote parts of Africa the very first chance he got.

He turned his gaze in my direction with a blinding smile

and brilliant eyes. No one else mattered—I floated toward him like I was caught in a tractor beam.

It seemed I'd always been in love with Henry, even from my first memory of him when we'd nearly given each other concussions jumping on the bed at five. Our parents had all but betrothed us at birth, leaving the matter somewhat decided, a joke between us that didn't really feel like a joke. But we'd never dated and had only kissed once.

We were eight.

On another night years later, we *almost* kissed, and he'd suggested that if we weren't married in a decade, we'd marry each other. And here we were, nearly ten years to the very date.

I was just as in love with him now as I'd ever been. And what *wasn't* to love? He knew me better than almost anyone. And on top of being brilliant, gorgeous, and clever, he oversaw a charity in Africa that built sustainable communities for orphaned children, putting his social work degree to good use.

Really—orphans.

He looked more rugged than he had the last time I'd seen him, which was a year ago now. Shaggy blond hair and a scruffy beard set off the tan of his skin and the brightness of his eyes. He'd stayed with me in London for a week before flying to Nairobi, and it'd been a week of bliss, despite my concrete place in the friendzone.

As always, he pulled me into his arms and kissed the top of my head. "Hello, Bits."

"Hello, Bobs," I said, doing my best not to nestle into his chest, a task made difficult with my arms around his waist. "You're here!"

A chuckle reverberated through him, into me before he kissed my temple, the warmth of his lips on my skin pure heaven. Instantly, I was comforted and relaxed. Henry, my sweet and kind man who didn't make me want to tear my hair out in chunks. Refined, civilized, polite Henry, who didn't make sex jokes that inspired inappropriate feelings in inappropriate places.

I sighed, feeling wonderfully at ease.

That was all I got before I had to make my rounds, kissing Davis on the cheek and having a little whispering moment with Cass as we hugged and giggled, still giddy to be near each other after so long. And then, we sat, settling in to catch up.

"Now, don't make fun of The Filly," she warned quietly. "It's the only restaurant within twenty miles with real napkins."

With a chuckle, we opened our menus.

"What's good?" I asked.

"Any of it, really, but I always get a filet," she said. "With cheesy broccoli and a baked potato. Fuck a wedding diet."

"I'll remember you said that when I can't button your dress," I teased.

"It has buttons?" Davis asked with one brow raised.

"That's your only hint," I assured him. I closed my menu. "I'll have what you're having. But I could use a glass of wine."

"Rough flight?" Henry asked.

I wanted to dive into his voice and swim around in it. "The flight was fine. It was what happened after that did me in."

Cass had a pointed expression on her face when she said to Davis, "She met Remy."

It was all she had to say for Davis to cast me an apologetic glance.

"And?" I prompted with no small edge of blame.

Cass winced. "And she has to stay with him."

"Oh, no," Davis breathed.

"Oh, yes. Thank you," I said as the server arrived with a bottle of wine. "I'm in desperate need of a drink."

29

With a wan smile, she poured mine first, disregarding the rules of table service. I couldn't have cared less, as it meant I didn't have to wait to sample mine. I tried not to make a face when it hit my tongue.

Cass and I shared a look.

"It's bad, isn't it?" she asked. The waitress made a face at her, and she added, "No offense, Brandy."

But in the end, Brandy shrugged. "None taken. Nobody'd accuse Remy of being a sommelier, but I'm sure he did the best he could with what God gave him."

"Remy ordered it?" Cass asked. "Well, that explains it. He should have asked me."

"Ask him to order whiskey, though, and prepare to have your world shaken," Brandy said as she finished pouring. "I'll give y'all a minute."

I sat back in my seat with a sigh, sipping my wine. Cass mirrored me, smiling with her lips together and eyes twinkling.

"I can't believe we're all here. We haven't been together like this in years, not since the last summer we spent at your parents' estate, Jessa."

"Ah, the grand graduation summer of debauchery," Henry said, raising his glass. "Cheers to that."

"The end of an era," Cass added. "Those were my favorite summers, though they were my mama's worst. I probably should have come home from Oxford, but . . ." She shrugged. "Chance of a lifetime summer vacations in Europe or spend the summers with my mother? I love the woman, but an aristocratic British estate will win every time."

Davis chuckled. "At least your parents wanted you to come home. Mine were more than happy to ship me off to Eton and leave me there. Dad was more worried about his legacy at the school than he ever was about me. In fact, I only came back to America twice through all of secondary school."

"Ugh. I hate them," Cass noted, scowling into her wine glass before taking a drink.

"They're paying for the wedding," he countered with a sad sort of smile.

"I *appreciate* them, but I hate them."

"The only thing that would have made university better was if Henry had been with us," I said.

"Ah, but Cambridge was the college of every great-grandad I've ever had. And as we all know, the legacy must remain intact." He blustered a bit, imitating his father. "Anyway, we didn't lack for time spent together, did we?"

"No, we didn't," Cass said.

I smiled at her. "How lucky was I to have you as my roommate first year?"

"It wasn't luck—it was fate," she insisted.

Davis groaned and rolled his eyes, but he was smiling a little too.

"What? It was and you know it. I was put with Jessa, Jessa introduced you to me, and you only knew her because of Henry. That's too much coincidence to be a coincidence."

"You're right. I love you." Davis leaned over and kissed her cheek, petting her hair.

She laughed. "Thank you for patronizing me, and I love you too. And now here we are, ten years after our first summer. Davis and I are finally getting married, and if I remember right, you two might be next. Isn't your little marriage arrangement about to come to term?"

Everyone laughed, but my cheeks were hot and my chest all fluttery at the mention.

Henry and I shared a secretive look, clinking our glasses together.

"It's true, Bits," Henry said, shifting to lean on the arm of his chair toward me. "Or did you forget?"

"How could I forget you, Bobs?" I leaned on the chair arm closer to him.

"I really don't know. I've been told I'm quite unforgettable. But I had to be sure. Can't trifle about when marriage is at stake, can we?"

Cass was so excited at the sight us, she looked ready to burst. "Maybe we should have waited a year, Davis? I would have loved a double wedding."

And just like that, everyone was laughing, and the moment slipped away.

"Well, I'm glad we're all finally here," Cass said as we settled back in. "Spending the day cleaning my cousin's dirty house was at the bottom of the list of things I'd rather die than do.

"Thank you for your sacrifice," I said. "I hate that it was you and not me, but I think I've been traumatized enough for one day."

Which I said too soon. Because in through the door walked Remy Winfield pushing a dolly of wine cases, and I decided it was quite possible that my day might never be over.

32

6
a little cheese with that

REMY

JESSA WAS the first thing I saw when I walked in the front door of The Filly.

Somehow, she looked shocked to see me, which was baffling. In a town of this size, there was no getting away from anybody.

Cass just rolled her eyes, and I jerked a chin at their table before heading to the bar. The Filly and the adjacent bar, The Horseshoe, came as a pair, so when my boss instructed me to order a metric shit-ton of wine to accommodate all the fancy attendees of Cass's wedding, I double checked he meant *me*. I knew as much about wine as I did about babysitting or knitting. Or cleaning, if you asked my mother. So the best I could do was pick something halfway down the price chart and hope for the best.

But both wine orders were delivered to The Horseshoe rather than The Filly, so here I was, dropping them off before the bar got busy. Should have figured when they said they were going to dinner that they'd be coming here.

Jessa turned to the rest of them, her shoulders rising and falling with a sigh. I knew Davis—he'd spent a couple of

Christmases and other holidays here with Cass, which left the big blond guy.

Henry.

He gave me an amiable smile that for some unknown reason, I hated. It was genuine enough. Maybe a little too pretty. But I had a hard time smiling back and was pretty sure it ended up closer to a sneer. Unfazed, he turned back to the table. And just like that, I was forgotten.

Just as well.

I wheeled my way to the back and unlocked the liquor cage. Jack, the bartender at The Filly, followed me in.

"Thank God you're here. We're about out—these fancy folks drink this shit like water. I miss the days when a case of this stuff would last us a year."

I chuckled, unloading the boxes. "I got another load in the truck, so you should be set for a minute. Red or white?"

"Both."

I set one of each aside and tore the tops open.

Jack took out a bottle of cabernet and inspected it. "One of 'em gave me hell because we only had one or the other. He asked for somethin' I never heard of. *Mal*-something or another?"

"Malbec?" I guessed, having been traumatized by that wine list.

He snapped his fingers. "That's it. Sounded more like a place than something you'd drink."

"They'll be gone soon enough," I promised. "Just smile and nod and say you're sorry."

"They're good tippers, at least. Even the cranky ones."

The swinging door into the kitchen flew open and hit the wall, and through the doorway rushed Brandy, one of our servers, with a worried look on her face and her phone in her hand.

I paused, concerned. "You all right?"

"No," she answered, her voice watery. "Billy fell off his

34

bike and Mama thinks he broke his arm. We've gotta take him to Sevierville." She was already pulling off her apron and shoving it at me. "I'm sorry, Remy. I'll make it up to you, okay?"

"Don't worry, I'll take care of it. Go on—go take care of your boy."

"Thanks, Remy," she said through tears, reaching up on her tiptoes to kiss me on the cheek. "I knew I could count on you."

"Let us know how he is."

"I will!" she called on her way out.

I sighed. "Guess I'd better find the boss," I said, and went in search of the manager.

I found him in the office, working on his laptop. When he looked up, he took off his glasses and rubbed the bridge of his nose. "Remy. Bring that wine over?"

"Yessir, but you might need to call in another one of your servers. Brandy's boy broke his arm, and she just took off."

He hissed a swear and rubbed his face like pizza dough. "I'll see what I can do. Is the dining room full?"

"Just about."

Another swear. "You busy?"

My face flattened.

He held out his hands. "I'll owe you one, I promise. If I can't get anybody in, we're gonna have to shut down part of the floor, but I need a little time to sort it out. Just an hour?"

I sighed again, wrapping Brandy's apron around my waist. "Yeah, I'll tend to her tables."

Relief washed over him. "Thanks, Remy."

"No prob."

As I made my way back to the floor, I pulled Brandy's waiter book out of her apron pocket, the inside pocket already stuffed with cash and her notepad scribbled with orders I couldn't read. The teenage hostess blushed and stammered as she showed me the floor chart.

"*Shit,*" I whispered on inspection.

Because my cousin's table just so happened to be in my section.

I straightened up and bent my neck to crack it. *Only way out is through.*

With a sigh, I put on a fake smile and wandered in their direction. Cass's face quirked as I approached, then crinkled into a frown when she saw the waiter book in my hand and an apron tied around my waist. The look on her face distinctly said, *Seriously?*

"Hi, folks," I started. "Brandy had a family emergency, so looks like I'll be takin' care of y'all tonight. Need a minute, or are you ready to order?"

Davis looked around the table. "I'm ready if you are." He smiled up at me. "Hey, Remy. Heard you had an interesting day."

"That's one way of putting it."

Jessa drained her glass.

"More wine?" I asked.

"Yes, thank you," she answered politely.

Henry gave me another of those friendly smiles. "You're one of the groomsmen, right?"

"Bridesmaid. Cass thinks she's funny," I deadpanned.

"Pleased to meet you. I'm Henry, the best man." He stuck out his hand for a shake, and I obliged, paying close attention to his grip. Annoyingly, he passed—not at all soft, but not too tight, just the right amount of force. The virtual Goldilocks of handshakes. "I heard Jessa's staying with you."

She stiffened. "I think you meant shackled."

I rankled at her disdain. "Aww, come on, Duchess. I'm not all bad."

"Just partly?"

"So you *do* get it."

"What percentage, would you say?"

I bobbed my head and glanced at the ceiling. "'Bout sixty-forty."

"Is sixty the good or the bad?"

At that, I gave her my most charming smile. "Guess you'll have to wait and see."

Cass rolled her eyes so hard, I was pretty sure she saw Mr. Greer picking steak out of his teeth behind her.

"So, how about dinner?" I prompted, pen at the ready.

They ordered, ladies first, Henry last by my design. And when they were through, I checked on Brandy's other tables and headed for the computer to get it all going.

I wasn't sure why I didn't care for Henry. Nothing about him seemed insincere, nothing suspicious. In fact, I didn't get anything but good vibes from him. Yet here I was, fantasizing about dumping him out of his chair so I could sit in it myself. I'd caught Jessa looking at him like he was Jesus with that pretty flush in her cheeks. She'd dressed a little smarter for the weather in a striped dress that made my head hurt for all the zig zagging black-and-white stripes. The neat little collar circled the long, white column of her neck, topped by a golden bun at her nape. Even without seeing her face, you could tell she was something different. Maybe it was written in the proud line of her shoulders or the arrow of her back—stiff, but not stuffy.

And all I wanted to do was unwind her. I imagined it was a secret sort of pleasure to catch a glimpse of something that tight when it's come undone. An image of her blasted into my mind—Jessa flushed and dewy, eyes closed and hair spread across my pillow, her face soft and satisfied, her naked chest rising and falling with every—

"You gonna stand there all day?" One of the servers asked from behind me.

Startled, my cheeks warmed up a touch. "Hey, whatever keeps me looking busy."

She chuckled, rolling her eyes as she swatted me in the

chest. Her fingers lingered. "You're impossible, Remy Winfield."

"Oh, I know it. Just ask my mama—she's been telling me so for years."

I left her at the terminal, watching Jessa out of the corner of my eye as I refilled drinks and got everybody caught up with what they needed. I might have eavesdropped a little on hearing Henry's name in the same sentence as the words *Africa* and *orphans*. No wonder she was all moony over him. Hell, with *that* kind of resumé and *that* face, I might have given him a shot. And I didn't even swing that direction. He was a catch, and right up her alley. British and everything.

Bet his house was clean, too.

Once I had the wine, I made my way back to their table, uncorking and pouring out while they talked. Henry was in the middle of a story about how they were building compounds for orphaned kids that reclaimed water and ran on solar panels. They even had a school and provided the kids clothes and everything.

I then decided that Henry Howard was an asshole for making the rest of us look bad.

I made it to Jessa last, poured her a glass that was a little more than her share. Wanting nothing more than to interrupt, I leaned in to get close enough to whisper. *"You look like a zebra."*

She turned her head so fast, our lips almost connected. We froze there for a heartbeat, neither of us breathing.

"And I suppose you think yourself a lion?" Her warm, sweet breath licked my lips.

I stayed put, savoring her eyes on my mouth. "Maybe so. But I dunno how anybody's supposed to catch you in that dress."

A little laugh bubbled out of her, but she remembered herself, clearing her throat and wiping her face flat when she noticed everyone was looking.

Gotcha. I smirked, lit up by the fact.

I couldn't have told you exactly why she'd sparked a mission in me the second I first saw her. Maybe it was the way she smelled, or the little curves at the corners of her lips. Maybe it was the challenge. Henry didn't help matters.

Maybe I just wanted to win her over.

I wondered if my mouth would help me or hurt me.

All I knew was that her little smile meant I had a shot and two weeks to make it. Plenty of time to *get to know* one another well and fully, and on many, many surfaces. Not enough time for anything more. No expectations. Just a good time, and afterward, she'd fly a million miles away.

Without Henry Howard.

I had fourteen days at my disposal and I was heading into battle with an arsenal of maneuvers to convince her I was worth a shot.

And I bet I'd have to use every one.

7
out of the park

REMY

THE CRACK of a bat against a ball was one of my three favorite sounds, right alongside the hiss of a freshly opened beer and the satisfied sigh of a woman. And when that sound of wood meeting leather was my own doing, it somehow sounded all the sweeter.

The connection reverberated up my arms, my swing coming to a natural close as I watched the softball sail across the field and hit the fence with a thunk. But before I could finish admiring my handiwork, Coach pitched another.

Crack. Sail. Thunk.

"Gimme a challenge, wouldya, Gray?"

Coach scowled and pitched again.

Crack. Sail. But no thunk—this one kept on going, landing somewhere beyond the fence.

"Come on, show-off," Wilder called as he exited the dugout, bat in hand. "We get it."

Noting my distraction, Coach threw the ball. That zing up my arms felt like a reward when he swore in my direction.

"You done?" I asked, smiling like a dickhead.

"Get the fuck outta here," he answered without any heat in his voice.

I shrugged, knocking fists with Wilder on my way to the dugout.

"You could at least pretend you have to try," Tate snarked, handing me a beer.

"I may be many things, but a liar ain't one of them."

"Don't listen to Tate," Shelby— one of our assistant coaches—said, twisting her golden hair into a fresh bun, her voice cheery. It always was when Tate's pride was on the line. "He's just butthurt he can't hit one over the fence. Just keep on trying, little buddy. You'll get it someday."

"Trust me, I'm not the one who's gonna get it," Tate promised.

"Oh, and you're gonna give it to me?" she challenged, one pretty brow arched.

"Shut the fuck up about my sister," Wilder yelled from the plate, pointing his bat in Tate's direction.

I clinked my can to Shelby's, who laughed at Tate's scowl but was smart enough to keep her mouth shut otherwise. By my math, she'd been giving Tate hell since elementary school and he'd been giving her noogies just as long. As close as Tate and Wilder were, they might as well have *both* been her brothers.

Shelby scooted down to make room for me, and I sat, watching Wilder through the chain-link. His form was perfect, the torque of his body supplying the exact force to knock the ball into the outfield without much effort, which was one of the many reasons he was a first-round draft pick after college. He'd played pro for a few years before tearing his rotator cuff. Never could pitch fast enough after that to stay in the majors.

Our piddly little softball team was damn lucky he decided to come back home.

The Roseville Ramblers were a competitive fast-pitch rec team stacked with all but a few ringers. Most of us had at least played through college, and all but one played on the high school team. Grayson, his dark hair shot with gray at the temples and his mouth full of bad attitude, coached our team and the high school boys, and Shelby coached the girls' softball team. We'd been winning competitions too, and the prize money that came with them.

I might not have been in the big leagues, but I had the Ramblers, and that felt like enough to me.

I took a pull of my drink, my mind wandering to a subject I couldn't seem to shake.

And she went by the name of Duchess.

Last night, I'd endured waiting on my cousin and her crew with the patience of a saint. Truth be told, Henry was the only thing that needed enduring. That, and the look on Jessa's face as she fawned over him. Once she'd had a couple glasses of wine, her cheeks were smudged with color, her eyes all sparkly when she laughed at whatever stupid joke he'd told. It was weird to see her like that, gone from fancy and classy to a flustered, giggling loon.

By the time they left, my boss had rearranged things, and I was able to get back to The Horseshoe for the rest of my night, which was nothing to write home about. When I made it back to the house, I walked in the door to a different place than I'd left. It was so clean, it was unrecognizable. Didn't know if it'd *ever* been so clean, despite Mama's best efforts to shame me into submission.

But everybody knew I was shameless.

"Y'all are ridiculous," Coach yelled from the mound as another of Wilder's balls disappeared behind the fence. "How about we give somebody a chance to learn something? Carlin —you're up. Wilder—go sit on the bench and think about what you've done."

"What, be awesome? No prob, Coach," he said, narrowly avoiding getting nailed in the ass with Coach's softball.

Carlin sighed, picking up all hundred and ten pounds of himself and snagging a bat on his way to the plate.

Shelby set her beer down to clap. "C'mon, Carlin! Just make a connection, that's all! You've got this!"

Carlin thanked her with a pale smile before turning his attention to Coach.

"Poor kid looks terrified," she said under her breath. "I wish he was here because he wanted to be and not because his mama made him."

"She's been pushin' him into sports since we were kids," Carlin's sister Trish, the other assistant coach, said from down the bench. "Mama's not a fan of his Star Trek obsession. The last time he addressed her in Klingon, she lost it. Told him if he didn't play, he didn't stay."

"Man, your mama must be some cook," Tate said with the shake of his head.

Trish snorted. "She does laundry real good, too."

I took another swig of my beer, grateful for the cold drink on such a hot day. The sun hit us like a radiator—everybody but Carlin and the women were shirtless. By the way Trish was salivating over Coach, I had a hunch the lack of clothes was the real reason she joined the team.

I didn't know much, but I knew a thirsty woman when I saw one.

Shelby elbowed me. "I heard you've got some sorta princess staying with you. A friend of Cass?"

"Ah, the duchess," I answered, smiling.

Tate wore a crooked smile, running a hand through his damp, dark hair before putting his cap back on. "I heard Beau trampled her when she was changing and she ran out of your house naked."

I gave him a look. "Where do y'all come up with this shit?"

He shrugged. "All the cashiers were talking about it at the grocery store. Janine almost knocked over a watermelon pyramid trying to listen in on Cass yesterday. I guess she came in for some fancy cheeses or something."

"Hate to burst your bubble, but I have not seen her naked," I clarified. *Sadly*.

"Yet," Wilder added as he entered the dugout, slapping Tate's hand when it was offered and hissing *Ow!* when his sister answered with a slap upside the head.

"Trust me—she's not interested," I insisted. "Pretty sure she hates me."

Shelby's gray eyes narrowed in thought. "Hate means you have a chance. It's indifference you've gotta look out for."

"I saw her yesterday," Trish noted, tearing her eyes away from Coach's glistening torso. "She's so pretty and perfect, like a doll fresh out of its box. What's she doing staying with you? I've seen your house. And the things that live there." She shuddered.

"Aunt Julie was in charge of everyone's boarding arrangements."

A knowing *ohhh* hummed through them.

"Worked out for you," Tate said.

"You gonna go for it?" Wilder asked.

I shrugged noncommittally and took a drink.

"If you don't, I will," Tate said.

A peal of laughter rolled out of me to cover a hot rush of dissent. "Please. You don't stand a chance."

"How about we bet on it?"

"How about you quit being an idiot before you get hit?"

A chorus of *Ooooos* sounded.

"Oh, grow up," I said. "She's too hot for the likes of us, least of all you, Tate."

"Please tell me you're not talking about my best friend," Cass said from behind us.

In unison, we turned to find my cousin and the woman in question standing outside the dugout.

I barely saw Cass. Jessa on the other hand was unmissable, all sexy smile and glittering blue eyes, arms folded to frame her pretty tits.

Not missing a beat, I answered, "Why? I'm pretty sure she'd agree."

Cass gave me a look. "About the hot thing or the part about being too good for all of you?"

"Both. Did you come to watch Coach tramp around without a shirt on like Trish?"

"Sir, I am a promised woman. Of course I did. I have a pulse."

"We were hoping you had a spare key with you," Jessa cut to the chase in that accent of hers. "I've run out of places to go, I'm afraid."

"I'll do you one better," I answered, snagging my bag and bat. "Howabout I come with."

"If you're asking," Cass said, "I say no."

One of my brows rose, and I turned my attention to Jessa. "And what do you say, Duchess?"

Her cheeks flushed prettily. "I suppose that depends."

"On what?"

"Whether you'll be a gentleman or not."

I rounded the dugout and stalked toward her with a hot smirk on my face. "Darlin', I'll never promise you that." The heat of her licked at me as I passed closer than I needed to, throwing over my shoulder, "But what I *can* promise is to keep Beau in line and off of you."

I threw my stuff into the open backseat of the Scout, turning to find the two of them having some kind of silent debate with nothing but their eyes and a few slight shifts of their heads.

Cass rolled her eyes. "Fine. But for God's sake, put a shirt on for once in your life. It's obscene."

They headed toward me, but I frowned as I pulled on my shirt and leaned against the Scout. "What's in your ass, Cassidy?"

Sparked, she narrowed her eyes and ate up the ground between us with long legs for her small frame, leaving Jessa

45

by the car. "I don't like leaving her with you. That's what's in my ass."

"You're just mad you had to clean my bathroom yesterday."

"That didn't help." She poked me in the chest, saying under her breath and through her teeth, "You'd *better* be a fucking gentleman. If you have any love and respect for me at all, you will not touch her. You will treat her like the treasure she is, or so help me God, I will ruin you. And you know all the ways I'll do it."

She was serious, that much was certain. But I also knew the warning wasn't as fiery as she was pretending it was. Cass was a sister to me. Which meant that she was asking and not telling me. And reminding me that she knew how to prank me to literal death.

I grabbed her finger and twisted her hand so that we ended up in a shake. "You know she's safe with me, Cass. I'm just messing around."

She softened a little, but her eyes were still narrow. "Well, cool it. You're stressing me out, and I have enough to be stressed about."

"All right, Squirt." I pulled her into a hug, further softening her bulldogging rage. "Don't worry. I got you."

She sighed and whacked me on the arm halfheartedly.

When I let her go and made sure Jessa was watching, I tossed my keys in the air and caught them.

"Well, come on, ladies. I don't have all day."

"Yes you do," Cass said over her shoulder.

I chuckled and climbed into the Scout. "You're right, I do."

She yelled something else at me, but I didn't hear over the rumble of my engine. I cupped my hand to my ear, but she rolled her eyes again and said something to Jessa before slipping into her Audi. Jessa laughed, her back arching to expose a little bit of her pale stomach between her cropped white top and the wide legged trousers she had on. My eyes lasered to the spot—I didn't know why something so modest made me salivate. Maybe it was because, outside of *Henry*, she seemed like a woman who was together all the time, in all circumstances.

And I was left with a rush of desire to see her undone.

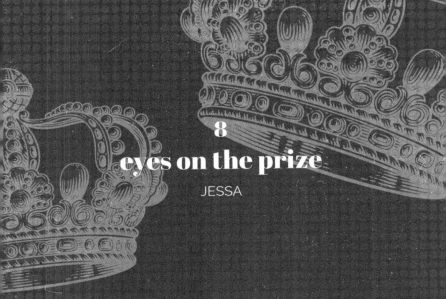

8
eyes on the prize

JESSA

IN THE FIVE minutes we'd been out of the car, it had turned into a sweltering hot-box.

Cass was going on about something, but I wasn't listening. My eyes were on Remy as he gripped his steering wheel, the muscles of his arms and shoulders bulging when he twisted to look back as he reversed the car. The vision reminded me of his strut off the baseball field in athletic shorts that did nothing to conceal the outline of what I knew to be his massive cock. Which reminded me of the pornographic dream I had about him last night that woke me with an actual, real-life orgasm.

This place left me entirely too hot for entirely too many reasons.

I blamed the firehose in his sorry excuse for shorts.

"Are you sure you're okay with this?" Cass asked, watching me.

"Do I have a choice?"

"There's always a choice. You could stay with me and I'll make Davis sleep on the couch. He won't mind."

"I won't kick Davis out of his wedding bed, but thank you for the offer."

"Maybe there's another couch out there for you to sleep on?"

"I think I'll take my chances with your brute cousin."

She chewed her lip as she pulled out of the carpark behind Remy.

"Why exactly are you so worried?"

"I don't really know," she answered. "It's not like you'd somehow fall for *Remy* when Henry is right there at your fingertips."

I laughed, slipping my sunglasses onto my face. "No, you don't have to worry about that. I don't think I've ever known anyone less my type, do you? Can you imagine?"

At that, she laughed too. "I honestly can't. Not like . . . on a date. But Remy doesn't date. He's a love-em-and-leave-em type. The local good-time guy. The trick is not to forget just exactly what he is. Despite that knowledge, many a friend has been blindsided." She paused. "I'd just hate for you to miss your shot with Henry because Remy wouldn't keep his shirt on."

"Have I been so weak?" I feigned offense.

"No, which is why it'd be even worse."

"I admit, he's fit. I've never seen anyone quite *so* fit. And I never seem to know what he's going to say, or what he's going to do."

"We call that a wildcard. Unpredictable underdogs with nothing to lose. They get you when you least expect it, and I guess I'm just afraid you won't see him coming."

"I shall be ever vigilant," I said with my hand on my heart.

"You'd better be, or I'll kill him. And don't look so excited —you'll be an accomplice to murder."

After a laugh, I looked out the passenger window, hoping I sounded nonchalant. "How was the rest of your night?"

"Boring. Henry and Davis were too busy catching up. I couldn't get a word in, ended up back in the house with

Mama and left them on the front porch talking half the night. But dinner went well, I thought. And we'll all be together every day. It'll be like our summers all over again."

I sighed. "Honestly, it's too much to hope for, isn't it? Henry and I, I mean."

"I fucking hope not," she started, the leather of the steering wheel squeaking under her palm as she squeezed. "He's the heir to the dukedom with no wife. You're his childhood friend who he has a marriage pact *that expires like right now*. There's literally no such thing as a better time than this. The stars have aligned."

"But saying and doing are two different things," I pointed out. "The pact could have been some sort of joke."

"It wasn't, and you know it wasn't. Also, I don't know if you know this, but you have gotten hotter in the last year. I don't know what kind of virgin blood you've got stocked to bathe in, but it's working."

I barked an unladylike laugh. "Thank you, but I'll never be Henry hot."

Her mouth popped open and her eyes cut to me. "Are you kidding? *You* are a *smokeshow*," she started, leaning into the steering wheel as she took a breath to fuel a rant. "Talk about fit—you are the most gorgeous woman I know. I'd do you, if you got me drunk enough. You're confident now in a way you weren't back then, sophisticated and kind times a million. You do charity work like him—"

"Not save-orphans-in-Africa charity. It is not like—"

"You know what I mean, Lady Jessamine Hastings. He'd be lucky to *have the motherfucking honor* of your attention. Honestly, it's getting ridiculous. Maybe this should be it. Last call. If he doesn't make a move now, of all times, he doesn't deserve you. As much as I'd love for Davis and I to be in the Howard-Hastings wedding party, I will skin him and sell his pelt to Buffalo Bill if he doesn't snap you up *immediately*."

Laughter filled the car.

"This is the time," she promised. "I can feel it in my very bones. It's you and Henry or bust."

Tiny wings fluttered in my belly at her certainty. "Well, your bones never lie."

"Amen."

The conversation turned to the Strawberry Festival and subsequent softball game, which dominated the rest of the ride. Our attendance tomorrow had been anticipated by my appetite for months now. Curiosity about the carnival rides and pie-eating contests had plagued me, and I wondered how much it would be like what I'd seen on the telly. By the time we pulled into Remy's long drive, said stomach was daydreaming of strawberry shortcake and funnel cakes, whatever they were. All I knew was that I wanted them in my belly.

"Dinner tonight at Aunt Linda's," Cassidy commanded, putting the car into park next to Remy's truck. "If you try to rely on the contents of Remy's fridge for sustenance, you'll starve to death."

"Color me unsurprised," I said, exiting the car and rounding my way to the boot for my luggage.

Cass stood between me and the stairs, her hand shielding her eyes as she looked at the cottage with mild disdain on her face. "Linda and I did our best, which is pretty damn good, considering the circumstance. I've never seen somebody clean like her—she even had a little toothbrush she detailed his sink with. The sheets are clean and so is the bathroom. The hordes of dust bunnies have been evacuated and the kitchen is dirty dish free." She sighed. "He wasn't always like this, you know."

"Like what? He's a lot of things, Cass."

She chuckled. "I mean, he's a man who's always played sports, so there's a level of stinky boy he's *always* had. But he used to . . . I dunno. Care more. A long time ago, he was fixing this house up for him and his fianceé, how wild is that? All he

51

wanted to do was take care of things. Me. His mama when she got sick. Chelsea. When she left him, something in him broke, and the pieces never went back quite right. And now?" Another sigh. "I mean, you've seen inside the mouth of hell. It's like he just gave up. The place was a disaster." She turned to me, nibbling on her lip. "Are you *sure* you want to do this?"

"I promise, I'll be fine," was my answer, since the truth wasn't an option. "Shall we?"

She took my bag with a sigh. "Yes, I suppose we shall."

My stomach twisted as we walked up the stairs and into the house, my eyes scanning for Remy but taking the time to pause over the bang-up job Cass and Linda had done. It looked like a different house—without the layer of grime, it was almost cozy.

Almost, I thought, stepping over a wayward pair of boots.

"Hello?" Cass sang as the back door opened and closed.

"Back here. Was just tying my asshole dog up."

He rounded the corner with a smile on his face, and I cursed myself for the involuntary drop of my gaze to the waggling anaconda his shorts highlighted so well.

"Here, lemme get that for you," he said, taking my things. "Your room's over here."

I followed the vast expanse of his back through a casing that led to a very short hallway. One bedroom stood at each end with the bathroom in the middle. We took a right into what I assumed would be my room. Once I could see around him, I found myself in a charming little bedroom with a brass bed. A lovely chest of drawers was topped with a mirror that reflected Remy and I back at me. I looked so small next to him. Without heels, I barely reached his shoulders. His arms were nearly as big around as my thighs, and his thighs were thick as my waist.

Absolutely ridiculous, the size of him.

He set my suitcase in the far corner and my bag in the

chair next to the window. Beyond it were the branches of a large tree, its leaves casting a dappled shadow on the bed in the slant of afternoon sunlight. I pulled aside the sheer curtain, my gaze sweeping the back of the property. The tree line at the edge of the yard was the deepest green brushed with darkness so complete, it was as if the light had been swallowed up by the forest.

Remy looked to the window, back at me, and scratched the back of his neck. "Hope it's okay. The room and all. I . . . I know you didn't want to stay here, but hopefully it's not too bad."

His uncertainty was a surprise. I smiled. "It's lovely, thank you."

"Shit," Cass hissed from the hallway, her eyes on her phone. "Is it really three? I'm sorry Jess, I've gotta go—the caterer needs to go over the menu one more time." She swept into the room and swiftly kissed my cheek, then hitched up onto her tiptoes to kiss Remy's, slapping it gently afterward. "Call me if he's a problem."

"I will," I said on a chuckle.

We waved our goodbyes, but when the front door closed, Remy and I seemed to remember we were alone.

"Well, I'd better—" he started as I said, "I think I'll—"

We'd moved in each other's direction, and in a terribly graceless fobble of arms, I ran directly into his solid chest, bouncing off of him like a pebble.

He caught me, smiling like he knew something I didn't, I noted from beneath my lashes. He smelled like freshly cut grass and sunshine, touched with the lightest musk of pure and absolute *man*. But I was too flustered to think of anything clever to say. Instead, I breathed, "Oh, my."

Remy laughed softly, the sound reverberating in his cavernous chest as he set me to rights and put space between us.

I straightened my back and smoothed my ponytail. "What, no quippy, inappropriate thought to share?"

A shiver ran down that straight back of mine when he leaned in, his lips next to my ear, and said, "Only the filthiest thoughts, Duchess. I'd share, but I don't want to set your panties on fire."

My mouth popped open, my gaze tracking him as he walked out, my body turning to keep him in sight. "You . . . you're . . . well, I say—"

"Doesn't sound like it," he said over his shoulder. I could hear him smiling, the bastard. "I'm heading outside to work on the truck—holler if you need me."

My mouth opened and closed and opened again, but before any words tumbled out, the back door sounded, marking his exit.

Fevered and ruffled, I turned to the chest of drawers, catching my reflection, absolutely *scathed* that my nipples were hard. Because the truth was, I might have done something silly if he'd said whatever filthy things resided in his brain. And as enlightening as that might have been, I had an agenda.

And Henry was at the top of it.

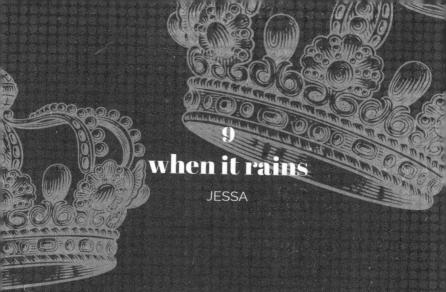

9
when it rains

JESSA

THOUGHTS OF HENRY tethered me as I began to unpack, filling the drawers and closet with my things. Most of my clothes were at the dry cleaner receiving emergency care, so I didn't have much, but it felt good to unpack them all the same. Perhaps I could even settle in here if Remy would stop hitting on me.

It seemed a herculean ask.

Part of me didn't even want to ask it.

I opened the window to let in the breeze, and it shifted the curtains, carrying the heady scent of magnolia on its currents. The ancient tree outside was the source, its waxy leaves providing the shade that would ideally help keep the room cool. I sat on the edge of the bed with a small smile on my face at the beauty and simplicity of this place. Not a small sort of simplicity, as if it was lacking. Far from it. Rather, it was uncomplicated. Easy and unhurried.

I found I liked it very much. Even the feral Remy, though I'd be hard pressed to admit it.

He was unlike anyone I'd ever met. Brazen and forward, and altogether too familiar with me. In the moments when he wasn't actively trying to unsettle me, I found him charming.

It'd have been so much easier to ignore my own feral impulses if he wasn't.

Country music played from the front of the small house, and I wondered just what he was doing. Perhaps he was half naked again, bent over that greasy engine with his shaggy hair half in his eyes.

Maybe I can see him from the front window.

Jessamine Hastings, get ahold of yourself.

Or I could get ahold of him.

With another swing of my mood, I huffed and stood, snatching my toiletries from my bag and a pair of shorts from their drawer. Fresh towels sat on the top of the chest of drawers, so I grabbed one of those too and made my way to the bathroom for a shower.

The washroom was actually lovely, with black and white penny tile floors and jade wall tiles. A clawfoot tub stood at the end of the room with a high window on the wall behind it, but the true wonder was a frosted skylight that set a brilliant glow to the room.

Once again, charmed.

When the window was open and the shower was running, I kicked off my shoes and slipped out of my clothes, folding them neatly before checking the mirror. My cheeks were flushed from the heat and dewy from humidity, leaving an unsightly sheen on my hair from perspiration. But I somehow looked fresher and more alive than I had in years. Younger even, like a version of myself I used to know.

It seemed Roseville agreed with me.

I slipped into the shower, setting my little bag of potions on the windowsill and sighing as I stepped into the lukewarm stream—anything hotter would have done no good in cooling me off, though I was beginning to wonder if the task was possible. I soaked my hair and soaped up my hands with shampoo, my thoughts wandering back to Remy as I lathered.

More pointedly to the cursed dream.

In it, I'd found myself standing inside his front door in my clothes from yesterday as he exited the bathroom naked in a cloud of steam. Water sluiced through the valleys created by his rolling muscles, dripping from his dark hair and ridiculous cock, a crooked smile on his wide, lush lips. He'd stalked toward me and said, *"You've never broken a rule in your whole life, but I'm gonna make you break every single one."*

And then he'd kissed me. An explosion of sensation shot through my body, lips to tits, to the deepest center of me. Instantly in this dream I was naked, and within a moment, we were in whatever my brain thought his room was without having walked there. He'd stretched me out in his bed, working his way down my body until his eyes were on mine, my thighs on his shoulders, and his hot mouth was occupied with my aching pussy.

Soap slid down my body and my hands wandered in its wake, brushing my peaked nipples. One hand stayed there, the other roaming on with the replaying dream. But my eyes were closed, and behind my lids was his face, soft and intent in his desire, devouring me with such desperation, I'd had an orgasm in the real world last night without him ever touching me.

My fingertips slipped between my pussy lips and slid up to find my clit, the swollen, aching thing that reveled in the pressure the dream lacked. A steady circle of my index and middle finger, and my legs twitched, my lungs squeezing, pulling in a sharp breath. Imagining his tongue circling my clit, my fingers did the job, and I bit back a moan. Electric heat zinged and crackled through me, my awareness shrinking to the point of connection. His lips latched onto me, my fingers in my slick heat, my heart thumping in my chest, my ears, my skull, so close that—

An ear-splitting crack preceded a shocking flood of water from the wall, the pressure so hard it nearly knocked me over. I screamed, turning toward the offense with my hands out, but when I opened my eyes, soap burned them shut again. Were I not afraid the pressure would detach my corneas, I'd have rinsed off, but as it was, I struggled to stay upright, backing away from the wall, screeching. Blindly, I searched for the opening of the circular shower curtain, but the assault and the acid in my eyes made this rather impossible.

This is how it ends, I thought. *Death by shampoo while masturbating to the last man on earth I should ever fuck.*

Which was exactly when the last man on earth I should ever fuck burst through the door.

"Jesus Christ," he said over my screaming and slipping. I heard the pops of the shower curtain tearing on each ring like a machine gun, and before I knew what was happening, he'd wrapped me up in it and was carrying me out of the house like a princess about to be roasted by a dragon.

His skin was hot against mine—as predicted, he was shirtless again—my arms instinctively linked around his neck. Parts of me touched him that should have been in the shower curtain, but I was too frantic to overthink my tit pressed against his blessed, godforsaken chest. He set me down on a stump somewhere outside and disappeared.

"Wait! Where are you going? Is there a towel? Your shirt? Anything?" Juggling the shower curtain, I wiped my eyes with my hands but still couldn't open them without hissing in pain. "Remy? Where the hell *are* you?"

"I'm here," I heard from the direction of the house, the words jolting like he was running. "Here," he said, panting in front of me. "Lemme help you."

He wiped my face tenderly with a towel as I adjusted the unforgiving plastic shower curtain.

"What the fuck were you doin' in there?"

The heat on my cheeks was radioactive. "Oh, I . . . erm, well, I was—"

A chuckle. "It was rhetorical, Duchess. Don't get your knickers in a twist. I mean, if you were wearing any."

The radioactive flush went atomic.

"Can you open your eyes?"

I pried one open and hissed again.

"So, no. Lemme get some water."

He disappeared again, and I sighed, sagging. What a mess I must have been, soapy and soaked and wrapped in a plastic sheet. A *clear* plastic sheet.

Never had I been so mortified in my life.

I heard footsteps in the grass and the splat of water. A hose was my best guess. "Put out your hands. It's cold."

Pinning the useless shower curtain under my arms, I held out cupped hands and leaned in, using both them and the stream to flush my eyes for a moment, wishing I could flush my humiliation. When I straightened up, I sloughed off the excess water and held out my hand.

"Towel?"

A towel landed in my palm, and I dried my face, finally able to blink my eyes open.

To find a Remy who was somehow both deeply concerned and highly amused.

"There she is," he said with that sideways smile on his face.

I groaned.

He laughed, bastard.

"C'mere." He took the hose and stepped around me. "Tip your head back."

I did as he instructed, looking through the leaves of the tree he'd deposited me under to the cornflower blue sky, ignoring the sliver of his face that I could see from the vantage.

"You okay?" he asked as he began to rinse my hair with frigid water.

"Other than my pride, I think I'll survive."

Another chuckle. I luxuriated in the feel of his fingers in my hair.

"I suppose it was only fair that you see me naked," I said. "I had a fair view of your cock the other day, so I reckon it's a matter of balance in the universe. And perhaps a lesson in humility."

He hmm'd, the sound appreciative and deeply thrilling. "I hope it's not too forward to say I hope your view was as good as mine."

A laugh burst out of me. "You're worried about offending me *now*?"

"Fair enough." A pause as he directed my head to tilt so he could get at my nape. "Did it really offend you, though?"

My own pause as I considered just how much to tell him. "Yes and no."

"Oh?"

"Don't pretend you didn't know you'd crossed the lines of propriety."

"I'll admit that was a good part of the point. I've found great pleasure in shocking you, Duchess."

His voice was deep and velvety and sinful.

"Then you have done your job, good sir. Congratulations."

The water and his hands disappeared. "There. All set. Here's your towel."

"Thank you," I said, taking it. But I was faced with the logistics of how on earth I'd manage my way into the towel and inside without open nudity. I died a thousand deaths sitting on that stump, dabbing my hair to stall. "What will happen in there?" I nodded toward the house.

He glanced in that direction and shrugged. "I shut off the water. Gotta go get a good look at it. Hopefully I can fix it."

"So you can just . . . plumb?"

A chuckle. "Sure, simple stuff at least. I'm good with a hammer and nail too. But I bet that doesn't surprise you."

His smile was so searing, he could have set the forest on fire. As it stood, he'd sparked a fire that started in my cheeks and tore through my chest like I'd been doused in petrol.

"You really do think highly of yourself, don't you?" I asked, glaring at him.

"Nah, but God do I love watching you squirm."

"Oh, do you?" I jeered, standing, holding the shower curtain like a Roman as boldness struck me like furious lightning. "Perhaps I can return the favor."

To my complete and absolute delight, his haughty smile melted down his chin as I unwrapped the plastic sheet and let it fall to the ground.

My ribs rattled with my heartbeat as I stood there for a moment. His mouth was open like a fish, easy enough to hook. But I savored the widening of his eyes as his gaze raked down and up my body.

When he finally met my eyes, his were aflame.

My work done, I turned and strutted to the house, swinging my hips and toweling off my hair. "Now I suppose we're even," I said.

But he was too stunned to answer.

And I'd never been so pleased in all my life.

10
slam dunk

JESSA

BY THE TIME I came out of my room, he was busy fixing the shower, whistling with grace I'd never expect from his mouth. I waved at him as I passed on my way to the front yard, book under my arm. He jerked his chin at me and kept on working, no trace of his thoughts on my nudity, which, based upon what I knew of him, was impossible.

He had plenty of thoughts about my naked bum, of that I was certain.

I'd seen a rickety old bench hanging from a tree just off the drive and figured I'd take the risk in regard to its sturdiness. Gingerly, I sat, and my luck held out, so I stretched out in the shade to read until he left for his shift at The Horseshoe.

Once again, he offered nothing to acknowledge the taste I'd given him of his own medicine.

Infuriating. Maddening. Absolutely exasperating that I couldn't rattle him the way he rattled me. I'd shaken him, but only about as much as this old swing in a breeze.

He shook me like a Pangean earthquake.

I didn't see him for the rest of the night. Cass picked me up to take me to Linda's for dinner, and I wondered again how someone so lovely could have ended up with a smartarsed bastard for a son. Through the meal, I worried he'd be at the house when I returned, but when we pulled in and the Scout was gone, I sighed. Mostly in relief. I think. And then I went to sleep wondering how long I could dodge him.

Shockingly, I didn't have another pornographic dream. Annoyingly, I was a little sad I hadn't.

The next morning, I snuck out of my room when Cass texted that she'd arrived. Through the sliver of his cracked door, I made out the shape of his outrageous torso and arms, sheets twisted around his waist. Beau lay sprawled at his feet, belly up, tongue hanging out of his open mouth and paws twitching in the air. With a smile I had not asked for, I tiptoed across squeaky boards to the front door, not breathing until I was outside where Cass waited.

I managed not to mention anything about sexy dreams or bare arses—mine or Remy's—listening instead to Cass rattle off wedding to-do lists and making notes on my phone like a good Maid of Honor. Nearly everyone intimately connected to the couple had made it to town for the festival. All the groomsmen and bridesmaids too, though outside of Henry and me, they were all cousins.

And they had a *lot* of cousins. Even Davis. And though many parents had arrived, his were still not here. Cass said they wouldn't be until the rehearsal dinner, which was likely why they were paying for the wedding. It was their favorite way to assuage their guilt for ignoring Davis, I supposed.

Brunch at the diner in town was lovely, Cass and Davis paired up opposite Henry and me. I spent the morning relishing in Henry's attention. His arm slung behind me on the booth. A kiss pressed to my temple. The rich sound of his laughter at a joke I made.

I haven't thought about Remy at all, I thought several times.

Cass looked quite proud of herself through brunch and

every minute after as we walked into the Roseville Strawberry Festival I'd heard so much about.

Everything was red and white with a splash of blue, from the sign to the tents to the Ferris wheel. They'd even painted the Ferris wheel cars to mimic a strawberry—green cap, seeds, and all. The air carried music and laughter and the hum of the crowd, with an assault of sweet and salty smells that set my mouth watering. Near the entrance, a pack of very little girls in foam strawberry costumes sang a song about summertime, and I dragged Cass to a halt in front of them so we could listen.

"They're precious," I said under my breath, my face soft.

"Those little girls are going into first grade, if I had to guess," she whispered back with a small smile that didn't reach her eyes.

"Your grade. I know you miss teaching, don't lie and say you don't," I warned.

"Well, that's the beauty. I can teach whenever I want. Davis just likes me home."

"Yes, but do *you* like being home?"

She shrugged, looking a little too blasé. "Do I miss working with kids? Absolutely. But I can go to Pilates whenever I want, and he makes more than enough money so I can otherwise lie around like a hoss cat. Anyway, you're not using your degree either. And you've mastered the job of hoss cat. You're basically a pro."

"Whatever would I use my art history degree for? Unlike you, I am not a natural teacher. I only got the thing because I love art, and to help with auctions."

"I guess that's fair." She linked our arms.

"You just seem a bit restless, that's all. Unfulfilled. A little lost."

One of her brows rose in my direction. "Pot, kettle."

I groaned. "At least we're young enough that we have time to sort it out, right?"

"God, I hope so. I'm really banking on it." She squeezed my arm. "Oh, I didn't even ask you how last night at Remy's went. I've been too busy blabbing on about myself. I'm sorry."

The flittering-fluttering in my stomach shouldn't have surprised me. "Oh, it went fine. He left straight away for work. Haven't seen him since."

She sighed, either in relief or annoyance. Maybe both. "Good. Hopefully it stays that way."

I shifted so I could give her a look. "You *do* like your cousin, don't you? There's no grudge or fight between you?"

"I love Remy, the dirty old shithead. Closest thing to a brother I have."

"You're just very concerned with us being near each other." *Same.*

"Listen—dozens of women I know have been casualties of that particular war."

My brows clicked together. "I thought he was engaged once? Surely he can be serious."

"He can be, he just avoids it at all costs. Honestly, Chelsea is probably why. Since her, the only thing he's been serious about is baseball. God, I hate her. It was so bad, he—" Frowning, she looked around. "Shit, we lost Davis and Henry. Come on."

My brain exploded with questions as Cass tugged me deeper into the fair, past booths of candles and necklaces and leather goods. Lemonade and pretzels and funnel cakes. My eyes hung on a passerby's plate and my stomach almost followed them, Remy and his mystery woman forgotten.

"Oh, there they are," Cass said, relieved as we walked up to an open area where Davis waved back and Henry smiled at me in that way that made me feel like the only woman in the world.

She abandoned me to bound over to Davis, launching

herself into his arms. He laughed, leaning back so he could press a long kiss to her lips.

Henry didn't seem to notice, instead beaming down at me. "Hello, Bits."

"Hello, Bobs." I beamed right back like a fool.

"Did the barbarian behave himself last night?" His brows drew together, his smile falling. "I don't like you staying with him."

I laughed, savoring the streak of jealously I saw in Henry. Not for cruelty, but because it gave me hope. "You and everyone. Don't worry. I'll be fine, and at least now it's clean. And if he tries anything . . . well, you know I'm quite capable of defending myself."

"Sometimes, when I'm having a bad day, I think about that time you nearly snapped a man's neck in a pub for grabbing Cass's bum. Classic." He sighed. "You, I trust. Him, I do not."

Jealous Henry had my cheeks warm and heart all fluttery. "He'll be a gentleman, I'm sure," I lied. "I've got nothing on Cass. Just think of what she would do to him if he doesn't behave."

At that, laughter burst out of us.

Cass and Davis were busy cooing at each other, so Henry hung his arm on my shoulders and turned me to the fair.

"Well, Bits, it's your first American fair. What shall we do first?"

I hummed. "I've always wanted one of those massive stuffed prizes. Think you could manage?"

"Manage? Darling, I'm a master." He winked, and I melted into a puddle and died happy. "Come on—let's start over there."

We'd stopped right in front of a red dunking booth painted with small black seeds where a little boy was making a valiant attempt at throwing a softball at the target.

Inside of that booth?

A mostly naked Remy.

Suddenly and instantly, all that happiness solidified into a dreadful, lovely sort of heat that lived at the apex of my thighs.

If the sight of his bare, hulking chest wasn't enough, his thighs were almost completely exposed, thanks to the nearly imperceptible inseam of his swim trunks. And if all *that* weren't enough, my eyes met his.

Remy sat on the platform with his hands balled into fists on those thick and taunting thighs, his back slightly curved, hackles up. But it was the violent sort of electricity with which he stared at me under Henry's arm that left me faint.

I leaned into Henry to keep my balance, and the dark look on Remy's face went pitch black.

The little boy's softball hit the booth with a thunk, and Remy let go of the tether he had on me with the shift of his attention. Almost instantly, his face was light as he cheered for the little boy by name, but his sizeable body was tight as a bowstring.

Jealous Remy inspired a completely foreign reaction in me. How I felt angry and proud and spiteful *and* hot for him baffled me. My ribs weren't big enough to hold it all—the feelings threatened to crack me open and blast out like fiery confetti.

Remy looked at me with an utterly wicked, slightly unhinged smile on his face.

"Hey, it's the Duchess," he shouted. "Has everyone met Her Highness?"

Everything he said was both horribly wrong and unwittingly right.

I gave an annoyed smile to Remy and a small wave to the crowd.

Cass fumed at him. "You're exhausting."

"Oh, come on," he said on a laugh edged with something hot and sharp. "We're raising money for the school library.

This is just part of the dunking-booth experience." He gestured to himself.

"When are you going to give us the shut-the-hell-up experience?" she shot back.

The crowd laughed and *oooh'd*, their faces swiveling from one to the other.

"I'm just saying. It's not every day we have royalty in town. Bet she can't throw for *sh*—" He glanced at the little boy. "For *anything*."

"And how would you know?" I asked, taking a step in his direction.

He shrugged. "Just a hunch." Before I could answer, he turned to the crowd. "How much do y'all wanna bet she can't dunk me? Come on, don't be stingy. Remember—all proceeds go to charity."

The surrounding people laughed, a couple of men holding up bills and shouting their bets.

Glaring at him, I folded my arms across my chest, which housed a steaming freight train.

Remy smiled like the devil, leaning to the edge of the booth to collect their money. "Come on, Lady Jessamine Hastings. Hit me with your best shot. Or are you afraid you'll break a nail?"

"Don't let him goad you," Cass said quietly. "Don't give him what he wants."

But my lips curled into a devilish smile of my own. "I've learned the best way to handle him is to rise to the occasion. You can't win the game if you don't play."

Chug, chug, chug went the freight train in time with my feet as I walked toward the grumpy-looking coach at the bucket of balls, ignoring the slant of his very small smile.

Delicately, I took the ball from his hand and curtsied politely. "Thank you, good sir."

I turned to the booth and narrowed my eyes at the

bullseye, lining up a throw that I hoped wouldn't embarrass me.

"Uh-oh, folks—she's serious," Remy said. "Shhh. Hush, everybody. Let her concentr—"

The ball left my hand wild. But in a stroke of sheer luck, it sailed close enough to his head that he shifted out of the way on instinct.

His surprise instantly shifted back into that smile. "Somebody get her a diamond tiara," Remy shouted. "Maybe it'll help her throw straight."

"I hope the water's cold," I shouted back.

I exhaled steam through my nose, my jaw tight as I wound up again and let go. This time, it hit the tarp around the bullseye, just to the right of my salvation.

The crowd *ohhh'd* at my miss. At least they were on my side.

It made sense. Who wouldn't want to see Remy eat his words? The whole town would likely root for me, even though they'd almost certainly bet against me.

"Third time's a charm, Duchess," he said. "Dunk me now or I might end up like you did after your shower—"

I'd never heard anything so satisfying as the sound of the ball smacking that bullseye, the cheer of the crowd, and the splash Remy made as he fell into a tank of water.

Those sounds were second only to the look of sheer shock on his face as the platform went out from under him.

I grinned so widely, I thought it might actually stretch from ear to ear. Remy emerged from the water with a whip of his head that tossed his hair all in one direction. And then the bastard hitched himself up on the edge of the tank and pulled himself out, all wet and slippery. His gigantic hands sloughed water along the curve of his skull, and then he turned to the crowd and waved.

And damn them all, they switched sides again, cheering for *him*.

But they couldn't rob me of the joy of my win. I tucked it away for safekeeping.

I headed for Cass. "He's a fucking menace," I said when I reached her, but my cheeks were flushed from the surge of adrenaline.

She was practically bouncing, her face alight. "Oh my God! You did it! I didn't think you could do it."

"Gosh, thanks," I said on a laugh as Henry pulled me in for a side-hug. I wound an arm around his back, trying not to be obvious as I inhaled his scent.

"Bits, you sneak. Where have you been hiding *that*?" he asked.

"I've always performed well under pressure."

He laughed.

I ignored the bubbling myriad of emotions Remy had set boiling in me.

"Now let's go pick a carnival game so you can get your prize."

But I didn't answer, instead smiling up at him as we turned for the games, wondering if he knew what the prize was.

I wondered if I knew either.

11
good girl
REMY

I GRABBED a towel and haphazardly dried off before snatching and throwing on my Hawaiian shirt, my eyes on Jessa as she walked into the crowd under that douchebag's arm.

Wilder gave me a look when he passed to take my place. "You okay, man?"

"Dunno. Where are my shoes?"

"Here." Shelby threw a pair of old flip-flops at me, and I slipped them on, flipping and flopping in Jessa's direction.

I didn't know what I was going to do when I caught up to them. I didn't know what I was doing a lot lately, especially since the scene she put on yesterday as she walked away from me buck naked. Honestly, I'd earned the payback, but Jesus Christ, she'd left me twisted. Soaking wet and shimmering like a siren, the smile on her face telling me all I needed to know—she liked me, and not in that *he's such a good friend* way. More of the *God, I want to ride that pony* way. And I'd just stood there like a fucking idiot, mouth hanging open and pants straining to contain the hard on I'd been sporting since I found her squealing and naked in the busted shower.

She was soft in all the right places, curved in just the right way to momentarily stop my brain function. Like the gentle slopes of her shoulders. The sweeping swells of her breasts. The arch of her back to her ass. The mound low on her pelvis that would fit perfectly in my palm.

Thank God she'd never caught me drooling over her. I'd never hear the end of it.

I'd rinsed out her hair while she sat in that useless shower curtain, her face tipped up to the sky so I could see down her throat when she talked. Unbidden, the vision of fucking her mouth flashed through my mind like lightning. This didn't help my boner either. But her strutting off like she did had my cock so hard, my fly dug painfully into the shaft.

I'd never admit what I did after that unless you asked or I found an opportune moment when it would make Jessa flush like I loved so much.

Fine, I jerked off. It took a whopping five seconds of my cock in my fist before I came so hard, I stood there behind the shed, one hand on the wall, shaking like a leaf and huffing like I'd run a marathon.

And today, here she was in a little yellow sundress with her hair loose, tucked into that shitbag's side.

The worst part was, I didn't even think he was an actual shitbag.

I didn't know why I saw red when I laid eyes on them—as bad as I wanted her, I had no claim. That slippery body I'd seen yesterday wasn't mine. And that hit me in a way I didn't expect . . . with jealousy and want and a fiery surge of protection.

So what did I do about it? Acted like a dickhead. Needled her until she did exactly what I wanted. Wasn't the first time. Probably wouldn't be the last. But it definitely felt the worst.

I caught sight of her yellow dress and wove my way through people, reaching Jessa and Henry just as they stopped in front of a booth.

Jessa looked smug, but I could tell by the tightness at the

corners of her mouth that she was pissed. Her lips usually lifted at the corners, like she was in a perpetual state of smiling.

I decided then that I didn't like those angry little lines and vowed to make sure I didn't see them again. Or at least not pointed at me.

Cass hit me in the arm. "You dickhead. What is wrong with you?"

"How much time do you have?" I defaulted to jackass. Had a smile to go with it and everything.

She groaned, her eyes searching the clouds for help from a higher power. "Pulling her ponytails won't make her like you, Remy."

I opened my mouth to say something rude about how I could, in fact, pull ponytails in such a way that could make a woman fall in love, but—

"It's fine," Jessa said, studiously ignoring me. "Come on, Cass—you owe me a strawberry shortcake."

Cass let out a breath that seemed to calm her down, but before anyone could speak, a gaggle of old church ladies crowded her and started yammering about the wedding.

I looked to Jessa, but she hooked her arm in Henry's.

"Strawberry shortcake can wait," she said, making hard eye contact with him. "*You* owe me an outrageously sized stuffed animal."

Henry glanced at me warily. "All right."

"Hang on," I said, before they'd taken two steps. "Jessa, could I . . . would you mind if I had a minute with you? Alone?"

Davis and Henry shared a look. Jessa eyed me.

"Why? What do you want?"

"To apologize."

At that, Cass's head whipped around in pleasant, albeit unbelieving surprise, but the old ladies had circled her like buzzards.

The tightness around Jessa's eyes eased, but her lips were still flat in the corners.

Hated it. Really did loathe it.

"All right." She nodded to Henry.

"I'll win you the grand prize, Bits," he said, shooting another warning glance in my direction before he and Davis headed toward the rubber duck ring toss.

His jealousy sent a violent surge of testosterone through me.

But I managed to tear my gaze away from Henry The Seersucker Mama's Boy and settled it on Jessa.

That violent surge ebbed when I looked down at her, arms folded, hip popped. Mad as all hell. A little wounded too.

"I'm sorry I picked on you back there," I started.

"It's fine. You're the one who's all washed up." She flicked my open shirt, and I didn't miss her lingering gaze on my bare torso.

I laughed, relaxing a little. "Never would have guessed."

"Neither would I."

"You mean you didn't know if you could do it?"

She rolled one bare shoulder. "None. It was dumb luck, really. I occasionally get a streak of it."

"I shouldn't have put you on the spot like that. Or heckled you."

"Then why did you?"

"Because you're cute as fuck when you're mad."

"Oh my God," she said, turning away from me.

I laughed and took a step in her direction. "I'm sorry, I'm sorry. Come on, Duchess. Let me make it up to you."

She stopped, half turning back with one of her brows arched. "What do you have in mind?"

I snuck a glance at Henry throwing rings at rubber ducks and knew exactly what to do.

So I snagged her wrist and towed her toward another booth.

"Where are we going?" she said on an annoyed laugh.

The feel of her slight wrist in my fist made my insides all fizzy.

I pulled her to a stop in front of a booth sporting tiered rows of creepy-looking stuffed clowns and a pile of bean bags.

"Down the Clown." I gestured to the dirty dolls with a flourish. "Go ahead and pick out your prize. I'll only be a minute." I slapped a soggy twenty on the counter and picked up my first bean bag. They were farther away than the guy down the counter from me figured. He couldn't hit one to save his life.

I wound up and tossed one, knocking it off its stand.

"Think you can beat Henry?" she asked, smiling.

"Blindfolded." *Thunk.* Down went another clown.

"Did Henry have anything to do with you acting like a twat?"

The word twat from her mouth in that accent killed me—my dick twitched to life in my swim trunks. "Twat, huh? I forgot the words y'all use without shame. Say cunt in a sentence."

I lined up to shoot as she came closer, stretching on her tiptoes. Her breath tickled my ear when she said, "*Cunt,*" the hard *T* sending shivers down to my balls.

God in heaven, the sound of the word in her mouth set my twitchy dick to a full salute in one very efficient heartbeat.

I threw the beanbag to distract myself.

She backed up, smirking as she watched me for a moment. "You really love baseball, don't you?"

"It was my whole life, in another life."

"How long did you play?"

"Through college."

She hummed. "Did you ever want to play professionally?"

"Almost did." *Thunk.*

"What happened?"

75

"Mama got cancer." I tested the weight of the beanbag before, *thunk*. The attendant set another stack on the counter.

When she spoke, I could hear her frowning, but I refused to look. "What do you mean?"

"There was no one to take care of her, so I did."

Silence for another throw. I watched the orange tuft of fuzzy hair as the doll flew into the air a little before falling. I didn't elaborate, but she still didn't speak.

"I'd been drafted to play for Atlanta—just got my contract. But instead of signing it, I came home."

Thunk.

"Surely they would have taken you after . . ."

"The offer was gone. Only other option was to walk on, and that's almost impossible." *Thunk.* "It all worked out." I smiled down at her, ignoring the cinderblock in my chest. "I got to be here to win you a . . ." I looked up at the prizes, my face screwing up. I didn't recognize a single creature. "Well, whatever those are."

"Why not try?" she asked, ignoring my deflection. "People like you are the reasons those opportunities exist. It's why the rules are in place."

"Rules," I scoffed, picking up a beanbag and soldiering on. "Aren't you the good girl."

The corners of her mouth were tipped down now. But it was still better than flat. "You say that as if it's a bad thing."

"I bet you've never done anything bad." *Thunk.*

"Define bad."

"If I have to define it, it wasn't bad enough."

She made a frustrated little noise that made me entirely too happy. "I've done bad things," she assured me.

"Oh yeah? Prove it."

I turned to her, tossing the beanbag a few inches in the air and catching it. God, she was pretty when she blushed.

"Prove it how?" she asked, squaring up as a terrible, wonderful idea came to me.

She'll never do it. Not in a million years.

But Jesus it'll be funny to watch her squirm.

"Give me your panties."

Her mouth popped open, her lashes fanning as she blinked. A rosy, pink flush climbed from under her low neckline, racing for her collarbone.

I shrugged, turning for the clowns. "Didn't think so." *Thunk.*

But when I turned, she was gone.

My smile fell. "Shit."

Now I owed her another apology.

You just can't keep your fucking mouth shut, can you?

I stepped out into the wide aisle, scanning for that yellow dress, swearing at myself. Henry was still at the stupid ducks, but she wasn't with him. Cass was trying to back out of the old lady rugby scrum with very little success, but no Jessa there either.

I glanced back toward the dunking booth, making the decision to head that way, when a pointy finger poked me in the biceps.

A very determined Jessa stood before me, her face set and lips tilted in another smug smile, the flush having made it all the way to her hairline. Confused, I opened my mouth to speak, but before I landed on exactly what to say—leaving it to chance usually gave me the best odds—she took my hand in hers and shoved a warm swath of fabric into my palm.

"Proof," she said, the words more breath than sound. Her chest heaved, her breasts straining at the neckline.

In a daze, I looked down at my hand where I held a sliver of silken fabric the color of her skin. And then I recited the roster and stats of the '98 Yankees so I wouldn't pop a full woody in these tiny swim trunks in front of my entire town. But no amount of Derek Jeter could stop the rush of blood to my cock. She could see what she'd done too—her nose was up, but her eyes were on my dick like a promise.

"Hey, you getting your prize or what?" the game attendant said.

I closed my fist around that sacred silk and put on my most obnoxious smile. "Pick anything you want, Duchess."

She stared at me through a couple of shallow breaths before turning to the attendant, and I took the opportunity to button the bottom half of my shirt so I didn't send the blue hairs into cardiac arrest with my unruly cock. Jessa marched up to the counter, and without hesitation, pointed at a pink monstrosity that looked like a cross between an octopus, a crab, and a kangaroo.

"I'll take that one, please."

He hooked it and handed it over. She thanked him and strode in my direction with some mixture of pride and lust and annoyance. At least my smile had worked.

"Satisfied?" she asked.

"Never." I answered inching closer. "So the good girl does bad things after all. Next time I make you prove it, I'm getting more than panties."

She looked up at me with hooded eyes, barely breathing. Heat mingled between us in whorls so potent, I hoped to God nobody lit a match.

We'd both go up in flames.

I broke the connection before I did something stupid like kiss her. Because don't get me wrong—if I hadn't been sure before, I was absolutely certain now. I was going to kiss her. But not here, and not like this, and God help us all when Cass found out.

I promised her Jessa was safe with me, and that was no lie.

But I never said I wouldn't fool around with her.

I caught Henry's eye and pointed at the bizarre stuffed animal in her arms with a smile.

"Don't worry," I shouted, hand cupped to my mouth. "I got it."

When I made sure he was good and pissed, I gave Jessa another smile.

"See you at home, Duchess."

And I strode off, swaggering away like I ruled the whole entire world, with her panties in my fist and a hard on that was about to be right behind them.

12
prove it
JESSA

I STOOD there like an idiot watching the back of that stupid shirt and tiny shorts disappear into the crowd, contemplating all the ways I might kill him.

Poison was too easy. Knives too messy. No—I'd like to kill him with my bare hands wrapped around his throat. Sitting on the topographical map he called a torso, his ribs between my thighs, Adam's apple in my palm. I'd bet he wouldn't even fight me. He'd likely slide his hands up my skirt to my bare backside and—

For God's sake, would you shut up already?

The deep breath I took trembled coming in and stuttered coming out. Never had I felt so out of control, not in all my life. But there was no anticipating Remy. The second I thought I had him, he managed to bite me in the bum.

Briefly, I wondered what it would feel like for him to bite my bum.

A noise somewhere between a roar and a groan escaped me as I turned for my friends.

I'd gone completely mental.

Cass was still stuck with the old ladies, so I slapped on a smile and squeezed in.

"Excuse me, ladies—I need to steal her back. So sorry!"

Her eyes sighed a thank you as she said goodbye and we stole away.

"What the just happened with you and Remy?" she whisper-yelled before we'd taken a second step.

There was absolutely no way to tell her I'd just given my underpants to her cousin. "Nothing. He was just being himself."

"That's terrible. I'm so sorry."

I chuckled, adjusting the stupid stuffed animal given to me by the wrong guy. Maybe I could suffocate him with it in his sleep.

"I thought Henry was supposed to win you one of those," she said.

"He was. And then Remy found out and beat him to it."

"Damn. He really is on a mission," she mumbled. "I don't like it—he usually gets what he wants."

"That doesn't sound like always, so I'll take my chances."

"Ugh, Henry looks pissed."

A sigh. "I know."

We stopped talking as we walked up to Henry and Davis.

Henry's brow settled low on his forehead, changing his appearance more than I imagined any expression could. But his gaze wasn't on me. It was on the hot pink fire hazard I had round the neck.

"What the fuck is wrong with that cretin?" Henry asked.

"Everyone asks, but no one seems to know," I said. No one laughed. "He gets off on upsetting apple carts. Don't let him get to you or it'll get worse. Trust me."

"It's *him* I don't trust."

Jealous Henry was my new favorite Henry. I linked arms with him. "I mean it. His mouth might be unmanageable, but I am perfectly safe from the rest of him."

Even staring at Henry, I considered Remy's unmanageable mouth and the body parts I could use to shut him up with.

Calculating the many, many months it had been since I'd last had sex, I made it a point to remedy the grievance immediately. Ideally with the man on my arm.

Henry didn't seem to believe me, but he let it go, taking the cursed prize so he could carry it for me like a gentleman.

With that, we were off to eat our way through the fair, leaving me glad I'd worn something without a waistband—I could eat all the shortcake and hot dogs I wanted. As convenient as the sundress was for my appetite, the downside was that it was a bit short to traipse around in on a breezy day. One of my hands hovered at my waist like a gunslinger, waiting for the wind to expose me to poor, unsuspecting children and elderly women.

I hadn't even considered how I'd sit down, not until I was directed to the metal bleachers around the high school baseball field for the annual festival game. Carefully, and with both hands, I smoothed my skirt over my bottom and held down the hem as I sat so my bare pussy wouldn't touch a public surface. It had been punished enough by Remy.

I wondered for a good long moment what it'd be like for Remy to *really* punish it. Really take it out on the poor girl.

And then I rolled my eyes at myself, deciding I needed therapy. Perhaps Jesus. Likely both.

Cass eyed me. "What's with you?"

"Too many hot dogs."

She elbowed me, leaning in. "Speaking of hot sausages, Henry was so jealous. Oh my God. File under: upsides to my cousin hitting on you."

We laughed, glancing at Henry. He sat on the other side of Davis, who was on the other side of Cass. He was Apollo in the flesh, shining and golden like sunshine, with a perfect, smiling mouth framing perfect teeth on his perfect face.

"I think he's going to make a move," Cass said from behind a sheet of her auburn hair.

"Did he say something?" I whispered.

"No, but I can tell. Gut feeling."

"I'll die. Absolutely deceased."

"Please don't die. I need you."

Another bout of laughter was interrupted by the loudspeaker announcing that the game was about to start.

We weren't so far away from the field that we couldn't see the players clearly as they warmed up, and I hated that I scanned them all for Remy's face.

I found him on the far side of the field as he threw a ball to another player, his body like a whip. When the ball was off, he glanced at the stands. From beneath the shadow of his baseball cap, his gaze landed on me like a grand piano.

I couldn't understand what he'd done to me, how the mere meeting of our eyes could set me on fire. And not a slow, simmering heat. An explosion, thick with danger and destruction and the promise of consumption.

A ball hit him square in the chest, and he flinched, blinking as he looked down. He picked it up and threw it, taking care not to look at me again. So I took the chance to catalog the sight of him in the tightest trousers I'd ever seen. The black baseball uniform hugged every curve of his legs, his tree-trunk thighs, the baffling and impressive shape of his backside. His jersey had been neatly tucked in, highlighting the taper of his waist from the barrel of his chest. Broad shoulders and arms like thick-corded rope caught and threw in a motion so fluid, it was clear he'd been doing it his whole life. His dark hair licked the back of his neck and ears, thick and wavy. The cap somehow emphasized the square, strong line of his jaw, framing the most masculine face I'd ever laid eyes on.

I caught sight of a small bulge in his pocket, and by God if my pulse didn't triple at the possibility that it was my underpants.

He was wound tight, hopefully trying not to be distracted by me. It gave me great pleasure to think I actually *could* rattle him the same as he did. Although I didn't think I could make him angry, not like he managed.

I wished I could have said I hated him. I suppose in moments, I very much did. But why? I had no reason to other than his audacity. And in sickening abundance. But what *really* drove me mad was that same audacity possessed the power to bring me to my knees if he wielded it right. Such as, if he'd kissed me at the Down the Clown booth, I wouldn't have just let him—I would have climbed him like an animal, kissed him until he was gone or I was. Probably worse. I might have lost all sense and let him fuck me stupid right there in front of Henry and everyone.

That's what he did to me. He left me disarmed by robbing me of all logic, driven purely by some strange, electric desire he sparked in the deepest, darkest, wildest spaces in me.

I squeezed my thighs together to appease the ache between and contain the wet slick the thought initiated.

The last thing I needed was to ruin the skirt of my dress.

The players lined up and took off their hats as everyone stood for the anthem, and once the song was over—and after a bit more careful skirt maneuvering—I was once again sitting between Cass and the hot pink, four-foot tall stuffed animal Remy had won for me out of spite.

Cass went on about the game, which apparently took place every year on this night of the festival with a neighboring town. Roseville's rivals were of a similar caliber —half of their team had gone pro, played through college, coached or the like. The other half, it seemed, was terrible. But the Ramblers were celebrities in Roseville. They sold out nearly every home game, though Cass suggested it was more for the handful of well-endowed single men on the team than it was the spirit of the game.

She was still talking when Remy stepped out of the dugout to bat, but I didn't hear a word she said.

His posture shifted, tightened as he stalked to the plate, his eyes dark and jaw set. I'd never seen him so serious, every molecule in his body at attention as he stood next to home plate, knees bent, bat drawing small circles in the air over his shoulder as he anticipated the pitch. *This* was a man who could have anything he wanted. He could win wars, conquer countries. He could find a way to survive any storm that dared cross him armed with nothing but will.

God help me if he turned that level of will on me.

I had no idea *this* existed in the brash, brazen, cavalier package he displayed with such pride.

His eyes stayed locked on the pitcher with a terrible determination, and when that pitcher threw, it almost happened too fast to see. Remy's body twisted in the most perfect motion, in the exact right mathematical equation to hit the ball with all the power stored in those roiling, coiled muscles.

The bat hit the ball with a crack, and a little white dot soared across the field. Everyone sprang to their feet, and I was glad. Because the vision of him hitting that ball and the sound it made when he did it left me with another slick rush of heat between my thighs.

What is the matter with you? Get a grip.

My pussy clenched watching him run the bases.

Ugh, not on that, ninny.

He ran across home plate to a throng of celebrating players, smiling like a beautiful bastard. I realized I was smiling back. As I celebrated the point with my friends, I saw Henry in a new light, one contrasted by Remy.

Henry was accomplished, steady, kind. Gorgeous. Familiar.

Remy was a parade of red flags.

And here I was, baton in hand and boots marching, the unwitting drum major leading us straight into the fiery pit where I'd either find heaven or hell.

I probably wouldn't know until it was too late.

By then, I wondered if I'd care.

13
true gentleman

REMY

JESSA'S PANTIES were burning a hole in my pocket.

I shouldn't have had them with me, but I couldn't help myself. The little bundle pressed against my thigh was a serious distraction, much like her presence in the stands, marked by that fucking toy like a blinking neon sign. I tried not to look at her. I really did. But the second I let down my guard, my eyes would slide in her direction. Which would remind me of her panties. Which would send impulses to my dick that I didn't have time for.

Should have left them in my bag. But I was beginning to think they might have to be pried out of my cold, dead hands.

The sun set as the game went on. We played these dickheads too often for my taste. Not only was Danville our high school rivals, but our town's, and now our softball team's too. I played against half their team in school, some even in college. These days, they were the only thing standing in the way of us making it to the state champs. If we won that, we'd qualify for regionals, then the championship. A new league had opened up a handful of years ago, and the billionaire who ran it had thrown all his weight behind it, getting sponsorship from the biggest brands, even landing the

World Series on ESPN 2. But the wildest thing was the cash prize—each bracket's winning team landed two hundred grand to split between them.

It might not have been that much money to some, but it could change the lives of more than a few of my teammates.

The score had been back and forth for nine innings, thanks to some unforced errors on our part. But we'd made up for it with enough good bats to tie us six-six. Wilder had pitched a shutout in the top of the ninth, earning us a shot at winning.

And then we'd struck out twice.

The crowd was out of their seats and screaming as I walked onto the field, but I barely heard them. I felt the thud of my heart, the turf under my feet. The bat in my hand as I walked up to the plate, drew a deep breath, and shut everything else out with the flip of a well-worn switch. I didn't see the glower on the pitcher's face, but I knew it was there. My eyes were on the ball in his hand as he turned it with his thumb, the moment of anticipation stretching out.

He wound up and let loose—*it's high, let it go*—the pop of the ball into the catcher's mitt sounding just before a ball was called. I stepped back for the throw back, then into the box I went, the bat squeaking against my gloves when I tightened my grip. Another pitch—*outside, leave it*—another ball. Nerves began to jangle in my belly, itchy to hit the ball and end the anticipation. Which was why I swung at something I shouldn't have. I knew it was too low the second it was too late to turn back.

"*Strike!*"

Which was probably why I let the next pitch go. Thankfully, it was low again.

I swallowed hard, teeth grinding as I positioned myself.

When he whipped the ball, it was so close, I didn't want to risk the strike, hoping it was another ball and would walk.

"*Strike two!*"

The crowd screamed encouragement at me at a thousand decibels.

"Fuck." I stepped out and turned, swinging a couple of times to shake myself loose and focus. Coach made his way over to me.

"Whatever it is, just fucking hit it."

I nodded.

He nodded.

And that was it. I headed back to the box. Felt my ribs expand and contract with a breath.

He pitched.

I swung.

Crack.

The hit was spot fucking on, and it sailed to the far right corner of the field as I ran like a motherfucker. Rounded first with my eyes on their outfielder as he picked up the ball. He threw it just as I approached second, and I stopped where I was, safe and sound.

As much as I'd have liked a homer, I'd take a stand-up double. Because Wilder batted next.

The beast strolled up to the plate like he owned the stadium, smacking his gum and shooting me a wink as he stepped into the box. He'd pitched for LA until a couple years ago when he was injured.

He might not have been able to pitch fast enough again, but the man was born to play.

He didn't even have to try, just swung with the ease and grace of a pro, hitting the ball with that glorious sound, a line drive between first and second that was too fast to catch. But when it hit the ground, the right fielder scooped it and let her rip for home.

I saw it all as I ran like hell for home plate, pushing hard when he threw, sliding as soon as I could—just as the ball fell into the catcher's mitt, which was on my hip, the two of us still in a cloud of swirling dust.

"Safe!"

And then all hell broke loose.

I bounded to my feet as the bleachers erupted, the catcher spinning around to argue with the ump. I didn't wait around, running toward the dugout where the team spilled out to meet me and Wilder. We ended up in the knot of our team, screaming and hollering and clapping shoulders and jumping on each other's backs. The crowd was still up and losing it. I threw a hand in the air, shit-eating grin on my face as I waved to the stands. I found Jessa, pleased to see her smiling and bouncing with Cass, a look of unbridled joy that only sports could bring on her pretty face.

I'd put that look there. And goddamn if that didn't feel even better than making her blush.

This was the feeling I craved. The win. The thrill. Standing at the plate, knowing just what I had to do if I wanted to feel this way.

I fucking lived for it.

But a shadow forever loomed, chasing down the high to swallow it up. Because there was a whole other life I could have had, one that amplified the high by a billion, one where I could eat, breathe, sleep what I loved more than anything in this world besides my mama.

For now, I basked in the glow, dead set on holding off the shadows as long as I could.

We got our shit together long enough to line up and slap hands with the Dusters. When we circled back toward the dugout, people had filed out of the bleachers, leaving it half empty. I frowned when I didn't see Jessa, but a quick scan found her behind Cass, waiting to get out of their aisle.

God bless that stupid fucking crab-oct-aroo.

I trotted to the dugout and grabbed my shit, slinging my bag over my shoulder. With a quick goodbye met with some confused expressions from my teammates, I jogged toward the gate to head Jessa off.

When I met them at the side exit, their faces lit up.

"Remy, you fucking showoff," Cass said, bouncing over to slap me a high five.

"Wasn't me. That was all Wilder."

"Yeah, it was," the man himself said, clapping me on the shoulder.

Laughing, we clasped hands and chest bumped.

Cass's excitement shifted into something shy and demure at the sight of Wilder, two adjectives I'd never in a million years associate with her. She took a step toward her fiancé and away from her ex with the weirdest smile on her face.

Davis didn't seem to notice, but Jessa did. She and I shared a look.

Wilder didn't miss a beat. "Hey, Cass. Good to see you, girl," he said as he approached her for a hug. He was so much taller than her, he had to bend down, and she hitched up on her tiptoes, stretching her neck so she could get her chin over his shoulder.

"You too," she answered with that weirdshit smile, patting him awkwardly on the shoulder.

When Wilder let her go, he pointed his movie star smile at Davis, extending a hand. "You must be the lucky guy."

"Nice to meet you," Davis said, obviously clueless as to who Wilder was.

They'd started dating in junior high, staying together all the way through the summer before we all left for college. Cass went to Oxford thanks to some old grandpa on her mama's side, and Wilder and I went to Auburn. And after that, Wilder moved to LA, keeping space between them when she moved back to the East Coast with Davis. She and Wilder had ended with more of a fizzle than a bang, and I couldn't help but wonder just how much unfinished business they might have left between them.

"Congrats, man. She's a catch," Wilder said. Cass's cheeks reddened.

Davis pulled her a little closer, looking down at her with pride. "She really is."

A knot of giggling women called Wilder's name, and like the hot shot he was, he gave them a smile that dropped the panties of all eligible bachelorettes in a solid radius.

"Gotta run. Good to see you, Cass. Y'all have a good one, okay?"

"Good game." I slapped him in the chest with the back of my hand.

He jerked his square chin at me. "You too, Ace." Off he jogged in the direction of the girls who'd made the mistake of calling his attention. Tomorrow, they'd be nothing but a pile of broken hearts.

Henry offered me a smile, suspicious though it was. "I have to admit, I didn't expect such a good game."

"I'll take that as a compliment, I guess. Glad we were able to meet your very high standards."

His smile disappeared. "I was trying to congratulate you."

"Oh, I caught that." I adjusted my bag, dismissing him. "Where y'all headed? I think everybody's meeting at the Horseshoe."

"I think we're going to go home, but thanks," Cass answered, all of a sudden looking at me like I was trouble.

"You too, Duchess?"

She opened her mouth to speak, first looking at Cass, then at me, then back at Cass. On reading her expression, she said, "Yes, thank you."

"Good. I'll drive you."

Cass huffed, pissed she'd gotten caught in the trap. "Aren't you going out?"

"You know, it was a rough game. I think I'll hit the hay."

"You're impossible. We'll take her."

"Why? That doesn't make any sense and you know it. I'm going there. She's going there. It's on the other side of town from your mama's."

"The town has a radius of four miles," Cass said, her face flat.

I shrugged. "Still. Save the turtles, or whatever." With a brow arched, I looked to Jessa. "How about we let Duchess speak for herself."

Something warred on her face as she adjusted her carnival prize, stalling. "I . . . erm . . ." Her gaze flicked to Cass, who looked worried. Jessa straightened up, smiling. "It's fine. He's harmless."

My cousin narrowed her eyes at me, leaning in to kiss Jessa's cheek. "He fucking better be. Can I talk to you for a second before we go, *Remington?*"

"Sure, *Cassidy,*" I answered as she grabbed me by the arm and pulled me aside.

"What are you doing?" she asked. She didn't spit it or snap it, she just asked with her eyebrows together like she was worried.

"I don't know what you mean."

"Stop it, Remy. I'm not dumb. You like her."

I shrugged. "She's likable."

"But she's not for you."

"And how come?"

"Because she's always been in love with somebody else."

"Who, Hank?" I scoffed. "Please. He barely knows she exists, the fucking idiot."

"That's not my point. *She* is emotionally unavailable. And *you* have a tendency to break women's hearts. She is my very best friend in the whole world, Remy, and I am asking you to please, *please* quit it. Because if the two of you ended up tangled up in something, one of you is going to get hurt. Or both of you. So just ... keep it in your pants. Please?"

She looked so worried, I pulled her into my chest for a hug, wishing I could promise her with certainty that I'd never so much as think about Jessa again.

"I love you, Squirt. Quit worrying so much."

She sighed. "I love you too, and I can't help it."

"Jessa's safe with me, remember?"

Another sigh. "Yeah."

"Good." I kissed the top of her head and let her go. "Now get back over to your man and let's get out of here."

"Hey—you really were great tonight. I'm sorry I've been on your case," she said, picking at her thumbnail.

"Cass, if I know one thing, it's that I have it comin'."

With her laughter, I'd been forgiven.

But all it took was one look at Jessa, and I instantly knew.

Cass shouldn't have let me off so easy.

14
bet your bottom dollar

REMY

SATISFACTION WASHED over me as Jessa said goodbye —until she got to Henry. That stupid fucker looked down at her like she hung the moon, pulling her in for a hug.

"See you tomorrow, Bits." He kissed the top of her head, and hot fury ripped through my chest. But I kept still, kept my face locked in the DGAF position.

"Night, Bobs," she said all flushed and breathy.

I almost picked her skinny ass up and threw her over my shoulder right then and there.

Cass hugged me, but pinned me with a look of warning.

Only the way I read it was that Jessa and Henry weren't so sure of a thing, or she wouldn't be worried about me.

I tucked that knowledge in my pocket right next to her panties.

The girls kissed cheeks and had a whisper conversation that ended with Jessa laughing too hard at what I assumed to be a joke at my expense. And with that, we parted ways.

"Lemme get that for you," I said, taking the toy from her. I held it out in front of me, making a face at its wonky eyeballs as we walked toward my Scout. "I don't know what the hell you call this thing."

"I was thinking of calling him Merlin."

"Because he has a face not even a wizard can fix?"

She laughed. My chest filled up.

"Do you have a better idea?"

"Hmm." I inspected him. "Kinda looks like a Bocephus to me."

That earned me a full on cackle. "That cannot be a name."

"In Tennessee it can. Never was there a name so hillbilly." I slung Bocephus over my shoulder by one of his legs. "It was Hank Williams Jr.'s nickname from his daddy. But I think it fits. Don't you?"

"It's perfectly ridiculous. Suits him."

"I'm over here." I nodded to the Scout.

We walked for a minute in silence. I wondered why I couldn't think of anything to say.

"Did you know that was my first baseball game?" she finally said.

"How'd you like it?"

"Surprisingly, quite a lot. The ending was wild. I've never felt that sort of excitement before."

"Not a sports fan, huh?"

"Not purposely. Just never had a reason to go before."

"Glad to give you a reason."

"Me too."

I kept quiet for a beat. "Still mad at me?"

"Only when I think about it." Thankfully, when I glanced at her, she had on a sardonic smile.

"I'll do my best not to remind you, then."

"Oh, I very much doubt that," she said on a laugh as we approached the Scout.

I'd put her top on as it was supposed to rain starting tomorrow, but the back window was down. I threw my bag in and stuffed Bocephus in the back seat before following her around to the passenger side to help her in.

"Here—lemme help you." I reached for her, sliding my

hands in the curves of her waist and hoisting her up. When her feet touched down, her skirt flipped a little in my direction, just enough to catch sight of the smooth curve of her ass.

A swear hissed in my mind as I shut the door and walked around to my side to hop in, feeling the bundle of her panties in my pocket like they were a living fucking thing.

The truck started with a deep rumble, and I pulled straight out and through the gravel parking lot to the road.

"You played well," she said after a moment. "I see how much you love it."

"So I managed to impress you?"

"It was a surprise to me too."

A soft chuckle.

"You're quite good. I think, at least. You made it look easy in a way the others couldn't seem to manage."

I preened at the compliment. "Years of practice, that's all it is."

"I don't know. It seemed so natural for you. I'm sorry you weren't able to play professionally. They'd have been lucky to have you."

"I appreciate that," I said earnestly.

We fell into silence once again, rambling down the road toward my house. I fiddled with the radio to give myself something to do, landing on an oldies country station.

As easy as she was to read, she was an enigma to me. Mostly, her putting up with my shit was the enigma, but the only thing I could figure was that she was enjoying this as much as I was.

The thought encouraged me. And the encouragement emboldened me.

"So what's the deal with you and Henry?" I asked, one hand on the steering wheel and the other on my thigh, the godforsaken underwear under my palm.

"What do you mean?"

I gave her a look. "You know what I mean. You've all been friends forever, but he's all lovey-dovey with you. Bits and Bobs? All the touchy-smoochy-ness? Are y'all a thing? Were you ever a thing?"

She folded her arms. "We've always been like this. I love Henry. I've always loved Henry, my whole life."

Why those words felt like molten steel in my heart, I couldn't tell you.

"Strong word, love," I said.

She shrugged. "I don't know what else to call it. No, we've never officially been a thing."

"Have you ever hooked up?" My fist tightened on the wheel.

A pause. "No."

Elation. I couldn't help but laugh. "I knew he was a dumbass, but I didn't think he was *that* dumb."

Her eyebrows pinched together. "Honestly, this is none of your business."

"Oh, *now* you're worried about manners? You weren't thinking about them overmuch when you handed me your knickers." Inadvertently, I patted said knickers.

She caught the motion and stilled, though I didn't get the feeling it was in anger. "Have they been in your pocket this whole time?"

"Damn near lost me the game a couple of times."

I chanced a look at her—I think she might have glitched out, her eyes blinking and wide.

"You okay, Duchess? Did I just break you?"

"I'm beginning to think that might be your life's purpose. You do know they're all worried about leaving me alone with you?"

"They'd be wise not to trust you around me."

She laughed. "Oh, that's not what they're worried about. It's *you* no one trusts."

"And how about you? Do you trust me?"

Jessa thought for a second. "I trust that you'd never touch me without my permission, which is their concern I think. I trust that you wouldn't hurt me, not on purpose. Drive me mad—that's another story."

I nodded. "You're right on all counts."

"What I can't sort out is why you're playing this game with me."

"Darlin', I'm not the only one who's playing. You've tried to top me at every turn. Only got me the once."

"The dunking booth?"

"Doesn't count. I got your undies fifteen minutes after." I didn't mention her giving me the garment got me harder than I'd ever been gotten in my life. "The shower curtain."

"Ah, yes. I was rather proud of that."

"I could tell. Maybe I'm waiting on you to make a move."

"*Me* make a move?" Her laughter was meant to be annoyed, but I caught the nerves in it. "Whatever makes you think I'd ever make a move on you?"

I gave her a look. "Are you serious? You ducked behind a carnival booth to take your panties off for me. It's only a matter of time, honey. You and I both know it," I goaded in the hopes I was right as I turned into my driveway.

"Please. You'll break far before I ever will."

I gave her a hard look, my lips tilted in a smile. "You really think you can outlast me?"

"I know I can."

"You already broke for me once. It won't be the last time, either And it's gonna be *so sweet* when you do."

"No, *you* will give in," she insisted. It was cute how right she thought she was. "And when you do, you'll be mortified when I don't give you what you want."

I pulled the Scout to a stop in front of the house and turned in my seat to face her, my hand moving to grip the back of her seat.

"It'll be you," I said, the words fire and smoke. "You won't be able to stop yourself, Duchess. And there's no fucking way I'll stop you, not any more than you'll stop me. So game on. Show me what you've got. Because the only thing in this world that'll be as sweet as winning is getting ahold of the sweet pussy that left her scent on these." I reached into my pocket and held up the scrap of fabric for her inspection.

I figured she'd either slap me or kiss me, but to my surprise, she just sat there with her lids heavy and breath shallow, staring at her delicate panties wound around my thick fingers.

After a slow blink, a smile curled on her lips. "That's what you think." She opened the door and half stood to hop out, parting her legs before she hinged far enough to have touched the ground. She flipped her skirt to her waist in order to expose her ass, which I'd seen. What I had *not* had the pleasure of viewing were the lips of her pussy, the line where they met begging to be parted by my tingling fingertips and cock.

And then she arched her back, and I caught a glimpse of the bud of her clit, and I thought my heart was going to explode from the tsunami of blood it pumped straight to my dick.

She hopped down, turning to give me a smile straight from the devil himself.

"Game on, you fucking tosser."

And when she slammed the door, I was pretty sure I fell in love.

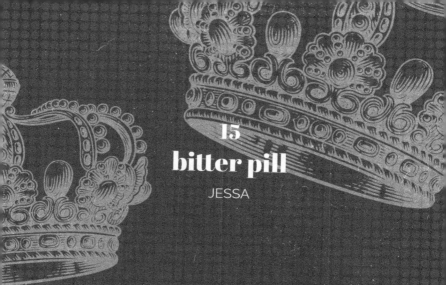

15
bitter pill

JESSA

MY FEET RESTED in Henry's lap, dangerously close to his cock.

Finally, all was right in the world.

We sat on Cass's mother's sofa, the four of us working on crafts for the rapidly approaching wedding, to the sound of raindrops on the roof and windows. It had rained for two days, confining us to Cass's house. Not only was it clean and cozy, but it smelled divine thanks to the four thousand candles her mother owned. Plus, it kept me close to Henry, which I'd very much needed.

For a moment, I'd forgotten all about him.

The man himself laughed at something Cass said as he tied another nude tulle sash to a strand of twine, and something jellified in my chest at the sound. Here, I felt like myself. Now, things were right and familiar.

I sighed my contentment, slipping a photo of Davis and Cass into the small frame that would be part of one of the centerpieces. We'd printed up dozens of photos of them spanning the years they'd been together. It seemed so long ago that they met, that we all came together with all the possibility our lives would hold still ahead of us. Ten years later, those windows of possibility were little more than cracked.

Time was slipping away. I felt every second as it passed.

Conversation had dwindled and then split, leaving Cass and Davis across the room talking quietly, happily, oblivious to the rest of the world. I wished for that with a longing so deep, it left a space in my chest. Henry set the ribbons next to my feet and stretched, his shirt creeping up to expose his abdomen. A flush crept through me, and I rested my head on the back of the sofa, smiling at him.

When he noticed, he smiled back, shifting so he could see me better. He rested a hand on my ankle, stroking my skin with his thumb.

"You look lovely there, like this," he said.

And there I went, *poof*. "Feeling sentimental, are we?"

"It's hard not to when I'm around you. Do you remember when we first kissed?"

I chuckled. "How could I forget?"

"I haven't been able to recall if we were eight or nine. It's been driving me mad."

"Eight. It was the summer in Barcelona."

He sighed happily. "Ah, yes. Inseparable as always."

"When we were together, which was tragically infrequent."

"Hadn't we snuck away from the nanny? I thought her head was going to pop."

"Wouldn't have been the first time."

"No," he said on a laugh. "It was a favorite pastime, as I recall, driving her batty."

We gazed at each other for a moment in perfect silence.

My thoughts rambled about as I wondered over him, the culmination of years of dreaming. Was he truly it? Could Henry really be my future? I'd been waiting on him for so long, and here we were, at the end of the line, and he'd said nothing.

It needed to be said. It must be decided.

And if he wouldn't do it, it was time that I did.

So I opened my mouth to say it all, but . . .

"Right, Henry?" Davis said, drawing our attention.

Instantly, the moment evaporated, and he was the same happy old Henry, answering Davis as if there wasn't a continent between us, even though my feet were in his lap.

Jenny, Cass's mom, had come in and sat on the arm of the other sofa, smiling the irreverent smile she'd given her daughter. Her hair was auburn like Cass, but faded with age and shot with gray at the temples.

Cass's brow quirked when she caught my eye, but she kept on talking, finishing a story about one of the photos, a holiday they'd taken in Bali and a mishap with a pineapple that had ended with them being propositioned by a much older couple. Davis shook his head, smiling and embarrassed. Cass thought it was hysterical, mostly because she was shameless.

It ran in the family, I supposed.

"Well, how's it coming in here?" Jenny asked, patting Davis on the shoulder.

"I think we've just about got it done," Cass answered, stacking up frames to deposit in a box. "Good thing it's been raining. Gave us a reason to sit still and knock all this out."

Henry shifted to stand, depositing my feet on the sofa, the cushion still warm from his bum. Which was quite a lovely bum, I noted with frustration as he walked across the living room to lay the garland he'd been working on in one of the other boxes.

"It looks terrific," Cass's mom said, picking up one of the frames from its box. "Look at how gorgeous you two are. I'm gonna have the prettiest grandbabies." She beamed at the photo, sighing before putting it back. "Are y'all ready for dinner?"

She'd only asked Davis and Cass—they'd been planning a

dinner with just them for days, leaving Henry and me to fend for ourselves.

"I think so," Cass said. "Let us just finish cleaning up."

"All right, baby. What are y'all doing tonight?" she asked me and Henry.

I was about to suggest he and I have dinner so I could say those pesky unsaid things, but he beat me to it.

"The groomsmen planned a little dinner for tonight."

I worked very, very hard to ensure my face remained pleasant through my disappointment. "Ah, well, back to the house I go."

Everyone wore a look of pity. I watched the war of manners on Cass's mom's face as she contemplated inviting me to her long-awaited private dinner.

"I'm looking forward to a quiet night. I've nearly finished reading my book, and I have takeaway from my heavenly dinner last night. Please, don't worry about me." I swung my legs off the sofa and stood, helping everyone clean up.

"Are you sure?" Jenny asked, genuinely concerned. "I hate to leave you with Remy like that. I love that boy, but . . ." She shook her head.

"Absolutely certain. Remy's not all bad. We have an . . . understanding." An understanding that had thus far involved more nudity than I would have expected, but an understanding nonetheless. "Anyway, he's working tonight."

Henry groaned. "Damn. We were planning on going to the bar."

"Go to the bar and make him work for once," Cass said. "Just be sure to tip him. Last thing any of us wants is to have to feed and clothe him."

We closed up the boxes, and I parted ways with Henry, to my utter sadness.

"Text me, would you?" I called after him in a pathetic attempt I hoped wasn't as transparent as it felt.

"Of course, Bits," he said with a wave and the smile I'd

spent so much of my life dreaming about as he walked out the door.

I followed everyone to the garage where we loaded the car and left for Remy's.

The drive wasn't long, and everyone was too busy visiting to ask me any questions. Thank God it hadn't been just me and Cass. Who knew what I'd confess.

What was I to do about Henry? Wait in aching limbo for him to tell me what I'd begun to wonder was absolutely nothing? Try in earnest to seduce him? I'd discovered I had new tools at my disposal for the task, but I didn't think baring my fanny to Henry would have the same effect as it did on Remy.

Remy. The man should come equipped with a tail and devil horns. Perhaps he did possess horns beneath all that hair. I'd wonder about a tail, but since I'd seen every centimeter of his body, I couldn't pretend not to know better. Unless one mistook his ridiculous cock for a tail at a glance, which wasn't out of the question.

Everything about that cock spelled trouble. It wasn't just an unmanageable length—it was an emergency room visit. That it belonged to Remy Winfield was its own problem, not only for his reputation of fucking girls and then fucking them over, but because he'd been expressly forbidden by my best friend, who was his cousin, and who *also* happened to be the bride I was busy filling picture frames for.

So why was it that I couldn't stop imagining the whole of that dangerous cock fitted—likely painfully—in the hot space between my thighs?

What I'd have given to fuck *that* without consequences.

I'd kept my secrets about Remy, which wasn't difficult with the wedding looming. The event was all Cass could talk about when we were alone, and when we weren't, the subject of Remy's dick was not at the top of the list.

Ashamed as I was to admit it, the secrecy made the game

we'd tangled ourselves up in more thrilling. No one knew Remy had seen my entire pussy, nor were they aware that he was in possession of a pair of my worn knickers. Silky and very, very small knickers. Lord, he'd even seen my fully naked body. Washed my hair with rough hands that didn't seem capable of tenderness. But they were, damn them, unexpectedly gentle and careful.

And not a soul knew.

My chest ached, my ribs squeezing a hot coal of desire that I had *never* felt with Henry. My love for Henry was quite practical and safe. My feelings for Remy were anything but. They were utterly feral, and my control over them was dubious at best.

I hadn't seen him much the last few days, a blessing and a curse. The space had given me time to cool off—the Night Of The Knickers, I'd had a very long multi-orgasm session with myself to stop me from doing something stupid. And I didn't know what Remy had planned to try and tempt me into losing, but despite my bravado, I couldn't guarantee my willpower would hold out.

Why I was involved in the whole mess was beyond me. Apparently, I was not above being goaded, too stubborn for my own good. What made it so terribly dangerous was that I *did* want him, but I had promised myself to Henry long before he'd ever asked. Henry, who I was no longer convinced would ever be mine.

Henry, my feelings for whom I wasn't too sure about after all.

It was quite confusing. The easiest way to handle Remy was to avoid him. And thankfully, he was working tonight.

Every thought in my head died when we pulled up to the house and his Scout was there.

My sigh was nothing short of defeated.

Cass nibbled her bottom lip. "Are you *sure* you can't join us for dinner?"

"Yes," I said on a forced laugh. "Go! Enjoy yourselves."

"Judo chop his ass if he deserves it. Just not in the face," she added. "I need him unbruised for wedding pictures."

At least that time when I laughed, it wasn't a lie.

I opened the door to torrential rain, throwing it shut behind me as I took off for the porch. But even in that short distance, my shoes were muddy and my clothes soaked. I waved goodbye like a wet raccoon and braced myself for whatever was going to happen with Remy.

Something *always* happened with Remy.

But of all the things I expected to discover beyond the door, I couldn't have guessed what I'd find.

16
truth is

JESSA

THE LIVING ROOM and kitchen were filled with a warm glow, the delectable smell of food, and the quiet strumming of country music from an unknown source. It was even tidy, complete with a throw hanging on the back of the sofa, not a shoe to be found in front of the door. Small lamps I hadn't noticed before were the source of the glow, dotting the living room and kitchen, giving the room the coziest ambiance. The scent came from the stove, where I found the biggest surprise of all.

Remy stood in front of a pot, large spoon in hand, half turned to me with a confused look on his devastatingly handsome face. A dark T-shirt stretched across his back and arms, his jeans hugging his backside and thighs, looser from the knee down to where they bunched at his bare feet. I'd never considered bare feet strong or masculine, or noticed a dusting of dark hair with anything but mild disgust, but here I was with Remy's sexy feet, questioning my mental health.

Beau's head lifted sleepily from his sprawl on the kitchen floor. On seeing it was only me, he flopped his head back down and sighed, instantly asleep again.

"What are you doing here?" Remy asked, still looking confused.

"I might ask you the same thing." I shook off my arms and twisted my wet hair to get it off my neck. "I thought you were working tonight."

"Boss figured we wouldn't be busy, what with the rain and all. I thought you'd still be avoiding me so you don't lose our little wager."

And there he was, good old Remy. I rolled my eyes, reckoning I was no better.

Really, I was a different person inside these walls than I was anywhere else.

"I haven't been avoiding you." I kicked off my shoes, leaving them in the doorway. I had to admit it was a liberating not to care. "We've been busy with wedding things. Crafting and such."

"Tell me you made a life-sized papier mâché Henry I can beat the shit out of with a stick."

A laugh bubbled out of me before I could catch it.

I hated that he was so funny. I really did.

"You eat yet?" he asked. "I think I've got enough for two." He gestured to the big stock pot with a sideways smile on his lips.

"That would be lovely. Is there time to change? I'm a little . . ." I held up my arms, looking down at my wet clothes.

"Soaked. And yeah, you have time."

"Thank you," I said, padding toward my bedroom and closing the door behind me.

The smell of whatever was in that pot had my mouth watering. I hadn't eaten since lunch, and though I'd told everyone I'd been looking forward to my takeaway dinner, the truth was I woke up to find Remy had already eaten it. My plan had been to scrounge around for some bread and meat, though I had my doubts as to the contents of his refrigerator. So to discover there was a hot meal waiting delighted me, even if it meant I had to share a meal with the one man I desperately needed to avoid.

Bocephus stared cross-eyed from his chair in my room as I dug through my drawers for something comfortable, settling on a tan lounge set I'd packed for just such an occasion. I was glad to have all my clothes back from the dry cleaner—and with only minimal damage, keeping Beau off the hook. Once I was in the wide-legged pants and tank, I slipped on the matching cardi and took a moment in the mirror to address my hair. While Cass had taught me the art of the messy bun, I couldn't bring myself to do it. Instead, I twisted it into a chignon with a little less chaos, binding it with a hair tie.

Since I was starving, I decided it to be well enough and made my way back to the kitchen.

Remy stood at the island with a mixing bowl steadied in one hand and a whisk in the other. When he saw me, the whisk came to a stop, his eyes sliding down, then up, ending with a slight shake of his head.

"Can we call a truce for tonight?" he asked, eyes on the batter in his bowl.

"Of course."

"Good. Close your cardigan because I can't sit through an entire meal with your nipples that hard."

I rolled my lips to stop myself from smiling, gathering the sides of my sweater and wrapping them around me.

"It wasn't intentional, I swear," I said, taking a seat at one of two barstools opposite him.

"I'd rather assume you were in there perking them up for me, if it's all right by you."

"Does it really matter if it's all right by me?"

He considered. "Probably too late for that, if I'm honest."

"*That* is perhaps your best quality—honesty. You only have to choose to use it for good rather than evil."

"Never," he said with that devilish smile of his.

"Also the unadulterated truth." I smiled despite myself. "What are you making?"

"Cornbread."

I must have looked confused.

"Sorta like . . . polenta?" He poured the mix into a greased cast-iron skillet and turned to put it in the oven. "This," he started, picking up his spoon to stir the contents of the pot, "is red beans, and there's rice in that smaller pot over there."

"It smells divine. I must say, I'm shocked to learn you cook."

"Well, you do know I love to shock you."

"And you excel at it."

"What can I say? I'm an overachiever." He replaced the lid and went to the cabinets in search of bowls. "Mama taught me when I was little. Plus, I owed you a meal since I ate yours last night."

I blinked at him, caught off guard. "Thank you."

"You're welcome. I make a mean gumbo too, though I haven't cooked much at all, not in years. I can also fry chicken so tender, you might find religion in a mere, buttery bite of it."

"I'll expect it tomorrow for dinner, thank you."

"Yes, ma'am." He set the bowls next to the pot.

I chuckled. "Ma'am," I said, flattening the As like an American would.

"How do you say it?" When I demonstrated, his face quirked. "Sounds like you're saying 'mom.'"

"I think that might be where you got it."

"Figures." He set out napkins and spoons. "Beer? Or wine?"

Genuine shock hit my face. "Wine? You have wine?"

Looking pleased with himself, he said, "Got a red and a white from the bar. Thought you might like them. Even stole a couple wine glasses so you wouldn't have to drink out of a jelly jar."

"A . . . what?"

"A jelly jar. Like this." He reached into the cabinet and pulled out what looked like a faceted juice glass with a thread on top for a lid.

I shrugged. "When in Rome. I'll take the white, please. In a jelly jar glass."

"Whatever suits your fancy, Duchess."

I watched him uncork the bottle, fascinated by the girth and vein density of his forearms. "It's all very thoughtful. Is this part of your plan to break me? Put away your boots and bring me wine?"

"Why, is it working?"

"I'll never tell." It was. "Anyway, we're in a truce tonight. I hope you're not cheating. It'd be an automatic loss."

"Girl, I am not gonna lose."

I shrugged one shoulder, sending my cardigan over the curve to hang on my arm. "We'll see."

"You'd better put that shoulder away or I'm calling *you* the cheater."

I pulled the thing back up, still smiling. Damn him.

He poured out as we talked and set my glass in front of me.

"No wine for you?" I asked.

He was already half in the fridge. "I'll have a beer, thanks."

I watched his big hand twist off the top and bring the bottle to his lips, hypnotized. The realization that I was perhaps the thirstier of the two of us stung. But it wasn't just that.

This Remy had charmed me much like the other versions I'd met, but the one who'd made dinner and tidied up without even knowing I'd be here was my favorite. I'd never felt this sort of fluttering before. With Henry, it was the nervous flicker of wings in anticipation of a thing I'd never have. But with Remy, the fluttering felt like possibility, as real and solid as he was. This anticipation held a promise I hadn't quite grasped. And to my wonder, I realized something.

Maybe Remy was exactly what I needed.

Maybe it'd never been Henry at all.

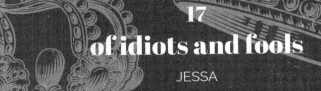

IN AN EFFORT TO distract myself from him, I glanced at the front window. "Does it rain like this often?"

Remy smiled like he knew what I was doing, if the banal subject of the weather hadn't given me away. "It does, though not always this many days in a row. The ball field is gonna be trashed for days."

"You practice a lot?"

"Three times a week plus games."

I took a sip of wine, surprised at the crisp finish. "Will there be another game before the wedding?"

"There will. Why, you coming?"

"It was thrilling. I do believe I'd enjoy another. You're I think what they call a natural." I paused, watching him for a beat. "I find it admirable that you sacrificed baseball for your mother."

He shrugged it off. "Couldn't let her go through all that alone. When I think of how hard it was for her, I can't imagine having been anywhere else."

"There wasn't anyone else who could have helped her?"

"Not the way I could. Cass's dad had died not long before —her mama couldn't move in with mine and care for her. Her grief took everything she had. Aunt Julie can't be trusted to remember doctor's appointments and medicine schedules, as you can imagine from her bang-up job organizing everyone's room and board for the wedding."

I breathed a small laugh.

"I thought . . . I don't know. I think part of me thought there'd be an open invitation back to the team, even though I knew better. I had a whole life right there, right in the palm of my hand. A pro career in the majors. A degree under my belt. Even had a girl on my arm set to marry me."

My heart buckled at the mention. But he just kept talking like he was telling me about average rainfall per annum or the price of eggs and milk.

"But when I came home, it all came unglued. Chelsea wouldn't come with me, balked at me giving up my spot on Atlanta's team, and a couple months of long distance later, she was gone."

"I'm sorry," was all I could say, and I said it softly.

"If she couldn't back me up where my own mama was concerned, she wouldn't back me up on anything that didn't serve her. Best I found out before I married her." He took a swig of his beer.

"How long were you together?"

Something behind his eyes softened, but the rest of him was as nonchalant as one could be. "Through college. We met freshman year."

I swallowed, shaking my head.

"Hey, don't do that. It's all right. Good riddance, you know?"

"No, *you* don't do *that*. Don't play it like it didn't devastate you. She left you when you needed her most, left you alone to watch your mother waste away and nearly die, for God's sake. And why? Because she was more upset about losing the promised life than you were?" I shook my head again. "No. Frankly, I say fuck her."

A deep, lovely laugh filled the space between us. "You know? I have said it many a time, but it sounds better out of your mouth."

A timer went off, and he set down his beer and slid his hand into an oven mitt to remove the skillet from the oven. Once it was on a trivet, he came back for the bowls to fill them up with rice and beans.

"I'm still reeling over the fact that you cook. And not just eggs or pancakes. Your mother suggested I'd starve if left here alone with you."

"Everybody likes to rib me for being a mess. At least if they're teasing me, I don't have to deal with their pity. I think they might feel the same, honestly. So I lean in. Having a dirty bathroom isn't usually hurting anybody but me."

He placed a steaming bowl in front of me, followed by a plate with a buttered slice of cornbread. I salivated as I opened my napkin and laid it in my lap, though I didn't lose the thread of what he'd said.

"And how do you feel about your life now?"

Remy walked up to the empty stool and set his meal on the island before sitting. "I love this town and the people in it. I'm close to Mama, and I get to play ball all week, nearly every week. I've got plenty of time to work on cars, fix things. I like fixing things."

"Of course, but are you happy? Satisfied?"

His gorgeous green eyes met mine. "Are you?"

I saw the deflection for what it was, but something about the way he was looking at me shook up my thoughts.

"I . . . I am."

"Don't believe you." He stirred up his beans, steam wafting off it in tendrils.

"Well, I don't believe you are either, so I suppose that makes us even." I took a bite, and a little piece of me died. It took all I had not to moan at the salt and spice of the meal.

"The older I get, the less I believe there's such thing as

happy. Or at least not like I thought would happen when I was a kid. Like one day we hit an age, ticked off a series of boxes, and boom, *happy*. It's not a thing. Never was."

I nodded, struck by his candor, though I'd learned this was just who he was. I only wondered if I'd ever stop being surprised by him.

"Life is weird," he continued, absently turning his food over with his spoon. "When we're kids, even in college, everything is possible. None of us know that all the little choices we make add up, or that sometimes one big choice can change your life in a way you can't come back from. It could give you the world, or it could strip you of everything. And you usually don't know which is which until it's too late to change your mind. Guess that's how cynics are born," he joked. But he wasn't joking. "This is my life. I wouldn't change the choices I made, not for anything. And so, I'm content, and that's good enough for me."

He took a bite, turning his attention to his food.

I laid down my spoon so I'd stop shoveling red beans into my mouth like an animal.

"I suppose I'm content too. College was my favorite time because of that sense of possibility. But then I moved back in with my parents as an adult. Which meant taking on my responsibilities there."

"Which is what?"

"Nothing," I said on a laugh. "I shouldn't say that. We mostly do charity work with my mother, and we're able to help so many people, but it just feels *empty*. I don't have loads of friends there, not true friends, and *none* like Cass."

"To be fair, there aren't a lot of girls like Cass."

"True. But . . . I don't know. I have a community, but I feel less and less like I belong. I thought things would click in and make sense, like you said. Tick the boxes and then you're happy. But I'm as lost as I was when I left for college. Just older. Which makes being lost sadder."

117

"What about your parents?"

"Father is . . ." I sighed. "He has very high standards and expectations of everyone, myself included. My older brother has been groomed for his position in politics since he was toddling around in a nappy. But I was schooled in the art of society, spending my time at teas and charity events. At least with my mother, there's champagne."

That earned me a laugh.

"My childhood was a strict, serious affair, but I wasn't a strict or serious young lady. Whimsies like love and romance were decreed impractical. Father thought me silly and was more likely to stand me up like a soldier and school me with a whistle like the von Trapps than read me a story or—heaven forbid—play with me. Did Cass tell you I was obsessed with the occult as a girl?"

"Like witches?"

I chuckled at the thought of my father finding me doing witchcraft. "No, just things like tarot cards and Ouija boards. It was all so magical, full of hope that my life—which had been carefully laid out for me long before I was born—could be whatever I chose. I loved to read fantasy, dream of other places. It sounds so silly coming from someone born with so much."

"No, I get it. It's hard to be put in a box, especially when the box is locked."

"Yes, I suppose it is. I'd smuggled contraband into the house, and when he found my cache, he lectured me in front of the fireplace as I was made to throw in the books, then the cards one by one, and the Ouija board last."

I remembered the flames eating it up until only one word was left unscathed: *No.*

"We make our fate, Jessamine. Hastings don't use foolish parlor tricks to decide our futures," I said in my best impression of my father.

"That's . . ." Remy's spoon hovered over his dinner for a moment. "Frankly, I say fuck him."

His attempt at a British accent was horrid. I couldn't help but laugh. And then I sighed.

"We're now in a place where the expectation is that I find a husband of good standing and breeding so that I might begin breeding my own successors."

He was quiet as I took a bite of my red beans and rice, a salty slice of sausage setting off a chain reaction of flavors in my mouth.

I was about to compliment him on it when he said, "So is that what Henry's all about?"

Supper went down my throat like a stone. I poked at my food. "I told you. I love Henry."

"Yeah, but does Henry love you?"

My cheeks warmed. "Of course he does."

"I mean like, *breeding successors* love."

"I . . . I don't know."

"Well, has he ever kissed you?"

"Of course." Indignance lifted my nose just a touch.

"When?"

"It doesn't matter when."

"If you don't want to tell me, it probably does."

My nostrils flared. "We were eight."

A laugh burst out of him. At my visible frustration, he held up his hands in surrender. "I'm not trying to be a dick, I swear."

"I'm sure you weren't, and yet." This time when I sighed, it was to vent the heat of my annoyance, unsure why I was even defending Henry. The script had long been written and recited, I supposed. "I think we're a lovely match and would be quite happy together. Our best friends are getting married. I could even move somewhere like Africa with him, my parents wouldn't care. It's *Henry*," I said, as if that explained it all.

"And you want to move to Africa?"

"Well, not if I don't have to. But—"

"I'm just saying, have you thought it all the way through?"

"I've been thinking it through since I was all of eighteen, thank you."

He nodded at his food. "Honestly, the whole thing makes sense now. I mean, I still think he's a dumbass, but I get why he'd fit the bill. He checks those pesky boxes. I mean, aside from not ever kissing you, but what do I know."

I stared at him. "And here I was enjoying your company, forgetting how terrible you are."

"Oh, come on, Duchess. You have to admit how stupid it sounds."

"I will not," I blustered. "You know nothing about me or Henry."

He set down his spoon, his eyes narrowing. My chest cinched tighter with every increment. "I know you're too good for some dipshit who won't even kiss you. Any man who wouldn't is a fool. That idiot douchebag has no idea what he's got."

I blinked, stammering quietly, "He . . . he's not an idiot or a douchebag."

"*I fucking know,*" he growled. Actually growled the words like an animal through his teeth. "But I hate him anyway. I watch you look at him like you do, and he has no clue. Not one fucking goddamn clue."

I stared at him with my lips parted, not breathing as I attempted to process the words that had left his mouth and the order with which they exited. Thoughts and questions exploded in my mind like fireworks, too loud and shocking to separate.

But I didn't end up needing to—a groan of wood from the direction of my room preceded a snap, followed by a wet whoosh of water and a crash.

REMY WAS off his stool and running toward the sound, and I hurried behind him, my jaw coming unhinged at the sight of the roof over my bed. Or, moreso, the lack of roof over my bed.

It looked as if a cannonball had been shot through the roof, the wood splintered, shingles hanging into the room. Rain fell hard, loud, and directly onto my bed.

I stood there staring at it as Remy swore and headed for the door, stuffing his feet in his worst pair of boots and throwing on a Carhartt jacket. And out he went into the torrent.

"*Shit.*"

I tore into my room, rushing to put on a pair of shorts and tossing my cardigan. Once at the front door, I pulled on my muddy shoes and grabbed one of Remy's heartier jackets, overwhelmed by the garment and the smell of him as it curled around me. And then I was out the door to do what I could to help.

I didn't see him out front or by the shed, so I hurried around the wraparound porch, finding him climbing a ladder to the roof, tarp folded up under his arms.

A crack of thunder and flash of lightning shook the house. My heart stopped at the thought of him on a metal ladder in a thunderstorm, but he remained unfazed, disappearing onto the roof.

With a quick prayer, I followed. Rain spilled in buckets, fat heavy droplets splatting on every surface, including me. When I could see over the roof, he paused, his face dark with rage.

"What the fuck are you doing?" he yelled through the wild rain. "Get inside."

But I climbed up. "No!" I took one corner of the tarp and moved to circle the hole. "Two of us means you're off the roof faster!"

The noise he made sounded a lot like a roar, but he sprang back into action, spreading out the tarp. A handful of errant bricks laid next to the chimney, and he picked them up, handing me two to pin the corners with. When the job was done, he stared at it, running his hand through his sopping hair before shaking his head and scanning our surroundings. A good-sized branch of the magnolia tree had split, hanging within reach, complete with offshoot branches and wide leaves. He grabbed it with both hands and snapped it off, carrying it to the hole, laying it on top to help divert the rain. And then he turned to me, shouting, "Go!"

We made for the ladder, and I hurried down with my knees knocking. As soon as I was clear, he all but pushed me under the porch overhang and picked up the ladder, carrying it onto the porch with him and tossing it next to the rail. Then he grabbed my arm and dragged me to the back door, shoving me inside.

"Jesus Christ, Jessa. You could have gotten hurt." The door slammed with another crack of thunder.

"So could you," I shot back.

"Next time I tell you to get inside, do it."

"Don't tell me what to do, Remy."

"Then stop being careless, Duchess. If you get hurt on my watch, I'll never fucking forgive myself. So if you won't do it for yourself, do it for me." He snatched a big bucket by the door, brushing past me as he stripped off his coat and kicked off his boots, leaving me dripping in the kitchen, staring after him.

When he moved for my room, I collected myself and discarded my coat and shoes too, hurrying behind him to assess the damage.

He was already pushing the ruined bed against the wall, knocking Bocephus askew. When it was out of the way, he set the bucket under the hole and took a moment to look up at it, finally letting go of a sigh that drained a little tension from his shoulders. And then he walked out, largely ignoring me as he stomped to his room.

When I found him, he was busy pulling a pillow off his bed and an extra blanket from the foot.

"I'll sleep on the couch."

"That sofa isn't fit for Beau to sleep on."

"I've had worse."

"There's a perfectly good bed right here. I won't let you sleep on that derelict sofa."

He stopped close enough that I could feel the heat wafting off his wet clothes. "How are you gonna stop me?"

I saw the fear behind his eyes and realized just how badly I'd scared him. I softened, shaking my head. "I'm sorry, Remy. I shouldn't have followed you, but I was worried about you, and wanted to be useful. That's all."

I wasn't only talking about the ladder and tarp regarding my usefulness, and he understood. Another sigh uncoiled him just a bit more. "Next time, the place you're most useful is safe. Okay?"

"Okay."

We stared at his queen-sized bed. As I considered how I hated the thought of him sleeping on the sofa, I realized that I knew a way to get him into bed with me where he wouldn't throw his back out.

A terrible little smile brushed my lips. "I understand. You're worried you'll be tempted, sleeping in bed with me."

"Damn fucking straight I am. And I'm *not* losing this bet."

Disappointment sank in my belly at the thought of him never kissing me. The thought that maybe he just didn't want me like that stung with surprising ferocity.

Until he turned to me, his voice thick with heat when he said, "I won't come in second place, Jessa. If this happens, *when* it happens, it'll be because you made a choice—*me*."

The electric chill that ran through me shuddered all the way down to my toes.

And then a terrible smile of his own played on his lips.

"On second thought, this might be the best idea you ever had." He threw his pillow back on the bed with a thump and tossed the blanket onto a chair. My eyes followed his giant hand as it moved for his belt, unstrapping it with a snap. "Just so you know, I sleep in the buff."

Pants half unzipped, he reached back to grab his shirt and pull it off over his head. The glory of his torso was on display, wet and rippling in the moonlight. I followed his abs down to the beginnings of a thatch of dark hair in the open V of his zipper.

When I'd regained cognitive function a moment later, I gathered my resolve and unbuttoned my shorts. "No problem."

He sucked in a breath through his teeth as I slid them down my legs and stepped out of them, leaving me in very small underpants and a very thin tank. As I pulled my hair out of the bun and combed my fingers through it, his gaze was as heavy as fingertips trailing up and down my body, his broad chest heaving. Another growl, and he raked a hand through his hair, moving for the door.

"Get in bed," he commanded.

My heart had stopped painfully, my mind firing a thousand guesses as to what he was going to do.

When he walked past me and out of the room, my heart started, but it had sunk somewhere near my stomach.

What are you doing? I wondered as I rounded the bed to climb in on the far side, sliding between his sheets. *Why are you playing this game? This was not the plan. None of this was in the plan. If you don't fold tonight—in bed with him, mind you—he will, and then what?*

My body knew the answer, responding with a prickling of my skin that tightened my nipples and sent a rush of heat straight to my pussy. I squeezed my thighs tight and my eyes shut as I listened to him bang around in the kitchen, presumably packing up our dinner. Likely trying to gain composure before calling my bluff and getting into bed with me.

Naked.

I didn't know who was stupider, him or me.

Me. It's definitely me.

What about Henry?

What about Henry? There's been no real indication that this time is different than any of the others. I have no need for a man who obviously doesn't want me.

Maybe he non-obviously wants you.

I sighed, opening my eyes to stare at the ceiling.

Would it be so bad to have a fling with Remy? It gets in the way of Henry, true, but where is that going, anyway? And then there's Cass.

God, she'd kill me. She's as determined to pair me and Henry as my parents are. Maybe more.

Don't decide now. Survive tonight. See how you feel tomorrow. Just don't sleep with him tonight or you're fucked in more ways than one.

Every atom in my body went still when Remy walked back into the room. He'd turned off the lights in the house—

125

all I could see was what the quartered square of light from the window touched. Beau's nails clicked on the wood floors, and the mattress dipped when he flopped his front paws on the end of the bed and whined at me for occupying his spot.

"Get down, Beau," Remy huffed, very much bothered.

Beau snuffed, but listened, collapsing at the foot of the bed.

Remy gave me his back, the jangle of his belt doing something wicked to me as he hitched his pants off his hips, then down that brilliant arse of his to the floor.

God bless him for being a man who kept his word.

Strategically, he turned in such a way that wouldn't fully bare him to me, putting him quickly in the shadows. But I could still see every hallowed bit of him drawn in shades of darkness, including the very hard cock he displayed.

And when he climbed into bed next to me, I battened down for the longest night of my life.

19
hot caulk

REMY

IT WAS the longest night of my life.

Neither of us spoke, not one single word. A thousand thoughts went through my head, but I was afraid that if I said even one of them, I'd kiss her and then fuck her, and then where would I be? I'd have lost the bet, for one, and I wasn't about to be the consolation prize because she couldn't have Henry.

She fell asleep first, the time marked by the slowing of her breath. I could feel her in bed next to me like a phantom limb. I could have drawn the shape of her body there in the dark because every cell was staring at her, pointing at her, reaching for her. And so I was up until the dead of night when the rain stopped and the room was quiet except for the sound of her measured breath.

After a fitful sleep, I woke before the sun was out, the room still cast in shades of purple. At some point, she'd shoved a pillow between our junk, and thank God. Because Lady Jessamine Hastings and I were tangled up in each other like a bowl of naked spaghetti.

Yeah, I was glad for the junk pillow. But that meant there was no boob pillow.

Her breasts were pressed to my chest with nothing between us but the thin fabric of her top, her ribs expanding and contracting in the circle of my arms. And beneath the junk pillow, my naked cock was so sensitized that when Jessa's leg shifted the pillow a millimeter, I jerked my hips back from the shock.

She had invaded my senses, from the feel of her glorious fucking body to the sweet smell of her hair. The silky softness of her skin against mine, the sound of her sighing when she shifted again. An inch, and I could kiss her. A solid flex, and I could fuck her. Heat tingled up my neck, through my chest—I had to get out of this bed before I came into my pillow like a teenager.

Carefully, I moved, and without waking she rolled over to face the window and tucked her hand under her head, sighing again.

My breath came heavy and thick as I climbed out of bed in inches. The second I was free, I rushed silently to the bathroom, turning on the shower for cover. I didn't know if I could control myself well enough to keep quiet—my cock was already in my hand, the weeping tip slicking my crown. I spit into my hand and sank into my fist, the smell of her on me. In me. My eyes slammed shut, my hand on the counter and feet apart, head bowed in prayer to the girl in my fucking bed who just might be my undoing. Her panties in my nightstand. The sight of her pussy, close enough to touch. I opened my eyes to watch my cock disappear, shining, into my fist at the thought of her bare ass in my clenched hand, spreading her to give my tongue access to that hot fucking slit, and that was it. I came, shuddering, into a towel that I wished was her cunt.

For a long while, I stood there panting like an animal. I was like a fucking kid for all I could control myself. When it came to her, I was a mess in a hand towel waiting to happen.

When my pulse dropped out of the red, I cleaned up,

taking the filthy towel with me to the laundry room where thankfully I had clothes in the dryer. Brooding, I pulled on a pair of jeans and a T-shirt and put on my boots, heading outside to find something to do with my hands that didn't involve my cock.

Fortunately, there was plenty to do.

The yard was trashed from the storm, branches and leaves strewn all over the grass. After picking up the bulk of it and tossing it into the burn pile, I headed to the shed for supplies to fix the roof. But even after I gathered everything I'd need, she was stuck on my mind with superglue. By then, there wasn't anything quiet left to do, so I rolled the dice and climbed onto the roof with my circular saw to remove the damaged decking.

I didn't know why I was counting the seconds until she woke up with a saw in my hand. Maybe I'd quit thinking about her if I accidentally lost a finger, but somehow I doubted it.

After a bit, I sighed and set the saw next to me.

"Morning."

I jumped so hard, I almost knocked the saw and myself through the hole in the roof. "Jesus Christ."

She laughed and bit her lip. I bit back a groan.

"Sorry," she said. "I called your name, but . . ." She gestured to the saw.

With the smirk I often wore as a mask, I said, "How'd you sleep?"

Carefully, she kept her face still. "Like a baby. You?"

"Never better." I turned to the hole and dusted off the rafter I'd exposed.

"Can I help?"

"Sure. This part's done—need to build a frame." I stood and waited for her to make her way to the ladder, my face quirking when I got a good look at her. "What the hell are you wearing?"

She looked down at herself and dusted off Mama's old overalls. Underneath, she wore a hot pink string bikini.

"Well, I found these in the back of your closet." She flicked the strap of the overalls. "But it's too hot already to wear all this denim, so I thought I'd wear as little as possible underneath."

I shook my head, pointing at the ladder, dying to know what the bottoms looked like. "I swear to God, Duchess."

She rolled her eyes. "Really? I look like a farmer in these overalls."

"Go." I pointed at the ladder again.

With a huff, she descended, mumbling something about pigs and cocks and me being a child, but I didn't ask.

Jessa waited at the bottom of the ladder with her arms folded, following me when I passed her. I'd set up in the front, table saw, two-by-fours, plywood and all.

"All right, come here—we're going to cut these to build a frame."

Her face lit up like a Christmas tree. "Ooh, I get to use the saw?"

"I oughtta make you put a shirt on first."

"Why, are you tempted?"

"You could get hurt from splintered wood. Also, yes. Put these on, at least." I handed her a pair of safety glasses and picked up a plank. Once it was in place, I stood behind her and guided her hand to pull down the blade and cut the board with a noisy zzzzt.

The laugh that tore out of her was a wild, giddy sound. "Again!"

I couldn't help but laugh with her as we cut the wood we'd need. I couldn't help but notice her ass against my cock, nor could I ignore the smell of her mingling with freshly cut wood.

"Now what?" she asked, grinning.

And it was with that eager disposition that we worked on

the roof for the next while, framing up the hole and measuring for the patch. She cut it all on her own with much whooping and many giggles before we headed back up to the roof with the plywood, shingles, and the rest of our supplies.

I'd laid it all out on the roof, and when I turned around, Jessa was squinting up at the sky, her overalls undone and the bib hanging off her waist, hand on her hip. Every visible inch of skin was glistening, and I watched her wipe her brow like she was in a *Sports Illustrated* spread.

She shielded her eyes and glanced at me. "What? Lord, Remy—you've seen me stark naked. Surely you can handle this."

"Surely." The word was rough, gravelly, low.

Something in her shifted at the sound, tightened in desire, curled in mischief. "It's so hot," she said matter-of-factly, unfastening the button at her hip. "I don't know how anyone can stand the heat."

Half of her was fucking with me. The other half was decidedly *not*.

I swallowed hard, turning to the patch. "You get used to it." Once I'd dropped the plywood into place and approved the fit, Jessa stepped into my periphery with a hammer in one hand, nails in the other, and nothing on her godforsaken body except that tiny bikini and a pair of muddy leather sneakers.

She ignored me completely, looking down at the patch, nodding like she knew what she was looking at. I did not ignore her. It was foolish to think I could have, not with the teeny-tiny triangles barely covering her gorgeous tits, the hard tips of her nipples leaving nothing to guesswork. The bottoms, God bless them, were also tiny, barely keeping her pussy contained and leaving three quarters of her ass on display. What fabric there was gathered just a little between her ass cheeks, spotlighting the split I'd have given my right arm to get inside of. The ties were high on her hips, and my eyes lingered on those stringy Bocephus-colored temptations. One tug, and she'd be naked.

The fire that ate its way through me was a force beyond my control. And when she laid out her overalls and got on all fours to get a good look at the seam, I almost lost it.

I had to touch her or I was going to fucking die. I'd combust on the fucking spot. There had to be a way to have my cake, eat my cake, and fuck it all night too.

A slow smile spread across my face as I stepped behind her, dropped to my knees, took a moment to admire her ass. And then I hinged, putting my hands outside of hers, caging her beneath me. Her breath was loud and shallow, the seam of my jeans shifting against her ass as I settled in behind her. The scruff of my beard rasped her cheek, my lips almost touching her shoulder as I nuzzled her. Goosebumps raced across her skin, and I smiled like the devil.

"It occurs to me that we never decided exactly what constituted losing the bet," I said softly, my lips grazing the shell of her ear.

"Didn't we?" she breathed, her back arching ever so slightly, hips shifting as she wiggled beneath me.

"We did not. "

"Oh." It was almost a whisper. I wondered absently if her pussy was soaked. My fingertips ached to find out.

"So let's say loser kisses the other first."

She stilled beneath me. "A kiss? That's all?"

"That's all. Just one little kiss on the lips."

"Which lips?"

Fuck, I almost died. "The ones on your face. The ones between your legs are fair game."

"So as long as I don't kiss you, I could fuck you right now and not lose?" she asked with a trembling voice, her ass grinding against my rock-hard cock.

"Mhmm. But we won't."

"And why not?"

I took a moment to drag my lips across her nape. "Don't wanna give the milk away free, do I?"

When I rolled my hips, I swear to God she almost melted right there beneath me.

"So, what do you say, Duchess?"

"Get ready to lose."

With my lips almost touching her ear, I said, "Don't be so sure."

I rose to my knees with my heart hammering my ribs, traced the curves of her waist and hips with my hands. Grabbed a handful of her ass like I'd been daydreaming about, only letting it go to slap it once, hard.

I hadn't intended anything more, not trusting myself to hold out in our little game of chicken.

But then she moaned, reaching behind her for my belt.

I snagged her wrist and forced her hand back where it was, keeping her on all fours. For a second I just stayed there, panting into her hair, my thoughts firing through a haze of vulgarity.

Somehow, I regained enough composure to back off her, though I only made it so far as kneeling again when she dropped to her elbows and looked over her shoulder, arching her back to point her pussy right at me.

I was right, she was soaked, the fabric darker where it was tucked into her lips. Before I could stop myself, I thumbed the line, cupped her, squeezed.

"What was that about giving away the milk?" she asked.

"I said I wouldn't give it away. I never said you couldn't have a taste."

The mewl she mewled hit me deep in the belly, tugging my balls toward the feeling.

"Do you know how bad I want to fuck you?" I circled her clit softly.

"How bad?" she rasped.

And then I was behind her again, my rigid cock against

133

her ass, left hand planted next to her. My free hand reached under to slide between her legs and cup her sex. "I've been thinking about this pussy ever since you gave me your panties at the fair, and now here it is, wet for me, just like I wanted. I want to fuck you so bad, I almost came into that fucking pillow you put between us last night." I pulled at the fabric until her lips were free, groaning when my fingertips touched their bare skin. "All you had to do was move. That's what you do to me."

I pumped my hips, wishing I was fucking her with my cock instead of my hand. I dipped my finger into her slick center and used what I found to coat her clit.

She gasped, her cheek pressed to the denim of her overalls. Her thigh twitched when her lids fluttered closed.

I curled my left hand on the back of her neck to keep her still. "Open your eyes, Duchess. I want you looking at me."

For once, she did as she was told.

"Good girl. That's what you are, you know that?"

This time, I slid two fingers into her silky heat, squeezing when I was as deep as I could get. Her pussy flexed around me.

"Never breaks the rules, never does anything bad. And here you are, getting finger fucked on a roof by me. *Me*. Who's fucking you, Duchess?" I asked, my rhythm slowly getting faster, the heel of my palm pressing, circling her swollen sex.

"You are," she whispered, her lids heavy and breath shallow as she ground her hips into my hand. Her pussy clenched again.

"And this? This is *nothing*. Next time, the taste you get won't be milk—it'll be my come in your throat."

She came with a gasp and a squeeze of my fingers, so hard my cock ached at the thought of how that would hurt exquisitely when she was full of *me*.

And that was it—if I didn't do something, I'd come in my

pants. With a shaking hand, I unfastened my jeans, wrapping my fist around my cock as soon as it sprang free. She reached between her thighs to take my cock, and then I went blind as I came in a hot stream, my legs jolting when she pumped, and I fucked the last of myself into her hands.

God, I wished she was naked. And *we* were naked. And not on the fucking roof. The urge to kiss her was deep and primal, but I'd already gone too far. So instead, I hinged to press a kiss to her salty back as I put myself away.

Blinking, she sat back on her heels and looked up at me, all desire and submission and invitation, with my come dripping down her stomach. All I could think about was the many ways in which I could fuck her and the many places I wanted to see my silvery seed. Fighting the compulsion to do just that, I reached behind me and pulled off my shirt, kneeling in front of her to clean up my mess. The air between us crackled, our breath still heavy as she watched me, smiling.

"No kissing. Very clever."

"Thank you. I'm full of great ideas."

"You're full of something, that's for sure."

And she laughed. And I laughed.

But neither of us admitted how much trouble we were in.

20
probably fine

JESSA

THERE WAS a time not too long ago when I thought I had been well and truly fucked.

I understood now that I had not, in fact. Thanks to Remy, I was now aware that I knew nothing. And he'd enlightened me without even using his cock, just one well-trained hand and the filthiest mouth I'd ever wanted to kiss.

The tender flesh between my thighs *hurt*, I wanted him so badly. And though I'd had my orgasm, I was far from satisfied. The way it had taken everything I had not to climb him like a tree and mount his face astounded me. And not just today, but every time we were alone.

It was uncanny, utterly extraordinary, absolutely arresting.

We were a powder keg, and he'd just lit a bonfire.

Why had I agreed to all this? Oh yes, the magnificent cock I'd met on that very first day. With the heft of it in my hands, there was little I *wouldn't* have done. If he'd tugged the strings on my bottoms and fucked me in front of the hole in his roof, I wouldn't have stopped him. I nearly undid them myself and begged.

Instead, I directed him to come all over me.

I could count the number of times that had ever happened on my—never. It had never happened. And I was desperate to have him do it again.

After a quick, albeit shaky cleanup in the loo, we finished the roof as if nothing had happened. A diddle in the shower after was only a finger in the dam, and I needed a good piping. When I was dressed, I stripped my soggy bed, and Remy came in to set the mattress up against the wall in an attempt to dry it out. Bocephus remained unaffected, still staring at me with his lopsided eyes from the chair in the corner.

Believe me, I know, darling. I'm crazy too.

The night had been eternal, my body zinging in such close proximity to so much naked Remy. It was true, I'd stuffed a pillow between us. Had I not, I'd have impaled myself. Somehow, I'd ended up wrapped in him, waking when dawn had barely broken. In the crush of his arms, with his steady heartbeat against my ear and his warm skin against my cheek, I knew without question that I wanted him beyond his outrageous body and what it could do for, and to me. I'd seen his tenderness and care, I'd seen his jealousy and fury. He'd opened himself up last night and given me a glimpse past the charm and the jokes, and it felt like a gift.

I'd heard him through the night in my mind, telling me how Henry didn't deserve me and what a fool he was. And he was so earnest, he'd convinced me too.

Henry *was* a fool. But here, right before me, was a man who'd already shown what he'd do to deserve me in a million little ways.

And so, the game between us was truly afoot, and I couldn't wait to break him. Mostly because if I didn't kiss him soon, I'd likely explode.

We worked that way for a while. I started the wash, Remy made us sandwiches as if it were a normal day. We talked and laughed as if he hadn't just shot a full load all over me. Beau watched us with curiosity, and I realized we probably smelled like a tsunami of pheromones. Poor dog. At this rate, we'd ruin his sense of smell before dinner.

Remy asked if I wanted to go to his softball practice with a tiny little touch of shyness that made that unholy ache between my legs worse. So, of course I agreed, texting Cass to meet me there.

I changed into another sundress, this one navy blue with little straps that tied on my shoulders. My hair I'd twisted into a high bun, and I'd worn little gold hoops and my freshly rinsed-off sneakers. With my purse in hand and my denim jacket slung over my forearm, I made my way out of the house. When I found Remy waiting for me on the porch in those slutty, slutty basketball shorts, a sleeveless shirt, and a baseball cap, I was terribly thrilled to catch the hitch in his breath when he saw me, accompanied by the slightest shift of fabric between his legs.

One of my brows rose, my eyes on the shadow of his cock. "Not wearing underpants, are we?" I slid my big sunglasses on as I walked past.

"Never. Why, are you?"

I smiled at him over my shoulder. "Never," I promised, throwing a little extra swing in my hips.

Really, I needed professional help.

He cleared his throat and trotted down the stairs behind me. "What do you have a jacket for?"

"Well, I don't know when we'll be back, and it might be chilly at dinner or the bar later. Plus—no knickers, remember? The other night at the softball game, I was worried I'd catch something dangerous from the bleachers. At least now I'll have something to sit on."

He made a sound somewhere between a groan and a sigh before helping me into the Scout. I didn't check to see if he'd taken a good long look at my legs on the way up, but I had high hopes.

I kept my smile in check as I gazed off, my elbow hanging out the window and gold bracelets clinking against the metal. He'd taken off the top again, and the sun covered us in glorious heat, kissing my shoulders. With a rumble of the engine, we were off for town and the day. Which would lead to the night. Lord only knew what *that* would bring.

He took us down the drive, glancing at me, one elbow resting in the open window with his hand on the wheel, the other hand on his gear stick.

"Wonder if we'll get carried away again tonight," he mused. "I don't know about you, but that wasn't nearly enough for my tastes."

"Probably," I answered, as if the thought of him touching me hadn't wrecked my vagina all over again. "Why, are you worried?"

"Only for you."

I laughed. "Worried for me? All I had to do was wear a bathing suit and you made up a loophole so you could touch me."

"You didn't seem to be complaining."

"Not at all, but I'll be damned if you can convince me to kiss that dirty mouth of yours."

"That's not all this dirty mouth can do, Duchess."

"And how much does it think it can get away with tonight?"

"Guess we'll see," he said, smirking.

"I suppose we shall," was all I said, smirking right back as we pulled onto the country road and headed into town.

It was too loud to talk, so I leaned over and turned up the radio, taking in the moment. The rush of musky, green forest walling the two-lane road. The heat of the sun, the heavy air, the warm wind licking my skin. The rumbling engine made the seat tremble as the tinny country song on the radio warbled from old speakers. And of course there was the beast in the driver's seat who'd very nearly convinced me to disavow a decade's worth of plans in favor of a new one that largely revolved around him being naked.

Through all of last night and the length of today, I'd thought a lot about seducing a man, but that man had not been Henry. I'd potentially gone and fucked the whole thing, hadn't I? Cass would kill me. Disown me. Cut me out of the will. Somehow, I'd gotten myself to a place of rogue sex on roofs, the road murky and thick with lewd thoughts. But here I was, sitting next to the most unlikely of suspects, quivering with anticipation. I didn't know what was going to happen or when, but something surely would, and it'd likely be nothing short of insane.

I didn't even care if Henry was there tonight. In fact, I realized I'd rather he not be there at all. He'd never wanted me, it seemed. And why had I even placed him in such high regard? Why had I ever agreed to the silly pact? Because he was clever and handsome? Because my family would approve? In the world my father lived in, Henry had the makings of an ideal husband. The woman Father wished me to be would have been perfect for Henry. I'd been groomed for him my whole life.

But what about *me*? I wasn't even sure who I was, though I knew I wasn't whatever my father had hoped for. I wished I could have been, for all our sakes—life would have been much simpler. Ever since I was a girl, I'd thought I could shave off corners of myself to fit better into his mold, but all I'd ever accomplished was scuffing myself up.

Here in Roseville, I felt more myself than I had, perhaps ever. Last night eating beans and rice in a little cottage in the Tennessee woods, I was at ease. Today, hammering nails and using an electric saw, I felt at home. There wasn't a single expectation on me here that I couldn't meet. How curious that nearly thirty years of life had passed without knowing how it felt to have an unconditional love for my place and myself.

How curious that I should find it here, with him.

Although it was quiet enough to talk once we reached town, we listened to music in companionable silence. I wondered what he was thinking as we pulled into the softball field parking lot—judging by his face, something was on his mind. He put the Scout in park and turned it off, and for a moment, we sat there, regarding each other. My heart skipped when something in his face changed and he opened his mouth to speak, but before he could say anything, Cass pulled up next to him and honked.

So we shared a smile and climbed out of the truck, leaving whatever he was going to say where it was. Which left *me* both relieved and disappointed.

Cass popped out of her car, her wild red hair in a bun on top of her head and sunglasses on her nose. I gave her a kiss on the cheek when I got to her.

"Heya, hot stuff," she said, slapping me on the bum.

I giggle-yelped, the sound drawing Remy's attention as he gathered his bag up and slung it on his shoulder. We shared a secret sort of smile while Cass reached into her car for her phone.

"Did you want to go grab lunch?" she asked.

"Oh, I ate already, thank you."

She made a face. "What did he feed you? A can of tuna and some stale Doritos?"

"He made ham sandwiches."

"Ham? Not SPAM?" When I nodded, she laughed. "Get outta town."

"Really. And last night, he even cooked an honest meal with pots and pans and everything."

Her mouth popped open, and she dragged her sunglasses down the bridge of her nose so she could make sure I wasn't lying. "Well, I'll be damned."

"Don't act so surprised," Remy shouted over his shoulder as he headed to the dugout where his teammates were already gathered.

"Did we have somewhere to be?" I asked. "I thought we might watch for a while."

Her brow quirked. "Why?"

I shrugged. "It's nice out."

Her face went dead flat. "Is this about Remy? I swear to God, Jessa—if you slept with him, I'm going to kill you both. Him twice."

I laughed, hoping I sounded unaffected as I hooked my arm in hers and pulled her toward the small set of bleachers. "No, silly," I answered, thankful I didn't have to lie. Yet.

Cass still eyed me with suspicion, but reluctantly, she followed.

My eyes were on Remy as he ran out onto the field where the lot of them were throwing the ball back and forth, his squarely round backside a glorious sight as he trotted away.

"What do y'all do over there all the time?" Cass asked. "I've been trying to figure it out, but I'm stumped. Never would have guessed cooking with Remy. I thought I had some ideas, but that one really threw me for a loop."

I chuckled. "Well, today we worked on the house. He showed me how to use a saw and hammer a nail."

She eyed me. "Jessamine Hastings, that'd better not be a euphemism."

One of my brows rose in challenge. I didn't dare say anything.

She sighed noisily through her nose. "Fine. I'm glad you didn't lose a finger. Or your dignity."

I put all thoughts of the indignities I'd enjoyed today as far from my mind as I could, which ended up being my lap. "Really, it's just things like that. His house breaks. A lot."

"Well, it's a thousand years old. Luckily, he's handy. It was our grandad's, did you know?"

"I didn't." But it made sense he'd stay there despite its structural integrity.

"His mom and my dad—and Aunt Julie—were siblings, and the house was their father's."

I frowned. "How do you have the same last name?"

"Linda never married Remy's dad."

"Oh," I said quietly, wondering if I could ask the thousand questions that had just popped into my thoughts.

But she changed the subject before I could ask one. "I hope you don't mind working on some more crafts today with Mama and the cousins. Then we'll have dinner at The Filly and drinks at The Horseshoe after. A slew of family made it to town today, so we've been busy getting everybody settled. I think we have near twenty for dinner."

"Well, that's a wonderful list of things, but how have the things *been*? We haven't been alone in an age."

"I hate it." She sighed, but this time, she relaxed a bit. "It's been . . . I don't know. Weird. It helps that we haven't stopped moving for what feels like a month. Davis is distracted, but I guess I am too. He and Henry haven't seen each other in forever, so he's always around. Don't get me wrong, I don't mind—it's *Henry*—it's just, I feel like I've seen Davis less than I've seen you, and I sleep with the man."

"There's a lot going on. Soon you'll be on your honeymoon, just the two of you. You'll be so tired of him, I'll have to fly back and visit to serve as a buffer."

Cass laughed. Then sighed once more, sagging a little. "It'll be over soon," she reassured herself. "Anyway, Henry's been talking about you nonstop. He *really* does not like Remy. It's the best."

I made a noncommittal noise as she continued.

"It's driving him nuts that you're staying with him, but when I nudge him into talking to you, he clams up. Dinner should be fun though—try to get a seat near him. And then tonight, there'll be music and dancing and drinking . . . the perfect ambiance for a good snogging."

Somehow, I doubted Henry would be the one snogging me, but I said nothing, not keen to tell her what I'd been doing with her cousin. I valued my life too much.

"Should be fun. Plus, I'm going to teach you how to line dance." She put her hands on her hips and jigged her feet around.

"Can't wait," I said, leaning back against the seat behind me.

Cass did the same. For a minute, we watched the team practice. Well, I watched Remy throwing the ball as hard as he could to Wilder, Cass's high school boyfriend, enjoying the pop the ball made when it hit his leather glove. I wondered who Cass was watching and figured it was probably him.

Wilder was, in many ways, her unfinished business. As she told it, they were mad for each other, started dating at thirteen and went on through the end of school. But Wilder was recruited to UCLA, and she came to Oxford, and things sort of . . . trailed off. Technically, they never broke up, just ghosted. I think she didn't want to admit aloud it was over, but it made no sense to keep up the effort when the two of them had no plans to be in the same place again, maybe ever.

Now here she was getting married, and he was busy sleeping with the female population of Roseville, if the rumors were true.

I wondered how much it bothered Cass. Judging by how little she'd said about it, I reckoned it was a lot.

"All right, that's enough of my cousin for one day," she said, standing as quick as that. "Come on, gorgeous. There's a hot glue gun at Mama's house with your name on it. That tulle isn't going to glue itself to itself, you know."

When she extended her hand, I took it and stood, gathering up my things. And as we made our way down the bleachers, I felt Remy's eyes on me. I turned to the feeling, and we shared a smile that Cass didn't see, however brief it was. Which presented a new problem.

If this kept going on, I'd have to find a way to tell Cass everything that had happened between me and Remy.

And God help us all when I did.

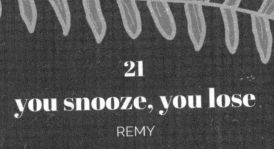

21
you snooze, you lose

REMY

I STARED at the door of The Horseshoe half the night waiting on Jessa to walk through it.

If I could have gotten off of work, I would have. Years ago, The Horseshoe and The Filly were connected, but they'd boarded it up in the seventies to class The Filly up. What I wouldn't have given to look in on the big dinner where Jessa was. The thought of her sitting next to that pretty, preppy punkass made my blood simmer. But soon enough, she'd be where I could see her. That was really all I wanted.

Okay, that was a lie. There were many things I wanted, and watching her was probably the least of them. Unless you counted watching her fucking herself. I wasn't picky either— she could use her hand or a toy or whatever she wanted, so long as I got to watch her do it.

I didn't just have it bad. I had it brutally. The wanting was eating me up from the inside like a sweet, sweet poison, and I was so obsessed with her I didn't even care. I'd die happy.

Getting inside of her had not helped. Her hands on my dick hadn't done me any favors. Our little fuckaround this afternoon was the dumbest thing I could have done. Because now I knew. And the knowing was close to killing me.

I liked looking up from practice and seeing her in the stands. I loved looking up from home plate and finding her in the crowd. As different as she was from anyone I'd ever met, she fit here. It didn't make any sense, but I think Roseville made her better, and I think she made Roseville better too. I could say with all honesty that I didn't want her to go. I had one week left with her before she hopped a plane and flew thousands of miles away. And I wasn't done with her yet.

I couldn't picture her in a stuffy ballroom with gray skies outside the window, drinking tea. She was sunshine on a pair of the prettiest legs I'd ever seen, and Roseville agreed with her. But she had no reason to stay. Cass would leave again and there'd be nothing to keep her here but me. That order was so tall, there was no ladder that could top it. I had nothing to offer her but a busted house and a bartender's tips. My charming smile might get me a long way, but convincing a fucking Duchess to hang around was too much to ask.

All the more reason to enjoy the time I had with her while I had it.

If today was any indication, she wouldn't hold out much longer. If she did, I was fucked because *I* wasn't going to hold out much longer either. And if Henry made a move on her before then, I just might have to kill him and tell God he died.

My replacement, Leo, was tying on his apron when the door opened, and my gaze snapped to the motion, heart in my throat. But it wasn't Jessa—it was a woman about my age who looked like a goddamn J. Crew model. Blonde, windswept hair. Crisp blue eyes. No makeup, tan, freckles on her nose and cheeks. Effortlessly cool, definitely rich, but a little sporty, like she belonged just as easily on a boat or a soccer field. Every set of eyes in the place looked at her. She didn't seem to notice as she sauntered up to the bar and smiled at me.

"Hi, I'm looking for the Winfield-McGrath wedding party. I think they were supposed to come here tonight?"

I nodded. "They should be here soon. Getcha something to drink?"

She glanced at the taps. "How about your favorite IPA."

I slung a little cocktail napkin onto the bar in front of her. "Comin' right up."

She took a seat and checked her phone while I poured, and I watched her, wondering who she was. One of Cass's friends, maybe? I certainly couldn't place her.

Before her beer was full, the party finally arrived, streaming in through the door. She turned on her barstool and watched along with me, jumping off her stool at the same moment my heart jumped back into my throat. This time it stuck there.

Jessa walked through the threshold under Henry's arm.

Her eyes locked to mine like she knew she'd find me right there, and her smile hit me in a thousand places at once, nearly knocking the wind out of me.

The beer spilled over, soaking my hand.

"Well, shit." I set the pint down and pulled the towel out of my back pocket to wipe up.

In the split second that took, the girl had run across the bar and launched herself into Henry's arms. But I wasn't looking at them. My eyes were on Jessa, who had stepped aside to give them room and was watching them say their hellos with a strange look all over her. The girl was holding Henry's face—they were kissing on each other and laughing while everyone tried not to stare at them.

But Jessa stared, hurt. And the cut was deep.

I left the beer under the tap and strode around the bar, through the tables until I was standing next to her.

"Annie, darling, I'm so glad you made it," Henry was saying, turning to everyone with his arm around the beaming girl. "For those of you who haven't met her, this is Annie, a friend of mine from grad school."

She waved.

It was then that I noticed Cass, who was in a hissing match with her fiancé. By the look of it, she was fucking *pissed*.

"What do you mean his plus one? He doesn't *have* a plus one," she snapped, turning to Henry and Annie. Her cheeks were cherry red and steaming, the hold on her tone tenuous and her smile tight. "It's nice to meet you, Annie. Henry— you didn't RSVP with a plus one."

Henry blinked. "Davis said it was okay."

Davis groaned as Cass whipped around on him and let 'er rip.

Annie looked miserable. "Oh my God, I'm so sorry. Henry, you idiot."

"What? Davis said it was fine. I thought she knew!"

I stepped into the fray to defuse the situation with everybody's favorite pastime. "Who's ready to drink?" As expected, I earned a few whoops and hollers. "Y'all head on over to the bar. Leo'll get you whatever you need. Pitchers are on the house!"

With some more happy cheering, the crowd made for the bar with the exception of Cass and Davis, who were busy fighting on the other side of the room. Henry and Annie were all googly and stupid, touching each other in as many places as they could at once. I half expected them to twist up like a pretzel and roll to the bar.

Jessa just stood there, watching them with an unreadable expression. Not because it was enigmatic, but because there were too many emotions to decipher just one.

"You look like you could use a drink," I said.

She blinked and looked up at me. "I . . . I'm sorry. I don't know . . ." Her gaze drifted in Henry's direction again. "I didn't know he was bringing a date."

"Yeah, I don't think you were alone." I jerked my chin in Cass's direction, and Jessa's face fell.

"Oh, no."

"Looks like Hank ruined everybody's night."

"Except hers."

"Who is she?" I asked.

"I don't know. I've never heard of her. But they look awfully familiar, don't they? I . . . I've never seen him like that with anyone."

If I didn't hate him before, I loathed him now for being the reason her voice was tight like she might cry. I'd fucking kill him, the dumbshit. He couldn't be this stupid—he had to know what he was doing to her. And if he knew how she felt and he was doing it anyway, he deserved the broken nose I was primed to give him.

On realizing I was a heartbeat away from beating the shit out of Hank in my place of employ, I grabbed Jessa's hand and pulled her toward the crowded dance floor.

"Come on, Duchess—dance with me."

She followed silently, and when we reached the dance floor, I spun her once and pulled her into me. Her body fit against mine so neatly, I nearly heard a click. She slipped into the two-step with me, but her mind was a thousand miles away.

"I didn't know you could two-step," I said.

"Oh," she leaned back to look down at our feet. "I didn't know I could either. You're that good of a dancer, I suppose."

"Don't tell anybody. I've gotta keep the bar low."

She chuckled, our bodies meeting once again. She softened a little in my arms, more still after a sigh.

"You all right?" I asked.

"Yes. I . . . I'm just surprised, I think."

"Who wouldn't be? For some godforsaken reason, you've had a crush on that shitass for a decade, and he showed up for Cass's wedding with a date nobody knew about. You're entitled to a little surprise."

She thought about that for a moment, then nibbled her lip. "It very much seems like they're together, doesn't it?"

I shrugged one shoulder. "Maybe Hank is just touchy-feely with everybody. Or he's the world's greatest prick."

"Do you think she's his girlfriend?"

As we rounded the bend of the dance floor, I got a good look at them. She was practically sitting in his lap with her arm on his shoulder, the two of them talking to another group with shit-eating smiles on.

My face must have given it away because she groaned, shaking her head.

"I'm such a fool," she whispered.

I would have stopped dead if there was a chance we wouldn't get trampled. Instead, I widened my gait, stepping us in an oblique toward the bar where there was space to stop, turning us as we went. She was breathless, her eyes bright as we danced, the speed spinning us with solid force. A little smile played at the corner of her lips, Henry forgotten.

I stopped once we were free of the dance floor, but I didn't let her go. With my free hand, I thumbed her chin, lifting it so she'd meet my eyes in the hopes that she'd really hear what I was about to say.

"Jessa, you are a great many things, but a fool is not one of them. Don't you dare let that dumb motherfucker's error hurt you. Don't let *him* hurt you. He's done enough of that." I looked in the asshole's direction, pleased as fucking punch that he was watching us. And I had another genius, moronic idea. "You know, he's not the only one who's here with someone else. I think it's high time you show him what he's missing."

Her lips parted softly, her eyes flicking to my mouth, sparking electricity where her gaze lingered.

"Make him jealous?" she asked quietly, her eyes still on my lips.

"Remember how mad he was at the fair? Make him think we're dating. He'll go crazy." *I'll go crazy. Hell, we all might go crazy.*

"I don't know if you're brilliant or mad."

I shrugged. "Bit of both."

She laughed, and anticipation shook me. I calculated a number of things—the distance between us and the wedding party, the wager I was so desperate not to lose, the pain I'd seen on her face, the way she felt in my arms, the way I wanted her—and I made a decision with intentional idiocy.

"All right," she said. "How should we go about it?"

"Well," I started, watching my hand stroke her jaw, "there's one easy way."

"Yes?" she breathed.

"I'm about to kiss you, Jessa, but I need you to know something first."

"Tell me."

"This one doesn't count."

I brought my lips to hers before she could speak.

And just like that, I was lost forever.

I'd intended a gentle kiss, something tender and sweet, and for a brief moment, it was. Her soft mouth opened with disarming shock and aching shyness. But when our tongues met, the match was struck.

There was nothing tender about the way I breathed her in, a violent, hungry inhale so deep, it didn't leave a millimeter between us. There was nothing simple about the way I drew her into my eager arms, crushing her into my chest. There was nothing gentle in the way our reckless tongues sought the depths of each other, hunting the source of this feeling—what she did to me, what I did to her. It lived somewhere in us. And like a fool, I'd let it out.

There'd be no putting it back.

Awareness came back to me at the same rate the kiss slowed. I enjoyed the heat of her mouth for a moment longer, basking in the way her body clung to mine, her arms a vise around my neck. I realized distantly I was holding all her weight, and with a great and terrible sense of loss, I set her feet back on the ground and broke the kiss.

Her eyes opened, though her lids were heavy, her lips swollen and red as she looked up at me, dazed. The smudges of pink on her cheeks were so pretty, I cupped her face to thumb one.

The corners of her lips lifted just a touch.

"Think they bought it?" she asked, her voice rough.

"I dunno. Should we try it again for good measure?"

Her laughter filled me up, bottom to top.

I glanced at the bar, my smile falling when I realized that near two dozen of our friends and family were staring at us with their jaws on the floor, scraping sawdust and peanut shells.

To my fucking delight, Henry was *livid.*

To my dismay, my cousin was about to have an aneurism. "Uh-oh."

Jessa turned to the crowd, her mouth stretching into a soft O to match her wide eyes when she saw what we'd done.

Cass marched toward us with murder on her face, scary enough that Jessa backed up until she was leaning into my chest. When she reached us, Cass sucked in a breath like the Big Bad Wolf, but before she could blow us down, Jessa put out her hand.

"Shhh, don't be mad! Look—it's just to make Henry jealous!"

Cass blinked so many times, I wondered if she was swearing me out in Morse code. After a second, she grabbed Jessa by the arm and dragged her toward the ladies' room, leaving me standing stupidly in front of the crowd.

So I did what anybody'd do—I threw on my cockiest smile and sauntered up to the bar, cutting in next to Hank and Annie.

"Heya, Leo—get me a whiskey, neat."

Leo nodded, smiling like a son of a bitch.

I turned, still leaning on the bar, to face Henry.

"What the fuck are you doing?" he asked through his teeth.

"I'm not sure I know what you mean, Hank." I picked up my drink and raised it in Leo's direction before knocking the whole thing back.

"I don't know who you think you are," he started, standing, nearly dumping Annie on her ass when he did, "but you need to stay away from her."

I sucked my teeth and set the glass on the bar. "Why? Are you afraid I'll hurt her?"

"Won't you?"

"Haven't you?" I shot, all levity gone. "Don't go throwing stones, Hanky. And don't be pissed she's with me—you had your shot for a decade. Finders, keepers."

I didn't expect him to lunge at me with his fist flying, but I managed to dodge him just the same. Truth be told, I did feel a little bad. But mostly, I wanted to take a swing of my own.

Honestly, I hadn't expected him to care so much.

I put up my hands and stepped back as a couple of guys wrangled Henry. "Hey, man—I'm sorry. But look, you're not with her, and she's a grown woman. She can make her own decisions."

Henry raked a hand through his hair, his eyes still a little wild. "Fuck you."

Davis's jaw was set, his eyes narrow as he stepped between us. "Maybe you should go, Remy."

I sighed. "Yeah, maybe I should."

"What happened?" Cass said from my elbow.

Henry pointed at me. "He needs to be taught a fucking lesson."

"Ugh, Remy! Get!" She shooed me to the door like she was my mama and dragged me outside with Jessa on our heels.

Cass didn't let me go until we were on the sidewalk. I rubbed my ear sullenly while she went off on me.

The gist of it was that I was an asshole, which I was, and that I should be ashamed of myself, which I also was. When she'd finally gotten it out, she sighed, drooping. She looked exhausted. My brows drew together in concern.

"You kissed her?" she yelled. "What the fuck, Remy!"

"It was just to—"

"Make Henry jealous? I wish I believed that was all you wanted. What I didn't expect was for you to kiss him back," she said to Jessa.

"Cass, really! It was only to make Henry angry, and look— it worked! He's furious. Absolutely mad with jealousy."

The way I hated hearing the words from her mouth ate me up from the inside.

Cass glowered, folding her arms. "That's true."

"Cass, please, don't be mad. I'm sorry," I offered, trying to pull her into a hug, but she flailed like an octopus and pushed me.

"Not now, Remy. Okay?"

"Okay," I said quietly.

"Is there anything I can do?" Jessa looked distraught.

"No," Cass said, taking her hand. "I'm sorry. It's just been a lot, and Henry throwing punches in The Horseshoe wasn't on my Bingo card."

"Was me kissing Duchess on it? 'Cause—"

"*Remy, shut up!*" they said in unison.

"Okay, okay."

"I'll come back in with you," Jessa said, but Cass shook her head.

"Honestly, I was ready to go home before dinner. Y'all go. It'll piss Henry off more if you leave together anyway."

Jessa nodded obediently and they shared a hug. When they parted, Cass lasered in on me, pointing a finger I was certain cast spells.

"Don't you dare enjoy this, Remington."

"I'd never."

With a huff and a final glare of warning, she headed inside.

"Think she'll be okay?" Jessa asked.

"I know she will be. Just maybe not until the wedding is through."

Jessa and I looked at each other from across the sidewalk. She nibbled her lip for a moment until I realized she was biting back a smile. When it broke free, it was followed by a string of laughter. She grabbed my hand, looking up at me with eyes I'd likely drown in.

"Well, what do we do now?"

And I smiled. Because I had just the thing.

22

out to dry

JESSA

IT HAD BEEN the weirdest twenty-four hours.

Somehow, I doubted the weird would be over at the end of the wooded trail behind the cottage that he'd taken me down. His hand was warm, so big it swallowed mine. So strange that a simple gesture could make me feel safe, but here I was, following him into the woods without a second thought.

I never knew what was going to happen next when I was with him, tonight included. He'd even kissed me at the bar just to make Henry jealous, which was the absolute last thing I expected. Although, I had my doubts as to how much it had to do with Henry outside of an excuse to kiss me like that.

He kissed me like I was air and he was fire. In the end, all that was left between us was ash.

The sting of seeing Henry with Annie still smarted, but truly it'd been more shock and affront than jealousy. I was angry with him for not telling me she was coming. I was angry with him for a lot, in fact.

But then Remy kissed me. And that was the end of that.

There was a magic in the woods tonight. Flickering glowworms hung in the air around us, appearing and

157

disappearing in the mist that had begun to gather along the forest floor. The musty smell of damp wood and fresh earth was a heady perfume, the sounds of the frogs and crickets a symphony.

The man in front of me was his own strange magic, and I was spellbound.

"Well, tonight could have gone better," he said.

Startled, I jumped a little and laughed. "Yes, it might have. You nearly took one on the chin from Henry."

"Trust me, Henry nearly took one himself. Was he unbearable at dinner like he usually is?"

"I wouldn't know—I sat by your mother. And I must say, I think I love her."

"Hey, me too. What'd y'all talk about?"

"You, obviously."

He gave me a look over his shoulder. "Obviously. How bad was it?"

"It wasn't bad at all, in fact. I was singing your praises and complimented her recipes. She couldn't believe the house was still clean."

"I'll deny it. Otherwise, I'm really gonna hear it when she comes by if it's not up to snuff."

"Deny it all you want. It's appreciated by me, and does anything else matter, really?"

"Not a goddamn thing, Duchess."

We walked in silence for a moment, lost in thought.

"I'm curious," I started, "What did you say to Henry to make him swing at you?"

For a few footfalls, he didn't answer. "I might have provoked him."

"Might have?" I said on a laugh. "It was very much unlike him, so I suppose you did."

"He was worried I'd hurt you. I pointed out that it was pretty funny, considering he'd been hurting you forever. I also reminded him he's had every chance with you and he blew it."

I frowned. "That doesn't sound like reason enough to get so angry."

"I might have also said *Finders, keepers*. I don't think he liked that."

A fleet of butterflies took off in my ribs.

We approached a split-rail fence with a large sign nailed to it warning us to keep out. Unfazed, Remy vaulted over it and once again extended that bear paw he called a hand.

My face quirked at the sign.

"Ah, ah, ah, Duchess. Think less." He wiggled his fingers.

And there was nothing to do but sigh and climb the fence myself.

"Good girl," he said in a voice so velvety, I could feel it in all kinds of places.

But sadly, we didn't linger. "It's bullshit," he continued as we started down the trail again. "Why does he get to string you along all this time and then fuck with you by bringing that girl? How come the mighty Hank gets to do whatever the fuck he wants, but the minute you make a choice he doesn't like, he has an opinion? Him taking a shot at me was less about you and more about his pride." He half turned so he could look at me briefly. "I don't mean he doesn't care about you—he does, that much is clear—but he didn't like that I saw through him. He liked it even less that I made sure everybody standing there did too."

I didn't say anything—words were all muddled up in my throat.

"I think it's worth noting something," he said, and I waited. "If the tables were turned—if somebody had kissed you in front of me like that, I'd do more than hit him, and it would only be about you."

This was the moment I knew without a doubt what was

going to happen tonight—I was going to fuck Remy Winfield's brains out.

The trail opened up into a rock clearing and the sound of rushing water. In a crescent around us stood a wall of stone, and in its heart was a misty pool of water fed by a waterfall.

The gasp I gasped.

Remy watched me take it all in, following me as I walked toward the pool in a daze. The air was charged from the waterfall, teasing every hair on my body. Cool fog licked my ankles.

I kicked off my shoes and kept walking, pulling my hair out of its bun. "This is incredible."

"Been swimming here since I was a kid despite Old Man Abbot's signs. He even called the cops on us once, but nobody really cares but his dog. So if you hear Kenny Rogers barking, you know you're busted."

My brows quirked. "The singer?"

He chuckled. "The dog."

I dipped a toe into the cold water, then stepped in. There was rock everywhere, the water clear, the center close and deep.

"We used to dive in from up there." He pointed to the top of the waterfall where a flat rock jutted out like a diving board. He then went on to start a story, but I was busy untying the strings of my dress.

He stopped mid-sentence when I pulled it over my head, tossed it onto the stone, and dove in. After the heat of the day, the cold water was a shock and a sigh, though it did little to cool the heat Remy inspired in my nethers. With him around, there was a fire in me so red hot, I didn't know if I'd ever need a sweater again.

I surfaced just in time to witness him drop his pants, his shirt long gone. He strode toward me and dove in, and I watched hungrily as his naked body disappeared into the black water. I saw him swimming toward me which was a good thing since he grabbed my foot, trailing his hands up my body.

"You got in before I could warn you about the snakes."

He only laughed for a second as I dunked him, but I glanced into the dark corners of the pool for slithering anyway.

He did that thing where he whipped his head, slinging his hair all in one direction. I must have looked nervous, because he said, "Don't worry. Only one's poisonous, the rest are harmless."

I made a face. "How many kinds of water snakes *are* there?"

"Nine."

"That's it, I'm through," I said on a laugh, turning for the edge, but he grabbed me and pulled me back until I glided into him, my back to his front.

He pressed a kiss to my shoulder before I turned to face him. We were close enough that I could have kissed him, but instead, I smiled.

"I told you from the start I'd win, by the way," I noted. "Which means I didn't just win—I was also *right*."

"That kiss didn't count."

"Like hell it didn't. Your lips were on my lips—the ones on my face even."

He lay back and floated with his eyes closed. "Nope. I called it, so it doesn't count."

I gaped, but I wasn't even the slightest bit angry. "You're unbelievable, do you know that?"

"People tell me all the time, Duchess." I splashed him, but he just laughed, clarifying, "I kissed you to make Henry mad."

"Liar. You manifested another loophole so you could kiss me, and that loophole was Henry."

At that, he opened his eyes and lowered himself back into

the water, cutting through the space where he'd drifted away until he was close enough to leave me breathless.

"It didn't count because you still have to choose."

"Haven't I already?"

The admission sparked something in him, but he didn't move. And in that silence, I heard a dog barking in the distance.

23
permanent press

JESSA

WE DASHED to the edge of the pool as the sound of an ATV joined the barking, its light appearing over the waterfall. As we scrambled out, the dog came louder, closer, and moving fast in our direction.

"*Grab your stuff and run!*" Remy shot as he snagged his jeans and scooped up his shirt, stuffing his feet into his shoes as he ran-hopped in the direction we came.

I was right behind him, the heels of my shoes flattened and flopping on my feet.

"*Remy Winfield,*" the old man yelled. "*I swear to God, I'm callin' your mama!*"

Laughter ripped out of us as we hurried away, bursting into the yard and through the back door of the house, panting and laughing and flushed, primed with adrenaline and the concoction of hormones we seemed to brew when in close proximity.

Remy was still naked, leaning against the back door, his chest heaving and eyes fevered. I'd haphazardly pulled on my dress, though it wasn't tied. I kept it up with one forearm, and not very well—one breast was all but exposed. I didn't really notice. I was too busy tracing the curves of his

163

shoulders in the moonlight, the shadows made by his pecs. The valley between plains of abs, the flat low on his belly between those two wicked lines that pointed straight at his considerable cock. It stood eagerly, ominously, the root nestled in dark hair, the sight of it sending a tremor to my pussy. I squirmed, eyes still on his cock. My mouth watered, wishing my lips were closed over his crown instead of pinned in my teeth.

In my haze, I'd unknowingly lowered my arm, fully exposing the one breast and half of the other—a tipping point, it seemed. Because in the span of a heartbeat, he descended on me like a storm. His mouth and mine were a seam, the sick rush between my thighs desperate. The thunder of his groan, trapped in his throat and chest as he cupped my breast and squeezed hard, flesh spilling from between his fingers, the sweet sting peaking my nipple in his palm. The sound of our breaths were noisy, needy as we labored for air. Lightning crackled beneath my palms as they skated his chest, his shoulders, his neck until my fingers twisted in his dripping hair. My arse slammed against the dryer, my hips pinned by his, holding with so much force, my feet barely touched the ground.

But it was his mouth, that smart, ill-mannered, vulgar mouth, slanted on mine like he owned me. That mouth held me captive, fettered me to him, kept me from oblivion as he fisted the front of my dress, testing its seams before tearing them, leaving me blissfully naked. One shoe was lost, the other dangling from my toe as he shifted his hips, lowered them until his cock was nestled against my clit.

I squeaked, my leg twitching and shoe hitting the floor with a slap as he devoured my neck, his tongue lapping my collarbone. To my utter sadness, he set me down, though I found consolation in his lips as they tracked south. His breath against my tight nipple before the silk of his mouth, the pull of his tongue and graze of his teeth. Remy's eyes were closed, his brow furrowed with intent, and I watched with aching reverence as he took a long moment with my breast, his free hand cupping my sex, both hands busy whipping my pulse to run, run.

He dropped to his knees, lids heavy, shoulders scratched up—*oh, that was me*, I realized from Pluto. Thick, rough fingers skated across my belly and down to my pussy, lips swollen with need, clit craving his touch. The veneration on his face was like a prayer, his eyes never leaving my cunt as he lifted one leg and slung it over his shoulder, bringing him close enough that his humid breath felt like a touch. His arm curled around my thigh, spreading me open, tracing the fluttering flesh with his fingertips.

He slid one into me, and I was so close to the edge, I nearly came.

"Jesus, Duchess—your pussy is so tight. I'm gonna tear you apart, do you know that?" I sucked in air like I was drowning, my lungs burning, pussy clenching around his finger.

"Not yet," he said, his voice so low, so deep. "Not yet," he whispered again, just before he opened his lecherous mouth and latched onto my hood.

A string of nonsense fell out of my mouth, all my weight shifting to my thigh on his shoulder as the other one gave out. He took it on, raising me up just a little, just enough to line his lips with mine so he could devour me at just the angle he wanted. The sweep of his tongue, the rapid tease, the hard pull that earned him a long whimper from me as I hung onto the dryer for dear life.

My eyes closed, my head lolling. A sharp, successive snap of fingers left me blinking at his hand, signaling me to look at him. And that was where I met my end—his eyes on mine, his tongue against my clit, the growl in his throat sending vibration all the way up my throat, escaping me as a scream.

STACI HART

He stood, palming my pussy, slipping his finger inside, curling it as I came.

"Come into my hand, Duchess."

Another hard pulse at his filth, a strangled cry.

"That's right, don't you dare fucking stop."

I writhed against his hand as my orgasm continued long after it should have been through, his finger stroking me from the inside. Flashes sparked at the edge of my vision until his hand finally slowed, releasing me from the hold of the never ending orgasm, then disappeared only to grab my face. His lips met mine in a bruising kiss, a kiss that marred me in a way I wouldn't soon erase.

I wasn't sure if it was time that was broken or me, but things moved in flashes—Remy turning me around, bending me over the dryer, the metal against my fevered skin everything. I sighed, savoring the feel of cool metal on my flushed cheek.

"Don't you fucking move," he said, his voice raw.

Beyond my thundering heart and noisy breath, I heard him rummaging around in the kitchen before he was back and tearing open a condom. I wanted to watch him, but I was too languid to move.

Panting, he laid a hand on the small of my back, his cock in his hand. His silken crown hit my slick center with a *slap, slap, slap*, and just like that, my body came alive again with a gasp and a rush of blood.

"You make me like this," he said, guiding his cock to trace the slit. "You do this to me. Once I fuck you, it's only gonna get worse—I won't be able to stop myself from wanting you."

He slid into me with the slow flex of his hips and a grunt to match my cry, filling me up by increment, shifting once he was seated as deep as he could get.

I panted, gulping air, too full to breathe, my body on fire, not knowing what he was going to do to me. His hips were still, restrained and tight as he palmed my arse, squeezed.

166

Took my hands, laid them by my sides. Arched over me to . . . reach past me to the dryer? Confused, I heard the click as he spun the knob, the slap as he hit the button to turn it on.

Later I would wonder if nerve endings could actually explode like fireworks and decided yes, they could, and yes, mine did.

My soul left my body as the vibration hummed through me at every point of contact, the most precious at my nipples, sending shocks racing to the point where our bodies met. My cunt trembled around his cock—he planted his hands on the top of the dryer for a moment, and neither of us moved. I whimpered and whined and whispered, but I didn't move. After a second, or an hour, or a week, he retreated as he took my hands, pulled as he pumped his hips, not stopping until he was deep. Then again, again. The torture was sick and sweet as he fucked me, every roll and flex of his hips heavy with barely contained control. The emptiness when he drew back, the suffocating fullness when he entered me again. The tip of him teasing my trigger from the inside, pressed even closer to his cock thanks to the unholy appliance quivering beneath me.

My breath came faster, the world dimming.

"Fuck, Jessa," his hips jerked as my pussy clenched, another orgasm close enough to taste the tang of it. "You're so fucking tight." The words were pained but my body didn't care.

Until he stopped, trembling behind me, and I broke.

"Oh my God, fuck me right now. Don't stop, I'll die . . . I'll die . . ." I babbled and cried and wailed and screamed when he gave me what I begged for, pumping his hips, his pace relentless.

I came with heart stopping pleasure-pain, but he didn't stop, grunting and growling, the slap of my arse against his body clapping over the din. And when he came, he swelled, pulsed, but neither of us could move or he really would tear me apart. I snapped onto my forearms, back arched, feeling every throb as he emptied himself into me.

He collapsed, his arms winding into the space my arms made, slick and breathless and spent. When he could, he pulled out, pressing a kiss to my back. I suppose he cleaned up, but I wouldn't have known. I lay down on top of the dryer deciding I lived here now, arse out and everything, forever and ever, amen.

"C'mere, Duchess," he said with tenderness as he coaxed me into a position where he could pick me up. Thankfully, he didn't even try to set me on my feet, just carried me to his room, unpeeled me from his chest, and laid me in bed, climbing in after me.

I rolled over as he opened his arms, our bodies coming together again, but this time to just breathe. I could feel his pulse still racing where my face touched his neck, our bodies sweaty and rain slicked and hot and careless. The only priority was to make sure as much skin was touching as possible.

He stroked my back with sure fingertips, my elbow cupped in his other hand, and for a long while, I lay curled up in his arms, wondering if he'd broken my brain. He'd definitely broken my pussy.

I giggled, and he leaned back to look at me.

"Yeah?" he said.

"I was just taking stock and think you might have broken my cunt."

He groaned, squeezing me closer. "God, don't fucking say that word right now."

I lifted up on my forearm. "You can't be serious."

"It's one of the few things I wouldn't joke about, darlin'."

Glancing at his cock, I found proof that he wasn't kidding. Why I had to fight the urge to bury my face between his legs when I couldn't even use my own, I didn't know. He'd turned me into a sex-crazed lunatic, and I was here for it.

"Really, I think I'm broken," I said. "Never has anyone spoken to me like you do when your cock is hard."

He tucked his hand behind his head, his brows drawn in confusion. "Seriously?"

"Really. Not even a little light chatter, never mind the obscenities that leave your mouth. I love it."

A laugh rolled out of him. "Now we've just gotta get you talking."

"Oh, I don't know what I'd even say." I blushed like a schoolgirl.

He shrugged one shoulder. "Whatever you're thinking."

My gaze slipped to his decadent cock, and I pursed my lips, wetting them. "Well, I was thinking how I wanted to bury my face between your legs."

The suggestive smile on his face did something to my insides that I couldn't sort out. "Go on."

"Earlier tonight, I wondered what you'd taste like. I wanted the tip of your cock in my mouth, hot, silky, salty. I want to taste you, that's really the gist of it."

His eyes had gone all smoldery as he reached out to cup my breast, fondling it. "What else?"

My nipple hardened beneath his touch, and I took a moment to admire his dick. "I suppose now it would taste a little like me, wouldn't it?" I trailed my fingertips up the shaft. "I want to feel you come in my mouth, every last drop." I wrapped my fingers around him and pumped.

"Open your mouth," he said, the words gravel.

Holding his gaze, I did, extending my tongue to my chin so he could see what awaited him.

His hand moved from my breast to cup my neck, his thumb stroking my throat. "I've thought about fucking that mouth so many times, Duchess."

"I don't know if you remember, but you promised me yesterday there would be hot come in my throat."

"Oh, I remember." A smile flickered on his lips as a groan left them. "Well, a promise is a promise."

He rose to his knees, and I sat, hands in my lap, looking up at him.

Remy stroked my hair, cupped the back of my head, his smirk in full bloom. "I didn't know you were such a greedy little slut, Duchess."

I shrugged. "I guess I am." But then I giggled, flushed and hot. "Why is it so hot when you degrade me like that?"

"I dunno, but I bet you're soaked."

"I am. Would you like to see?"

A thick breath. "Not yet. First, you need to tell me if my cock tastes like you hoped."

I shifted to put myself where I could get to him, handled him with curiosity, enjoying the feel of him in my hands, the weight of him, the way his skin moved. And he stroked my hair, watching me.

"Open your mouth again, Duchess, and this time wrap it around my cock."

With his shaft in my fist, I extended my tongue and took his silky head into my mouth, relishing in the feel, moaning a little.

He snapped again. "Up here. Look at me."

I swirled my tongue around, sucking gently, releasing him with a pop. Unhappy with my angle, I got on all fours. But I wasn't happy there either. I backed away, sitting on my feet, pouting.

"It's not quite what I hoped for. Too much work to enjoy it."

He smiled, taking my chin in his thumb and forefinger. "Then tell me what you want, and you'll have it."

"Lie down."

He did, propping himself up on a pillow, hand behind his head again. He was, without question, the most beautiful man I had ever seen, and in more ways than even the obvious. Like the artful way his hand hooked behind his head, his biceps fanned next to his face. The size of those hands, one of which rested on his chest, rising and falling with his breath. His legs, casually splayed. He looked like he belonged in a dirty magazine, not in bed with me. But in bed with me he was, looking up at me with hungry eyes.

Never had a man wanted me like this, either. There was a quiet power in that knowledge, and as I nestled my body between his legs with his eyes on me, I felt it in every blood cell.

I took my time, running my nose up his shaft, skimming my lips down, the lightest touch of my tongue up to the cleft in his crown. And I closed my eyes, kissing the tip, bringing my lips together. It was a slow admiration, the enjoyment of how he felt, how he tasted. My mouth watered, spit dripping down his shaft and to my fist where I held what I couldn't take. He'd started to breathe heavier, his hand finding my face. I looked up at him through my lashes to find his eyes closed, chin tilted, wrist on his forehead. Without stopping, I raised a hand and snapped twice at him, earning me a smile and a hot look that only made me work harder. When I'd teased him as long as he could take it, I took him deep, feeling the swell of him against my tongue, in the back of my throat. I braced myself, eyes watering, his hands in my hair as he fucked my mouth.

"I'm gonna come," he whispered, giving me a chance to back out.

But I wasn't about to lose this one either.

He came with a cry, his legs shaking as I milked him until there was nothing left.

I didn't let him go until he was laid back and panting, and I had to swallow three fucking times to get it all down. Truly, I was lucky I didn't choke to death. The thought amused me, and I smiled, getting on my hands and knees to crawl up to him.

But he sat, turning me over, pressing me into the bed, kissing me, his tongue sweeping my mouth to taste himself. He only let me go to lean over and dig into his bedside table for another condom, and this time I had the pleasure of watching, my fingertips circling my breast as he rolled the condom on. The sight of his cock slipping in and out of his fist sent a shock to my pussy, but when I wriggled and reached for him, he filled my arms. He pushed my thighs apart with his knees, fisted his cock at the root, fitted his crown between my lips, and flexed into the aching space until I was full.

I rose, meeting his lips as he angled for mine. The kiss was deep and hot and slow, my hands roaming, wanting to touch him everywhere all at once. There was too much to feel. The weight of him on top of me. The sweet command of his lips. The way he felt inside of me. The way he touched my face, like I was precious. The way my skin tingled, the blood rushing to my core, the world fading away.

The stars behind my eyes when I came.

The sight of him when my eyes opened.

He kissed me again, this time softly, gently, with gratitude and adoration. I could have lived forever in that kiss. Except that I couldn't.

So I decided to collect as many as I could while they were here to take.

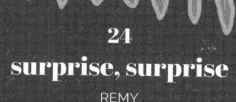

24

surprise, surprise

REMY

MY FAVORITE PLACE in the whole fucking world was the hot space between her thighs.

Through all of last night and now into a much needed shower, I had lived in the depths of her, and I wondered if I'd ever be satisfied. Somehow, I very much doubted it.

Steaming water rained down my back and shoulders, the water trailing down my torso to my bare cock that disappeared inside of her, the tight squeeze of her body punctuated by the slap of wet skin. Thanks to a conversation last night spurred by the annoyance of a condom, I could feel every millimeter of her sweet, sweet pussy around me.

I thought I'd wanted her before, but now I was downright impossible. I couldn't be anywhere but inside of her or I'd die on the spot.

She was hinged, her hands on the back edge of the clawfoot tub, tits bouncing and hair swinging in a curtain as I thrust into her, trying like hell not to come yet. Soap slid down her sides, gathered in the valley of her back, slicked her hips and ass beneath my hands. The notch of her waist was so sinful, I should have prayed for salvation. But there was no need—I was saved right then and there by the slick flesh squeezing my cock as I came deep and hard and messy inside her. It wasn't until I'd caught my breath that I pulled out.

"Stay there," I commanded, my voice rough.

She arched her back, sliding her hand between her legs.

"Look what you did," she said, spreading herself open. A pearly bead of come dripped out of her, and by the time my groan ended, a slow, thick stream had followed.

"Goddamn you," I rasped, grabbing her arm to turn her around. Our lips crashed, one hand cupping her face and the other splayed across her back, holding her to me. The feel of my cock against her soft stomach was everything. When the kiss broke, she smiled up at me, lips together, lids heavy. "You'd better not keep that up or we might never leave the shower."

"You're lucky we made it out of bed."

"I really am, aren't I?"

"You really are." I kissed her nose and made sure she wasn't still soapy before turning off the shower. Then I grabbed a towel, opening it up to dry her off.

She looked as happy and smitten as I felt, laughing as I ruffled up her hair beneath the towel. Overnight, she'd somehow gotten even more beautiful. Maybe it was just that I'd become acquainted with every square inch of her body. In my exploration, I found so much to admire that I hadn't seen before, just when I thought I'd cataloged it all. And though I couldn't plant a flag on her, I could plant something else.

So boy, did I.

I kissed her smiling mouth and grabbed a towel of my own, drying off and stepping out of the shower before helping her out.

"Hungry?" I asked without letting go of her hand.

"Famished."

"I'll cook us something up."

I kissed her again as briefly as I could, which was not very, and we parted ways in the hallway—her for her room, me for the mudroom. The second I saw the dryer, my dick was ready, willing, and waiting to get back inside her. The vision of her bent over in the moonlight would haunt every load of laundry I did for the rest of my life.

Sighing, I reached into the dryer for a pair of jeans and pulled them on, whipping off my towel and throwing it into the bin. Beau came sauntering in, leaning down to stretch his paws in front of him like he'd just woken up.

"You hungry too?" I asked, and he smacked his lips in what I assumed was the affirmative.

I clicked on the radio, busying around the kitchen, feeding the dog first and making our breakfast after, listening to Jessa get dressed and ready for the day. Those simple, mundane sounds filled me with a comfort I hadn't felt in a long, long time. There was someone here with me, someone who wouldn't just leave when the night was over. It was her presence, bolstered by the unspoken understanding that we were on the same page. That I wanted her and she wanted me, but not just bodies. I wanted her smiles. I wanted her laughter. I wanted the feel of her hand in mine and the curve of her body against me when I slept.

God, I was in deep shit.

She came in as the biscuits were in the oven and the bacon was sizzling, smoothing her hair as she took a seat at the island. When I turned to get a look at her, she was smiling at me, and then I was smiling at her. Or maybe I already had been. Who knew.

Her hair was in a low, slicked back bun, her gold jewelry glowing on her tan skin—newly acquired, thanks to the summer sun. But the best part was that she had on the yellow dress from the carnival.

Her hands folded on the island. "Seems dangerous to be frying bacon without a shirt."

"Listen, sweetheart—I like to live on the edge."

A quiet laugh from her direction as I pulled the bacon out and cracked some eggs to fry in the grease.

"Can I pick you up after you meet Cass at the venue? I wanna show you something."

I could hear her smiling behind me when she said, "You always seem to have something to show me, don't you?"

"What can I say? I'm full of surprises."

"I've never heard anything truer."

"So what are y'all doing over there at the venue?" I stuffed my hand in a potholder and pulled out the biscuits.

"Oh, last-minute things. Where the caterers will be, the best places to take photos, the layout for the wedding outside and reception in the barn." She chuckled. "A wedding in a barn. I've never."

"It'll just be you and Cass?"

"Maybe Davis, but I somehow doubt it."

"And Hank?" I plated Jessa's eggs and bacon, adding the piping biscuit last.

A pause. "I don't know. But I hope not."

"Hey, same." I offered her plate, and she took it with hungry eyes.

"I feel like I haven't eaten in a year," she said, picking up a piece of bacon with delicate fingers. When it was in her mouth, her eyes closed and she groaned.

"Quit making sounds like that, Duchess," I said as I built out my plate.

"Or else what?"

She wore a mischievous smile, watching me as I approached and took the seat next to her.

"You know what," I said matter-of-factly, popping a piece of bacon into my mouth.

Another groan. "I would do terrible things to you right this minute if I wasn't so hungry."

I laughed, tucking into my breakfast and repeated, "Hey, same."

For a moment, we ate to the sound of Dolly Parton over the radio. Well, she ate. I wolfed it like I'd never had a hot meal.

Half a second later when I'd finished, I grabbed her seat and pulled until she was between my legs.

She laughed, pulling her plate with her so she could keep eating.

"Hey, look at that—you're almost done," I said, leaning over to press a kiss to her neck. "What time do you have to meet Cass?"

"Oh, an hour or so," she said, the words all breathy and hot.

"Mmm." She smelled like flowery soap and fresh laundry, and I inhaled deep like a creep.

"Are you counting all the things you could do to me in that amount of time?" She took the last bite of her eggs, I noted.

"Why, are you?"

She turned on the stool until she was facing me. "Always. So far I've counted at least ten."

"Is that all?"

"Do you think you can do better?"

"Psh. Absolutely."

"Care to wager?"

My smile must have been wicked, from the look on her face. "Depends. What does the winner get?"

"Whatever they want."

My fingers trailed down her neck to her breast where it stayed for a moment, keeping itself occupied with ease. "Anything?"

"Anything."

"It's too easy, Duchess. Who knows what I'll ask for if I win." I leaned in slow, angling for her lips.

"Who says you'll win?" She stroked my face, then my chest, ultimately reaching for my waistband.

"Ten sexual acts in an hour is nothing. I figured you'd know that about me by now."

"But how do you know you'll last that long?" Her lips grazed mine with every word, her hands making quick work of my jeans button.

I would have laughed if she hadn't kissed me, even if she was right.

Her slender hand was down my pants and around my cock when Beau went nuts out in the front yard.

The kiss broke when we both looked in that direction. Sadly, she reclaimed her hand, and I begrudgingly zipped up my pants, frowning when I saw a black Bentley coming up the gravel drive.

It looked like it belonged here as much as Jessa had when she came hobbling in my direction and into my arms.

Jessa went still. "Oh, no."

"Who is it?" The car came to a stop next to the Scout. When the door opened, one long leg appeared, then another, followed by an elegant genetic copy of Jessa.

"My mother."

Fear gripped me with a cold fist in my guts. "*Shit.*"

Jessa smoothed her skirt, reaching for the doorknob with a weird smile on her face. "Shit is right. *Mummy!*" she called as she hurried onto the porch.

For a second, I stood there staring. When a droplet of sweat slid down my spine, I remembered I had no shirt on.

"Shit."

I trotted to the mudroom, cursing the dryer, though I was grateful for its contents. Once I'd pulled on a shirt, I heard the barking.

"*Shit!*" I took off in a run, tearing out the door and toward my goddamn dog, who was trying to get around Jessa to the horrified woman in the white pantsuit and sunglasses.

"Beau!" I snapped, grabbing him by the collar when I got to him. "I'm sorry about him. Lemme put him up."

Beau writhed and flopped around so hard, I nearly had to pick him up and carry him like a baby to his doghouse to tether him. My heart hammered from exertion, sure. But mostly because Jessa's real, actual life had just pulled up in a car that cost more than just about anyone in town could make in a decade.

And I did not fit into her real, actual life.

I raked a hand through my damp hair, hurrying back to the house with no idea what was about to happen, but I seriously doubted it'd be good.

This was confirmed when I found them in a quiet argument next to the car. I hung back for a second, not sure what I was supposed to do. Jessa saw me and put that weird smile back on.

"Mother, this is Remy, Cass's cousin. Remy, this is my mother, Lady Grace Hastings."

I couldn't see where she was looking for her sunglasses, but I got the sense it was all over me. Her lips were tight, I noticed as I stepped up and took her offered hand, which was palm down and limp.

I shook it, then wondered if I wasn't supposed to do that. Should I kiss it? That didn't seem right either.

"How do you do?" she asked all regal, taking her hand back and holding it funny.

"Nice to meet you."

But she'd already turned back to Jessa. "Really, Jessamine. This?" She looked the house over briefly.

"It's fine, Mother. Look, I'm in one piece and everything."

"Not to worry, I've arrived."

Jessa looked at her mother, whatever she felt well masked. "Yes, what *are* you doing here?"

"Ah! I was absolutely devastated to turn down Cassidy's wedding invitation, so when I was needed in New York for a charity event, I thought—why not surprise them all?"

"Well, Mother, I'm very much surprised."

Lady Hastings smiled at her daughter. "Oh, goodie. Gather up your things and let's get you to civilization, shall we?"

"I don't understand," Jessa said. "There's nowhere to stay in town."

"Yes, of course, but your father is acquainted with the CEO of a rather large chain of grocery stores, and he happens to have a house in these little mountains. He was more than happy to oblige."

"I see. And how did you find me?"

"I called Cassidy's mother. Though when she told me you were staying in a cottage, I'll admit this is not what I imagined. Now, if you're through, we should go." She stepped toward the rear doors of the Bentley, which was still running. "Run along, darling. Pleased to meet you, Remy."

She said my name like it was another language. "Yes, ma'am. You too."

And then she disappeared into the car, the door thumping closed behind her.

Jessa and I walked back to the house in a daze.

"I'm sorry," she said quietly as I followed her into her room.

"Sorry for what?"

"I . . . I don't know."

I put her suitcase on the recovered bed and unzipped it. "I don't want you to go," I said to my hands as I readied it for her.

"I don't want to go." She sounded like she might cry, and something in my chest broke.

I gathered her into my arms. "Hey, it's all right. We'll just have to sneak around a little."

She nodded against my chest. "This is so stupid. I should just tell her I want to stay."

That cold fear licked my spine again. "I dunno. I really don't want to piss off your mom—she doesn't seem to think much of me as it is. Maybe just . . . play along for a minute. We'll figure it out."

After a heavy sigh, she left the circle of my arms, but that niggling cold did not. Not while we packed her up, not as she drove off with her mother.

Certainly not after she was gone.

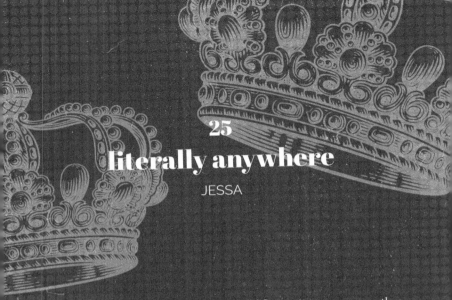

literally anywhere

JESSA

MY INSIDES WERE A ROILING, boiling mess as the driver pulled away from Remy's house.

Lady Hastings's presence did not help.

"Really, I don't know how you've survived with that beastly man and that beastly dog," she said to the window.

"It was no trouble."

Her head swiveled to look at me. "I do hope he was a gentleman."

My eyes swept the ceiling, but I had to stifle a laugh. "You act as if Cass found him on the streets. He's her cousin, not a stranger."

"Did you know him prior to this?"

"No, but—"

"Then he is, in fact, a stranger. I find it hard to believe there was nowhere else for you to stay. Soon enough you'll sort out how to take care of yourself, but in the meantime, you have me."

"Yes, well, it all worked out, didn't it? How was your flight?" I asked, suddenly exhausted and desperate to change the subject.

"Well enough. Our usual jet and its crew had been

chartered out so I had to deal with new staff, but I've had a rest and am fed, thankfully. I wasn't sure what we might find to eat here in the country. Tell me, how are things with Henry?" She turned in my direction, her smile bright and genuine.

I'd never noticed how awful it was before.

"Things are fine, same as they always were. He's brought a date to the wedding."

Her smile fell. "A . . . date?"

"Yes, a girl called Annie." An idea sprang to mind, and then I was smiling too. I'd hate for Mother to be surprised when Remy kissed me in public. "In fact, Cass, Remy and I have a little game going—we're pretending to date to make Henry jealous. It's driving him completely mad."

My stomach flipped and wriggled at the lie, but my heart was warm at the thought of the truth underneath.

"It's brilliant. Though couldn't it have been someone else? *Anyone* else?"

"It was convenient, that's all," I lied, wishing I still had the excuse to sleep in his bed.

"And you say Henry's gone mad?"

"As a box of frogs."

She laughed, and I suddenly felt much better. Then I realized her approval had sparked the feeling, which made me feel much worse.

"He even threw a punch at Remy last night."

"You don't say." She leaned in, her eyes wide.

"It's true. Took several men to hold him back."

"That is promising. Did Cassidy not know about this Annie girl?"

I sighed. "No, Cass was furious. Annie remains a mystery."

"How unlike him not to RSVP for her."

"Neither did you."

She scoffed.

"I know him as well as I know my own children, and we've always known you're perfect together, darling. It's only a matter of time until he decides to settle down, and then there you'll be. Although I appreciate your initiative with the little gambit with the barbarian. *Remy.* And what does that stand for?"

"Remington."

"How distinguished for such a creature."

"He's been nothing but surprises." I bit my tongue lest I say more and muck up the whole deal. "I still can't believe you're here."

She reached for my hand, squeezing it as if we were bosom buddies. "I'm so glad. I've missed you. Work and social callings aren't quite the same without you. After all these years of going it alone, I thought I enjoyed myself, but having you as a companion is much more agreeable." Her smile faltered a little before she looked back out the window as we turned onto a steep incline. "It really can be such a bore. But you make it easier."

Her candor surprised the words out of my head, just like that.

"But we're together again, and soon enough you'll be home and things will be as they should. While we're here, we'll attend whatever functions Cassidy has planned. I've already told her mother I'll pay for the catering. It's the least I could do, arriving unannounced. There will, of course, be the rehearsal dinner and wedding—what else should we plan for?"

"*Shit.*" I scrambled for my purse, checking the time on my phone.

"Jessamine," she warned, digging in her own purse for a mirror.

"I'm set to meet Cass at the ba—er, venue in just a bit."

"Well, where is it?" She cleaned up the edge of her lipstick with a tissue.

"Not terribly far," I hedged, not wanting to tell her the wedding would be in a barn on a farm. But then I realized she'd find out anyway, and wasn't it best to tell her where she couldn't offend everyone in earshot? I cleared my throat. "It's actually at a farm. In a barn."

Mother stilled, then looked at me. "A barn."

"Yes, a barn. I thought you might want to prepare yourself. It's only used for a venue and has been renovated, of course. And it's really quite beautiful."

"How . . . provincial." She snapped her mirror shut as we pulled into the drive of a massive home. "Ah, here we are. Take the car down to your . . . barn. We'll have supper tonight at eight, at the house, so please be sure you have time to come home and wash the muck off you beforehand."

"Yes, Mother."

She took my chin in her thumb and forefinger. "Good girl. I really am thrilled to see you." She opened the door and exited, leaning back in to say, "Give Cassidy my love, would you? I'd say have fun, but . . ." She gave my shoes a pointed look. "Well, at least you're dressed appropriately."

When the door closed, I slumped back in my seat, damning my luck.

"Where can I take you, miss?" the driver asked.

To which I said, with an exhausted sigh, "Anywhere but here."

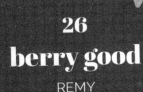

26
berry good
REMY

I'D ITCHED to see Jessa before, but this time was different.

As I leaned against my truck outside of the wedding site, my thoughts chased each other in circles, just like they had since she'd ridden away with her mother that afternoon. I wasn't sure why, but it felt like an ending of some sort, and just when we'd begun.

Life was not fucking fair.

The universe seemed to enjoy proving the point. As if I didn't know.

Jessa's mother carried herself with that poise I'd always imagined in high society. The kind of woman that came to mind when you heard words like *lady* and *duchess*. But my Duchess was nothing like her mother. Sure, I could see the resemblance— they were both beautiful and had smartass mouths—but when it came to her attitude, Jessa was nothing like that woman. Funny her name should be Grace when she possessed so little of it.

And there was no mistaking how she felt about me.

I couldn't say I blamed her. I knew I wasn't fit for her daughter just as well as anybody—take one look at us together and you'd see. Ask us to speak and it'd be over.

A little ways off, Jessa walked out of the open barn with Cass and Davis . . . *and Henry* in tow. A dozen feet behind them, Annie exited with her attention on her phone and an annoyed look on her face. The rest of them caught sight of me at the same time. Jessa lit up like a lightbulb. Henry fumed. Cass glared. Davis's eyes were bouncing off the points of our little fake love triangle. Annie finally looked up, glanced at Henry, and sighed.

I waved.

Jessa seemed to say goodbye, then headed in my direction, beaming, a big floppy hat in one hand and her purse across her body. When she got to the parking lot, she took off in a run, and I pushed off the truck so I could catch her if she flung herself at me. And thank God I had, because not only did she launch into my arms, but her legs wound around my waist.

I started to laugh, but she kissed me, the greeting so fine, it took me a minute to realize I was holding her bare ass in my hands. In a panic, I felt around for underwear, relieved when I found her thong. Last thing I needed was Henry to see what he was *really* missing.

She broke the kiss, lips together in a smile. "Hello, Darling."

"Hello, Darlin'."

Jessa flushed, laughing as I set her down. When I looked up, Henry had broken from Davis's grip with the jerk of his arm and was marching toward us. He got about two steps before Cass grabbed him by the shoulders and veered him in the direction of her car.

"Uh-oh. Hank's pissed," I said.

"Well, we needed to make sure it was believable, didn't we? I'm not keen on bearing Cass's wrath, are you?"

"No, but I seriously doubt we're fooling anybody with a kiss like that."

She laughed, and I slapped her ass before helping her into the truck.

"Man, poor Annie," I said, frowning at Cass and the gang as they got in her car, Davis in the driver's seat.

Jessa frowned too. "It's awful. The whole time, he was in my ear about you, ignoring her completely. I don't understand. It seems she thinks she's here as a date, but he's oblivious."

"You can say that again," I said, making my way around the Scout, waving at the carload of oglers as they drove by. Cass's jaw was set, and I saw her pick up her phone, thumbs flying.

My phone vibrated in my pocket as I climbed in next to Jessa and texted her back.

Cass: Stop enjoying yourself.

Remy: No idea what you're talking about.

Cass: OMG dude, I'm going to throttle you.

Remy: Look at Hank rn. How pissed is he?

Cass: Super duper core of the sun pissed.

Remy: See? It's working. Trust the process.

Cass: aewkfhlwfafwoeiaj;

"EVERYTHING OKAY?" Jessa asked.

I turned on the truck. "Yeah, just getting in trouble with Cass."

"I hate that part of it."

"Me too." When I put my hand on the back of her seat to

back up, I couldn't help but lean in for a kiss. When she sighed, I added, "Worth it."

We pulled out of the parking lot and onto the road, turning away from town.

She looked like a million bucks sitting there in my beat up old truck, floppy hat in her lap, her expression all wistful as she watched the forest roll by.

"Where are we going?"

"It's a surprise."

"Your favorite."

"It's true. So how'd it go with your mom?"

At that, all the pep slid out of her. "As well as could be expected, I suppose. The house is ridiculous, though how ridiculous it is, I don't know. I only ran in for the loo before coming here. I believe she's hired a chef, the driver of course, and who knows what else."

"Aren't you used to that sort of thing?"

"Well, yes. It's just . . . different now."

I glanced at her, confused. "How so?"

"I dunno. I suppose being here where things are easy. *There* everything feels too big. Too grand. Too complicated. *There* is jammed with expectation and responsibility. Here just . . . is."

"Vacation brain."

"Pardon?"

"Vacation brain. You know, where you glorify a place because you're infatuated with it."

"Oh. Then do I have vacation pussy too?"

A laugh shot out of me. "Jesus Christ, Jess."

She shifted to put her back against the passenger door, her finger between her teeth and a sly look on her face. "Your cock has been glorified in the highest, and I am most definitely infatuated with it."

Her legs parted a little, and I caught sight of said infatuated pussy, barely contained by her thong.

"You'd better cut that out," I warned.

"How come?"

"You keep asking me like you don't know."

She laughed, setting herself right. "I don't know what it is about you. I swear to you, I've never said or done such things."

"That vacation pussy is wild."

"She is, and starving to death, apparently."

"New topic. Because I want to take you somewhere before I give that hungry cunt of yours the attention it deserves, and if you keep it up, I'm not making it another mile."

"Fine, fine. Have it your way. Let's see, new topic. Oh, I did learn a bit about Annie."

"Mmm," was all I could muster.

"They went to grad school together, as he said. They've been friends ever since, and she lives in Nashville, so he asked her to join him as his date. She's staying with him and everything."

I noted happily that she didn't seem too upset by the fact. "So he was bent out of shape all day?"

She rolled her eyes. "Mostly, he just wanted to talk about how upset he is by the thought of me with you. Hopefully he got a good look at your hands on my bum. I'd love for him to know just how much you enjoy me."

"Not as much as I would," I said, enjoying the chuckle I earned. "And how about your mom?"

"I already hate staying with her, not only because I'll be *with her*, but because I won't be with you. I'm absolutely furious she's just shown up and whisked me off when I'd finally won our bet."

"You did not win."

"Oh, yes I did. Twice."

"Did not. What'd your mom say about everything?" And by everything, I meant me.

"Did too." She sighed, sagging a little again. "Nothing,

really. She criticized my clothes and was appalled that the wedding is in a barn. Honestly, I can't wait for the photos. Everyone will die when they see her with a champagne flute in her hand, feathered hat on her head, in a *barn*. Outside of stables, I'm not sure she's ever *been* in a barn, never mind eaten a meal in one."

"Sounds like it'll be a night to remember. If she doesn't want to go, why not bail?"

"Because she's already shown up and offered to pay for the caterer. She'd make an arse out of herself to leave now, and God knows she'd never do that intentionally. So she'll stay, and she'll smile, and she'll have all her meals prepared by the private chef in whomever's silly house it is we're staying in."

"Silly, huh?"

"The toilet had buttons and meters all over it. It's not so complicated a device that one should need instructions to use it. I did rather enjoy the heated seat, though."

I spotted the derelict driveway I was looking for and pulled in, slowing to adjust for the forest that'd reclaimed so much of it. The shade was deep, and Jessa peered outside with her lips parted.

"The forest here is like nothing I've seen," she said with reverence I felt in my heart of hearts. "Where are we?"

"You'll see."

The driveway opened up to a clearing acres deep, walled in by encroaching woods. At the end stood an abandoned house, its windows busted, the glass just maws of jagged teeth. I drove us around the house, stopping in the shade beneath the canopy of a cluster of trees.

"This place used to be a strawberry farm," I started, cutting the engine. "Old Murphy died a few years back and his kids have been arguing over the land ever since. Funny, 'cause by the time they figure it out, it won't be worth much anymore."

An excited smile spread across her face and lit up her eyes. "Are we going to pick strawberries?"

I reached into the back for a bucket and handed it to her.

She honest to God squealed as she took it.

"Come on," I said on a laugh. But she was already halfway out the door.

She put that silly hat on her head and headed for a grassy meadow concealing a strawberry field.

"This way." I offered my hand, my heart stirring when she took it.

Looking around, I found where I thought the beginning of the field was, happy when I found it without too much fumbling.

"See?" I pointed into the grass where a bundle of fat, red berries were waiting to be picked.

She gasped, kneeling to pluck one and hold it up for inspection. "Oh, it looks divine." Her eyes cut to mine. "We shouldn't eat them, should we?"

I shrugged and took it from her, inspected it for dirt or worms, and popped it in my mouth, biting off the crown. "It's organic." I chucked the waste and took a moment just to watch her.

She licked her lips, picking a strawberry and inspecting it like I had. When approved, her lips closed around it in a way that nearly drove me feral, especially when the juice dripped down her chin like a bikini girl in an eighties music video.

"Humuguh," she said around her bite. "Dish sho goot."

I laughed, figuring that was probably the rudest thing she'd ever done, and I was honored to have witnessed it.

Tin bucket hooked in her elbow, she took turns saving one and eating one, and I watched her like she was living art. There was plenty to admire. Like her delicate hands, her long neck. The prim bun of corn silk hair, the golden curve of her sun kissed shoulders. But while I appreciated all those things, the ones that affected me the deepest had nothing to do with her body. It was the light in her sky-blue eyes, the joy in the high apples of her cheeks. It was her excitement, her happiness that filled me up with happiness too. Experiencing it all through her struck me in the deepest, darkest, most deserted places. It had been a long time—a long, *long* time since that dust had stirred.

And I'd found the feeling with a girl so out of my league, she might as well live on Mars.

When she left, it was about how far away she'd be.

I shook the thought away, picking a strawberry of my own to get the taste of it out of my mouth.

We wandered deeper into the fields, the berries still largely growing in rows. Jessa finally slowed down the conveyor belt into her mouth, then stopped, laying a hand on her belly.

"I think I ate about a hundred," she said, still bending here and there to pick more. "What will we do with all of them?"

"Aside from snack on them until we're sick? We could make a strawberry pie or two."

"That sounds lovely, though I don't know how. Do you?"

"Sure do. It's a date."

She groaned, bending to pick a mutant strawberry that looked like three mushed together. "I hate that we have to set dates for anything." She inspected it, looked to me for direction, and tossed it in the bucket when I nodded. "I should be home with you, not with my mother."

I hated that I ached at her calling my place home. "We really should play nice. She hates me already, I can tell."

"Hate is a strong word." She tromped a little farther down and knelt at a bundle of berries.

"Hey, I can't say I blame her. I'm no catch."

"Ha! Sir, you are indubitably a catch. Shall I count the ways?"

"The bartender from the podunk town in nowhere,

Tennessee? Somehow I doubt your mom would ever approve."

"Well, lucky for us, she has no say." We walked a little ways down, this time both of us kneeling to clear a patch. "And anyway, is it really what you want to do forever?"

"What, would you rather I did something more palatable for your friends and family?" I did my best to hide the sting, but it wasn't good enough.

"No, of course not," she answered, her eyes wide and brow furrowed. "That isn't what I meant. I just wondered what you *wanted*."

"I gave up the things I wanted a long time ago, Duchess."

"Just because you gave them up doesn't mean they're not still there."

"But they're not. Sometimes you hit a point in life where those things you wanted are *gone*. As in literally impossible."

She frowned. "I can't imagine you playing baseball for a living is *impossible*. What do they say? The chances are low but never zero."

"There are kids coming straight of college, young and fresh and ready to play hard. I'm twenty-eight. Making the majors is a one in a million shot."

"Is there another league?"

I paused. "Well, sure. The minors, which has a whole bunch of levels."

"So, why not try? What would it hurt?"

"My pride?" I really was trying to joke.

Jessa rolled her eyes. "Really, Remy. Can you *really* not see that you're the only thing in your way? You've already given up."

"But the odds—"

"Are low, but *never* zero."

"Fine, little miss know-it-all. What do *you* want?"

She didn't like that. It made me feel better. "I don't know. Isn't that the difference? You know exactly what you want,

194

therefore there's a solution. You only need the means to do it, which in your case is the nerve. My problem is unsolvable."

"Listen, I've got plenty of nerve."

"And don't I know it," she said, chuckling, her eyes on her hands.

"Why not figure out what it is you want? That feels like step one, but what do I know?"

"Trust me, I've spent a decade trying to sort it out. More, I suppose. But it doesn't matter anyway because I have obligations. *You* do not have such obligations."

"Those obligations are made up, Jess. Nobody dies if you don't go back to work in charity. So your mom's pissed— sounds to me like she might be pissed by default. What, would they write you out of the will or something?"

"Well, yes."

I blinked. " Just for deciding you wanted to do something else?"

"As I said. Obligations. My parents have very specific expectations of me, and I've only ever met the bare minimum. Truly, I don't know if anyone could be who they wanted, because it's only a caricature, an idea. My brother's only expectations are to work with my father and have children. I, on the other hand, have been jumping through their hoops my whole life, and it feels like the older I get, the smaller the hoops. So it doesn't really matter if I want something else. I can't have it, so why torture myself?"

"Pretty bleak, Duchess."

"Perhaps. Or perhaps practical." For a moment, neither of us spoke, just kept filling up the bucket. But then she sighed and said, "I'm sorry. You brought me to this beautiful place to pick these luscious strawberries, and I made it bad."

"You could never make anything bad."

"Awfully forgiving today, are we?"

"When it comes to you? These days it's every day."

She gave me a little smile, then looked into the bucket. "Well, this is more than we could possibly eat. Shall we go?"

"Unless you wanted to walk around a little more."

"No, thank you." She stood, dusting off her knees. "I've got a hungry vacation pussy to feed."

First I laughed, then I growled, and then I was chasing a squealing Jessa toward my truck with that pussy on my mind.

27

fuckin' truckin'

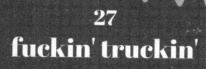

REMY

SHE CLIMBED into the open driver door and bent to set the bucket in the back, putting her ass at the perfect height to eat. I grabbed her thigh when she started to move.

"No. Stay right there."

She went perfectly still, panting.

"Good girl," I rasped, one hand sliding her skirt over her ass, the other finding her pussy hot and wet and waiting. "You ready to find out what happens when you fuck around, Duchess?"

"Yes, please," she breathed, bracing herself on the passenger seat.

I hooked my fingers in her G-string and pulled it to the side, and there was my salvation. I dipped a finger into her slick slit. "Your pussy's hungry, is it? For what?"

"You know what for."

"Yeah, but I wanna hear you say it." I stroked her.

"Your cock."

I leaned in, opened my mouth, extended my tongue, and took a long, sweet taste.

She gasped. "I want you inside me."

I groaned into her cunt, found her clit with my hand.

197

STACI HART

A low moan. "More than that," she whispered. "I'm empty, Remy."

I let her go with a wet pop. "Get the fuck in the truck."

In a daze, she did, and the second the seat was clear I was in it, the door shut behind me. I slid the seat back and reclined it, unzipping my pants, unleashing my cock.

I didn't have to ask—she was in my lap, her lips against mine, her hips rolling. My cock was barred from her, straining against her panties as she dry fucked me. But I didn't care. For a minute, the only thing that existed was her mouth, her lips, her tongue sweeping mine.

She broke away, reaching between us.

"Need you." It was barely audible, her hands finding my cock, raising it. I pulled her panties aside, and she guided me to the split, lowered her body, her heat swallowing my crown. I snatched her skirt up so I could watch as she took all of me.

Twin moans, and our lips met again. I held her there, not letting her move, wanting to feel her. My cock throbbed inside her—she was so full of me, she felt the pulse and whimpered at the feeling.

She leaned back, breaking the kiss. Her face tipped up to the roof and eyes closed as she swayed her hips, grinding when her clit met me. She took her pleasure, and I took mine, sliding the straps of her dress off her shoulders to bare her breasts. Her rosy nipples were pebbled, and when I took one into my mouth, she panted, bracing herself with her hands on my shoulders.

"That's right, Duchess," I breathed onto her slick nipple. "Are you full enough?"

A low moan. She opened her heavy eyelids. "Never."

I flexed my hips to put myself deeper, deep enough that she cried out. "You sure?"

"Oh, God," she whined, taking every grind with intention.

I filled my hands with her ass without stopping the flow

198

of her body. "Greedy, greedy. I love watching you come, Duchess. Are you gonna come?"

Her hips sped up, her eyes slamming shut. "Yes."

"Come all over me, and then it's my turn."

"Fuck," she squeaked, then gasped, then let out the most perfect sound as she came just like I wanted.

"Such a good girl." My heart slammed against my ribs as I took her breast in my hand, took her nipple with my mouth, let her ride me all the way down from her orgasm.

Her fingers slid through my hair, guiding my lips to hers with a tug. The kiss was long and deep, the sweep of her tongue tangled with mine, until she finally broke away with a smack and a smirk.

"Your turn."

With a growl, I held her to me long enough to dump her in the passenger seat so I could climb in back. The cab of the truck was humid, despite the slight breeze drifting in through the open windows, but neither of us seemed to care. By the time I'd kicked off my shoes, she was kneeling between my thighs, tugging my jeans out of the way. Panting, I watched her hand grip my cock, slick with her. When she opened her mouth, her eyes met mine, and she extended her silken tongue to lap my crown. A shudder rolled through me when I disappeared into her, and my eyes slammed shut, hand gripping the back of her neck. The moan from her throat reverberated down my shaft to my balls, stars bursting behind my eyelids. My head fell back, my fingers cupping her head as she pumped. I lost time for a while until she backed all the way off and kissed the tip of my cock, slow and hot.

"You taste like me," she said before kissing it again with the swirl of her tongue.

"Do you like that?"

She hummed an affirmation. "It means you're mine," she said so easily before closing her lips around me and lowering until I hit the back of her throat.

I hissed, hips flinching against my thin restraint. *Mine, mine, mine.* The word reverberated in my skull with every pump of her head and hand fisted around my root until I couldn't take anymore. When I stopped her, my wet cock rebounded with a slap against my stomach. My mouth was already on hers, noisy and impatient. My hand found her throat and held her there, her hands hooking my forearm, her face soft, bent in pleasure.

"Your pussy's hungry? Well, my cock's thirsty, and you're so wet." I reached between her legs to prove it to her. "Come here and gimme a drink, Duchess."

She nodded, crawling into my lap, kissing me as soon as she could. She tasted of salt and sex and seed, and my tongue didn't stop until it had all mingled in my mouth so I could taste her always. Jessa kicked off her shoes, then gathered up her skirts and pulled her dress off over her head, tossing it on the floorboard. I savored every inch of her as she dropped her panties, every millimeter of skin as my gaze followed her hands skimming down her naked neck, her breasts, her thighs, my cock. Again, she took control, raising one leg enough to guide me into her until I hit the end.

My mind raced, the feel of her pussy hot and tight and too much. I curled into her, burying my face in her neck, her arms draped over my shoulders and fingers in my hair as I fucked her slow.

Goddamn her. Goddamn her for making me feel so much.

With a noisy breath, I kissed her. And although I didn't believe I could hide anything from her, I hoped she didn't know what she'd done to me all the same. Because she was leaving and I wasn't going with her, and what that might do to me was a conversation I never wanted to have.

I broke the kiss, shifting to put myself behind the passenger seat. With a stretch and a flick of my hand, I inclined the seat and laid her down until she was leaning back on it, her ass between my thighs and her feet against my chest.

"Hang on," I commanded as I pulled off my shirt, and she fumbled around for the seatbelt, fisting it when she found it.

Cock in my hand, I guided my crown until it was inside her. My eyes on the seam of our bodies, I leaned and spit on her clit, thumbing it as I pumped my hips. I don't know what noise I made, something between a growl and a howl, my hand hooked on her ankle as I thrusted, watching her pussy swallow me over and over and over, the slap of skin ringing in the cab. She mewled, the sound jarred by the pounding of my cock, her tits bouncing from the force. I should have made it last. I wanted to make it last. But then she looked at me through lust drunk eyes and said, "Come on me."

My vision blacked—I was almost too late, pulling out just in time, stroking my cock as milky seed surged in streams across her naked skin. Her breasts rose and fell as she struggled for air, come dotting one. A white bead pearled on her pink nipple. I gathered her up, pulled her to me, felt her stroke my jaw as I dipped to lick that bead from her salty skin.

She sagged, languid, to kiss me in quiet worship. And I did the same, holding her in the hopes she knew she was cherished, treasured. Even if it was just by me.

Even if I couldn't keep her.

28
for the bride

JESSA

MY MOTHER MIGHT HAVE BEEN TALKING, but I'd been thinking about Remy's dick long enough that I had no idea what she was talking *about*.

It wasn't my fault. I'd been infected, and the only cure was more D.

Cass sat next to me, nodding at whatever Mother was saying, which was good. At least someone was listening. I moved my eggs Benedict around my plate with a fork, noting that mother had barely touched her brunch. The way she complained on the way to The Filly, you'd think I was dragging her to luncheon in prison. But for Cass, my mother suffered what was actually quite a good meal like a true hero.

Cass was so busy today that this was the only window in which we could meet up. She'd refused my help, but I couldn't fathom why when it was so clear she needed a hand. While she looked lovely—red hair shining and thick, skin dewy and lips rosy—an exhaustion lived behind her eyes that I'd never seen before. I only wished she'd tell me what was going on, because I believed her wedding excuses less and less every day.

"... and so I finally found a spa, though it's nearly an

hour away," Mother was saying. "Would either of you ladies care to join me?"

"I couldn't possibly," Cass answered. "I'm meeting with the florist after this, then the caterer, and after that, I have to go back to the farm to meet with the band so they can figure out how they'll set up. Then I have to hurry back for the baseball game."

"So there's time for a baseball game but not a massage for the bride?" Mother asked.

"Yes, ma'am . . . not only will the whole town be there, but Davis really wanted to go. We've been running in different directions for a week and I'd just really like to spend a little time with him." I realized the second she opened her mouth that she was about to cry and gave her a quizzical look. But she just shrugged and took a long, slow breath.

"I understand, but that's a shame," Mother said, tutting. "And you, Jessamine?"

"I promised I'd be at the baseball game too. But you're welcome to come with us."

Mother's nose wrinkled. "No, thank you. Well, suit yourselves."

When our server made eye contact, Mother flagged her with one finger in the air and requested the check. While she searched her handbag for a credit card, I tried to start a silent conversation with Cass, but she just shook her head.

Thankfully, my mother excused herself, and Cass and I had a moment alone for the first time in what felt like years.

"What is going on?" I asked quietly. "The truth this time."

She opened her mouth and took a breath, but closed it again, pinning her bottom lip between her teeth.

A hard look finally convinced her.

"I don't know," she started, her voice trembling. "It's just that we've been so busy and Davis is, like, *nowhere*. Mom has been helping some, but honestly, I think I just want to be alone. I don't get it. I waited a fucking decade for him to propose and now he's off running around with his friends and leaving me to everything, coming in late and drunk. Maybe it's my fault. He probably just proposed because he felt sorry for me."

"Cassidy Winfield. That is a bald-faced lie, and you know it."

"I don't know anything. I thought I did, but now . . . I'm just . . . I'm annoyed and I'm hurt and I'm not even sure what's going on except that I have a shitload of things to do."

"Why haven't you let me help you?"

"I don't even know! I think part of me was hoping Davis would pitch in, but when he doesn't, I'm usually so pissed I don't want to see anyone. It's so stupid. He's just being a guy."

"Let me come with you today. We can talk."

"No. I want to, but I'm afraid if I let whatever this is"—she gestured to her chest—"out of the box, it's going to ruin everything. Just . . . give me some more time. I've been avoiding picking a fight with him, but I guess today's the day. Which means I need to write a rage speech." Cass's phone buzzed, and when she picked it up, her face lit. "It's Davis."

"Good man."

Her thumbs went on a little rampage as she texted him back. "He's going to come with, so I guess we can fight and then hopefully fuck our premarital brains out because 'ya girl has been needing some one-on-one."

I kicked her under the table as Henry and Annie walked through the restaurant behind a hostess.

Henry stared at me, his eyes haunted. He looked like he'd barely slept, veering in our direction when he saw me.

Annie glared at the back of his head. "Seriously, Henry?"

Henry blinked over his shoulder at her. "I'm only saying hello."

She looked furious, her cheeks flushing and eyes flashing.

She muttered something under her breath and marched to catch up with the hostess.

Cass glanced at me, one brow flickering.

"Hey, Henry. I thought Davis was with you?"

He wore a strange smile. "No, I think he's running errands with you today, isn't he?"

She sighed happily. "Yes, and thank God. I was going to riot if we didn't see each other alone soon."

"Jess," he started, his attention already back on me. "I'm desperate to speak with you. When can we—"

"Good morning, Henry," Mother said from behind him, and he swallowed whatever he was about to say. "Whatever are you doing here?"

"Having breakfast with Annie," he answered, looking back at Annie, who was on her phone again, typing with too much force to be anything but angry. "Actually, I should probably be getting back. You'll excuse me."

But before he left, he touched the back of my chair, leaning in to speak into my ear.

"Please, can we find some time to talk, Bits? I need you."

Caught off guard, there was nothing to say but, "Yes, of course, Bobs. Good luck with Annie."

He let out a heavy sigh and dragged himself to her.

"My, that's awkward," Mother said, taking her seat to sign the slip. "Doesn't seem to be going well for dear Annie, does it?"

They were already having a quiet argument, and Henry had yet to sit.

"Probably for the best," Mother said, moving on. "You look cheerful, Cassidy. Did something change?"

The way she could eviscerate you with a compliment was artful. But Henry was instantly forgotten, and once again Cass was so happy, the well-veiled insult bounced right off her.

"Davis texted!"

"Ah," she said with a smile. "Not to worry, things will get easier soon. The day will come and go so swiftly, you'll miss it before it's even through, and this will be nothing but a happy story to tell."

If my mother was going to say something else, the words died in her throat, her face flattening.

I was confused until I heard, "Morning, ladies."

That velvety voice had said some of the filthiest things I'd ever heard spoken aloud, a handful of them just yesterday. My smile was absolutely mental.

Remy stood behind Cass, and I was happy to see her smile too, a promise that whatever she was feeling was temporary.

Mother offered little beyond a thin smile and, "Hello, Remington."

"How was breakfast?" he asked.

"Perfectly adequate, thank you."

Cass stuffed her phone in her purse and beamed up at Remy. "Grace offered to take us all to the spa today. You should go."

He made a face. "A spa?"

"Yeah, get your dogs all cleaned up. I bet your feet are so gross."

"My feet are not gross," he assured her. "And I don't need somebody handling them either."

Cass stood, smiling. "Can't wait for the game tonight. Maybe we can hang after? I feel like I haven't seen you since I've been home, and you're holding my best friend hostage. Well, you were."

Remy smiled, but it was a little sad at the reminder we were separated. "Yeah, we can hang anytime you want. I miss you too, Squirt."

"Sorry about the other night. I was just . . ." She waggled her hands around.

"I mean, I fake-kissed your friend in front of everybody. You were a little caught off guard," he said.

"And you're still enjoying yourself a little too much, but it's genius, really. I mean, look at Henry."

We all did. He looked miserable.

Cass sighed. "I swear, this wedding cannot come fast enough. I'm ready to be on a beach with a fruity drink in my hand. Preferably in a coconut."

"What are you doing today?"

"Running errands with Davis. Which—speaking of, I'd better get going. Thank you for breakfast, Grace!"

"It's my pleasure, dear," my mother answered.

"Y'all have a good day! See you at the game." Cass hopped on her tip-toes to kiss her cousin's cheek before bounding out of the door like a kangaroo.

Leaving the three of us staring at each other in The Filly.

"Well, Jessamine, if I can't convince you to come with me, shall I drop you off at the house?" Mother asked, gathering her things and standing. "I should be on my way to Asheville."

"I could take her, ma'am," Remy said with a sheepish look about him.

"Thank you, but that's all right," Mother answered, pushing in her chair.

"Actually, Mother, it might be better if I go with Remy." I stood, busying myself with my handbag so I didn't have to look her in the eye. "That way I won't miss the game, and Cass can bring me home after."

I put on a polite smile and met her gaze, which shifted between Remy and me. "And whatever will you do all day?"

Remy cleared his throat. "Well, I, uh, got some strawberries and thought I'd show Jessa how to make a pie."

Mother's eyes narrowed as she processed the words she'd not heard together before in reference to me. "Pie?"

"Oh, that sounds wonderful," I said, turning to Remy.

"Jessamine—"

"Enjoy the spa today, Mother," I called over my shoulder

as I pushed Remy toward the door.

She was following, frowning and blinking, but we hurried to his truck and climbed inside, leaving her on the sidewalk, Hermès bag hooked in her elbow and eyes full of questions I didn't want to answer.

And then, blissfully, we were off.

The second Remy turned off Main Street I climbed into his lap, the both of us laughing. And then I was kissing his neck. And then I just curled up there and sighed, not even caring that my knee was jammed into the door. I was too busy savoring the feel of his big hand on my back.

"I missed you too," he said, and my insides turned to goo.

"It's sick, really. I saw you less than twenty-four hours ago, and yet . . ."

"And yet." His chuckle rumbled through me.

"Really, I saw you just last night. Or at least I saw your cock."

"God bless technology."

"I've seen a lot of dick pics, but never one so majestic as yours."

"Think it could pass for royalty?"

"In the right circles, perhaps."

With a sigh and great care, I peeled myself off of him and got back in my seat so we didn't get arrested. "Are we really going to bake a pie?"

"If you want to. Got all the stuff for it."

"Yes, please."

"Wanna know something?" he asked, a sinful smile on his face.

"Always."

"I love it when you're all polite."

"Oh, do you?"

"Mmhmm. With your *pleases* and *thank yous*. Makes me want to make you beg a little. Or a lot. Depends on your behavior, I suppose."

I groaned, wriggling in my seat. "Seriously, you can't just say things like that when you can't do anything about it."

"Sure I can. Just did."

"Well, then I'm going to masturbate."

I had my shorts half off my bum before he grabbed my wrist, laughing.

"All right, all right. Touché." He threaded his fingers through mine, and I decided I might not have been so happy in all my life as I was right then.

I leaned my head on the rest to watch him drive, the wind dancing through his hair, the lines of his jaw and brow bold and strong. How had I been so lucky to have met him? To have had fate dump me in his lap like this? To find a man like Remy when I least expected it was the best gift the universe had given me.

But the universe giveth, and the universe taketh away. In a few days, I'd leave on a plane that would put me thousands of miles away from him. But what else could I do? Cass and Davis would be leaving same as me for their honeymoon. I had no ties here beyond that, no reason to stay. Remy had no reason to go. And neither of us could ask for such a thing.

There just hadn't been enough time, and there wasn't enough left, and I hated every single thing about it.

Well, except that I had him now. I shouldn't have been greedy, but Remy seemed to inspire that in me. He challenged me to take what I wanted in ways no one else ever had. He'd emboldened me. And I was all the better for it.

He turned into his driveway, noticing I was watching him.

"What?" he asked, his lips tilted in a smile, brows quirked.

"Oh, just considering all the ways in which I'm about to get fucked."

His laughter felt like a million-pound reward.

"But first," he said, parking in front of the house, "let's make some pie."

29
end game

JESSA

MIRACULOUSLY, we made it through baking two pie crusts, whipping cream, and making the strawberry sauce without mounting each other like animals.

I stood opposite Remy with the island between us, listening as he told me a story about college baseball. A pile of cut strawberries laid in the center, the tops in a steel bowl as we made our way through the mountain of berries we'd collected yesterday with little snicks of our paring knives.

The way his face changed when he talked about the sport did something to my heart that I couldn't quite place. He came alive, his voice full of passion and his eyes sparking with ardor. I wanted that for him always. I wished it could be his.

Remy shook his head, laughing before shifting his gaze to his hands. "You look like you're thinking about something interesting."

I looked at my hands too as I sliced the top off a small strawberry, then halved it. "I just love listening to you talk about baseball, that's all."

"Well, how about that. I've made a fangirl out of you."

"It must be the uniforms. Your arse is out of control in those trousers."

He looked over his shoulder. "I mean, if it gets you to games, I'm all for it."

"You like having me there?"

"I really, really do."

"I enjoy being there. When you pitch, well, I've started biting my nails, I'm so nervous. When you're at bat, my stomach is twisted into knots. The anticipation is terrible. I absolutely love it."

"I like looking up into the stands and seeing you there."

"Wish I could go to all of them, but I suppose I'll just have to settle for one more."

The truth of that statement hung between us like a living, breathing thing.

"Anyway," I continued, "thank you for coming to get me today. And for teaching me how to make pie."

"You'd better believe I'll come and get you anytime it means I get to see you. And really, the pie was just an excuse."

"For my mother?"

"So I could put whipped cream on your tits."

A laugh shot out of me, my cheeks instantly hot. I threw half a strawberry at him. "You're awful."

"You like it. Throw another one." He crouched just a little with his mouth open. So I tossed another half strawberry into the air, and he caught it with ease.

He bowed as he chewed, I clapped as I laughed, happy and miserable all at once. I wondered if it would always be this good. If I stayed, how long would we go on like this? We barely knew each other, but that didn't seem to matter—the thought of leaving gutted me.

One of Remy's brows rose. "Your face is dong that thing again."

"Well," I started, avoiding his eyes, "I was only thinking about how I have to leave in a few days."

"I do my best not to think about that at all."

"You're a wise man, Remy Winfield. Has anyone ever told you that? Beside yourself, that is."

"You think you're so funny, don't you?" His smile twisted wickedly as he stalked around the island.

"I really am." I stayed right where I was just to see what he'd do if I didn't react at all. "I considered a career in comedy, but I reckon if I'm a glutton for criticism, I could just call my mother. *Ahhh!*" I squealed as he wrapped his arms around my waist, burying his scratchy scruff in my neck.

I set down my knife and turned in his arms, leaning back against the island, my chin tipped so I could gaze up at him.

"I hate that I'm leaving."

"I hate that you're leaving too. But I sure am glad to have you now."

My heart broke a little at the ease in his words. It occurred to me then that he might only see me as a fling from his cousin's wedding, and the thought cut deep. It was quite likely he'd never considered us beyond these few days—that to him, it might not be anything more serious than a tryst. And here I was, pining and mooning over an unavailable man.

It seemed to be my lot, falling for men I couldn't have. And I'd been so sure this was different simply because I'd never felt this way, not ever. Meanwhile, it could be just another summer for him.

Cass warned me about this. I'd had ample opportunities to take her advice. If I really hadn't wanted to stay with Remy, I'd have slept on someone's floor, but I didn't. I stayed because I knew what would happen. I suppose I just thought it would happen to him too.

"I was just thinking how lucky I was to have found you," I said, shoving my feelings deep down into my heart where I could ignore them. "I only wish I'd slept with you from the start like you wanted."

"Hey—who said I wanted?"

I gave him a look. "You. You literally said so."

"Well, you always say you value my honesty."

"It's true," I said, laughing. "But since I can't time travel, I suppose I should make the best of what I have right now."

Lips tilted in a smile, he leaned in and said, "Now that's the spirit."

His breath was hot as he nipped my lip, teasing me only briefly—he didn't seem to have the patience for it either. His lips captured mine, mouth opening, tongue sweeping, and I melted into him, boneless and dazed.

No one could kiss me like Remy could.

Today, it was the combination of his playful tongue and purposeful lips, masterful and simple in design. I was breathless, my hands roaming his face, his neck, his silken hair. When my arms were around his shoulders, he picked me up, swiping away utensils and strawberry heads before setting me on the island with the slap of my bum against the surface.

I laughed, breaking the kiss, but Remy had moved on. His eyes were dark but his smile roguish as he gazed upon the skin he exposed when he pulled my tank off, setting it aside so it wouldn't get dirty. With a reach and the flick of his fingers, my bra unclasped, and he slid it down my arms, leaving it with my top. My ribs were too tight, only allowing sips of air, my nipples peaking with the shallow rise and fall of my chest.

I moved to reach for him, but he snagged my wrist and put my hand back on the counter.

"I want you to sit there like a good girl, Duchess." He reached for the bowl of whipped cream, and a slick rush dampened my underpants. "The game is, you can't touch me with your hands. But I can touch you."

To demonstrate, he cupped my breast and leaned in to put his hot mouth on me, drawing my nipple in for the most delectable moment. I gasped. I wiggled. But my hands remained where they were, gripping the edge of the counter.

"That's right," he said, giving my breast one more squeeze before dipping a finger into the whipped cream. It crested on his index finger, fluffy and wet, and I watched it disappear into his perfect lips and come out clean.

"It's good, Jess. Wanna try?"

With another swipe, he offered his creamy finger.

I opened my mouth.

"Say it. *Yes, please.*"

"Yes, please."

"Good girl." He slid that thick finger into my mouth as my reward, and I licked the sweet cream off of him, wishing very much that it was his cock instead.

I sensed he did too, judging by the moan in his throat.

"I told you how much I love your manners." He set the bowl next to me, scooped out a dollop with the hook of two fingers and settled the cream on one of my nipples, then the other. "So polite."

Breast in one hand, he brought his mouth to one nipple, licking and sucking and lapping the cream from the tender peak. I hissed and writhed, hanging onto the counter with one leg twitching a little. My eyes had rolled so far back in my head, I wasn't sure they'd find their way back. In the brief moment it took for him to switch breasts, I gulped a breath, and thank God because he sucked every bit of air out of the room when he debauched my other nipple with that criminal mouth of his. He let it go, leaving it slick and shining, my breast giving a little jiggle from its sudden release.

"Jesus, fuck," I rasped.

"What do you say, Duchess?" The question was expectant, and I smiled.

"Thank you. May I please have another?"

214

His laughter was evil and wonderful. "Yes you fucking may. But take those goddamn shorts off or I'll ruin them."

"Too late," I answered, shimmying out of them.

"Goddammit," he said, grabbing and throwing them on the pile of garments he'd collected, leaving me naked and at his mercy.

And then he was covering my breasts in whipped cream so he could devour them. Only this time, his free hand found its way between my legs, fingertips circling my clit. And like the good girl he claimed I was, I kept my hands to myself, hanging onto the counter so tightly, my fingers ached.

I whimpered when he backed away, hooking my leg around his waist to pull him close again.

"Lay back," he commanded on a laugh, picking up a fat, fresh strawberry and dipping it into the whipped cream. With one hand, he spread my legs, taking a good long look at my pussy, drawing his bottom lip into his mouth to wet it.

I ached, fighting the frantic urge to maul him and get what I wanted. But I wanted to torture myself more.

And so, I whimpered, doing my best to keep still as he dragged the wet end of the strawberry up the inside of my thigh. He met my eyes, biting into the berry before lapping up the creamy trail. By the time he reached the end, I was a quivering mess.

"Can I touch you?" I begged, hands fisted.

"Depends on what you want and how nicely you ask," he said from between my thighs, tracing my pussy lips, dipping into me with fluttering fingers, one tease after another after another.

"Your cock in my hands, your mouth on mine. May I *please*?"

"Anything you want," he said roughly, reaching for me as I rose to meet him, our lips colliding in a noisy, violent kiss. Our hands fumbled blindly with his jeans until they were gone. I wasn't sure when the kiss ended, but I watched my hands fist that glorious cock as he pulled his shirt off in my periphery. Though I didn't get to look as long as I wanted— he was kissing me again, hand cupping the back of my head, his tongue seeking the depths of me.

As much time as I'd spent thinking about his cock, and as much teasing as he'd done, touching him wasn't enough. I wanted his dick in my face. I wanted him in my mouth. I wanted to taste him and feel him and tease him. So I urged him back with my hands on his chest until there was enough room to climb down, my eyes on his cock again.

"You took what you wanted," I said, dropping to my knees. "Now it's my turn."

I reached for his dick, but he backed off, smirking a little, his eyes lust drunk and voice gravelly. He took it in his fist and pumped. "Didn't say the magic word, Duchess."

With a breathy laugh, I looked up at him through my lashes, chin low. "Please, put your cock in my mouth before I fucking die already."

As he came closer, I opened my mouth and stuck out my tongue, closing my eyes. He snapped for me to open them again.

"I want you to see what you do to me," he said, holding his cock by the root to slap my tongue with the crown.

It was all I needed. I leaned in, swallowing him, one hand on his hip and the other fisted around his shaft. He made an animalistic sound that urged me on, his fingers slipping into my hair. When he squeezed and pulled, the sensation trickled down my spine, spoking at my nipples and pussy and all the way down to my toes.

But it was his silky, salty cock in my mouth that tightened the ache between my thighs.

He pulled away with a pop and picked me up, and before I fully sorted it out, I was back on the counter with his hips between my thighs. He kissed me until we'd calmed down just a little, just enough, and guided me to lay back. I lay languid on the island, watching him drag a hand down my torso, pausing to fondle my breast before moving on. When he reached my clit, he leaned in reverently, dropping his lips to take a long moment with my cunt. The sight of his face between my thighs was nearly too much. I writhed and wriggled and begged him with the pleases he was so hungry for, until he stood and gave me what I wanted, slipping his cock between my pussy lips and pumping his hips.

And he didn't stop. He brought my legs up to rest against his chest as he fucked me, one hand on my ankle, his other forearm and hand clamping my knees together. Remy closed his eyes, never stopping his easy pace as he kissed the top of my foot, drew my toe into his mouth for a handful of heartbeats, my body tightening at the knowledge that his hot mouth felt like my hot pussy, that I was inside of him when he was inside of me. With hooded eyes, he watched his fingertips skate low on my stomach, then flattened his hand and pressed, thrusting still harder. My lungs shot open at the sensation of his palm against my G-spot from the outside, his cock stroking it from the inside. My vision blacked, hands gripping his wrist as I held on, chin tipped, the world shrinking to the point where our bodies met and flying apart in shattering pieces as I came.

He was right behind me, pulsing and throbbing inside me as he exploded, hips rolling and thighs trembling. The feel of him pressing, squeezing, cock pumping, stroked my orgasm on so hard, I urged him to slow down or I might fall apart, so sensitive I might break.

Panting, he parted my legs, pulled me into his arms, kissed me like he fucked me. Touched me like he needed me. Held me like he cherished me. Then looked into my eyes, holding my face.

"You're gonna be the end of me, Duchess."

And when he kissed me again, I hated how I wished I was the end of him, if it meant I could keep him.

30
head in the game

REMY

I'D PLAYED like shit the entire game, and it was all her fault.

I stood just inside first base as Wilder pitched a game that shouldn't be this close. To the casual spectator, I looked tuned in and ready for whatever came at me.

I wasn't.

My mind was on the girl in the stands.

My thoughts were a dog chasing its tail. It'd start with flickers of fucking her on the kitchen island, leading into the sound of her laughter and the pretty way she talked as we tidied up and left for the game. Which would leave me reliving the strawberry fields. The swimming hole. The goddamn dryer I might never be able to use again without getting a hard-on. The way she smiled. The smell of her hair. The feel of her in my arms.

The fact that she was leaving in a few days.

And then, after a quick spiral, it'd start all over again.

The batter connected, the sound snapping me back to the task at hand. Thankfully, it was a pop-fly to right field and not my responsibility.

Grayson eyed me from a few feet away, his arms folded and brows together. "Fuck's got into you?"

"What? I'm doing my job, old man."

He rolled his eyes with a *ha* to the heavens. "Watch your mouth. And get your shit together."

And for a second, I did. But while Wilder was throwing balls, my mind wandered off and started the chase all over again.

Probably shouldn't have had her panties in my pocket either, but we won last time. Wouldn't be the worst good luck charm I'd ever had, that was for goddamn sure. At the thought of that silky slip of fabric, I felt her eyes on me and met them. The connection hit me in all kinds of long abandoned places, shining her light where the light had been forgotten.

The memory of what it was like to have a *person* had been lost to me until Jessa showed up on my driveway. The thing was, I'd never felt like *this*. I'd been infatuated plenty of times, but there was always an empty space in the middle, clear signs it was temporary.

This didn't feel temporary.

This felt like when she left, she'd gut me, snatch my heart out of my chest, and fly it to the other side of the world.

I didn't even know if I'd see her again.

The thought was a knife to the belly, starting the cut for her.

As much as I loved her body and all the time I got to spend in her, that wasn't even in the top five things I'd miss about her. I wanted her sitting in my kitchen with Dolly on while I cooked. I wanted her in the bucket seat next to me, laughing as she tried to keep her untethered hair out of her face. I wanted her sitting right there in the stands, looking at me like she was. I wanted—

Crack.

By the time I turned to the sound, a ball was sailing just

over my head, and some motherfucker was sprinting up the line in my direction.

I missed a catch that should have been an easy out, to the tune of a couple hundred people bitching me out—Coach the loudest—but recovered, zipping it to Tate at second to hold the runner. My gaze was on the dirt, hands on my hips as I headed back to first, shaking my head.

"Do I need to pull you?" Coach snapped.

"I'm good."

"You sure? 'Cause you look like shit."

"I said I'm good," I shot back, turning to the game.

I put Jessa as far from my mind as I could, which was not very far at all, turns out. When the inning was over, I even thought about putting her panties away, but in the end, I couldn't do it. My mistake was indulging myself between plays and at bat with thoughts of her. Because once the tail-chasing started, there was no stopping until it was too late.

I was taking my swings on deck when Grayson pulled up next to me and spit in the dirt, eyes narrowed.

"Is this about that girl?"

"I don't know what you're talking about." I swung the bat, pretending to be unfazed.

"Don't bullshit me. Is her being here fucking you up?"

"Why would that fuck me up?"

"Don't play dumb either. What needs to happen for you to lock in?"

I considered as I swung again and inspected the bat like I had something to look for. What needed to happen was her sticking around for a little while. What needed to happen was she should be back at my place every night instead of in that mansion with her mom. What needed to happen was—

"Hey!" Coach snapped his fingers. "What in the fuck, man. You've got it bad."

"Tell me about it." *Swing.*

"Figure it out or you're going to lose us this game."

With that, he stalked back to the dugout, and Tate hit a line drive past first that got him to second base.

And then it was my turn.

Inside the batter's box, I found the peace I'd been looking for. Nothing existed except me and my bat, the pitcher and his ball. The noise of the crowed muffled, the sound of my heartbeat loud in my ears, my breath even and measured as I waited for the pitch.

When he let it loose, I swung.

Crack. Sail.

No thunk, because that motherfucker went over the fence.

Tate and I trotted around the diamond, the crowd on their feet and cheering. I had been redeemed, and so I was smug, smirking and waving and celebrating with my team when I made it back to the dugout.

"Told you I was fine," I shot at Gray with an asshole smile still on my face.

And he sighed, shaking his head, eyes on the sky. But he let it go.

For now.

I was able to lock in for the rest of the game, even if it was half-assed—at least until the last inning. Thank God we were batting and I wasn't up because what little focus I'd mustered went to shit as I inched closer to spending what was left of the night with Jessa.

As soon as we won, I snagged all my shit and was calling goodbye over my shoulder as I made my way to the gate where the crowd exited the stands. I got a few accolades for a good game, but not nearly as many as usual. They weren't wrong to deny me. I'd played a shit game and gotten lucky a few times. And why? For a girl I barely knew?

That girl I barely knew caught sight of me and beamed like the goddamn sun itself, running in my direction as soon as she could get through the crowd.

I caught her when she jumped, kissed her the second her

lips were in reach, grateful Hank was around so we could get away with it without sending Cass into a fit of hysteria. That, and I loved rubbing his blue-blooded nose in the fact that she was *mine*, and he'd missed his shot.

He was mad again, even with Annie at his side. I decided then that he definitely *was* a shitbag.

Jessa laughed as I set her down.

"Well, Cass and Davis have a date, so it seems she can't hang out tonight after all," she said.

I had to admit, I was disappointed. I missed her. Hell, even when I was around her, I missed her. She was so stressed out, I barely recognized her anymore.

"Bully for her, I guess."

"It's a good thing," she assured me. "They needed a day just the two of them. But the good news is, now I have you all to myself. What shall we do?" she asked.

"In that case, I want to show you something."

"Oh, I love it when you say that."

As I tucked her into my side, I realized just how true it was. I wanted to show her everything in the hopes that if I did, she might find a reason to stay. I wanted to show her things she'd never seen just so I could be the one to witness it. I wanted to show her I might not have money or power or status, but I had fireflies and strawberry pie and an insatiable need for her.

I just didn't know if it was enough.

By the time Cass and the gang finally made it to us, we stood waiting patiently, my arm around her shoulders, hers circling my waist, her face against my chest.

Cass was suspicious. Davis was concerned. Hank was pissed. And poor Annie just looked left out.

I wanted to give him a piece of my mind. And maybe a piece of my fist. But instead, I smiled.

Cass rolled her eyes. Davis narrowed his. Hank huffed. And poor Annie just sighed.

"You played like shit," Cass said with a wink in a singsong voice, kissing me on the cheek as she passed.

"Love you too, Squirt."

Davis eyed me. Hank opened his mouth to say something, but Davis gave him a little nudge in Cass's direction.

Poor Annie just gave me a sad smile and followed the rest to the parking lot.

"Goodie, they're gone," Jessa said. "Now, where will you take me tonight?"

"You'll see." I kissed the top of her head and we headed for the Scout.

"Another surprise? I love your surprises."

I hmm'd happily.

"Will there be pie?"

A laugh bubbled out of me. "No pie. You're not afraid of heights, are you?"

She pulled away enough to give me a concerned look.

But before she could say anything, a man in a suit approached and said, "Lady Hastings, your mother has sent me to fetch you."

Every bouncy little bit of joy Jessa had slid out of her and onto the gravel. "Oh, I see. Thank you."

The man didn't move at the dismissal, just stood there watching, looking bored and mildly judgmental.

Under his scrutiny, we separated, and I was robbed of a goodbye kiss and a solid night of messing around.

"Well, goodnight, Remy," she said all politely.

"Night, Duchess."

Her cheeks flushed a little, and she smiled before following the stiff to the Bentley.

And just like that, she was gone.

31
do it again

JESSA

THE VERY LAST thing I wanted to do was walk into my mother's house. Well, the house where she was staying, which was just as bad because she was here and Remy was not.

"Hello, darling," she said as she stepped into the entryway to meet me.

"Hello, Mother."

"You're late for dinner."

"Yes, I'm sorry. The game ran late."

"And how was it?"

One of my brows arched. "You really want to know?"

"Of course," she lied.

I sighed. "We won."

"Oh, lovely. There's food in the kitchen if you're hungry. Would you care to watch the telly with me?" She leaned in, smiling.

But all I had for her was a halfhearted smile. "No, thank you. I think I'll eat a bit and clean up for bed."

She looked so disappointed, I nearly felt bad. Until I remembered she'd summoned me with a driver and ended my night earlier than I'd hoped.

"All right, dearest. Rest well."

"Thank you, Mother."

Into the kitchen I went, leaving her in the entry, trying not to feel guilty. But I was sour. And I wasn't over it well enough to watch guilty pleasures with her.

A plate of dinner sat in the fridge, but it was so terribly formal—squab for God's sake. So I scrounged up a sandwich instead and trudged upstairs, nibbling on it and pouting. I pouted as I undressed, pouted as I showered, pouted as I toweled off.

And all the while, resentment flickered underneath.

My mother's arrival had brought with it the reminder that my freedom had always been conditional. As long as I remained inside the boundaries set up for me, I could do as I pleased. It was an illusion, a gilded cage. I didn't think of it in my normal life, never needing to breach the bounds.

But then I came here.

I met him.

And now I saw what little freedom I had and bucked against it like a wild thing, eager for escape.

My phone buzzed on the counter.

> Remy: Your mom really does know how to spoil a party.

Poof, my pout was gone. I snatched up my phone, smiling as I typed back.

> Jessa: She's the absolute worst for that. I'm sorry.

> Remy: Don't be. I'm sorry I couldn't see you a little longer.

I sighed and flopped into bed, adjusting my towel, wet hair sticking to the pillow.

> Jessa: Me too. I wish I could see much more of you.

> Remy: That can be arranged.

> Jessa: Then arrange it.

Seconds later, a photo came through of his rolling abs, and his massive hand fisted around his massive cock.

I pinned my bottom lip between my teeth.

> Jessa: This is exactly why I get turned on every time my phone dings. Really, sir, you have no right.

> Remy: Well, you said you were in the shower and this happened. There's only so much I can do.

> Jessa: Wish I was there. I'd do it for you.

I giggled, my cheeks flushed as I shimmied to bury myself a little between the pillows. A hot flush tingled its way down my body—I'd scrolled back up and was very busy zooming the picture, starving to catalog the details of his cock. With my free hand, I undid the tail of the towel.

> Remy: I hate that you're there when you could be here where I can do filthy things to you.

I sighed.

> Jessa: Me too. I was thinking about you in the shower and now I'm all hot.

Rolling onto my side, I fiddled with the towel, exposing myself quite artfully, I thought. I sent the picture as soon as I snapped it.

Remy: Jesus Christ, Duchess.

Jessa: I never thought I'd say this, but I love it when you call me that.

Absently, my fingertips brushed one nipple as I waited for his response.

Remy: Good, 'cause there's probably no chance of me stopping.

Jessa: Guess what I'm touching and I'll send you a photo.

Remy: Look at you, being all nasty. Please tell me it's your pussy.

Jessa: Aren't you ambitious? Sorry, darling. Not it.

Remy: Tits.

Jessa: Close.

Remy: Ah, those rosy nipples. Tell me they're hard.

Jessa: Of course they are. I'm almost certain when your cock is hard, you've done the same to my nipples.

Remy: Quit gabbing and send me the goods, Duchess.

I laughed, twisting so my back was nearly flat and did as I'd been told.

Remy: Good girl. Now I want that hungry finger on your clit.

Jessa: Already there.

> Remy: I wish it was the tip of my cock. The only place in the world I want to be is inside of you.

Oh, how my heart trembled.

> Jessa: But you just had me this afternoon.

> Remy: Wasn't enough. It'll never be enough.

My fingertip dipped into my cunt and I used my own wetness to slick my clit. My trembling heart went faint.

> Jessa: When you say things like that, you leave me soaked.

> Remy: Prove it.

Another thing I'd never done—sent a man a photo of my cunt. But here I was, propping myself up in bed and tousling my damp hair, positioning my legs just so, squeezing my tits between my upper arms. And then I took a short video, letting out a pleasure sigh as it ended.

I rewatched it, quite proud of myself. I looked bloody *hot*.

Seconds after I sent it, my phone rang with a video call from him.

Laughing, I answered when the phone was out of my vagina.

He was devastatingly handsome, mostly naked and absolutely perfect.

"Hello, darling."

"Hello, darlin'."

I reached for the bedside table and one of my ear pods—the last thing I needed was for my mother to walk in because she heard a man in my room. And then I nestled back into the pillows, my left hand finding its way back to my aching pussy.

I couldn't see his cock, but I noted his hand was missing, his arm moving slowly. For a minute, we just watched each other even though we couldn't see exactly what we were doing. The rosy blush on my cheeks deepened.

"You've ruined me, you know," I started, my voice breathy. "You've made me insatiable."

"How do you feel?"

A soft sigh slipped out of me. "My body? It's slick and hot where I'm touching myself. My heart? I wish you were here."

"Me too, Duchess."

My cunt squeezed, and I giggled up at the ceiling, cupping my sex to squeeze back. "God, just thinking about shagging you has me drenched."

"Show me," he commanded.

I sat back into the position I'd been in for the selfie and propped my phone up with a pillow before getting back to work.

He groaned, his biceps flexing. "Goddamn, girl."

"I want to see you too."

"Ask nice," he said with a depraved smirk and hooded eyes.

"Please, may I see your cock? I think I'm addicted to it."

He chuckled, shifting around as he propped up his phone too. I nearly came right there on the spot when he spat thickly into his palm like he had in the truck and slicked his cock. The view from between his knees was glorious. All he had on was a pair of gray joggers, which were pulled down so he could stroke his shaft. He tucked his free hand behind his head and looked down the long line of his body at me.

"You're beautiful, Jessa." The words were smoldering coals. "Every goddamn inch of you. I don't think I've ever wanted anybody more."

"I know I haven't." My eyes were locked on his hand as it pumped, the sight of his shining cock appearing and disappearing into his fist, my fingers circling my clit in rhythm. "Remember when we fucked in your truck?"

"Mmhmm."

"And remember when you came all over me?"

He groaned, his lids fluttering, his hand picking up speed.

"It was everywhere. On my stomach and tits and nipples in creamy ribbons, pooled in the hollow of my throat."

"Jessa, fuck."

"The look on your face when you licked a bead of your come off me was the hottest thing I've ever seen."

He didn't say anything, just stroked a little faster, his abdomen tight, every muscle in high relief.

I split my index and middle finger so my clit was between them and stroked harder, hot tension twisting deep in my belly.

"Do it again, Remy," I breathed. "Come on your chest so I can imagine it's me.

On command, he grunted, fucking his hand, his balls drawn tight. Alabaster come jetted from the tip of his cock in streams, streaking his tan skin, sliding into the valleys made by his muscles. A thick spurt ran down his crown and onto his hand, dripping down his fingers.

And that was the vision I came to, the orgasm gripping my lungs, tightening until it hurt, until there was no air, no space, no room for anything but sweet release.

Remy's head hung back as he panted, his chest heaving, his hand still around his dick. I was too tender to touch, but I squeezed, feeling the orgasm through my fingers as it slowed.

He lifted his head like it weighed a thousand pounds, but reached for his phone and stood, making his way through the house.

"Put your fucking clothes on, Duchess."

"Huh?" I sounded drunk.

"I'm fucking you tonight, Jessa. To-fucking-night. So put your fucking clothes on and be outside in ten minutes."

"You're crazy," I said on a laugh.

"Crazy about you. Be right there."

He hung up the call, and for a second, I lay there catching my breath, a silly, half-drunk smile on my face.

I was going to sneak out. I'd only ever snuck out of my room, never the grounds.

Of course Remy would have me break the rules.

And for him, I'd do it every time.

32
for me

REMY

THERE WAS nothing in the whole wide world as perfect as fucking Jessa in the moonlight.

She lay splayed across the pillows and blankets I'd thrown in the back of the Scout, her skin pale in the full moon's light. Her pretty lips were parted, her head lolling, still riding down her latest orgasm. Her hair was twisted in my fingers like corn silk, her breath sweet, her body small and delicate beneath mine. Her folded leg was tucked in my side, her knee cupped in my shoulder as I came like hell and thunder into her.

When I was spent, I collapsed, my face buried in her neck. Her arms draped lazily around my neck, lips against my jaw, hands in my hair. My heart banged painfully, flinging itself in her direction as I tried to catch my breath, my hips still rocking. I kissed her neck gratefully, thankful I'd ever found her and luckier than I'd ever been that she'd let me con her into my arms.

I didn't know how I'd ever let her go. Didn't know what I was supposed to do when she left. My life didn't seem to make much sense anymore if she wasn't in it.

It didn't make any fucking sense.

Ask me if I cared.

With a sigh, I lifted my head, angling for her lips, taking them slowly. I had to drink her in sips to make it last.

She hummed, her hands cupping my neck, then my jaw. When I broke the kiss, she just smiled up at me in that way she did.

"I'm so glad you stole me away," she said, her gaze tracing my face.

"Every chance I get." I kissed her swiftly, then backed off and cleaned us up. The first round, I'd made a mess all over her like she asked, and goddamn. I'd never been into it before, but my God if there wasn't something about my come all over her that didn't fuck me up. Maybe it was because she was so pristine. A lady, a good girl, and dirtying her up with the chaos from my cock felt like writing my name on the *Mona Lisa*.

I couldn't explain it. I only knew it'd be the last thing I saw before I left this earth—Jessa stretched out in the moonlight with my come spattered across her like a Pollock.

I'd be spoiled forever now that I knew her. There'd be no coming back.

"So, did you just bring me out for a shag?" she asked, pulling on her knit shorts, then the matching spaghetti-strap top with an adorably useless pocket over her breast.

"I want to show you something. Maybe break another rule or two."

"You're going to land me in trouble, Remington."

"That's the idea," I said with a wink, nearly dressed.

She laughed, stuffing her feet into her sneakers and tying her hair back. I hopped out of the topless Scout and helped her down, keeping hold of her hand.

"This way," I said, and she followed.

We walked in the comfortable quiet, the crickets and frogs singing their songs in the summer night. When we stopped at the foot of the water tower, she looked up at it with her brows clicked together.

"Surely we're not going up there," she said.

"And why not?"

"Well, I doubt it's legal."

I shrugged. "Nobody comes around here but high schoolers anyway, and none of them have gotten busted. Our cops might be bored but they're not bored enough to jeopardize their deaconship at the church by hauling in the congregation's kids. You're not afraid of heights are you?"

"No. Damn, if I said yes would it get me out of it?"

"You tell me." I took her hand and dragged her toward the ladder. Her eyes were still up, her expression dubious.

"Come on. You first."

"Why me?"

"So if you fall, I can grab you like in a spy movie."

She tried to walk back to the truck, but I grabbed her around the waist, nuzzling into her neck as she laughed.

"Don't be a scaredy cat. Kids do this, Jessa."

"Well, they don't really understand mortality, do they?"

I laid a look on her, and she must have realized there was no way out because she sighed.

"Oh, all right," she muttered.

"Now we're talking." I picked her up so she could get onto the high ladder without much effort, then made a jump for it, pulling myself up.

The higher we went, the faster the wind until we were past the tree canopy, then up some more. After a minute, we reached the platform, and Jessa stopped at the railing, her face touched with awe, hair flying loose from its tether in strands.

I'd never seen anything so beautiful. Not in my whole life.

"It's incredible," she breathed. "Look—you can see the big mountains over there. The trees look like broccoli heads." She laughed, pointing. "Do you see?"

In the light of the full moon, I saw well enough and laughed.

"Oh, and look over here! There's town, isn't it? How lovely," she said quietly with a small smile.

"Worth the climb?"

She tore her eyes away from the scenery to smile up at me. "Every time you have something to show me, something amazing happens."

"Wow. No pressure."

We sat, dangling our feet over the edge, the rails perfect for hanging my elbows on.

For a little while, we just looked over the valley and the town as the moon made its climb.

"Well, I had something to tell you," she started a little sheepishly. "I maybe did a little research online about some things, but you have to promise not to get mad."

My face flattened. "Jessa . . ."

"Yes, yes, just listen. So, I was looking at Tennessee minor league baseball teams—"

I sighed. "Jessa—"

"—and I'm sure you know there's a team in Sevierville. They're having open tryouts in September."

"Is that all?" I asked after a second.

She picked at her thumbnail. "Well, I don't know. It was all much bigger in my head. They said you have to run the"— she wrinkled up her forehead remembering—"sixty meters in less than 6.8 seconds. I asked, and Coach said you're well under that."

"When the hell did you see Coach?"

"At the market. That's not important. It's easy enough, and you qualify. I wanted to ask if you'd try out."

"And why would I do that?"

"Well, for me."

She said it so simply, so quietly, the words speared my heart like an arrow.

"I know it's not for me to ask, really. It's none of my business what you do, and you owe me nothing—"

"Okay."

She paused. Blinked at me. "O-okay?"

"Okay."

Another pause. "I admit, I thought that would take much more convincing. Perhaps even sexual favors."

I laughed. "Maybe I should change my answer."

"No, no don't!" She giggled, leaning into me. Her arm wrapped around my biceps and her head came to rest on my shoulder. "Why was it so easy, Remy?"

I rested my cheek on the top of her head. "I'm starting to realize I'd do a lot of things for you." The words were out before I could reel them back in. I kept talking so she wouldn't ask more questions. "You're the first person in a long, long time to believe in me like this."

"What about your mother? Cass?"

"They believe in me. But they also gave up on me. It wasn't their fault—I pushed them to leave me alone about it. All I wanted was to close the door on all of that, so they finally let it go and let me pretend like I didn't want it. But I do. Probably always will. At least if I do this, I'll have done something. And if I'm honest, it's easier to do it for you than for me."

"I understand," she said softly. "Thank you."

"Will you come back for tryouts?"

"Of course. I'm sad I won't see another game before I go."

"It's probably for the best. You nearly cost me the last one."

"Me? What did I do?"

I didn't want to answer with the whole truth, so I said, "Gave me your panties. They're my new good-luck charm."

"Oh my God," she said on a laugh.

"So if I try out, what are you gonna give me, Duchess?"

"Hmm. I'll have to think about it."

"It'd better be good. Top shelf sexual favors at the very least. And you'd better think fast. We don't have much time left."

We fell quiet at the mention of her leaving.

She broke the silence. "I was thinking about telling Cass. About us."

My head swiveled to look down at her even though she couldn't see me. "Really?"

She sighed. "I'm tired of keeping it from her. She's my best friend, after all. That, and I'd like to dance with you at her wedding and not leave everyone thinking I'm trying to make Henry jealous. I've realized I don't care a fig about Henry after all."

"Did you realize this before or after the roof?"

"Before, actually. Over beans and rice with this brutish baseballer I met."

I chuckled. But my smile fell. "Cass is going to be pissed."

She sighed. "I know."

"I mean, *pissed*-pissed."

"Yes, I suppose."

I chewed the thought. "Like, she'll be pissed for longer than you'll be here."

At that, she said nothing for a second, still leaning on my arm, looking out over the town. "That's probably true." She sounded so sad, something in my heart fissured.

"Her wedding is in a few days too. Do we want her to be pissed at us then? She's already stressed out."

"Are you saying you don't think we should tell her?"

It was my turn to sigh. "I want to tell her, Jess. I just don't know if we should drop it on her *now*."

She considered it. The air between us was filled with all the things we couldn't say. "You're probably right. I'm leaving anyway."

"Yes, you're leaving."

Christ, I hadn't been so sad about something in years. Just

237

the thought of her being gone left me with a tear in my chest so painful, I rubbed my sternum absently.

Jessa sat up, giving me a resigned smile and smoldering eyes. "Then we'll drive Henry mad instead."

"You know that's my new favorite hobby."

She gathered up her legs and crawled into my lap, putting her back against the rail. "And we'll enjoy what time we can without upsetting Cass." She hooked her arms around my neck.

My hands slid up her back. "It's a good plan."

"Have you ever fucked on the water tower?" she asked, her lips inching toward mine.

"Not even once."

Her hands were already undoing my jeans. "Good. Then you can do something bad too."

The kiss was deep and unrelenting, her hands freeing me, then sweeping the leg of her shorts to the side and guiding me until my tip slid into the wet heaven I'd come to need so insistently. And then she sank down my shaft, inch by fucking inch.

I don't know how long she rode me, only that I was already too close to coming. Her strap was down her arm, her breast in my hand.

When the whoop of a police siren sounded below our feet.

33
the audacity

REMY

IT WAS near three in the morning when Jessa's mother bailed us out of jail.

If it'd been anyone but Jessa, getting arrested for fucking on the water tower would have been funny. But sitting next to her in the back seat of Bailey's squad car just made me feel like an asshole and a chump. I'd sullied her once again with a first I never wanted to give her.

As much as I enjoyed getting her filthy, I hated to tarnish her like this.

I told her not to call her mom, but there was nobody else to ask if we wanted to keep things under wraps. The last thing any of us needed—Cass least of all—was to have my stressed out, bedraggled cousin screaming at us in front of the Roseville Police Station in the middle of the night.

Jessa was certain her mother would be discreet, which I didn't doubt. Our reputation was her reputation too, and she was the kind of lady who cared too much what people thought of her. But discretion wasn't my concern.

I was more worried about how much Grace would hate me after landing her daughter in jail for the first time. And when we walked out of holding, I hated to find out that I was right to be concerned.

Grace Hastings stood beneath the fluorescent lights of the police station, proud nose in the air. Her tired eyes were narrow and her lips a flat line, just like the expression I hated to invoke on Jessa. She wore silken loungewear with a tan trench coat hanging from her shoulders, and underneath, an expensive-looking bag was hooked in her elbow, her hand elegantly poised.

Her cool eyes cut from Jessa to me, narrowing a sliver farther.

She said nothing, turning on her heel to march out of the station. Jessa and I shared a worried look and followed.

Grace stopped next to the Bentley's backseat door, held open by the driver. She stared Jessa down.

"Get in the car," she said, the words clipped.

Jessa hesitated.

"Mother, I appreciate your coming, but—"

"Do not test me, Jessamine. Get in."

"But—"

"I will not hear a word from you, not after disgracing our family as you have tonight. I wonder if I even know you—the daughter I raised wouldn't have been caught fornicating in public for God's sake. She certainly wouldn't have been arrested. So spare me your excuses and get in the car."

My brows drew together. "You should go with her, Jess," I said quietly.

She turned to me, her expression hurt. "And why should I?"

I glanced at Grace, then back at Jessa. "I'm already in enough trouble with her. It's bad enough I got you into this mess—I don't want to be the reason you fight with her too."

"A bit late for that, don't you think?" Grace said. "It's your fault we're here at all. And here I stupidly believed your lie—you were pretending for Henry's sake, were you? Seems that you were out for your own interests all along. I can't say I'm surprised, not by you. It's my daughter whose judgment is compromised. Never did I think she'd lower herself in such a way, despite your charm and despicable influence. Jessamine Hastings, get in this car *right now*."

"No," she said from my side, her voice trembling with fury. "I'm not a child, Mother."

"Then stop behaving like one." She stepped forward to grab Jessa's arm, but she shook her mother off.

"That's enough!" she shot, her cheeks pink and shoulders bunched. "I'm a grown woman—you can't order me about as if I were a little girl. I'm going with Remy. You've found us out—we're sleeping together, though I don't know why you care or why it matters."

"It matters for the sake of your decency and self-respect. You have debased yourself with this . . . man. Which was horrid enough when you were lying, but utterly loathsome as the truth. When your father finds out you've been in jail, I can't imagine what he'll say. The disappointment of discovering his only daughter is a whore might undo him."

Rage flamed in my chest as I stepped around Jessa, putting myself between them.

"I think you'd better leave, Mrs. Hastings."

Her head cocked a notch. "Or you'll what? Shall we add assault to your charges for this evening?"

"No ma'am, but I think you should reconsider your words. I may never be good enough for Jessa, and I sure as hell don't deserve her, but she's no whore. You have no right to hurt her like you do."

"No right?" She scoffed. "Were it not for me, young man, you'd still be in that putrid cell, waiting for someone to save you. Half of your town would know by first light, had I not taken care of the deputy. Including Cassidy, who I suspect would be deeply upset to find out about whatever this is. The only one with no rights is you. Now, release my daughter to me."

She reached for Jessa again, but I shifted, keeping myself in front of her. "If she doesn't want to go with you, she's not going."

Grace's nostrils flared. Jessa hooked her arm in my elbow, looking around my biceps at her mother.

"You animal," Grace spat. "How dare you interfere. How dare you corrupt her. At least you know you'll never be good enough for her. You'll never have her for your own. So enjoy your little romp. It's the last you'll ever have of her." She whipped around and stepped toward the car, pausing at the open door. "Jessamine, see me in the morning. The conversation *will* happen. Best it be by your choice."

A bitter laugh escaped Jessa. "Choice. I've never had a choice. Why should I trust you'd give me one now?"

"Tomorrow," Grace said, pinning Jessa with a look, then me, her expression thick with spite and disdain. With that relayed, she ducked into the car.

We stood there until she was nothing but taillights.

I heard Jessa's breath hitch and looked down to find her crying. I drew her into my arms and held her for a long while, feeling her body tremble with rage and adrenaline and frustration. Sadness.

"Don't cry," I said softly.

"I-I've never disobeyed her before."

I paused. "Never?"

She shook her head against my chest. "I'm so s-sorry she said such a-awful things about you. She doesn't know you. She doesn't know me. She doesn't know *anything.*"

"Shh," I soothed, rocking her gently. "It's all right. Don't let her get to you—I know I didn't," I lied.

"We should have called Cass," she said, sniffling. "I'd rather have argued with her than be dressed down and called a whore by my mother."

"I'm surprised she even bailed me out."

"Me too, after all that. I'd have come back for you, though. If I'd only had my bag, I could have done it myself and no one would have been the wiser."

"I'm sorry," I said, feeling miserable. "This is all my fault."

"No, it's mine."

"If I hadn't taken you to the water tower—" I started.

"If I hadn't wanted to fuck you so badly—"

"If I hadn't fucked you in the first place—"

She looked hurt. "You regret that?"

"God no," I said on a laugh. "Never regretted anything less. But it sure has been a whole lot of trouble for you. That's what I can't stand."

She sighed, backing away, taking my hand.

"Don't worry about me," she said. "I made a choice, remember? You made sure of it. And I've never regretted anything less either."

I stopped, pulling her back to scoop her up and kiss her for a moment, wishing things were different. Easier.

But they weren't. And they seemed to keep getting more complicated by the day.

"Come on, Duchess. Let's get you home."

And with another brief kiss, we did just that.

34
these dreams

JESSA

I HATED WAKING from lovely dreams.

I was in Remy's arms, tangled up in bed. The sun hung in the afternoon sky, cicadas hissing in the heat beyond the open window. His fingertips drew shapes on my bare skin, his body warm and vital and alive against me.

I only wished I could stay in this dream forever—it was the best dream I'd ever had. But the clock ticked incessantly on, despite any wishes and dreams I'd been cursed with.

A sigh slipped out of me, and he tipped my chin, shifting to kiss me, slow and luxuriating.

"You need to go talk to your mama," he said, though he looked even less enthusiastic about it than I did.

I groaned and pulled the duvet up over us.

He laughed, a low, raspy sound that rumbled around in his chest. "I know. But the sooner you go, the sooner you'll be back. Unless she convinces you to stay with her."

"I'd rather die, thank you."

"How bad do you think it's going to be?"

"I don't really know. I have no precedence."

He sighed. "Another first I wish I hadn't instigated."

I did my best to sound blasé. "Really, it's all so silly, I

mean, I'm leaving in a few days, anyway." Approximately zero percent of that ended up blasé. I sounded rather whiny, in truth, and tried to recover my dignity. "I just can't imagine why she cares so much."

"In my experience, most mothers do. About nearly everything."

"It's none of her business who my vacation pussy decides to gorge herself on." That earned me a laugh. "I shouldn't have called her—that's all there is to it."

"We didn't have many options if we didn't want the whole town to know."

I leaned back to look at him, one brow arching. "You're awfully concerned about people finding out about us, Remy."

"It's not that. I just . . . if you were staying, it'd be different. But it'd be this whole ass thing, you know? And if I'm honest, I think it'd be harder. You know, when you leave."

My heart broke a little at the sadness in his voice.

"Anyway," he continued, "we'll be too busy the next couple of days to think about it overmuch, and we've got our bases covered thanks to Hank. Bachelor/Bachelorette party tomorrow night at The Horseshoe, then the rehearsal dinner, then the big event. Tonight, you're going to Cass's to help her pack, and this afternoon you've gotta talk to your mom."

I groaned again, this time flipping the duvet down and reaching for my phone. Cass was busy all morning with family, thank goodness—I didn't have to explain why I'd been in bed all day, however anxious I was to tell her. Though I understood Remy's logic, I despised keeping it from her and loathed the fact that he didn't want her to know. He didn't want *anyone* to know.

It was fine. It made perfect sense. Really, it had nothing to do with him being ashamed of me. Probably.

"I don't even know what I'll say." I sat up and swung my legs around, putting my feet on the floor. "Will she just shout at me and make me feel stupid? Am I supposed to argue? Stay quiet? What's the purpose?"

He propped himself up in bed and tucked his hand behind his head. The sheets pooled at his waist in the most inviting way. It took all my will not to slither back into bed with him. Instead, I busied myself with getting dressed.

"She probably just needs to get it off her chest, whatever it is. But don't take any shit from her. Whatever she says about you, it's not true."

"What about what she says about you?"

One corner of his lips rose. "Oh, I'm sure it's on the nose. She's not happy her daughter's sleeping with a scoundrel, and I guess I couldn't blame her. Tell me if she calls me that, would you? I've always wanted to be one."

"I think you were born one," I assured him. "Anyway, the whole thing is silly. I can't wait to be done with her, and then with Cass. And then I'll be back here with you. Will you be late?"

"Nah. I'll be here when you get home—I can get out of pretty much anything if I set my mind to it."

"Don't I know it."

Once dressed, I made my way toward the bathroom, pausing to kiss the top of his head as I passed. His hand curled around my biceps as he pressed a kiss to it, his fingertips hanging on to trail down to mine as I walked away.

The space in my ribcage ached, warm and painful.

I couldn't stay in Roseville, could I?

What excuse could I possibly give? How would I tell Cass?

Would she truly be upset—long lastingly upset—or was she just being Cass about it?

I sighed at my reflection as I did my best to tame my hair. It was ridiculous, really. I barely knew Remy. Staying would be ludicrous. There were a thousand reasons not to.

But I could think of at least a hundred to stay.

Saying I didn't know him felt like a lie, and he knew me. I'd never had someone care for me like he did without shackling me. And though perhaps I didn't know everything about him, there was something intangible between us. Something magical, riotous, utterly perfect.

Which was why I was loath to leave him.

He doesn't even want you to, ninny. He refuses to tell a soul, and why do you think that is?

Surely he planned this to be a holiday affair. Based on everything you've heard about him, it's exactly what you should have expected. It's exactly what Cass told you he was like.

The thought left me preternaturally sad.

The Remy I'd come to know was too attentive and obsessive for this to be a fling. Flings were founded on detachment, and Remy was anything but. Unless the attachment was somehow part of the dating game for him, which would frankly be sick and twisted.

But anyone would agree that I didn't know Remy. Maybe he was sick and twisted in ways I'd not yet discovered.

I spiraled on like that as I brushed my teeth and freshened my face. By the time I was through, Remy was dressed and ready to go, leaning against the front doorframe, spinning his keys around his finger.

Waking from lovely, perfect dreams *really* was the worst.

It was a beautiful day, though it was nearly gone, dusk creeping in behind the sun as it disappeared beyond the horizon. Neither of us said much, just enjoyed the wind and the sky and the brief joy, our fingers entwined in his lap. When he pulled up to the house, my smile faded. I suspected I wouldn't see that smile for some time.

I took a deep breath, kissed Remy goodbye, and climbed out of the Scout, watching him drive away from the front step.

It took another sigh, a second deep breath, and some muttered words of encouragement to open the door and hunt for my mother. It was a sprawling house. The main rooms had sweeping ceilings with hallways spoking the middle, lined with a dozen bedrooms. In the back was a pool with a massive veranda, which was where I found her.

She lay stretched out on a lounger in her bathing suit, sunglasses on and a large hat providing shade for her face and shoulders. With a glance in my direction, I saw her chest rise and fall heavily. She closed her book and stood.

"I'm here as you requested," I said when I reached her.

She pulled on her kimono. "Yes, well, you must have been quite busy to have taken all day to finally come."

"Despite you being my mother, I'm not obligated to answer your summons. I'm not even sure what there is to discuss that wasn't said last night. Or did you have more names to call me? Have you told Father yet what a whore I am? I'm desperate to know what he thinks."

She paused, watching me incredulously. "What on earth has come over you?"

"I had the nerve to spend the last week saying exactly what I thought, for once. I've found it restorative, actually."

"This is all to do with that man. And what of Henry?"

"What of him? He brought a date to the wedding, Mother. Still, he's never so much as crooked a finger at me. If nothing else, I'm glad to have finally seen us for what we are. Friends."

"It's preposterous, Jessamine. Ever since you were little—"

"—you and Father and everyone else have groomed Henry and me for each other. I have been prepared, reminded over and over again how perfect we are, how well suited we would be. But nothing has come of it, despite all the hopes you've pestered me with since I was still in a nappy."

"You just have to—"

"Oh my God, Mother! I just have to *nothing*."

She was silent for a beat. "And this is all for your little fling?"

"No." I sighed, taking a seat and dropping my head to my hands. "I mean, yes in the sense that I now know how it feels for a man to truly *need* me. But no. I . . . I can't stay here, and it's not as if he's coming to England anytime soon. We're resigned to the facts."

Something in her loosened, her shoulders unbuckling just a touch. She sat opposite me and took off her sunglasses.

"No, you can't stay here, and he's hardly suitable," she said softly, never realizing what a shit she sounded like even when she was gentle. "You're quite certain about Henry?"

"Mother . . ." I groaned.

"Yes, all right, all right." She eyed me over a pause. "You truly don't intend to continue to see this Remington?"

My face screwed up in frustration. "I feel you should know that if things were different, I absolutely would. I'd see him and perhaps even get arrested again. Maybe I'd even move in with him. What would you say, Mother, if I moved here to live with him in the quaint little cottage you're so fond of? What would Father say if I *married* him?"

There was a sequence of blinking and mouth gaping as she tried to grasp what I'd said. "You couldn't possibly."

"I suppose we'll never know. But it's not for lack of wanting."

"Well, then, I'm glad we're leaving."

"I'm sure you are." I was instantly exhausted, despite having slept all day. "I understand why you're like this. I hate it, but I understand it."

"I don't know that you do."

"Of course I do. This was the world you were brought up in. We marry at least *near* our station. Someone with accomplishments and careers and degrees, and a pedigree too, if we're lucky. Remy is none of those things, but I don't love him any less for it."

Her eyes widened at my casual use of the word love.

"Oh, don't lose your mind, Mother. I've already told you

—we knew what it was when we started. I've no idea know how he feels about me, only that I have a devastating need for him and—oh, not like that. Well, actually, like that, but also simply for his company."

"But this is exactly my point, darling." She reached across the space between us to lay her hand on mine. "A little fling can bloom and grow until it chokes every flower in the garden. I would know well enough." I must have looked confused because she said, "Yes, of course. I haven't told you that I once had a Remington of my own."

My mouth opened. No words came out.

She let out a breath and retracted her hand. "I was younger than you are now, and he was a little bit older. He was my riding instructor one summer—I was twenty, and life was all figured out for me, you see. But then I spent my days with him and learned about him. I learned the way his lips curved when he smiled. I learned what he wished for, what hopes he held. I learned how it felt to give a man your heart. And I learned what it meant to give up something I loved. Do close your mouth, Jessamine."

I snapped my mouth shut.

"Thank you. It begins with the most innocent conversations. A brush of a hand maybe, and before you know it, he's all you can think of. Then you're kissing, then worse. I love your father, I do. But I *loved* Peter. I'd never wish the pain on you of having to give Remington away, should you decide to drag out the affair."

"But why did you give him up?"

"Because he was never mine to keep."

"That was a choice you made, Mother. You could have chosen differently."

"Oh, of course. It was so simple, was it? Disgracing my family, destroying my inheritance? I had responsibilities, Jessamine, as do you. There was no running away simply because I loved a man. The rest of my life was too big for something so trivial."

"A true romantic."

"Darling, it isn't that I wish anything but happiness for you. I wish you love, of course I do."

"Conditionally."

She shrugged. "It's the nature of things."

"All this time you were trying to protect me when I . . . well, I thought you hated Remy."

"Oh, I do. He's beneath you in every way. He's a horrendous influence and couldn't tell a salad fork from a port glass. I was hard on you both, but really, I was furious. And with every right, I might add. But it terrifies me to see you with him. I understand intimately what trouble he could be."

"Because of my feelings for him."

"Because of his feelings for you."

"Oh," was all I could say in my surprise. Just a hint of a word on a puff of air.

"Surely you know."

"I suspected. But Mother, he doesn't want me to stay."

"Has he said so?"

"Well, no—"

"Of course he hasn't, because the suggestion is absurd. You barely know each other. He'd sound like a fool if he mentioned it."

"But . . . well . . . he doesn't want to tell anyone either. Not that we're really seeing each other. Only fake seeing each other."

"And why is that?"

"Cassidy will murder us both."

"Ah, yes. I could see how she'd be unhappy with you sleeping with her cousin. But none of this proves he doesn't care for you. He does, which is why what you're playing at is so dangerous. So please. Detach yourself. Leave the boy where you found him when we go home in a few days," she said as she stood. "And for God's sake—don't tell your father I had an affair with a horse trainer. I'll never hear the end of it."

With that, she left me sitting on the chaise, listening to the trickling water of a fountain dribbling into the pool, trying not to think about my mother having sex with a man tasked with teaching her equestrian show jumping.

All this time I thought she hated Remy because she was a snob.

Well, she was a snob, but she was also worried about me.

Her behavior last night was inexcusable, but something pricked my heart at the knowledge that she was trying to protect me, in her way.

Lord, the bar was so very low.

I picked myself up and carried myself to her driver, requesting a ride to Cass's. But for the entire ride, all I could think was how very confused I was.

35
floppy squids
JESSA

AS I FOLDED the tiny knickers Cass was taking on her honeymoon, she paced the length of her bedroom, reciting her vows with her veil whipping behind her and her wedding shoes clipping on the hardwood.

"I, Cassidy Winfield, promise to love you, Davis McGrath, unconditionally and forever. I vow to stand beside you through life's ups and downs, to commit to a . . . partnership of equality, trust, and respect. On this day, I choose you as my husband, and together, we will forge our path in life—why are you looking at me like that?"

I smoothed my face. "Like what?"

"Like something smells funny."

"Well, it's just . . . that sounds awfully . . ."

She groaned, slapping the sheet of paper on her thigh when her arms flopped. "Boring? Like a wedding manual? Like a robot wrote it? Ten years I've had to figure this out! Ten stupid years waiting on this day, and the best I could do was rip off a bunch of stuff from *The Knot*."

"You could have at least used AI."

"I'd laugh if I wasn't freaking out." She flopped into the

253

chair at her childhood desk. "Watch, Davis is going to say the perfect thing, and all I'll have to offer is a tax return."

"Well, let's try and sort it out. Do you have a pen—oh." She threw the paper and a cup of pens in the bin. "Later, perhaps?"

She huffed and stood again, walking to her floor-length mirror to inspect her reflection. "Everything just feels wrong. Does everything feel wrong to you?"

I frowned, my hands pausing mid-air, a silky, hot-pink scrap of underpants dangling from my hand. "Does . . . what?"

She fussed with her hair. Smoothed her shirt. "I've eaten too much cornbread since I got here. Damn Linda and her demon recipes. Look—I'm getting a pimple too." She stretched her face out with the jut of her jaw. "Shee? Right dare. *And* I started spotting! I have an IUD, haven't had my period in a year, and now that I'm about to be in *Greece on my honeymoon*, here comes the crimson tide. Look, even my stupid shoes are rebelling." She kicked off one heel at a time and displayed her ankle. "I've been wearing this terrible footwear around for a month and they still give me blisters. I think I'm jinxed. Do you think I'm jinxed?" She whipped around and rushed over, her blue eyes wide. "Oh God. Maybe I'm jinxed, Jess."

I laughed, grabbing her by the shoulders. "Whoa, okay. Let's take a breath, shall we? There we go." I waited for her to complete a cycle. "No, I do not think you're jinxed. I think you're stressed and exhausted, but certainly not cursed."

She let out a long breath, her shoulders relaxing a little as she gathered up the lacy hem of her veil. "Davis left to stay with the guys. You know, so our wedding night would be more special."

"Whose terrible idea was that?"

"Mine," she said, groaning. "I know this is supposed to be

the happiest day of my life, but I cannot wait for it to be over. I wish we'd just eloped."

"Well, hindsight and all that."

"And now I have to stay here all by myself. Although, I *could* take the opportunity to watch some preparatory porn. You know, for science."

"Of course, science," I said, chuckling. "It's going to be perfect."

Her eyes went all big and glassy. "Promise?"

"If I have anything to do with it, absolutely."

She sighed, pulling off her veil before flopping back on her bed.

"You're doing an awful lot of flopping."

"Well, I can't help it," she whined. "I'm floppy."

When she flailed her arms a little, we started to laugh. Then we were cackling.

"I'm a fucking furious squid," she said between gasps and the wild thrashing of her arms as she flopped about like a fish. Which set off a new round of laughter. When we finally calmed down a little, she wiped her eyes, her face still all scrunched up and red. "I think I'm broken."

Instantly, her smile turned to tears as a deep and terrible sadness overcame her. She began to cry in earnest.

"Oh, darling, no. Come here."

I tried to get her to sit up, but she went dead weight and started to giggle again between sobs, halfheartedly flailing her arms.

"Furious squiiiiiiiid," she wailed, cry-laughing.

"I think you really are broken," I said, laughing again as I tried to intercept her arms so I could grab her around the waist. Finally, I gave up with a sigh, the stone in my chest heavy with concern.

"Will you stay with me until the wedding, Jess?" She sounded so small, like a little girl. "I don't want to be alone."

Being here meant not being with Remy. My heart split and

splattered, but there was nothing to do except say, "Of course," as I stroked her hair.

"Thank you." She sniffled, finally picking herself up. "Although honestly, it might not be for long." She waggled her brows as she reached for a tissue.

"What do you mean?"

"Well," she started, blowing her nose. "I overheard Davis and Henry talking about you last night. Henry's going to make a move on you! Maybe you'll end up staying with him after all."

I blinked. "What?"

"I know! It's finally happening!"

My thoughts had exploded into teeny tiny bits of what the fuck. "But . . . what about Annie?"

"He said they're just friends. There's nothing going on with them. He said . . . let me make sure I got it right." She glanced up at the ceiling. "*It's time. I'm finally going for Jessa. Maybe we'll be married this time next year, too.*" Cass squealed and giggled and bounced and I did my best to pretend to be excited. Mostly I just sat there with my mouth gaping.

"He . . . where did you hear this?"

"Through a door over where the guys are staying. I was supposed to be asleep, but I'm a nosy, nosy liar. Well? Aren't you excited?"

"No, yeah. I'm just shocked, that's all."

"But like, good shocked, right?" She nudged my arm with her elbow conspiratorially.

"Yes, of course." I paused. "It's only that . . . well, I've been thinking."

She waited. "About what?"

"Well, only that I'm not sure if I really want Henry after all."

Her face melted into some form of quietly confused fury. "I'm sorry, what?"

"Cass, think about it. I've held him on high my whole life.

He's been the pinnacle, the cherished thing I could never have because let's be perfectly clear—I could *never* have him. He brought a date to your wedding, and he must know how I've felt about him. We had a marriage pact, for God's sake, one that expires immediately. All he's done my whole life is string me along, and like a fool, I followed him around and waited. Well, I'm through waiting, that's all."

She stared at me for a long moment. "Does this have anything to do with my cousin?"

"What?" I laughed. My heart made a valorous attempt at climbing out of my throat. "No! Why would you suggest such a thing?"

She leveled her eyes at me. "Jessamine Marjorie Hastings, tell me the truth."

"Seriously, Cass. Whatever would I do with someone like Remy?"

"You didn't answer me."

So I leveled my eyes back at her, making sure I was facing her as fully as possible. I even leaned in so she could get a good, strong look at my pupils while I lied, the guilt sour in my stomach. "This has nothing to do with your cousin."

It wasn't a *total* lie. Remy was merely a catalyst for something I should have realized long ago—I didn't want Henry, and he didn't want me.

"I've seen you French," she reminded me.

I blushed, laughing, and lied, lied, lied. "I like Remy. He's a decent man after all. And clearly he's an exceptional kisser, but there's nothing to it."

Her eyes narrowed a tick, but she relaxed. "Good. I know I joke about him, but I really wouldn't forgive you. Not ever."

The words were a physical blow. I tried to laugh them off. "That's . . . really, that seems a bit far, don't you think? We've been friends for ten years. We've been through everything that's mattered together. You'd really never forgive me?"

"I'd really never forgive you."

"Am I so fragile that you should be *this* worried about Remy breaking my heart?"

"Yes, and you should be too. But . . . well, that's not the whole truth about why I don't want you seeing him."

"Well, say it then!"

The look on her face was a little bit hurt, a little bit angry, and whole lot of sad. "You'd survive Remy. Remy wouldn't survive you."

The vise around my heart tightened.

"He's been through too much, lost too much. Had his heart broken so bad, he never put it all the way back together. And if he fell for you—which he inevitably would, how could he not?—only for you to ditch him here and go back to England, I don't know if he'd ever recover."

I didn't know what to say, my mind a whirl. I hadn't considered I'd hurt him. I hadn't considered he could be hurt, not by me, at least.

"Warning you off him was easy—he proved my point the second he opened his mouth. But what Remy went through with Chelsea was . . ." She shook her head, looking down at her hands as she picked at her nails. "We thought she was it, Jess. He was all in, proposed in the gazebo in town and everything, had started fixing up the old cottage for them to stay in when they visited. But when Linda got cancer and Remy came home for good, he came home alone. He wouldn't tell us much, only that they broke up, and she didn't want to move to Roseville. So I called her myself."

I listened, stunned silent.

"We got in a huge fight after she told me that she didn't sign up to take care of his sick mom or live in a shitty old house in the middle of nowhere. She said she was too young to be stuck, and she said she was sorry. I think she meant it. But fuck her. Fuck her all the way to hell for being so selfish and leaving him like she did." She sighed. "At least she was honest, and at least he found out before marrying her and having kids and all. But . . . it did something to him, Jess. He threw himself into taking care of Linda alone—Mama and I were trying to get over Daddy dying and didn't have any space left for anything, not even each other. Remy lost everything with the snap of God's fingers, and it was too much to handle. So he didn't. He packed it up and resigned himself to stay here because everything else was too hard." She shook her head. "That summer changed him irrevocably. For all the girls and for all his talk, he's the loneliest guy I know. So, no. If you fucked around with my cousin and left him here alone, I'd never forgive you."

I nodded. Swallowed the stone in my throat. Put on the façade with my stomach hollowed out. Worried I'd inadvertently ruin Remy, if I hadn't already.

"You have nothing to worry about."

She relaxed, smiling as she said "Good," and jumped into ticking off a list of things she had to do tomorrow before the bachelor/bachelorette party. And while she talked, I packed her suitcase with militant exactitude.

She might not have had anything to worry about.

But I did.

36
would've, could've, should've

REMY

IT'D BEEN MORE than twenty-four hours since I'd seen Jessa, and I was crawling out of my skin from all the waiting I'd done.

She texted last night that Cass had asked her to stay, and I hated it the second I read her message. I hated every minute I sat at home with Beau alone. I hated every long second of the night that I lay in my cold, lonely bed wishing she was there to keep me warm. I'd hated every stupid hour that passed today like a dripping faucet, second by second, waiting until I'd see her tonight. By the time she came to the house to change and pick up some things, I was already gone for the mid shift at The Horseshoe. And when that shift was over, I had a beer at the bar and waited some more.

I didn't have enough time left, but I couldn't think of a reason for her to come home that trumped her best friend begging her to stay over through the wedding jitters.

The whole thing was a horrible, terrible load of horse shit, and I fucking hated it.

The relief I felt when she finally showed up with Cass and a handful of our female cousins was instant and complete. The pack of them bounded into the bar, giggling with Davis,

Hank—with a hopeful Annie on his arm—and a bunch of dudes right behind them. I was grateful for Henry's presence as it gave me an excuse to kiss Jessa hello in front of the whole crowd. I wrapped my arms around her and stood up straight, taking her with me, burying my face in her neck.

"Missed you," I said into her hair.

She squeezed my neck. "Missed you."

For a second, I considered throwing her over my shoulder and marching out, but didn't figure it'd go over too well with anybody but me. So I set her down, watching her with a dumbass smile on my face. One of the cousins handed her a huge tote bag, and she wore the wickedest smile as she dug into it, passing things out of its maw to the group.

My smile flattened when I realized what she was passing out, hand over fist.

Cass laughed, making a show of a satin sash that said *bachelorette* before draping it around my neck.

"For you, madam," she said.

I flicked a pink plastic penis on her headband, and it boinged around. "Nice dick."

"Don't worry, there's one for you too."

I stood there like an excellent fucking sport while a gaggle of women—one of whom I wanted very badly to fuck—adorned me in penis accoutrements. Necklaces. Straws. Bracelets. Sunglasses. Suckers and candies, and all kinds of edible weenies. There was even a penis whistle, which Cass shoved in my mouth and told me to blow.

The bachelors stood behind them laughing at my expense, beers in hand. I took the tail of the pink boa Cass adorned me with and tossed it over the opposite shoulder, blowing my dick whistle like my life depended on it.

The girls all cheered and bounced and clapped. I adjusted my penis sunglasses and turned for the bar.

"Gimme a scotch, neat. And make it a double," I added, absolutely certain I was going to need it.

Buddy Ray was in the DJ booth, and when Flo Rida started in about apple-bottom jeans, the girls took off toward the dance floor screaming every word, one of them holding a six foot inflatable cock like she'd won it in battle.

Jessa wiggled her way up to me rapping, dressed head to toe in penis apparel. The penis antennae wiggled when she got low, and goddammit if it wasn't the cutest thing I'd ever seen.

I shook my head and laughed, tossing back the scotch too fast—it scorched a trail of hellfire down my esophagus, but I didn't care. I grabbed Jessa's hand and dragged her to the dance floor, hoping to get a minute with her, but the rest of the bachelorettes circled me like a maypole. I wasn't sure how many times I'd ever had so many women dancing with me at once, but I was damn fucking sure none of them had ever been my cousins.

I managed to use Jessa as a human shield, and soon they lost interest, thanks to Nelly and his commentary on how hot it was in here and what we should do about it.

Jessa turned around, laughing as she slung an arm on my shoulder and straddled my thigh, swaying her hips in time to the music. So I did what every red-blooded straight man would do—I grabbed her by the hip and kept her beat, enjoying the feel of her grinding my thigh more than I should have for being in public.

She looked so happy, still laughing and smiling and lit up from the inside.

"You look good in dicks," she said.

I smoothed my shirt. "I get that a lot."

"I don't know if any of them would have been such a good sport about so much plastic penis."

I glanced at the bachelors, who all seemed to be laughing at me, and shrugged. "They're missing out." I put the dick whistle in my mouth and went ham on it.

She just kept laughing, finally pulling it by the chain. It popped out of my mouth with an audible noise.

"You look kinda hot with a dick in your mouth," she said.

"I get that a lot too."

She laughed again, and goddammit, I'd do anything to hear the sound. Even adorn myself in phalluses.

"Think we can sneak off at some point?" I asked.

Her mouth quirked. "Don't know. I hope so, but . . ."

"Yeah," I said, very clearly disappointed. "How'd it go last night?"

She sighed. "Oh, fine. Although . . . I think Cass might truly come unhinged."

"What happened?"

"She's convinced she's jinxed, said that everything feels wrong. One minute she's laughing, next she's crying."

"She's not pregnant, is she?"

"Oh, God. No. She actually started her period."

I flinched. "Good to know. She seems all right tonight."

We looked in her direction as she bounced and rapped and wiggled around like she was eighteen and not twenty-eight.

"I hope so," Jessa said.

"How'd it go with your mom?"

Something in her shuttered closed. "Fine. You were right —she just wanted to talk at me."

I frowned. "She didn't say anything shitty?"

"She always says something shitty, but no. She was fine."

Two fines? Felt like a lie.

I didn't push it.

I was too worried about what I'd find out if I did.

"Well, good. I'm glad you talked to her."

"Me too."

The conversation stalled. My concern rose.

"I hate that my last nights won't be with you," she said, toying with one of my dick necklaces.

"Not nearly as much as I hate it."

"How can you be so sure?"

"At least you have Cass. I just have my asshole dog to keep me company, and he's a terrible conversationalist."

She chuckled. "We'll have the wedding night together."

"Good. Rest up and eat a good dinner. You're gonna need your energy."

"Yes, sir."

"Ah, now don't start that, Duchess, or we're both in trouble."

She ground her hips a little harder, her pussy pressed against my thigh. "What? Shouldn't I call you sir?"

"Try it and find out what I do to brats."

I could have drowned in her as she laughed and looped both arms around my neck, bringing us closer. "I really do hate that I'm leaving."

"So maybe you should stay." The words were out of me before I could reel them back in. I knew it was what I wanted.

I had no idea I'd just blurt it out like that.

Her face flickered with hope, uncertainty, and something else I couldn't place.

"Just for a little while, at least. A week, maybe."

She didn't answer. A piece of me died inside.

"Or not. Just an idea."

"What about Cass?" she asked.

I shrugged. "She'll be on her honeymoon. What she doesn't know won't kill her. Anyway, it's fine. Like I said, just an idea."

"No, it's not that, I just . . . let me think about it."

"Sure," I said with a liar's smile. "You need a drink."

"Oh, I can get it—"

"Nah, let me. Besides, if you leave me here alone, I might end up getting molested by a cousin. Despite what you might have heard, it's not really a thing we encourage around here. Gin?"

"Yes, please," she said on another laugh, sounding relieved. I kissed her cheek and left her on the dance floor, doing my best not to panic as I made my way to the bar.

Something had happened in the time since I'd dropped her off at her mom's, but I didn't suspect she'd tell me what. Call it a hunch. But if I'd asked her to stay yesterday when we were wrapped up in each other's arms in my bed, I thought she might have said yes. Maybe she'd have laughed it off, but she wouldn't have frozen like that.

I ordered her drink, cursing myself. This was only supposed to be a fling. Just a couple weeks of fun. Just a game we were playing to kill time. But then she went and knocked the dust off my heart and shocked it back to life when I thought it was long dead.

And now, here I was, wanting a girl I couldn't have.

Needing a girl I shouldn't want.

Losing a girl who wasn't mine.

I raked a hand through my hair, forgetting about the dick headband, catching it in my fist. I slapped it onto the counter, my jaw clenching so tight my teeth squeaked. And I thought real hard about her leaving and never coming back, and just how bad I'd fucked up.

But most of all, I thought about what the fuck I was going to do about it.

I barely registered her drink being set in front of me, but picked it up and turned in her direction, desperate for answers, hoping to find them in her eyes.

But instead, I found her in Henry's arms.

37

100% nope.

JESSA

REMY STOPPED dead at the sight of me with Henry, his headband clenched in his giant fist and my drink in the other.

Henry was talking. I didn't hear what he was saying. All I could hear was my thundering heartbeat, 50 Cent booming, and my heart telling me to run. Cass watched Henry and me like it was *her* birthday 50 was rapping about. Remy watched us like he was going to bust the glass in his hand, imagining it was Henry's neck.

"Do you know what I mean, Bits?" Henry asked, frowning down at me. "Did you hear what I said?"

"I . . . erm . . ."

He laughed off my inattentiveness. "That's one of the many things I love about you—you're a bit mad."

I laughed awkwardly.

"I was saying," he started, holding me close, hips swaying against mine, "that I've realized a lot since being here. I can't pretend that seeing you with that buffoon didn't jog something in me. But it did. I love you, Bits. Always have, always will. So what do you say? Will you give me a chance?"

I blinked up at Henry. The words were all wrong. The man was all wrong. "A chance at what?"

Again, he laughed, pressing a kiss to my temple. "A chance at *us*."

Of all the things I expected when Henry finally confessed his feelings, horror was not one. "Whatever do you mean?" I asked, wondering if perhaps I played dumb, he'd let it go.

I couldn't be so lucky.

"Tomorrow is the rehearsal dinner. Let me take you. Be my date. Let me prove to you that my feelings are true. I know it's taken me a long time to finally realize that it's you— it's always been you. But I'll make it right, if you'll give me a chance."

I shook my head to clear it. "Why now? After all this time? You've seen me date men before—this can't all be about Remy."

Henry's face darkened. "Can't it be? I've never seen you like you are with him. It . . . it makes me insane, Jessa. I can't stand it."

"What about Annie?"

"What about her? She's just a friend."

"Then why did you bring her as your date?"

"I never said she was my date. I never said we were together. You assumed."

"Because you were practically snogging her in front of all of us, Henry! Don't be dim."

He looked genuinely confused. "I don't know what you mean. We've always been like that."

"You're just like this with everyone then?"

"Bits, you're acting strange."

"You may not think she's your date, but I get the sense she does."

I nodded toward Annie, who was storming toward us. I backed away just in time for her to slap him squarely across the face.

"That's *it*," she shouted, her face pink and scrunched. "All you've done since I got here is talk about her. All you do when she's around is talk *to* her. I'm so fucking stupid—I didn't realize you were in love with her all this time. Well, good fucking luck. I'm *out*."

She turned on her heel, shoving people out of her way as she charged toward the door and exited the building.

Henry stared after her, stunned.

"You really didn't realize she was hopeful for you?" I asked him.

He shook his head.

"Well, now I suppose I *really* need a date," he said.

Cass appeared at my elbow. "You can take Jessa."

"Now wait a minute—"

"But what about Remy?" he asked.

"Oh, that's fake," Cass blurted, pushing me in Henry's direction. "They were just doing that to make you jealous. She's only been in love with you her whole life."

"*Cassidy!*" I screeched.

"Brilliant!" Henry was beaming.

"Hold on a second—"

Before I could finish my sentence, Henry scooped me up and pressed a brief kiss to my lips that shocked me mute.

"You won't be sorry, Bits. Thank you. Thank you!" He spun me around again, and I thought I might be sick. "I'm going to go tell Davis. He'll be so pleased. I'll be back, all right? Don't go anywhere."

Cass squealed and squeaked and bounced and hugged me as I stood there, completely dazed as I tried to collect my wits. When she let me go, I laughed and excused myself for the loo, meeting Remy's eyes on the way. He was still standing there with my drink in his hand, dick whistle around his neck and sunglasses on his face, though the headband seemed to have broken and lay in pieces at his feet. I pushed into the bathroom, which only had room for one, but before I could lock the door, Remy shoved it open and locked it shut behind him.

In a breath, I was pinned against the wall with Remy arched over me, our noses barely touching, our breath noisy and thick and mingling.

Another breath dragged me into him, our lips colliding. It wasn't a kiss—it was a claiming. It was a hot brand, his name singed into my soul by way of his lips. He gripped my face, my hips tacked to the wall by his. There was no air that wasn't him, no breath that wasn't his—he owned me for a long, relentless moment.

When his lips finally let me go, I realized distantly that my legs were wound around his waist, my hands scrabbling against his chest, his shirt fisted in my hands.

"He fucking kissed you," Remy whispered, the words licking my mouth.

I nodded stupidly.

"He doesn't get to kiss you. What did he want?"

"I . . ." My thoughts found no purchase. Remy'd kissed me into oblivion.

He snapped his fingers. "Jessa. What did he want?"

"To . . . he asked me if I'd be his date tomorrow night."

"And what did you say?" he asked through his teeth.

"Nothing. He and Cass decided without me."

He disappeared so fast, I nearly fell to the ground. For a moment, he faced the opposite wall, his hand in his hair.

"Remy?" I reached out to touch him but he stepped away.

He whipped around and grabbed me by the arm. "I was wrong. Let's go tell Cass. Let's tell her right now."

"Remy, wait!" I dug in my heels and pulled him to a stop. "We can't."

"Why not?"

"Because . . . well, because last night, she said again she'd never forgive me, and she meant it." I didn't know where the tears came from, only that they started in my throat, choking me quiet. I swallowed. "She said she'd *never* forgive me."

"You're not going on a date with that fucker, Jess."

"If I go out there and say no, Cass will sort it out. She'll know we're together."

The muscles in his jaw flexed.

"It doesn't mean anything. I want nothing to do with him, you know that." I reached for him slowly, like he was a wild animal. He looked much like one.

His nostrils flared.

"Remy, listen to me. It's all for show. It's one silly little dinner, and then the next night, I'll be with you."

"And then you leave."

Choked, completely. The tears squeezed my throat closed again. "You told me I could think about it."

"No. You said you needed to think about it and I didn't argue. What happened last night, Jess? What aren't you telling me?"

I could lose my best friend.

I could lose you.

My mother could be right about everything.

I could hurt you more than you could ever hurt me.

The tears made it to my eyes, clung to my bottom lashes.

The breath he exhaled must have clocked a thousand degrees. "All right. Okay. Don't cry, Jess. Please, don't cry. It's just one night, and then you're mine, okay? *Mine*, for as long as I get to have you. Go on the date with him. But you need to know something."

He took a step in my direction.

"It was one thing to pretend we were together. I could do that all day. But to act like I don't care is too much. I might accidentally rip his fucking throat out. I won't even mean to. He'll just get too close and—" He squeezed his fist in front of him and pulled. Then he closed the space between us, backing me into the wall. "Do whatever you need to do. Go on this date with that stupid asshole fucker. And about staying? Come find me when you figure it out." His lips were a breath away. "But if he kisses you again, I'll kill him. Got it?"

I nodded, my lips tingling in anticipation for a kiss that, once met, I could have made a whole life in. But it ended too soon. He pushed off the wall and stormed out, leaving me panting against the bathroom wall, knowing what I wanted.

I just didn't know if what I wanted was what was right.

38
whisky river
REMY

COME FIND *me when you figure it out.*

What an idiot. Now I had to wait.

Jessa and Henry entered the church together as the preacher led everyone through the motions. I burned holes in the back of Henry's head with eyes like lava lasers from where I waited in the threshold of the sanctuary.

The sight of the two of them walking down the farm's chapel aisle made me want to pop his head off and shove my boot down his throat.

Cass should have been on my arm, as I was the one giving her away, but she was busy at the front of the church in everybody's business. I pulled my flask out of my sport jacket and took a heavy pull, noting that it was nearly empty. One of my teenaged cousins elbowed me and wiggled her fingers for the flask.

"Ha—I'm not getting bawled out by your mama tonight. No thank you."

She pouted to the back of the pews as the preacher waved me on. I walked down the aisle with ghost-Cass at my side. Paused at the front to hand her off to real-Davis, then took my spot right next to Jessa.

Goddammit, I could smell her. I inhaled as discreetly as I could, masking it as a sigh through my nose, and the hairs on my arms stood at full attention and leaned in her direction.

I'd left the bar the second I came out of the can, swinging by Cass to tell her Mama's truck had gotten stuck and she needed me to pull her out, making a note to tell Mama so I didn't get busted. But I couldn't stay. Selfish as it was, there was no fucking way I was going to be able to sit still for the rest of the night.

I should have for Cass, but she was half a bottle of Fireball deep, and judging by the bags under her eyes tonight, she probably didn't remember when I left anyway.

Since getting to the church all of ten minutes ago, all I'd done was seethe and nurse my flask. It'd been the longest day, full of *nothing*. Not a phone call or a text or a goddamn word from her direction. I spent two hours chopping wood just to give myself something violent to do, not stopping until my arms were jelly and my hands were too slick from sweat to hold the axe. I tinkered with the Camaro for a while. Took two showers. Tried to eat but just ended up poking at my food. Every bite was sawdust in my mouth.

It wasn't even the date that bothered me.

Okay, it bothered me, but it wasn't the heart of the matter —tonight was going to be eternal if I had to watch Henry put his arm around her like he owned her. Touch her hand like he had any fucking right. I considered learning the names of all the hand bones just so I could recite them to him while I broke them one by one, but who had that kind of time?

Oh yeah. Me. I did.

So tonight was already bullshit. But it wasn't what really had me twisted.

I fucking liked her.

A lot.

Like, a whole lot.

Like, a "maybe you should stay forever" whole fucking lot.

Like, a "I can't say I love you because I barely know you but I'm pretty sure I do" entire goddamn motherfucking lot.

And now she was standing next to me, smelling like actual, literal heaven, studiously listening to the pastor go on. I probably should have been listening. But I was busy staring at the length of her neck, exposed and offered directly to me, thanks to her bun.

Except I couldn't touch her. Couldn't have her. Had to pretend.

Should have known that would backfire.

We shouldn't tell Cass, I'd insisted. What a fucking dick.

I'd said it was for Cass, and it was—girl was unglued and flapping looser by the day. It wouldn't have been pretty to tell her I was nailing her best friend, but she'd have been fine. Eventually. I was pretty sure. But then there were all the other things. Jessa's mother, who hated me on sight, who'd actually said out loud that I'd never see Jessa again. Jessa's departure, which was looming like a goddamn hurricane, creeping in at five miles an hour.

She didn't want to stay.

I didn't deserve to keep her.

She'd never stick around with a guy like me.

God, I had never been so fucking dumb as to fall for a Duchess.

My longing was a hot knife in the heart.

I'd spent all day thinking about what might have happened (Jesus Christ, she smells so good I could eat every inch of her right here in front of God and everybody). Her mom was my first thought—I couldn't imagine she did anything but warn Jessa off me, potentially with threats. Maybe she'd lose everything, her inheritance and good standing, or whatever else British ladies lost when they married beneath them. (I could wrap that loose lock of hair at her nape around my little finger—wait, married?)

I brushed the thought away, chalking it up to the goings-on around me and the almost empty flask in my coat pocket.

Cass had said something to her, she'd admitted that much. But I couldn't imagine what she could have possibly said that affected Jessa so much she *cried* in the bathroom when she talked about it. Sure, I'd been around. But it felt like cruel fucking sabotage that my own flesh would get in the way like this, with the one thing I actually gave a shit about.

Of course, she didn't know I gave a shit, which was probably part of the problem.

I'd considered just coming out and telling her, blowing the whole thing open. But I trusted Jessa, and she asked me for this. I knew she didn't want Hank. I knew she didn't want him the first time I ever saw them together, not for real. I'd gotten a hotter look from her right off the bat than I'd wager Hank had *ever* received. She *had* just seen my entire naked body, cock and all, but I wouldn't call that cheating. Maybe an unfair advantage, but I wouldn't have admitted it out loud.

I trusted her, I did. I was just mad as fuck about the whole thing, which was my God-given right.

Honestly, Hank was lucky he got out of that bar alive after putting his hands on her like he did. Don't even get me started on his bitchass mouth.

I really, really wanted a drink, but didn't think it'd go over big with the pastor to pull out a flask in front of Jesus's burden and all.

The second we were released for dinner, I took my first breath in twenty minutes, turned on my heel, and hauled ass toward the exit.

But I was stopped by a small hand in the crook of my elbow.

Goddamn. There she was, fresh as a fucking daisy, her

eyes all big and sad and shiny. She was wearing the zebra dress. I wanted to take it off her *real* bad.

She smiled. "Hey."

"Hey."

We stood there stupidly for a second. Her mouth opened, then closed, then opened again.

"How was your day?" she finally asked.

A laugh shot out of me. A couple of people turned to look.

"Did you just seriously ask me about my day?"

"Well—"

"It was fucking terrible, Jess. How about you?"

"Also terrible. I missed you. I spent all night thinking about you and us and everything, but I didn't have a second to myself to text you except half a message I typed out in the loo before Cass barged in."

I sighed. "I'm sorry."

"Why are you sorry? *I'm* sorry. I mucked the whole thing up."

"No you didn't."

"Yes I did."

"No you—"

She pinned me with a look.

"Okay, you mucked it up a little. But it's okay. I trust you, Jess. Whatever else there is, let's figure it out tomorrow. Okay?"

She opened her mouth to say something, but Cass interrupted, ignoring me.

Jessa sagged a little. I wanted to gather her up in my arms, smooth the lines between her brows, kiss her until she sighed for happy reasons and not . . . whatever this was.

I noticed Henry was looking around for her, and when he found her standing next to me, he looked furious.

I smirked, resisting the urge to kiss her like a porn star to see if he'd try to hit me again. This time, I'd let him. Otherwise, I couldn't hit him back.

276

And *God,* did I want to fucking hit him.

I raised a hand. "Hey, Hank. I got her—she's right here."

Cass glared at me as I took Jessa by the shoulders and turned her in his direction, leaning in close to her ear.

"The second I get you alone, Duchess, I'm gonna fucking wreck you. Get ready."

Her cheeks flushed, and a little shudder wiggled down her spine before I let her go.

"See ya at dinner!" I shouted at Henry. "I'll save you a seat."

He scowled. I laughed.

And then I left, seething.

39
abominable hankman

JESSA

DINNER WAS UNBEARABLE.

Henry holding my hand? Insufferable.

Cass watching us with more enthusiasm than she had for her own wedding? Abominable.

Remy watching from across the room with murder in his eyes? A little bit hot, if I was honest.

How drunk he was? Worrisome. Not because I cared how much he drank, but because I didn't know if he was all right or not. I suspected *not*.

Never in a hundred million years would I have imagined that Henry's affection would be so contemptible. But here I was, skin crawling, a false smile on my face, and not nearly enough champagne to get me through the evening unscathed.

Everyone was milling about The Filly with champagne flutes in hand, a table of appetizers set to the back of the room. I kept close to Cass's side, and Henry kept close to me, never letting me out of his reach. He wouldn't stop touching me either, as if I were a toy someone might steal if he happened to set me down. When we finally took our seats, I was grateful—there were fewer places he could hold on to me if we were sitting, and fewer places I could wander to, I supposed. Remy didn't sit with the wedding party. Instead, he took a seat back a ways with his mother. His eyes were a tangible tether—I could feel them on me no matter where I was or where I was looking.

I hated his torture. I'd have given anything to end his suffering and tell Cass the truth. My only hesitation was that the wedding had driven Cassidy Winfield clinically insane. Ship her off to the madhouse. Diagnosis: hysterical wedding jitters.

Last night, I'd laid in bed with Cass spooning me all night, staring at the ceiling while she snored softly in my ear, a common side effect of her drinking enough liquor to down a thoroughbred. And all I could think of was Remy.

Yesterday had been a whirl of drama and admissions. Public indecency. Jail. Learning my mother had nearly run off with her riding instructor. Cass digging in her heels about Remy, and for the sake of *his* heart even more than mine. Henry pursuing me. Remy's pain. Had it not been for all that, I knew exactly what I wanted and would have been able to answer him without hesitation when he asked me to stay.

Because I wanted desperately to stay, and for as long as he'd have me.

I no longer gave a damn if people thought we were crazy. Knowing he wanted me to stay was enough. The absolute last thing I wanted to do in the whole entire world was fly home.

I'd have gotten up right then in the middle of the night and texted Remy, but Cass had taken our phones and put them in her bedside table for some "phone detox" she and Davis had come up with. And apparently I had to suffer in solidarity. I tried to sneak off, but she wrapped her arms around me like a chimpanzee and muttered something unintelligible with cinnamon liqueur on her breath. I hadn't been exaggerating when I'd told Remy I couldn't even finish a text to him without her barging in on me. I hadn't had a moment to myself, even in the loo.

And then I was about to tell him at the church, but neither Cass nor Henry could stand for me to be within Remy's earshot. And now I didn't know when I'd have a chance to talk to him. But it would all be over soon. The second Cass didn't need me anymore, I'd find him. Which likely meant after the wedding. It wasn't the worst plan—we could resolve the whole matter as soon as she was down the aisle and preferably too drunk to land a hit. I could change my flight back and stay for a bit with Remy, call it an extended holiday. Everything would be all right.

In twenty-four hours, all would be well.

We just had to survive this blasted dinner.

Our first course had been delivered when Henry stood at my side, tapping his champagne glass with his knife.

Cass, Davis, and I turned to him, surprised and a little uncertain.

Cass wasn't the only one to go mad, it seemed. But she did hold the title of maddest.

"Good evening," Henry started, smiling brilliantly. He really was beautiful. Objectively, academically beautiful. "I hope no one minds if I say a few words. Don't worry, I'll save my speech for tomorrow night."

A little light laughter was all he got.

Unfazed, he looked down at me.

The hairs on the back of my neck stood on end. *Oh God. What's this? Please, don't do anything stupid.*

"I have had the pleasure of knowing Jessa and Davis for most of my life. Jessa and I were practically raised together, Davis and I met at Eton as boys. They were both vital to me, but it wasn't until quite recently that I realized just how much." He smiled at me. I wanted to melt into the floor and disappear. "Sometimes, the thing you want most has been right in front of you all along. All you have to do is say yes. So thank you, Jessa, for saying yes when I've been a fool for so long." He raised his glass to Davis and Cass. "May you say your yeses before it's too late, and may those yeses bring you all the happiness. Cheers!"

The crowd echoed, *"Hear, hear!"* and we took sips of our drinks. Cass and I shared a look that was really a conversation.

That was weird. Her eyebrows said.

Well, he's been a bit weird lately, hasn't he? I answered with the flick of my gaze in Henry's direction.

I don't know, I thought he really came to his senses recently. Her head cocked.

He's coming on a little strong though, don't you think? I asked with the narrowing of my eyes.

I think he's just enthusiastic, she said with a shrug and a sip of her champagne.

And then Henry interrupted our very important conversation with his very, very stupid lips. They pressed to mine gently, briefly, just enough to set my skin crawling and drop my heart before he took his seat again.

Oh my God. He's dead. He's a dead man. Everything will fall apart right here in front of Cass's entire family because Remy is going to tear Henry's limbs off and beat him to death with them.

With horror, I swiveled to the room, braced for a very large, very angry man to charge over the table and dismantle Henry.

But there was none.

In fact, Remy was nowhere to be found.

40
forget it
REMY

I WAS SO FUCKING MAD, I could barely see where I was going.

When Hank gave his stupid fucking toast and *fucking kissed her again (imgoingtokillhim)*, my vision had dimmed to a pinpoint, my ears ringing. I had the wherewithal to get up and leave the room before I punched that motherfucker's lights out and ruined Cass's wedding pictures.

I was chugging toward the door, nostrils flared like a bull, when I ran into Grace.

Literally. I didn't see her stepping out of the restroom hallway and slammed into her hard enough that she yelped and bounced off of me.

I grabbed her before she stumbled. "Whoa, there. I'm sorry, Mrs. Hastings. Are you all right?"

She blinked up at me for a second before straightening herself out and taking a step back. "Good lord, what in the world has gotten into you?"

My jaw muscles bounced when my teeth ground together. "Nothin'. Just need a little air."

Grace Hastings assessed me for a long moment, her eyes

calculating whatever puzzle she saw in me. "You're flustered over my daughter, are you?"

"Yes, ma'am. She tends to have that effect on me."

"You've made quite the impression on her. In fact, you've distracted her from her responsibilities and goals completely."

"Wasn't my intent," I answered honestly.

"It never is in times like these. How much would it take for you to walk away?"

I blinked. "Excuse me?"

"What's the number? "

My jaw was popping again, my fists balled up until my knuckles strained. "You don't have any idea who she is, do you? You've spent her whole life telling her what to do, robbing her of her choices. It must eat you up inside to think she'd make a decision on her own. Especially if that choice meant lowering her standards for me."

"Really, no number is out of the question," she said, otherwise ignoring me. "Use your imagination. Name your price."

My eyes narrowed as I leaned over her for a heartbeat.

"There aren't enough zeros," I said, brushing past her for the door.

I shoved it open so hard, it hit the wall, the glass wobbling in the frame.

I took two steps and turned into The Horseshoe, ripping off my tie as I stormed to the bar. Leo eyed me as I approached.

"You okay?"

"Whiskey," was all I said back.

He nodded and got to work.

I stood there fuming, planning all the ways I'd murder that limey bastard for kissing her again. All I could do about her mom was hate her.

"You got it bad too?" someone asked from my side.

STACI HART

Shocked, I blinked. "Wilder? What the hell are you doing here?"

"Judging by the look on your face, same thing as you."

My brow quirked as Leo set a shot on the bar. I took it to the dome and sat next to Wilder.

He looked miserable, hunched over a glass of scotch, eyes tired.

I jerked my chin at Leo for another drink. "You all right?"

"Nope. You?"

"Nope."

"Your duchess?"

"Who else? Thanks, Leo" I kicked back another shot and sucked my teeth. "Howabout a scotch?"

"You've got it," Leo answered.

I sighed. "It's a long story."

"I got time," Wilder said.

I scratched at my chin. "Well, I fucked up and fell for her."

"That's your long story?"

I shrugged. "I wasn't supposed to. In fact, I wasn't even sure I had a shot at a hookup. But then . . ." Another sigh.

And then I launched into the whole thing. It took me three fingers of scotch to explain how we were flirting, then playing chicken, then fake dating, then real dating, but everyone who mattered thought we were fake dating. How we were fucking with each other, then fucking each other, and then falling for each other. I told him about Hank and his bullshit, her mom and her audacity, Cass warning Jessa off me so hard, she'd nearly bolted. How Jessa didn't listen, because she never listened when it really mattered, and I loved that about her. I explained how Henry had somehow become the lynchpin in our relationship, and how she had to go on some stupid fucking date with him tonight so we wouldn't blow our cover. And how he'd kissed her. In front of me.

Twice.

Mostly, though, I talked about how I didn't want her to go.

284

Wilder spun his glass around slowly on the bar for a minute when I quit talking. George Strait crossed his heart and made promises to the girl he loved over the speakers, and I listened to the lyrics with my nose stinging.

"You're an idiot," he said.

"I know it."

"You shoulda agreed to tell Cass when Jessa wanted to."

"Yup."

"But you didn't want Cass to know, did you? That'd make it real."

I swallowed hard. What I didn't do was answer.

"Last time you had feelings, you got your heart curb stomped, so you figured it was easier to keep Jessa on the low than admit to yourself you were afraid."

"We've already agreed I'm an idiot. No need to prove any points."

"I mean, I get it. She's leaving. I'd be getting hammered too."

"She hasn't said she's leaving."

"Did she say she's staying?"

"No."

"I mean, why would she? Roseville doesn't have much to offer in the way of sophisticated living. Plus, sounds like her mom is pissed and her dad is going to hate you."

I gave him a look. "Who's side are you on?"

"Sorry, sorry. It's just that . . ." He sighed. "They're too good for the likes of us, Remy."

"I just don't know what I'm supposed to do. Beg her to stay? Go with her? Hell, I don't even know if she wants to see me again after the wedding. I asked her to stay last night and she said she needed to think about it, which is what people say when the answer is no but they don't want to let you down."

"If you want her to stay, then yeah. Get on your hands and knees like a dog and fucking beg her. Do whatever you have to do and lock her down or you'll lose her forever. Take it from somebody who knows."

I frowned, glancing at him. Jesus, he looked miserable. Forlorn and dejected and very drunk.

There was only one person he could have been so wretched over.

"Cass?" I breathed, stunned.

He nodded at his glass.

I gaped. All the girls Wilder went through, how calm he was around Cass? He hadn't mentioned her name to me in ages.

I hadn't even considered that he was still in love with her. But looking at him, I had no doubts.

"She's getting married tomorrow," he said. "In twenty-four hours, she'll have somebody else's name. She's on the other side of that wall right there, sitting next to the guy who did what I thought I had time to do myself. I shoulda locked her down. Don't be me, man. Don't ever be me when you can be you." He took a swig of his drink. "But we're not talking about me. We're talking about *you* and what you've gotta do to keep your girl."

"But, Cass—"

"*Nope. We're talking about you.*"

He looked like he might hit me, so I sighed, sagging. "She's leaving, man. I trust her, I do. I know she doesn't want that dickhead. But I tortured myself all night watching them together, and why? For her to leave and never look back? Her mama was right. I'm a bad influence and a worse catch. She'll come to her senses soon enough, and then I'll never see her again."

"How come?"

"Why would she ever come back here? She's an heir to a fortune. The daughter of a fucking Marquess, whatever the hell that is. She's somebody. And I'm nobody from nowhere,

slinging drinks at the only bar in town. She shouldn't stay—
it'd be the worst mistake of her life."

"But—"

"So I've got a plan. If you wanna hear it."

"All right," he said after a beat.

"I've got tomorrow night with her and most of the next
day. Plan is to get through the wedding and then try and stop
time long enough to get my fill. And then I'm gonna put her
on a plane and say goodbye."

"And why the fuck would you do that?"

"Because I think I might love her."

His brows drew together, his face screwed up in
confusion. "Then why the hell would you let her go?"

"Because I love her enough not to put what I want above
what's right for her."

Wilder sighed, shaking his head as he picked up his drink.
"You're gonna regret it, man."

"Maybe so. But it's still the right thing to do."

"If you fucking say so."

"I fucking say so. I've got a plan for tonight too. If you
wanna hear it."

"Let's have it."

"Leo—bring me that bottle of Johnny Walker, would you?
Thank you, sir." I poured Wilder a finger and poured myself
two. "And now, we're gonna get so blackout drunk, we forget
women ever existed."

41
carte blanche

JESSA

THE NIGHT WOULD NOT bloody end.

Dramatic as it was to say, I suffered through dinner with nine-tenths of my mind on Remy. Thoughts circled around in my brain—where he was, how he was, if there was any way for me to make it better. Which was a silly thought because I knew exactly the things that would make it better. I wished I was performing them instead of being subjected to Henry in this new and unflattering light.

At the moment, we were walking along the river downtown with Cass and Davis, though they'd pulled ahead of us. I watched with longing as the distance between us lengthened.

Henry was blathering about something and took my hand. I tried to retrieve it.

"Oh, sorry. I'm cold," I said in hopes of stuffing my hands in my pockets where he couldn't reach them.

"I'll warm you up," he answered with a smile, angling for my lips.

I backed away with an awkward squeak. "Henry, please stop."

He frowned. Really, it was more like a pout. "I . . . I thought this was what you wanted?"

I sighed heavily, squeezing his hand and pulling him toward a bench. "I thought so too," I said as I sat.

Henry sat next to me, the bench so small that we were arm to arm. "Is this about Remy?"

"Yes and no. Mostly, it's about how I don't think I love you after all."

"At . . . at all?"

"Well, of course as my friend. Though that word feels a bit thin, wouldn't you say?"

"I can't think of a better one either."

"I know I've left you in a lurch with your father and how anxious he is for you to settle down, but I . . . I just don't think it can be me anymore. And I don't think *you* think it should be me, either. You don't love me, Henry. Not the kind of love required to maintain a marriage."

He was looking at my hand threaded in his. "No, Bits. I don't. You're right. And truthfully I don't know if I'll ever truly make my father happy. Do you know why he wants so badly for me to get married? Why he's leveraged my inheritance on it?"

My brows knitted together. "Because he wants you to prove you're serious?"

He shook his head, his eyes down. "Because he . . . he found out I-I'm . . ."

I laid my other hand on top of ours, my heart tight. "Henry, it's all right. What is it?"

He finally lifted his gaze, his crystalline eyes meeting mine with a depth of sadness I couldn't fathom. "Because I'm gay, Bits."

A cold tingle spread across my cheeks and hands, my breath catching, my mind racing.

"You're . . ."

He nodded, looking back at our hands. "He caught me,

you see. I'd brought a friend home on holiday, no one else knew. No one else *knows* other than the men I've been with. I've never . . . I've never said it out loud before. But Father . . . I suppose this is his way of wedging me into whatever life he designs."

"How long have you known?"

One shoulder rolled in a shrug as he played with our fingers. "Always, I suppose. I'm sorry to string you on all this time. You were the only chance I had at being happy *and* fulfilling my duties. Because I do love you, Jessa. I even thought we'd be quite happy together—who wouldn't want to marry such a good friend? But it isn't fair to you. I thought if I could buy myself a bit of time, another answer would present itself. It didn't hurt to have you around in front of my father, either."

I shook my head to clear it, my supper creeping its way up my throat. "So you used me."

"I was sure I had it sorted. A happy ending would fall into place for all of us with a neat little click. But I don't think I'll have mine after all. I certainly can't stand in the way of your happiness. It was easier when you didn't have someone else."

"So your jealousy of Remy was simply because you saw your opportunity fade?"

"Truly, Jessa—I fucking hate him and would rather see you with a number of predatory wild animals," he said on a sad sort of laugh. "I had committed to you in my mind—you were mine. You were the key to my future happiness, and he stood in the way. So in that sense, yes. But I was genuinely terrified he'd take advantage of you. Hurt you. I never want to see you hurt."

"Unless it suits you."

A sad sigh. "It wasn't fair. I know it wasn't fair. I'm sorry. Can you forgive me?"

I searched the jumbled up feelings in my chest, trying to assess the mess. All these years, he'd used me. He knew how

I felt and kept me on the back burner just in case. He'd lied in that sense, gravely. He'd hurt me profoundly. I'd been but a pawn and wondered briefly if I knew him at all. If he truly loved me in any way.

As appalled as I was by what he'd done, though, I also understood him. As hurt as I was, as much as I mourned the years I'd spent waiting on him, I was also hurt for him, for his secret. My childhood friend who had been living a lie for so long. I mourned with him for the happiness he'd never have if he wanted a future with his family and estate.

Beneath it all, I didn't think anything could stop me loving him.

"Eventually, I think so," I admitted. "But I'll need time."

"Of course. Have I hurt you very badly, Bits?"

I laughed. "By lying to me our whole lives and promising me to be your beard for the rest of mine? Yes, Bobs, I've been quite betrayed. But . . . well, I'll be all right. More all right than if you'd told me this a few weeks ago, certainly."

"Because you have him now."

"Yes. But that's been its own challenge, hasn't it? Between you, Mother, and Cass, there've been quite a few obstacles." I sighed. "I fell for him anyway, though. And now I'll have to face it all if I want to stay."

"You're staying?"

A smile spread on my face, slow as dawn. "For a little bit. Longer, if all works out."

"So tonight with me was . . ."

"An appeasement for Cassidy's sake. We were planning to tell her once the wedding was through. Didn't want to upset her. She's gone batty."

"Completely mental."

"I'm desperate to tell Remy—he doesn't even know I've chosen to stay. We haven't had a chance to talk at all without a gaggle of people around."

STACI HART

He watched me for a moment. "You really care for him, don't you?"

"I really do."

"He *is* a handsome bastard. I loathe the poor bugger, but I can see the appeal." A pause. "Think you might . . . love him?"

"I think I might. If not now, then soon."

Henry stood, tugging my hand to pull me up. "Come on. You should go."

"I can't just leave Cass—"

"Yes you can. Cassidy will survive without you. He must be going mad not knowing. And with me"—his face opened up with regret—"oh, God. Oh, God, I'm sorry."

"It's not as if you knew. And anyway, she expects me to stay with her tonight."

He took me by the shoulders, hunching to look me in the eye. "Cass will be fine, darling. Please, go and ease that man's suffering."

I glanced at Cass and Davis. "Really?"

"Go! But wait!" He pulled me into his chest and squeezed. "Thank you, Bits. For everything. I love you, you know."

I wrapped my arms around his waist and breathed him in one last time. "I love you too, Bobs."

And then I took off in the direction of Main Street, reaching blindly into my handbag for my phone.

"*Jessa!*" Cass screeched. "Where are you going?"

"I'll tell you later!" I shouted over my shoulder.

"Tell me now!" She started after me.

"I've got to find Remy!"

"*Why do you have to find Remy, Jessa?*"

"Because I might be in love with him!"

At that, she took off running in my direction, but Henry caught her and held onto her. I would have felt bad sticking Henry with the task of explaining, but he owed me.

I took off my shoes and ran to The Horseshoe, texting

Remy and praying I didn't trip, but he wasn't at the bar and I didn't see his truck anywhere on Main Street. I paused, panting, scanning the street as I tried to sort out what to do. It wasn't as if Roseville had Uber. I texted Remy again. Still nothing. Called—went straight to voicemail.

"*Damn!*" I hissed, stomping a foot.

"Uh, you okay?"

I turned to find Shelby, one of the softball coaches, eyeing me.

"Oh, thank goodness. Could I beg you for a ride somewhere?"

"Of course," she answered. "Where to?"

"Would you take me to Remy's?"

One of her brows rose.

"I swear, I'll answer any question you have on the way."

Now both brows were up. "Anything at all?"

"Anything you want."

"Well, what are you waiting for? Hop in." She was already heading for her truck.

"Oh, thank you, thank you, thank you," I said as I trotted to the passenger side and climbed in.

In the few minutes it took to get to the cottage, Shelby was able to ask a startling number of questions, none of them appropriate and all of them amusing. It seemed Remy was a man of mystery to most, but I had every answer. And I discovered I'd come to know him much better than I thought. A comforting realization, considering I was practically about to move in with him.

My heart was in my throat as we pulled into the drive, but when we rounded the bend to the clearing, my heart slid into my lap.

His Scout wasn't there.

I bit my bottom lip so I wouldn't cry, not even knowing why I was about to cry. Only that I was desperate to see him and he wasn't here, and that was the absolute *worst*.

Shelby glanced at me. "Want me to take you back to Cass's?"

"No, that's all right. I'm sure he'll be back any time now. Or maybe he'll answer his phone. Hopefully."

"Hmm. Well, let me give you my number. I'll come get you if you need anything, okay?"

"Thank you. Thank you so much, Shelby." I launched myself at her for a hug, and she hugged me back, chuckling.

"Well, aren't you enthusiastic."

We exchanged numbers, and I climbed out of her truck to head inside, grateful the front door was unlocked, although off the top of my head, I knew exactly which windows were likely open, should I need to shimmy in. The house was dark and quiet, so I flipped on a lamp. Beau didn't even bark, just trotted in, yawning and stretching before nuzzling my hand.

"Hello, Beau. I missed you too."

It smelled like Remy everywhere, I knew because I made my way through the house like I hadn't seen it in a decade. His shoes by the door. His coffee mug in the sink. The kitchen island where I'd been fucked silly. The blessed dryer, topped with fresh towels. The saggy sofa I wouldn't let him sleep on. The missing shower tile where the pipe had burst. The fresh patch on the roof over the bed I'd first slept in.

And then I was in his room.

I could picture him there, twisted in the sheets in the dark. And before I knew it, that was where I was—curled up in his bed, hugging his pillow, waiting for him to come home so I could tell him I wanted to stay.

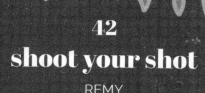

42
shoot your shot
REMY

MY HEAD HAD BEEN SPLIT open like a melon. It had to have been.

I cracked my eyelids and groaned, closing them again as I tried to figure out where I was. Based on the millisecond of a glance I'd gotten, and the fact that I'd started the whole ordeal off with Wilder, I figured we were at his place.

I braved another glance, shielding my eyes.

"*Faaahhhck,*" I groaned again, the contents of my skull sloshing around when I sat up. The heel of my delusional hand pressed into one eye socket in an effort to stop the thrumming.

Jessa's face slid into my mind, and I sighed. This whole fucking thing was such a mess, and I'd done it to myself. The second I first saw her, I knew it would be a mess, but I couldn't help myself. I wasn't even upset about it. I'd do it again in a heartbeat if it meant I got to have her.

I'd do it twice if it meant I got to keep her.

My phone was on the coffee table, dead as a brick. Next to it was a glass of water I'd had the foresight to get but not drink, and I snatched it, guzzling it down. I still had my shoes on, and my back was stiff from sleeping on the couch, but I figured with a little ibuprofen and a couple more glasses of water, I'd be right as rain.

Last night came back to me in flashes at first, then waves as I remembered everything in reverse. Slamming shots with Wilder on his back deck around his fire pit—*shit, did we put the fire out?* I got up and checked, relieved to see we had. The bar had happened, I'd told him my whole sob story, and he admitted—

Oh God, he's still in love with Cass.

"Faaahhhck," I whispered, dragging a hand through my hair. He had it so much worse than me. At least I had hope.

He was fucked.

Let's see, Jessa's mom tried to bribe me, and I was mad because—

Instantly, my body coiled up like a bag of snakes at the memory of Henry kissing Jessa again.

It's fine. She doesn't want him. She wants me. Even though she's leaving. And she sees Hank all the time. But it's fine. She wants me. I think.

I filled up my glass and downed the water, looking at the time.

My sleepy eyes shot open.

"Faaahhhck!" I was late. Not too late, there was time. But the bridesmaids were all set to be at the church with Cass at nine and I'd have to shift if I was going to get myself together and to the bridal suite.

Heading for the door, I patted my pockets—keys in the front and wallet in the back—snagging my deadass phone on my way out. It was a gorgeous day, perfect for a wedding. Not a cloud in the sky and the weather mild. I was glad I had the forethought to leave the top on the Scout. My eyeballs might have exploded from the sun exposure.

I rolled through everything I had to do this morning as I plugged my phone into the ancient charger hanging from the cigarette lighter port and got going. Showering, that was the big thing. Had to get my tux on and pick up coffee for everybody. My job today was errand boy/messenger, tasked with serving the ladies of the bridal party.

At least Jessa would be there.

My stomach lurched—I didn't know whether it was anticipation or whiskey. Bit of both, probably.

I needed to hear how the rest of the night went with that motherfucker Hank. I also needed to touch her and wondered if there was somewhere we could sneak off to before I starved to death for her.

I also wondered if she'd decided whether or not to stay.

My stomach lurched so hard this time, I almost ralphed.

If she didn't stay, I didn't know what I'd do. Scrounge up money to buy a ticket to England? If she even wanted me to come. If she even wanted to see me.

It was driving me crazy, the not knowing. But I'd rather get twisted for a minute than lose her forever. Hell, she could take all the time she wanted if it meant there was a chance.

I'd have done just about anything for a chance. That was all. Just a shot.

I couldn't remember the last time I'd taken one. Who knew—maybe the universe would do me a solid.

Maybe I'd even make it.

She was all I could think about as I drove to the house, pulled into the drive. Walked in, wishing she was there. I didn't know how lonely it was here until I didn't have her, and now I could barely stand to be there for the silence.

I sighed, reaching between my shoulder blades to grab my shirt and pull it off as I walked into my room and—

I froze, shirt half off, staring.

Maybe I was hallucinating.

Maybe I was still drunk.

Jessa couldn't really be asleep in my bed.

She was curled up in a ball around one of my pillows, her golden hair spilled across another. And she was still wearing that zebra dress with all the stripes on it that hurt my brain.

I fucking loved it.

My heart kickstarted to life in my chest. I tore my shirt off and threw it as I crawled into bed, caging her beneath me—she stirred at the contact before her eyes popped open and she gasped through a smile.

"You're here," she said, her voice raspy. Her hand cupped my face.

"You're in my bed."

"It smells like you." She moaned, her eyes rolling back in her head. "I can hardly stand it."

"Goddammit, I missed you." My lips were just a few inches from hers, my hands bracketing her face.

"I missed you too. I . . . I have things to tell you." She was smiling.

I was smiling. "Tell me you're gonna stay."

She tipped her head and laughed. "I'm gonna stay."

I breathed for the first time in days. "Oh, thank God."

And I crashed into her like a tidal wave. We were a crushing of lips, a tumbling of tongues. Hands seeking, hearts happy.

I didn't think I'd been so happy in my whole life.

I breathed her like I was suffocating, noisy and greedy and relieved. And then we were a tangle of arms and legs and stripes.

She giggled, breaking the kiss, but my lips kept themselves busy tasting the skin on her collarbone.

"We've gotta go, Jess," I said, palming her breast.

"Oh, what time is—oh!" she breathed when I flexed my hips into hers.

"Late. It's late. But I'll go crazy if I can't touch you all day."

"Well, I think maybe you can. Touch me all day, that is. Church appropriately, of course."

I lifted my head with a question on my face.

"I might have told Cass last night."

I froze. "You . . . told her?"

She nibbled her bottom lip, toying with my hair. "I was so excited, I sort of . . . blurted it out."

"And how did she take it?" My hips rolled on their own. I had no self-control.

"Mmm. Mmhmm. Well, Henry caught her before she could maul me. I ran straight for you, but I couldn't find you."

I put enough space between us to get her pussy in my palm. "I was at Wilder's. Jesus, Jess—you're drenched."

"I missed you—" She gasped when I stroked her through her panties. "Shelby gave me a ride, but you weren't here. So Beau and I fell asleep waiting."

"My phone was dead. We should be glad—if I'd known you were here, I'd have been too drunk for anything gentle."

"Oh. Think you'll get drunk tonight?" she asked hopefully.

I laughed. "Whatever you want, Duchess. But I can throw you around drunk or not, if you want me to."

"I want you to."

"Deal. But not now. We're on a timeline, darlin." I knelt to pull her panties off.

"I'm so tired of timelines. Come here." She opened her arms, and I filled them, gazing down into her face.

"Well, we don't really have one after today, do we?"

"Depends. How long do you want me to stay?" she asked.

"Forever," I said, kissing her gently. Gentle turned into determined, and that turned into something hot and rough. She bit my lip as we parted.

"God, I love this fucking dress," I mumbled, running a hand down her ribs. "Take it off."

"Would you help me?" She propped herself up and twisted. "The zipper's back—"

"Oh, fuck it," I said and ducked under her skirt.

She giggled. "Remy wait, take off my—*oh!* Oh." She sighed, melting beneath me as I ravaged her pussy. But it wasn't enough just to taste her. I wanted to drown. I slid my arms under her thighs and rolled over until the weight of her was pressed against my mouth. She yelped in surprise, then moaned, riding my face while I gripped her thighs. I couldn't breathe, didn't want to. Added *smothered by Jessa's cunt* to my short list of preferred ways to go. She somehow managed to get her dress off, and thank God—with it gone, I could look up her body, past her tight nipples, up the column of her neck to the base of her jaw. She propped her hands on the mattress above my head, brows drawn, lips parted. I knew that look—she was close. So I loosened my grip and let her lead as she fucked my face, licking and sucking to the rhythm of her body. And then she sped up. Her body went tight, her pussy went tight, and then she exploded in a burst, a cry, a gasping moan as she came all over my tongue.

She sagged—I flipped her over and climbed up her body.

"Later, I'm taking my time with you," I started, unbuttoning my jeans. "But we've gotta go, Duchess."

Jessa mewled, struggling to free me as I pulled my pants over my ass. We both sighed when my cock was in her hands, then dipped in her pussy, then sheathed inside of her. For a second, I couldn't move. She was too tight, she was too beautiful. She was here. She was staying.

She was *mine*.

I took her mouth as I took her cunt, thrusting my hips with her legs tucked into my ribs, my fingers tangled in her hair. She was warm and wet and whispering in my ear, the sting of her nails on my back sweet as she spurred me on. The tug deep in my belly set a prickling across my skin, squeezed my lungs, dimmed my vision. Pulled me deeper.

Stopped my heart.

I went blind, my vision flashing, ass pumping, cock

throbbing, pouring myself into her drop by drop until I was empty, and she was full.

I collapsed onto her, slick with sweat and trembling. It was all too much. And it wasn't enough. And she was everything.

And she was mine.

I kissed her so deep, I knew she knew it, too. And when my heart had slowed enough to function without having a heart attack, I broke the kiss.

"We've gotta go," I said before kissing her again.

She whined into my mouth.

"Cass is getting married today."

Her eyes widened, and she blinked. "Shit. We're late."

I laughed. "We're so late."

"And she knows."

My smile fell instantly. "Shit."

"Yeah. We need to shower."

I pulled out of her and climbed out of bed, then picked her up before she had a chance to get up.

"Come on. We'll get cleaned up, get to the church, and let her yell at us."

"I really, really wish we had more time," she said as I set her down next to the tub.

I smiled at her, lifting her chin with my thumb and forefinger. "Duchess, we've got all the time in the world."

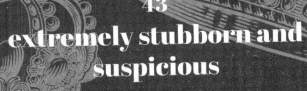

43
extremely stubborn and suspicious

JESSA

REMY and I stood hand-in-hand outside the church, staring at the massive wooden doors.

"Think she'll throw anything?" he asked.

"No. We're taking photos too soon for her to risk hitting one of us in the face. I wonder what Henry told her?"

He stared at me. "You let *Hank* tell her?"

"Well, yes because . . . oh!" I'd forgotten he didn't know. "Oh." I'd forgotten I couldn't tell him. "Trust me, Henry is not an issue for you."

His face quirked. "How can you be so sure?"

"Because . . . of reasons I can't share because it's not my secret. You *do* trust me, don't you?"

Remy sighed, but he was smiling. "I do."

"Good. I promise, he told her the right thing. He owes me. Come on," I said, tugging him toward the doors before he could ask more questions. "Time to face the music."

We followed the sound of the noisy cousin bridesmaids, my heels clicking on the terra cotta tile of the old church floor, my silky nude pink dress swishing and my hand sweating in Remy's. Or maybe his was sweating. Either way, our hands were damp as we approached the bridal suite and stood stupidly again, staring at it.

My heart thumped painfully.

"You scared?" he asked.

"A little. You?"

"A little. But I have you. Everything else feels easy."

I stretched to kiss him, and he bent to meet me, our lips connecting sweetly, briefly. And with a heavy sigh from both of us, we walked through the door to hell.

The room was an explosion of shades of nude fabric and talking girls, many of them teens. Makeup and shoes and bags were scattered about the room and every surface, and every seat was occupied with another cousin with red hair and freckles. One of them was playing "End Game" on a small speaker, and two of them sang along at the top of their lungs. Aptly, I might add, as they went on about the size of our reputations and conversations and what they'd heard about us.

Cass turned in her chair, one half of her head in big velcro rollers and the other half looking like a bird's nest. She was a silent storm with wild eyes.

Terror struck me. I glanced around for anything she could use as a weapon and noted too many hot curling irons for my comfort.

"You're late," she said too calmly as she stood. Her eyes cut to Remy's hands. First the empty one, then the one occupied by my hand. "And you forgot the coffee."

He swore under his breath. "I'll go get it right now. I'm sorry, Cass."

"*AH—*" It was more punctuation than a word that left her, her finger pointing at him when he took a step toward the door. "Don't you move, traitor. And *you*." She turned on me. "You lied to me. You've *been* lying to me."

I swallowed hard. "I know. I'm sorry. You made me promise—"

"That's right. You *promised.* I told you the truth, and you promised, and the whole time you were lying to me. And poor Henry—"

"Henry does not want me," I said as definitively as I could.

"Why, because he said so? That idiot doesn't know what he wants," Cass said, laughing like a maniac.

"All right, then you should know I don't want him."

"How do you go your whole life loving one man only to change your mind when you meet my stupid cousin?"

Three of the girls said, "*Hey!*" then giggled. Cass ignored them.

"And *you,*" she said, her finger out again as she took a step in Remy's direction. "This is your fault. I told you to leave her alone. You swore you'd leave her alone, Remy! And now? Now you're holding hands, and she refused Henry, and you like each other. Look at you! You *really* like each other." The pitch of her voice climbed, her madness made wilder by the chaotic nature of half of her hair. "Your mother is here, and she's going to take you away. You're going to leave, and he likes you, and *I can't believe you two did this to me behind my back!*"

"Hold on, Cass—we didn't do anything to you," Remy said, which was a mistake.

Her cheeks were red, her nostrils flared like she was going to exhale fire and smoke. White shone all around her eyes when she turned them on Remy. He was so startled, he took a step back when she took one forward.

"You lied to me, you dirty liar."

"Cass," I tried to interject.

"Don't you dare Cass me, Jessa! It's my wedding day and you're late and you're sleeping with Remy and you don't love Henry and—" Her brows clicked together. She touched her cheek with her fingertips. "Why am I crying? Is my face broken? Did you break my face on my wedding day too?"

"Cass!" I took the opportunity to close the space between us and took her by the shoulders, hoping I could stop her from smacking me if things went in that direction. "Cass, I'm not leaving."

She blinked. "What?" Her voice sounded small.

"Darling, I'm not leaving. I'm going to stay with Remy." I looked back, extending a hand for him. He stepped up and took it. "You're right, we do really like each other. Really, *really* like each other. I can't leave. I don't know what I'd even do with myself but be miserable."

"But your mother—"

"Sod my mother."

"But what will your dad—"

"Sod Father too."

"Even if they take your inheritance?"

"Cassidy, I have a degree from Oxford. I can find a job, and I'm perfectly capable of working. You've spent so much time worrying about what Remy and I would do to each other, but you never considered the possibility of us being exactly what the other needs."

"Because it's ludicrous." She laughed.

"Absolutely deranged."

"Completely demented." She snorted, firing up even thicker laughter.

"Totally mad, Cass."

"Mad for each other," Remy added.

The cousins went "*Awww!*"

For a moment, she took us both in wistfully. "You're really serious?"

"As a fucking heart attack," Remy answered.

"Remington Winfield," Cass's mom snapped. "You are in the house of God."

"Sorry, Aunt Jenny."

But Cass's eyes were all shiny and big and her smile all bent up as she tried not to cry. "My best friend and my cousin might be even better than Henry. I hate you two so much," she said, reaching for us both to pull us into a hug. "Don't ever lie to me again."

"Never," we promised.

When she let us go, she wiped her face and sniffled. Crazy Aunt Julie supplied a tissue out of thin air and put it in Cass's hand.

"You," Cass said, nodding at Remy, "Go get us coffee." She blew her nose with a honk.

"Yes, ma'am. Text me your order," he said, touching the small of my back and pressing a kiss to my temple before he left.

"You," Cass said again, this time hooking her arm in mine to pull me toward the vanities, "Come sit next to me and get your hair done while you tell me *everything*."

One of my brows arched. "Everything?"

"Not that. Please, God, not that. Everything else."

I pulled her to a stop. "Cass, I really am so sorry."

She assessed me for a beat. "Last night, you said you might be in love with him. Is that true?"

"It's absolutely absurd. Perfectly preposterous. Infinitely insane. And yes, I very well might be."

She launched herself at me, throwing her arms around mine, and I circled mine around her waist, noting that she was crying again.

"Please, don't cry."

"I love you, Jessa. Take care of each other so I can retire my hit list, okay?"

"Okay," I agreed on a laugh. "I love you too."

She let me go, taking a step back to look at me. "And if you ever talk like Mary Poppins again, I'll slap you."

44
something borrowed, something blue

JESSA

I STOOD at the back of the murmuring pairs of bridesmaids and groomsmen outside the chapel, waiting for our turn in the procession.

It had turned into the absolute best day.

Henry smiled at me from my side, patting my hand in the crook of his arm. A glance over my shoulder bought me a smile from Remy. He looked so absolutely magnificent in his tuxedo, his handsome jaw freshly shaven and hair neatly combed. The fit was immaculate, highlighting the breadth of his shoulders and the taper of his waist, not to mention that ridiculous arse of his.

Resplendent suit.

I couldn't wait to take it off of him.

Cass's hand was hooked in his elbow. She looked terrified —white as a sheet, eyes wide, lips thin—but that seemed to be her default of late. I hoped once a ring was on her finger in a few minutes, she'd feel much better and we could celebrate properly.

There was so much to celebrate.

I was going to stay for a while. Remy and I would have a chance at something here together. Cass knew, and Remy and

I both still had a pulse. Henry had told me the truth, effectively ending any lingering expectations.

And today, our best friends were getting married.

The deacon nodded to us, and Henry and I began the walk to the pulpit. I caught sight of my mother, the only one in the chapel wearing a hat, and certainly the only one who'd wear a hat with a feather out the top of it. A stern, disappointed look hardened her eyes when our gazes met, though she wore the appropriate smile. The reminder that I had yet to tell her my plans wobbled my stomach, but I was an adult. It would all work out, I was sure of it.

But then I noticed Wilder.

My heart jolted when he turned to look past us to Cass, his face carefully schooled. But there was a flicker of grief behind his eyes that sent the hairs on my arms on end. I longed to know what he was thinking and prayed it wasn't about doing anything stupid.

Really, the next twenty minutes couldn't come fast enough.

Henry deposited me in my spot and kissed my cheek before taking his place, and then the music changed.

Remy and Cass stepped into the aisle as the whole church turned in their pews. They wore wistful smiles, their eyes shining, some of them crying, some of them with their fingertips to their lips.

Cass looked spectacular, and she'd found a smile, even if she was clutching Remy's arm like she was about to drown. I frowned when I saw she was crying a little.

And it wasn't an I'm-so-happy-I'm-marrying-the-love-of-my-life kind of cry.

Davis stepped forward to receive her, shaking Remy's hand. Cass hugged her cousin and pressed a kiss to his cheek before taking Davis's hand and stepping up to the preacher.

The preacher began to speak of love and marriage as Remy took his place next to me and settled in, smoothing his coat front and smiling at me so brilliantly, I forgot for a moment that I was worried about Cass. I couldn't discern from the back of her how she was feeling, but Davis's concerned expression didn't give me any confidence. The wait was eternal.

"Cassidy Winfield and Davis McGrath, do you stand here together today to give yourselves to each other in marriage?"

"I do," they said.

The preacher looked out over the crowd with an amused smile. "If anyone knows a reason these two should not be joined in holy matrimony, speak now or forever hold your peace."

I held my breath. Cass looked back at the church pews, and so did I, finding Wilder immediately.

"I object."

Wilder's lips hadn't moved.

The sound had come from one of the groomsmen.

From *Henry*.

Gasps and murmurs rippled through the crowd. Remy tensed from behind me—we'd all turned to face Henry. He stepped out of line, his chin lifted proudly, his breath shallow, judging by the quick rise and fall of his chest.

He was in love with Cass. He'd lied to me about everything because he was in love with—

"Davis, I can't let you do this. You have to tell her. She can't marry you until she knows."

Davis's face broke in anguish, his chin trembling, hand shifting as if to reach for Henry, but he dropped it again.

Cass's voice was quiet, hard, and trembling all at once. "What's going on?"

Henry's Adam's apple bobbed with a hard swallow. "I've been in love with Davis since Eton, and he's been in love with me."

"Henry—" Davis started.

"No!" Henry snapped. "No more. It ends now." He turned

back to Cass, completely broken. "We've been together since high school, Cass. We've always been together."

A pink flush crept from the top of her sweetheart neckline and bloomed on her cheeks. "You . . . what?" She turned to Davis. "Is that . . . is he . . . he can't be. You can't be. Oh my God, Davis. *Oh my God!*" And then she was crying and screaming and beating Davis with her bouquet. Flower heads popped off and flew into the air like shrapnel until Remy grabbed her, held her. She sagged in his arms, sobbing.

My shock was total. My devastation for Cass was absolute.

In my periphery, I saw Wilder stand, but Remy shook his head. Wilder just watched Cass, looking torn.

"How could you?" she rasped. "How could you do this to me?"

Davis shook his head—he was crying too. "Cass, I—" his voice broke. "I love you."

"You love *him!*"

He looked older in that moment. Now that the burden had been lifted, the toll it had taken was plain as day.

"Yes. I love him too."

Cass wailed, twisting in Remy's arms to bury her face in his chest, and he gathered her up protectively, glowering at Henry.

"Say yes. Choose me. I'll give it all up. Just say the word."

Davis stepped into Henry. "Yes," he breathed.

Henry caught his face, their lips colliding, the pain on their faces etched deep in the furrows of their brows, the tears on their cheeks. It was a meeting of hearts and souls long quieted, grave and urgent.

Several women cried out, people began to talk and stand and gasp. Crazy Aunt Julie stood, then immediately fainted into a little bubble of chaos as the people nearby tried to catch her. Others marched directly out.

Davis and Henry were forehead to forehead, whispering

to each other. The preacher gaped, staring as his glasses slowly slid down his nose. A couple of men started to march violently toward them, and Remy passed Cass to me on the way to intercept.

I could barely hold her up, her body shaking with sobs, her face in the crook of my neck as if she could hide there. Her mother was instantly at her other side.

"Come on, let's get you somewhere you can have a moment, shall we?" I asked, already heading toward the bridal suite.

"How could he do this?" she asked, her voice rough and broken. "Always. They-hey've *always* been . . . they've b-been —" A fresh wail slipped out of her.

Jenny and I shared a concerned look and hurried her back. We had her sitting down a moment later with a box of tissues. When Remy entered, it was with a bottle of Johnny Walker. He uncorked it and handed it over without preamble. She took it silently and tipped it for a long drink, coughing when she came up for air.

"Want me to kill him?" Remy asked.

"Yes, please." She blew her nose with a honk.

"Cass!" Davis called from the hallway, past Wilder, who stood watch in the open doorway. "Cassidy, please. Please, talk to me."

"Fuck off, asshole!" she shrieked, crying again.

Her mother's lips flattened, but she said nothing about the swearing.

Wilder's hand on Davis's chest barred him from entry. "What do you want me to do with him, Cass?"

"Murder him. There's a graveyard out back." She brought the bottle to her lips and swallowed three times before she set it back down. But then she hinged, the back of her hand pressed to her mouth. "I think . . . I think I'm gonna be sick." She dry heaved, giving me long enough to put a small wastebasket in her lap. She wrapped her arms around it and vomited.

"Please," Davis begged, broken. "You have to let me—"

"I don't *have* to let you do anything," Wilder said through his teeth.

Cass panted into the bin for a moment before sitting up, eyes closed, hand on her stomach. "Let him in," she finally said.

Wilder's eyes narrowed. "You sure?"

"Mhmm." Her hand migrated from stomach to mouth. Her eyes were still closed.

Jenny had been rubbing a slow circle on her back. "Honey, what do you want us to do? We can stay with you."

"No. No one should be here for this. Tell Jesus to put on his earmuffs, okay?"

We filed out, Jenny first, Remy last, and the look on his face must have been something else, because Davis blanched.

And then he slipped into the bridal suite and closed the door behind him.

45
the cluster to my fuck

REMY

WILDER AND I had our ears pressed up against the door.

"Can you hear anything?" I asked.

"I think she threw something a second ago. Pretty sure I heard her yell *dickhead* too."

"Get away from there," Aunt Jenny said, swatting my arm. "You should be ashamed of yourself. You too, Wilder. Get." She shooed us away from the door and into the small crowd that had gathered outside the bridal suite that included Annie, all the cousins, and a couple of groomsmen. The rest, it seemed, had left.

Henry was a little bit down the hall, leaning against the wall looking fucking miserable.

I slipped my hands into my pockets and made my way over to him. When I was leaning against the wall next to him, I said, "Heya, Hank."

"Come to gloat?"

I shook my head. "I think I get it now. Annie, Jessa? Did you bring Annie here just to piss Davis off?"

He nodded.

"And the whole show you made of Jess, and you kept kissing her—I swear to God you're lucky to be alive—Davis

313

was always right there. You wanted to make him rethink his choices."

"It worked too, once he saw Jessa and me together. He was livid last night. I thought . . . I thought he'd tell Cass and have it done once and for all. But of course he didn't."

"So you outed him in front of God and everybody?"

"I didn't know what else to do." He scrubbed his hand over his face. "Cass needed to know before she married him, don't you think?"

"Sure, but I can't agree that objecting to her wedding was your best move."

He sighed, and it seemed to add years to him. "This was always the plan. He would marry Cass, I would marry Jessa. We could be together all the time. It was going to be perfect."

"That's fucked, man. You were going to use them?"

"Davis loves Cass, and I love Jessa. I'd happily have a family with her, and I like to think I'd have made her happy too. But I'm in love with Davis. I always have been. And last night, our grand scheme came apart. Jessa couldn't marry me. She fell in love with you."

Something climbed up my throat and stuck there.

"I won't pretend to understand, but it's true. She no longer wants me. When she did, it felt like . . . permission. But she doesn't."

"I'd like to say I'm sorry about ruining your plans, but fuck you."

He nodded. "Get married to Jessa, or lose my family. My legacy and inheritance. Today, I made that choice. I'd rather have nothing than lose him."

"I know the feeling."

A ruckus came from the other end of the hallway and Davis's parents stormed around the corner. Well, his dad stormed. His mom was running behind him, trying to snag his arm, saying "*Andrew!*" over and over, like the number of times he heard his name was crucial to stopping him.

314

Judging by the look on his face, *nothing* was stopping him.

"You! How dare you!" he shouted, purple-faced, fist cocked.

I grabbed him, but the little fucker twisted, slipping out of my grip before throwing himself at Henry fist first.

Shock had Hank's guard down—he took the whole force of it straight to the nose. A sick crunch preceded a burst of blood down his mouth and chin and the front of his tuxedo.

I'd already grabbed pops, wrenching his arms behind him. "Easy there. Can't run around hitting everybody who makes you mad."

"Like hell I can't! That queer turned my son! Kissed him *in a house of God!* He's ruined *everything. Everything!*"

I pulled his arms so tight, he called out, arching his back to ease the pressure. "Hank here had it coming, but not from you, and not for that."

The door to the bridal suite flew open and Davis dashed out, fear painted all over him. He rushed to Henry, handing him a pocket square before taking Hank's face in his hands.

"What did he do to you? God, I'm sorry. I'm so sorry. I shouldn't have forced your hand, Henry. Forgive me. Please, forgive me." They were forehead to forehead again, and I thought they might be crying, and they weren't the only ones. Half of everybody in the hallway was sniffling and dabbing at their noses.

The other half was glaring at Andrew.

Davis wheeled around and marched up to his father, his face twisted with spite, furious tears stacked on his lower lids. "Why did I ever put on a show for you? Why did I care so much what you'd think of me, what you'd say?" His laugh was dry and bitter. "You abandoned me at Eton, left me with Henry for the summers. I didn't even know if you'd show up today, on my *wedding* day. So maybe you should take your part of the blame for all this. Part of me . . . part of me hoped that . . ." Davis swallowed and shook his head. "I hoped

315

you'd understand, even though I knew better. You couldn't be bothered to call me on my birthday. I shouldn't have hoped you'd accept this."

"How dare you do this to us," his mother sobbed. "Your father and I have done everything for you! We've given you everything—"

"If you can't give me your love without conditions, does anything else matter? So I guess I'll say thank you for the opportunities you gave me. If you ever want to talk, I'll always be here. Until then, you should leave."

I turned his father for the door, steering him by his pinned elbows. "Let me show you the way out, sir."

Wilder and I nodded at each other, and he followed me outside and toward the barn, Davis's mom still shrieking Andrew's name. When we made it out, I let him go with a little push that almost knocked him over.

Whoops.

"Now, you're gonna go ahead and get in your fancy car and get the fuck outta here, all right?"

He started to come at me, and Wilder stepped up.

"You really want to think long and hard about going back in there. Because you won't just have Hank to deal with. You'll have the two of us, too."

Andrew's face was beet red as he tugged the bottom of his jacket. "Let's go, Sheila."

She sniffled, trotting after him, still saying his name all watery and sad.

"Man, what the fuck," Wilder said as we watched them walk to the parking lot.

"No idea. Come on—we'd better get back in there. Didn't know I'd be playing bouncer today, did you?"

He looked pensive, hands in his pockets. "I hoped not, at least."

Before I had a chance to ask what the hell that meant, we were back inside. Davis was tending to Henry. Cass was watching them from the doorway, but turned in a whoosh of skirts and disappeared into the suite. Jessa and Jenny followed, and I picked up my pace, walking in behind them and closing the door behind me.

Cass sank into a chair and reached blindly for the bottle of whiskey. Her face was all puffy and red, and she couldn't breathe through her nose.

Aunt Jenny knelt in front of Cass, smoothing her hair. "What do you want to do, baby?"

"I wanna go home." She sounded like a little girl.

"Okay. We can do that."

Jessa moved for her bags. "I'll come with you."

"No," Cass said.

Jessa's brows clicked together. "Are you sure? We can talk."

"I'm sure. I love you. I don't wanna talk—I just want my mama."

Jessa swallowed back tears and nodded, helping Jenny get Cass up and free of the chair.

"I'll take care of everything—we'll drop off your things later," Jessa said. "Okay?"

Cass nodded, shuffling toward the door. I walked over to Jenny.

"What can I do?"

She offered a sad smile. "I'll text you. For now, just help Jessa get everything together here. I've got her."

"Okay. Let me at least escort y'all out. Who knows what the f—*heck* is gonna get in the way next."

The good news was that nothing else got in the way. When we passed Davis, he made a move like he was going to try and talk to Cass, but I shot him a warning glance and shook my head.

Once they were pulling out of the parking lot, I headed back inside, finding the place almost empty. Henry and Davis were off to God knows where. Cass's honeymoon, maybe.

317

I decided to keep the suspicion to myself indefinitely.

My headache from this morning was back, or maybe it was a new one. All I knew was that I was ready to be done with this and home where it was quiet and no one was bleeding.

The cousins, Jessa, and I cleaned up the bridal suite and got all Cass's things together, finally heading out of the cursed room for good.

Only to find Grace waiting for us in the hallway.

The sigh I sighed came all the way from my fucking toes.

Jessa tipped her chin up bravely and approached her mother. "Mother, I'm not going home with you. Now, please don't—"

"I know."

Jessa stared at her. "You know . . . what?"

"That you're not coming home, although I've no idea what I'll tell your father."

Jessa and I wore matching expressions of confusion.

"I don't understand," Jessa said slowly.

"It's quite simple, really. You have found what seems to be a perfect man, his only fallibility is his station. Did he tell you we spoke last night?"

Jessa glanced at me. "No."

"I offered him *carte blanche* to end things. Would you like to know what he said?" When Jessa didn't answer right away, Grace's lips curled into the smallest smile. *"There aren't enough zeros."*

Jessa looked up at me with soft eyes and stepped to put herself in my side. I opened my arm and tucked her in.

"I must admit, I expected a different answer," Grace continued. "I couldn't say the man I once loved would have done the same. I'm not even certain your father would. Remington, you said that she was going to make her own choices now, and I . . . I hope she does. I was never afforded the chance. I assume you'll take immaculate care of her?"

"Yes, ma'am."

"Excellent. Well, darling, I must be off. The jet can leave tonight, and after all of . . . *this*, I'm eager to be home."

"All right," Jessa answered, shocked sheepish.

She glanced at Henry, and a strange expression washed across her face. "Well, they do say never to put all your eggs in one basket. His father is going to be furious."

"You're not going to tell them, are you Mother?"

Grace laughed, a pretty, tinkling sound, waving her hand with a pair of gloves hanging out of her fist.

"Absolutely not. I only hope he'll be happy. It's more than most of us can get."

Her smile was sad, but she didn't hesitate to kiss her daughter on both cheeks and shake my hand before she clipped off toward her car, the feather in her hat bouncing.

Jessa leaned into me. "Well, I never."

"Me neither."

She sighed, smiling up at me. "Now can we go home?"

I leaned in for her lips. "Absofuckinglutely," I said before I kissed her and kept my promise.

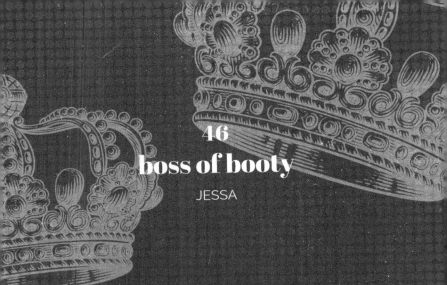

46
boss of booty

JESSA

IT WAS dark by the time we got home.

When we dropped Cass's things off, we hadn't bothered to knock on Cass's door, just left them on the porch and texted Jenny so we didn't disturb them. Then we swung by Sonic for food, since we were starving to death—our tots and patty melts were gone by the time we pulled into the driveway.

My feet ached as I passed the threshold. Beau trotted into the living room—I petted him while Remy closed the door. While I was down there, I unfastened my shoes and stepped out of them with Beau licking my face.

"Ahh," I said when my feet flattened on the cool wood floors. "That's wonderful. It's good to be home."

Remy chuckled, stepping behind me to wind his arms around my waist. I leaned back and sighed, covering his hands with mine.

"Home," he echoed. "I like that."

"As do I. What should we do now?" I asked.

"Fuck?"

"After that. Tomorrow. The next day."

"Fuck." His low laughter sent a little chill through me.

"You know, when I first saw the cottage, I had the strangest desire to—"

"Fuck?"

I pinched his forearm. "Take care of it. Restore it. I enjoyed working on the roof."

"Yeah, I bet you did."

I turned in his arms. "Really, be serious for just a moment."

He nodded and pulled me in tighter.

"We could work on it together, if you'd teach me."

His eyes went soft. "You'd want to do that? You'd want to stay here?"

"Well, provided there's a new sofa in the near future."

"Consider it done."

"We could fix the sagging porch, maybe. A fresh coat of paint? A new roof?"

"So, the little things then."

"Could we do it on our own?" I asked.

"I think we could manage it. Might need to have somebody come in and double check my work, though."

"Perfect. If we're to stay here, might as well fix her up."

He looked down at me for a moment. "We can stay here as long as you want, Duchess."

"Forever is on the table, isn't it?"

The humor in his face slipped into earnestness as he thumbed my cheek. "It is."

"Thank goodness. However could I leave? This is the only place I've ever felt as if I could be unconditionally me. In fact, you've never let me be anyone else. You made sure I spoke for what I wanted and chose for myself. You made me break all the rules, and it taught me something vital."

"And what's that?"

"Who I am. Who I want to be. This is the place it all began. You're the one who struck the first match."

"You mean when I won the bet?"

A laugh bubbled out of me and he smiled. "Oh my God, never. You will probably always beat me, but in that, darling, I won fair and square."

"I know. You're just cute when you're mad. Your nose scrunches up"—he booped my nose—"and your cheeks flush. Your eyes go all fiery, glittery. Reminds me of that day you gave me your panties."

"Must everything be about sex?"

"Not because of sex."

I gave him a look.

"Okay, not *just* because of sex. But because I know you can take care of yourself. It makes me proud. And possessive—not of you, but of . . . of your heart." He swallowed, his brows coming together a millimeter in uncertainty. Had I any armor left, he'd have disarmed me. "Remember when I told you I had it all in my hands once? My fingers were just closing over it all when it slipped away. And that was all right, I decided. If that was the price I had to pay to keep my mama, I'd give it up every time. I'd resigned myself to it. But then you showed up on my doorstep, and suddenly, I almost have it all again, right there in the palm of my hand. And is scares the shit out of me, Jess."

"Well," I started with a twist in my chest, "Despite my love of a good crystal ball, I don't know what will happen. But here's what I hope. What I want. First, I'd like to fall madly in love with you and stay here with you forever." I looped my arms around his neck. "Secondly, I hope when you try out for the baseball team, you make it without question and get picked up for the majors right after."

He laughed and opened his mouth to argue.

"Hold please, I'm not finished. Thank you. Lastly—since we'll be madly in love by then and all—I reckon we'll also be married. Maybe even have a pack of beastly little boys with dirty cheeks and your smile. In conclusion and in summary, I would like to assure you that I will honor and respect you above all. My greatest hope is that gets us to forever."

One corner of his lips rose a touch. "What if I want you to disrespect me a little?"

"As long as it's in the bedroom, I'll allow it." I smiled. He pulled me a little closer. "I don't know what will happen, but my hopes feel like a promise, if that matters."

"It does."

"Perfect," I said, adjusting his lapels. "Wait, I don't want this tidier. I'd like it dirtier. On the floor, if possible.

He chuckled, shrugging out of the jacket and tossing it onto the hardwood. "Better?"

I stepped back and tapped my lips. "Closer. Undo your buttons, darling."

"You know, I didn't think I'd like you bossing me around." I watched his thick fingers loosen his tie and get to work on his buttons, putting half the room between us.

"Oh, it's so rare, do give me this. Lovely. I've been thinking about this tuxedo rumpled on your floor all day, you know."

He tugged his shirt, loosing the tails from his trousers before unbuttoning it all the way to the bottom. "I swear to God, Duchess—I almost took that dress off you the second you walked out of the bathroom in it."

"Pity we were late."

"What now?" he asked, amused and very clearly humoring me. I shuddered to think what he was going to do when he got his hands on me.

"Take it off. Throw it next to your coat."

He pulled his shirt off one shoulder at a time, exposing his glorious chest in halves.

"Mmm, lovely." I hummed, stretching to expose my neck as I hooked one thin strap of my dress and slid it over my bare shoulder.

He watched my hand like a dog eyeing a bone—hungry and hopeful despite the cavalier cock of his jaw.

I let the neckline drop until my breast was exposed. Absently, I traced my collarbone, then my nipple, fondling it absently.

Remy wet his lips, pulling the bottom one into his mouth.

"Unzip your trousers, please."

A moan rumbled in his throat, his hands fumbling with his belt.

"Cock in your fist," I commanded, dropping the other strap of my dress. The silky slip whispered down my body, pooling at my feet.

He rolled both lips, his eyes dragging up and down my body, pumping his cock. For a moment, I watched, mesmerized.

"Yes, that's it, darling."

"I want inside you, Duchess," he said, his voice rough.

"I know, and you will be. But you promised you'd take your time tonight, didn't you?" I rolled the bud of my nipple, bringing it to a hard point.

He groaned. "I'm gonna make you pay for that."

"I hope so. My turn first."

"Are you sure you want to test me?"

I strode toward him as I let my hair down and shook it out with my fingers. "I'll take my chances. It's unfair how hot you are, really. You know what I was thinking about the whole way home?"

"Tell me," he said, stroking his cock slowly.

"How I was going to give you the wettest blow job." I stopped in front of him and dropped to my knees, adjusting his trousers to give myself access before taking his cock from him.

He slipped his fingers into my hair and squeezed, forcing me to look up at him. "Really? Because I was daydreaming about the sight of your lips around my dick."

As I stroked him, I licked the tip of his cock, then opened wide to kiss it, taking his silken crown into my mouth. I pulled off with a pop, cupping his balls, fingering the space behind. "Glad we're on the same page," I said before descending.

His hands fisted my hair, the feral noise he made stoking something hot and desperate in me as I explored the length of him with my tongue and lips, taking as much as I could, the rest in my fist. Saliva gathered around my lips, then slipped down my chin in a river.

He throbbed in my mouth—I moaned, lips closed around him, my eyes fluttering closed.

Remy snapped to get my attention, holding my gaze while he fucked my mouth.

"God I love the sight of you on your knees, Duchess. The feel of your hot fucking mouth around my cock." He grunted, his chin tipping up for a moment.

I snapped at him. He chuckled once, the sound sliding into a moan as he met my eyes again.

"I'm gonna come. Do you feel it?"

I did, his cock swelling, throbbing.

"I'm not coming on you this time like I know you want. No—this time, you're gonna drain every last drop from me." His voice went breathy, his fingers twisting in my hair as he held me still and pumped his hips. I held his eyes, watching him come closer to orgasm in stages. The tightening of his body. The speed of his breath. The way his hands felt against my stinging scalp. The unbearable size of his cock.

When he came, it was with a hiss and a groan, his cock pulsing against my tongue as he unloaded. My mouth was filling up too quickly, and I looked up at him as come dribbled down both sides of my mouth onto my breasts.

He watched, transfixed, panting.

Unexpectedly, he pulled out, bringing with him a spume

of milky come. Before I could close my mouth, he grabbed my face, slipping two fingers into my mouth.

"Good girl." He dipped his fingertips into his seed and toyed with my tongue. "Get up."

As I did, he commanded, "Suck them clean," sending a hot tremble through me. And I swallowed him, everything that was left.

He grabbed my chin, smearing the come with his thumb, trailing it down my neck. He squeezed. "I want to feel how wet you are," he said, tipping my face and slipping his hand between my thighs in the same motion. His hand around my throat squeezed gently. His other hand stroked me with purpose as he backed me into a wall.

He dropped to his knees.

My heart stopped.

His eyes were on my cunt as he played with it, spreading my lips to expose my clit, drawing a deep breath as he latched onto me.

My hips bucked at the contact, my lungs shooting open as he sucked and teased, sliding his shoulder under my one leg, then the other until I was slung over him, my pussy in his face and my shoulder blades against the wall. I looked down my body, dotted with pearly come, as he drew me into his mouth and pulled. Parted his lips and dragged the flat of his tongue up the length of me. The tip found my swollen bud and drew hard circles, fucking it slowly with the purposeful stroke of his tongue. When he broke the connection, it was to watch his fingertips run up and down the length of my hood with my clit in between, squeezing it gently, worshiping it slowly.

My lungs emptied, my head lolling.

"I could get drunk off you," he said, lapping me. "Off your pussy. It's fucking perfect." He latched on again, sucking my cunt into his mouth. I moaned, my hands scrabbling for purchase, finally sliding into his hair where I could hold on.

"Perfect," he whispered once more against my lips, "and *mine*."

He didn't say anything after that, his mouth too busy, his pace relentlessly slow, my orgasm racing toward his tongue.

"I'm going to come," I whispered.

I thought I'd experienced the peak of his skills. This, I was sure was the pinnacle. But on knowing his job was nearly through, he drilled into me with resolution, speeding up, brows together, his lashes dark crescents.

When he moaned, the sound vibrated through my aching clit.

I came painfully in his mouth, my legs twitching and spasming, my ribs contracting, electricity sweeping across my skin as I gasped and moaned and unraveled until there was nothing left of me. I sagged against the wall, unable to catch my breath.

Remy shrugged out from beneath me, catching me with the hook of his arm before my legs gave out. Holding me there, he arched, leaning in to grant me a long, reverent kiss. I licked the salt of my body from his bottom lip before he scooped me up and carried me to bed. When he laid me down, I watched as he kicked off his shoes and dropped his trousers, savoring the reveal of his bare skin. And then he retrieved a folded hand towel from the stack on his dresser before climbing into bed and pulling me into his arms.

He clutched me to his chest, my ear pressed against his skin so I could hear his racing heart. His hands were in my hair, and he leaned back, sliding them to my face. His touch was gentle as he tended to me, wiping my chin, then my chest, cleaning me with adoration. When his job was through, he held me for a protracted moment as if he had something to say, but instead, he kissed me again. It was a kiss of possession, of the ownership one reveled in when surrender is freely given. Of the brand on my heart, of the brand I placed on his.

When the kiss slowed, he sat, pulling me into his lap, guiding my legs around his waist. He held me close, locking his arms around my back, and I held his face, our hips grinding gently as I spent a moment searching his eyes. And then I brought my lips to his.

For a long while, we kissed slowly, sweetly, until he guided me to lean back. Our eyes were on his cock, nestled between my pussy lips, as we rocked, his shaft slick with me. Remy grasped his base, guiding his tip to trace my wet slit, pressing with his thumb to dip it inside me, then use his glossy crown to circle and pat my clit before he'd dip inside again.

Inch by inch, he went deeper, my thighs hooked on his as he crawled to hover over me, his arm under the small of my back to keep my pussy where he could reach it, guiding the tip of his cock into me slow, our gaze locked. He was trembling, our lips almost touching, our breath mingling, his cock seated deep inside of me.

Our mouths brushed, our noses grazing as he pumped his hips slow. The tip of his tongue skimming my lips, then my tongue. He tightened his grip, grabbing me and taking me with him as he sat, my legs around his waist.

It was the perfect position to grind, and he looked up at me as I rolled my hips, his eyes hooded.

"I've never needed anyone before," he said, his fingertips trailing my neck. "I'm glad it's you."

I kissed him, my arms slung over his shoulders as I rode him, his hands roaming my backside. One squeezed while the other reached under my thigh to touch the seam of our bodies until his fingers were slick, then slid those wet fingers back to my puckered hole and pressed.

I cried out, my hips speeding at the rush of contact, his finger knuckle deep inside of me.

"Don't stop until you come, Duchess."

"*Fuck*," I breathed, my pussy flexing. I mewled when his finger curled.

His lips dragged my neck, his tongue trailing "I love the way you feel. I love the sounds you make when I'm inside you. That's right, baby," he said against my skin when I sped up, orgasm slipping over me. "You're so tight, I can feel you come. I want to feel it, Jessa. Come on. That's it." He slapped my backside and I yelped, gasped, my body flexing. But when he closed his lips over my nipple and sucked, that was it.

I came with a cry torn from my throat, a shuddering, panting sound racked with the motion of my wild hips. The wave began to subside, but Remy wasn't through with me, managing to pull out of me and flip me over. He grabbed me by the bend where my thighs met my hips, jacking my arse and pulling me to him.

"Spread your legs, Duchess."

I did, panting.

"Good fucking girl," he growled, pulling me onto his cock. And then he bore into me, fucking me so hard, the bed thumped against the wall. His cock stroked my G-spot, reviving my orgasm.

"*Yes*," he hissed, swelling inside me. "Goddammit—you're so fucking tight, I can't . . . I can't handle it."

I writhed beneath him, the orgasm going on and on.

He groaned, our skin slapping until he buried himself as deep as he could get, held still, then sucked in a noisy breath as his hips pumped. Moaned long and deep until he was empty, still throbbing inside me. Hinged to press his torso to my back, burying his face in my hair. Swept it out of the way so he could get to my neck. Kissed and nuzzled and sucked my skin, his cock still pulsing inside me.

We lay like that for a long while as I tried to find my way back to my body. When he pulled out, he turned me over.

Climbed up me. Kissed me. Then he watched me for a moment, and I watched him.

He brushed a lock of hair from my face.

"I'm glad it's me too," I said, smiling.

"Never thought it'd be a duchess, though."

"I'm not a—"

"Yeah, I know. But you are to me."

"Perhaps I should come up with a name for you too."

"How about Commander of Cunnilingus? Or Sultan of Slapass?"

I giggled.

"No, I've got it."

I waited patiently.

"The Dictator. Get it? *Dick-tator?*"

A laugh shot out of me. "The Dictator and the Duchess? What a pair we make."

"We really do," he said, descending for a kiss.

And we really did.

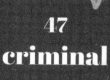

47
criminal

REMY

THE SMILE I smiled when Jessa started singing along to Dolly, paintbrush in hand on the front porch, should have been illegal.

Nobody should be allowed to be this happy.

She had on her overalls, her hair in a loose ponytail with one of my old bandanas tied into a kerchief. Her hands were flecked with black paint as we worked on the trim.

It was September and had finally cooled off after a sweltering summer.

Thankfully, I hadn't needed many clothes. I'd spent all my time wrapped up in Jessa.

Everyone had gone home within a day after The Ordeal, except for Jessa, who'd moved in with me. And Cass, who'd moved in with her mama where she could lick her wounds in peace. She'd even decided to stay, got a job at the elementary school and everything. While Davis and Henry were on her honeymoon—*not* a topic to bring up, and I had the scar to prove it—she flew back and packed up her stuff. Davis had even tried to give her money, like him leaving with Hank deserved some sort of severance package, for fuck's sake.

Either way, she was settled back at home in Roseville and doing okay.

Not great. But she was doing okay.

Jessa and I, on the other hand, were getting on like a house on fire.

The initial deal was for a week, which quickly turned into two. Then it was a month.

We hadn't talked about it since.

I was pretty sure that meant forever.

When I wasn't at work, I was either with Jess, working on the house, or at ball practice. She'd gotten a work visa thanks to a local charity and her connections. Coach had me training like crazy for the Mountaineers tryouts I'd just attended in Sevierville, and now we were in the don't-sleep-until-you-hear-from-us part of the process, which I was pretty sure was giving me an ulcer.

I looked up at the house, humming along with Jessa as she wiggled her ass. We'd done a lot so far—fixed the porch, put on a new roof, installed a new bathroom cabinet and fixtures. The kitchen was on the list, but that was gonna be such a pain in the ass, I kept pushing it to the bottom. Once we painted the rest of the house, I figured we could do the inside and maybe refinish the floors.

Jessa had been bringing home paint and fabric swatches since she decided to stay, outfitting the house with new curtains and rugs. But the couch was first, as promised. Nearly had to wrestle her to let me pay for anything—she insisted it was her way of paying rent. Easy enough since her dad didn't end up cutting her off after all. I guess Grace convinced him to let her go—he was so scandalized by Henry and didn't have a better option for Jessa, so Grace's stamp of approval on me was enough for him.

For that, I was more thankful than just about anything. I didn't know how I'd have handled coming between her and her family, and I was glad never to find out.

My stomach flipped at an unbidden reminder that I was waiting on my fate with the baseball team. Jessa suggested I get in touch with the team's scouts, which turned out to be easier than I imagined—one of them had seen me play in college and remembered me well enough. We got him to come to some of our Ramblers games over the summer, which would hopefully give me an advantage in tryouts. But who knew.

It was anybody's guess.

I'd never been so fucking nervous as I was running drills with a bunch of kids fresh out of college. Never felt so old either. But I kept up with them, which felt like a big deal. And there were only a couple who could hit a ball farther than me.

So things could have gone worse.

It made me feel better seeing Jessa in the stands. My magic feather.

I'd never have done it without her.

I was so glad I did.

I was so happy she was mine.

She turned during Dolly's chorus and pointed her paintbrush at me, still singing. Until she saw my expression.

Her brow quirked, but she was smiling. "What's that look on your face?"

"What look?" I closed the space between us, taking the brush from her.

She didn't fight it, just kept on smiling up at me. "This one." She brushed my nose with her dirty finger.

"I was just thinking about how much I love you."

Her cheeks flushed as she laughed, wrapping her arms around my neck. "Lucky me."

I pulled her closer, savoring the feel of her body against mine. "I'm the lucky one, Jess. Remind me to thank Aunt Julie for the screwup that put you on my doorstep."

"You thanked her at dinner on Sunday."

"Well, remind me to thank her again."

Another giggle.

"I love you," I said again quietly, brushing a lock of hair from her face.

Her face softened. "I love you too."

"I want to keep you forever. Can I?"

She peered up at me sweetly. "I'm yours, darling."

"Good. Because someday soon, I'm going to ask you to marry me, and I'd hate to make a fool of myself."

She laughed again. God, how I loved the sound. "Well, rest assured, when the time comes, I will most certainly say yes."

"Perfect."

She picked at my T-shirt collar. "So, you said soon?"

"But not too soon."

"And I'm to just . . . wait for it?"

"That's usually how it works."

She groaned. "But now I know. It's cruel, really."

"I know. It's gonna drive you nuts."

"Would you at least make sure I'm dressed pretty?"

"What if I asked you in bed? You wouldn't be dressed at all."

"Please don't ask me to marry you when we're naked."

It was my turn to laugh. "All right."

She stared me down for a second. "Promise."

"I promise."

Jessa relaxed in my arms, sighing. "Thank you. Now, kiss me, please."

I cupped her neck, dipping her as I brought my smiling lips to hers. "Yes, ma'am."

I'd never get tired of kissing her, not as long as I lived. For a long moment, I enjoyed that kiss for just what it was, with no expectations. But Jessa deepened it with the widening of her mouth, the sweep of her tongue.

I lost myself in her.

I was in the midst of pawing at her, one of her overall

straps off and the other button in my fingertips when a truck pulled into the clearing and honked.

"Ugh, shit," I huffed, setting her down before looking a little harder at who was honking. "Who the hell is that?"

She gasped, her fingers snapping her strap back on when she said, "Remy, I think that's Bill!"

The scout. My heart jumped into my throat.

I nearly puked it out when he stuck his arm out the window and waved a contract.

Jessa screamed, and I whooped as we flew down the stairs toward Bill's truck.

"Damn, son—don't you ever answer your phone?" He smiled, putting the truck in park.

"Sorry, sir. We were painting and—is that a contract?"

"Sure is," he answered proudly, handing it through the window frame.

I took it reverently with Jessa at my elbow, scanning it to find my name. The team's name. A salary number, however small it was.

It was something.

It was everything.

The paper trembled as my hand shook.

"So what do you say?" Bill asked. "Would you like to play for the Mountaineers?"

"Yes, sir," I answered roughly. "I'd like that very much."

"Then look that over and call me with any questions. Have a lawyer look it over too, you hear?"

"Yessir."

"Good." He tried to stifle a smirk unsuccessfully. "I won't keep you. Looks like you might have some celebrating to do."

"Yes, sir," I said again, reaching through the window frame for his hand. "Thank you, sir."

"Pleasure's mine, Remy. I'm glad Jessamine here convinced you to give us a try."

I smiled down at her. "How about that—me too."

He chuckled, shifting into reverse. "See y'all soon. Welcome to the team!"

"Thank you, sir!" I called after him, and we stood there for a second, watching him drive away.

And then all hell broke loose.

Jessa started screaming and Beau ran out of the house barking and jumping. I hollered, picking Jessa up and throwing her over my shoulder, running around the yard like an idiot, trying not to cry while she laughed and laughed and smacked my back with both hands like a drum.

"You did it!" she said, half laughing and totally out of breath.

I set her feet on the ground, grabbed her by her pretty face, and kissed her with my whole heart. I kissed her from the bottom of my toes to the tip of my nose, poured everything into her in gratitude and joy.

And I had everything I ever wanted, just like that.

epilogue

JESSA

One year later

IT WAS a beautiful day for a ball game.

I sat in the stands with half of Roseville to watch the Mountaineers play in their championship game, the Smoky Mountains all around us and the sun high. Cass sat at my side with her hand in a bag of peanuts and a pile of shells at her feet, stress eating, as the game had been close. Her feet rested next to mine on the backs of the empty seats in front of us.

On my other side were my very uncomfortable parents.

They'd come to town twice now since The Ordeal. The first when I informed them I was staying indefinitely in an attempt to convince me otherwise. It wasn't as bad as it sounded—in fact, they left happily and with respect for Remy, which was as unexpected as it was absolutely perfect. I wasn't at all surprised that he won them over in the end.

It was his specialty, after all.

It had been an age since I'd seen them though, so when Mother had to come to America for business, Father came as well, and they decided to stay a bit and visit. I'd convinced

337

STACI HART

them to come to the game with the promise that it would be thrilling, and it had been.

Father had taken to eating peanuts like Cass, his eyes a bit buggy as the innings wore on. Mother was less interested but had been a good sport. She even ate a hot dog. With an expression of disgust and a fork, but she ate it, and I'd never been prouder. Father had eaten nachos with his hands, which disgusted Mother even more than her hot dog. The sound of her giggle-shrieking when Father threatened to touch her with his gooey cheese hands was something I never imagined I'd hear. But here I was, laughing like a loon as my parents acted like children.

It was brilliant.

The whole day had left me feeling effervescent. I could have floated away.

It came as no surprise. The whole year had been like this, ever since I first saw Remy.

All we'd done was love each other desperately. Of course, he'd played baseball and we'd renovated the house—we'd even decided to buy the old abandoned strawberry farm, though we hadn't sorted out what to do with it yet. But mostly, it was just the loving that we did. It seemed our instincts were right—we were so well suited, I couldn't imagine tiring of him. I couldn't imagine being without him.

The game was nearly over, and we were up by one. One more out would do it. And so we sat on pins and needles, leaning in as the pitcher threw.

Bat hit ball with a crack. We gasped and held our breath as we watched the ball drive up first and . . .

Straight into Remy's glove.

The stadium erupted in noise. I shot out of my seat, jumping and cheering and grabbing Cass. We screamed into each other's faces, pink cheeked and wild. Even Lord and Lady Hastings were jumping around, mother's handbag swinging from her elbow. Father accidentally knocked her

French twist loose, but she didn't even notice, likely because Father dipped her for a kiss.

I grabbed Cass's hand, gaping at my parents, then giggling, then celebrating again, singing along with the crowd to "She'll Be Coming 'Round The Mountain," which I'd learned all five verses to and sometimes sang in my sleep.

The stadium calmed a little as we all sang, do-si-doing in the aisles. The teams made their way back to their dugouts, and when the song was through, the announcer came on.

"Thank you all for coming to the Southern League championship game, and congratulations to the Mountaineers for their win! We'd like to page Lady Jessamine Hastings to the field, please. Lady Jessamine Hastings—please report to the field. Everyone, say hello to our favorite Duchess as she passes."

I blinked, then looked back at everyone. "Me?"

Cass laughed, nudging me toward the field. "Yes, you!"

People waved and said hello as I trotted down the stairs. The team had gotten me a Mountaineers jersey with Remy's number three on it and DUCHESS across the back, and it was how everyone had come to know me. Remy had become something of a celebrity, and by proxy, so had I. So as many of our regulars said hello, I knew them by name, including some of the other wives and girlfriends of the team.

Really, I'd never felt more a part of anything.

When I reached the gate to the field, the security guard opened it up for me.

"Thank you, Dale."

"No problem, Duchess."

"Where am I to go?"

With a crooked smile, he jerked his chin toward the pitcher's mound where Remy stood smiling at me, tossing a ball into the air and catching it.

There wasn't any thought to it—one minute I was

walking, the next I was jogging. He opened his arms, and I jumped into him, meeting him nearly lips first for a kiss.

The crowd whooped and whistled, and I laughed as he put me back on my feet.

"Hello, darling."

"Hey, darlin'."

"And what's all this about?"

"Well . . ." He tossed the ball again and caught it. "First off, I got a call before the game from the scouting director."

I gasped, my hands flying to my mouth. "Oh my God. About Atlanta?"

A smile broke out across his face. "I made it."

I screamed and jumped and launched myself into his arms so I could kiss and kiss and kiss him, and cry a bit too, but mostly kiss him.

"You're amazing," I said against his lips.

He let me have my kiss and set me down. "I couldn't have done it without you. I wouldn't have done it without you. So I wanted to give you the game ball." He took a step back and handed me the ball he'd been tossing. My brows drew together—something was written on it, coming into view as I turned the ball over in my hand.

Written in Remy's square, solid hand were the words: *Will you marry me?*

When I looked up, stunned, he wasn't up. He was down. On one knee. With a little velvet ring box opened and a vintage ring nestled in the cushion.

My hand flew to my mouth, tears pricking my eyes and nose.

"I thought I knew love, Jess, I really did," he started, his voice shaking and eyes shining and hopeful. "But then I met you, and you showed me I didn't know a goddamn thing. Now I can't live without you. Can I have you forever? Will you marry me?"

"I'm already yours," I said, flinging myself at him, my

arms around his neck and my lips crashing into his. He wrapped his arms around me and held me close, stood and spun us around. I realized distantly that the stadium had gone mad. But it was just him and me, standing on the pitcher's mound as he took the ring out of its box.

"It's not worth anything, I don't think—not in dollars and cents. But it was my great-grandmother's, passed down through my mama's family. If you want something fancier—"

"Oh, no—not ever," I breathed as he slid it on. It fit perfectly.

And then he was kissing me again, and my heart was on fire, and I knew I'd never, ever been so happy.

He set me down, still kissing me, and when I broke away, I laughed.

"God, do I love you," I said, holding his face in my hands.

"Hey, same," he said as he so often did.

There was no talking after that. Only love.

So much love.

And there always would be.

epilogue 2

WILDER

I WAS SO FUCKED.

The crowd cheered around me in a hundred and eighty degrees as I stood on the pitcher's mound, turning the ball in my hand behind my back.

In that roaring crowd, sitting next to her best friend, was Cass.

Cass, who I'd been in love with since I was thirteen.

Cass, who'd almost gotten married two months ago.

Cass, who decided to stay here in Roseville to lick her wounds after getting left at the altar.

It'd have been easier if she'd just left.

I wound up. Let out a breath. Threw the ball.

"Strike!"

Tate tossed the ball back, and I turned, adjusting my baseball hat as I reset.

I'd have said it'd be easier if she'd just gotten married, but that would have been the mother of all lies.

Had I been pining after her since she made it to town?

You bet your ass I had.

I'd been pining after her since my very first boner, and

until we left for college—hers in England and mine in California—I'd had her for my own.

Maybe that was my first mistake. Getting a taste for something I couldn't keep.

I shook my head at Tate's pitch signal. Shook my head at the second one. A curt nod to the third, and I threw a knuckle ball that hit Tate's glove with a pop.

"Strike two!"

I snatched the ball out of the air and reset again.

That last summer, we all took a road trip to Vegas—me and Cass, Remy, Tate, my sister Shelby, and a handful of other classmates. We stayed off the strip in some shitty roach motel and got hammered all weekend while we gambled all our money away.

It was one of the best times I'd ever had, and I'd had some good fucking times.

God, I'd been sick over Cass. The thought of leaving her, of her leaving left me gutted. Ruined. There was no reason to tell her, mostly because there was no way to change anything. She was going to *Oxford*, for fuck's sake, and my pro career depended on my college career. Sure, maybe we'd be able to wait four years. Or maybe we'd both be single by the time we had our degrees. But the truth was bleak. So what else were we supposed to do?

Nothing. There wasn't a goddamn thing we could do, and we both knew it.

I straightened up. Wound up. Let her rip.

"Ball!"

With a sniff, I caught the ball again and circled back to the mound.

We'd always thought we'd get married, talked about it all the time, but as senior year went on, we brought it up less and less. But our last night in Vegas, Cass and I passed a little wedding chapel. We stopped and stared at it for a long time, her arms around my waist and mine holding her close.

"We should do it," she'd said, and I laughed. *"Just for tonight—we can annul it in the morning. But ... I love you, Wilder. This way, I could know what it was like, even if it was just for a night."*

I never could tell her no.

So we got married by an Austin Powers impersonator in a room that was wall to wall, hot pink shag carpet and laughed through the whole thing, all the way up until the kiss.

There was nothing funny about that kiss. It was a kiss born from a thousand dreams we'd never have, of hearts that were broken by the knowledge. This was it.

But for one night, she'd be my wife. And at least I'd have that.

That night was easily the best night I'd ever known.

I sucked in a breath and let it out slow. Pitched.

"Ball!"

The next morning, we filled out the paperwork and signed it, laughing and joking like we didn't hate every fucking minute of it. And I took that cursed piece of paper, folded it up, and put it in my bag, promising I'd take care of it.

I swear, I had every intention to.

Thing is, I never did.

I stood straight, eyeing Tate, turning the ball around and around in my hand.

I'd almost objected at Cass's wedding, but Henry beat me to it.

She couldn't marry Davis, even if the whole thing did end up falling apart.

She was already married.

To me.

And she had no idea.

"You're out!"

thank you

Much like Remy, I thought my dreams were lost to me.

Several years of writing through personal trauma broke me. Broke my creative spirit. Broke my heart. And for a long time, I thought that was it. The damage done was irreparable. There was no way back to my dream.

I just had to let it go.

I never thought I'd get it back.

One of the great gifts in my life are the people who love me, and it's because of two of them that this book exists.

I don't think I'd have written another word if not for Kandi Steiner and Kyla (K.A.) Linde.

These two women found a little coal of hope in me and nurtured it with care. They held space for me. They listened. They supported me in a way no one else probably could.

Kandi was the first to spark a flame. She's been generous with her time and her love as she always is, but this time she went above and beyond. She didn't push, didn't pull, just offered her hand and waited for me to take it. And then she brought me into a place I never thought I'd see again.

Kyla has tended that little baby fire with the vigilance of a saint, showing up every day for me, offering her time, her brain, her support and encouragement. That flame would be long dead if she hadn't been feeding it every day, stoking the coals, fanning the flickering flames that, at first, constantly threatened to gutter out.

But thanks to these two incredibly hard working,

dedicated, and loving women, I am writing the end on a book I love desperately. A book that I enjoyed writing more than anything I've ever published. Those two little words have never meant more to me: the end.

I have to thank my husband Jeff as always, but this time, it's for encouraging me to try again without any expectations or desires of his own beyond my happiness. He watched firsthand as I grappled with the loss of my identity, the loss of my career, a kite without a string, whipped away into a storm. All he wanted was for me to find my way back, and that meant everything. Where Kyla and Kandi made space in the world for me, Jeff had the herculean task of making space here in our home, in our lives. I've never been so lucky as was when I found him.

I'd like to thank a few others as well: Nicole McCurdy for the stellar content edit, Emily Hainsworth for the excellent copy edit. Good Girls PR for all the hard work you've done on this release and the support you've provided. And thanks to Devin McCain for the gorgeous interior formatting.

To my early readers—Frances, Allison, Amy, Lisa and Carly (who helped fix my Brit speak), and Chase (my queer sensitivity reader), THANK YOU for all your feedback and hard work!! It's because of you that this book shaped up to be what it is, and I'm forever grateful!

Thank you to every blogger who read, reviewed, shared. I've missed you all so very much.

And to you, dear reader—thank you for waiting for me, for remembering me, or for finding me and reading my words at all. Thank you for letting me into your heart for a few hours. Let's do it again soon.

also by staci hart

CONTEMPORARY STANDALONES

Small Town Romances

Bet The Farm

This lactose intolerant sunshiny city girl inherits a dairy farm with the grumpy farmhand, and neither is ready for the fireworks.

Friends With Benedicts

She's been in love with him since the first time she laid eyes on him. But they have one summer together, and they've got to keep it casual. Except their hearts don't get the memo.

Blum's Bees

For Love Or Honey

When the dark and devilish suit from the oil company comes into their small town looking to acquire the mineral rights to their bee farm, she's certain the only trouble she'll have is how fast to run him out of town. Too bad her heart has a mind of its own.

On The Honey Side

No one can have brooding Keaton Meyer, least of all sunshiney Daisy, but that won't stop her from falling for the the most unavailable bachelor in town.

Run For Your Honey

He left their small town and never came back, until now. And he's running against her for mayor. All she has to do is remember why she hates him so much.

Bright Young Things

Champagne Problems

Everyone wants to know who's throwing the lavish parties, even the police commissioner, and no one knows it's her … not even the reporter who's been sneaking in to the parties and her heart.

The Bennet Brothers:

A spin on Pride & Prejudice

Coming Up Roses

Everyone hates something about their job, and she hates Luke Bennet. Because if she doesn't,

she'll fall in love with him.

Gilded Lily

This pristine wedding planner meets her match in an opposites attract, enemies to lovers comedy.

Mum's the Word

A Bower's not allowed to fall in love with a Bennet, but these forbidden lovers might not have a choice.

The Austens

Wasted Words (Inspired by Emma)

She's just an adorable, matchmaking book nerd who could never have a shot with her gorgeous best friend and roommate.

A Thousand Letters (Inspired by Persuasion)

Fate brings them together after seven years for a second chance they never thought they'd have in this lyrical story about love, loss, and moving on.

Love, Hannah (a spinoff of A Thousand Letters)

A story of finding love when all seems lost and finding home when you're far away from everything you've known.

Love Notes (Inspired by *Sense & Sensibility*)

Annie wants to live while she can, as fully as she can, not knowing how deeply her heart could break.

Pride and Papercuts (Inspired by *Pride and Prejudice*)

She can be civil and still hate Liam Darcy, but if she finds there's more to him than his exterior shows, she might stumble over that line between love and hate and fall right into his arms.

The Red Lipstick Coalition

Piece of Work

Her cocky boss is out to ruin her internship, and maybe her heart, too.

Player

He's just a player, so who better to teach her how to date? All she has to do is not fall in love with him.

Work in Progress

She never thought her first kiss would be on her wedding day. Rule number one: Don't fall in love with her fake husband.

Well Suited

She's convinced love is nothing more than brain chemicals, and her baby daddy's determined to prove her wrong.

Bad Habits

With a Twist (Bad Habits 1)

A ballerina living out her fantasies about her high school crush realizes real love is right in front of her in this slow-burn friends-to-lovers romantic comedy.

Chaser (Bad Habits 2)

He'd trade his entire fortune for a real chance with his best friend's little sister.

Last Call (Bad Habits 3)

All he's ever wanted was a second chance, but she'll resist him at every turn, no matter how much she misses him.

The Tonic Series

Tonic (Book 1)

The reality show she's filming in his tattoo parlor is the last thing he wants, but if he can have her, *he'll be satisfied in this enemies-to-lovers-comedy.*

Bad Penny (Book 2)

She knows she's boy crazy, which is why she follows strict rules, but this hot nerd will do his best to convince her to break every single one.

Game of Gods

Greek mythology meets Gossip Girl in a contemporary paranormal series where love is the ultimate game and Aphrodite never loses.

Game of Gods

Blood of the Beast

Dead of Night

The Hardcore Erotic Serials

Read for FREE!

Hardcore: Complete Collection

A parkour thief gets herself into trouble when she falls for the man who forces her to choose between

right and wrong.

FREE bonus content! Click here!

about the author

I was the kid who stayed inside to read.

As a four-eyed nerd with a bad perm, I was no one's dodgeball pick, but I had a lot of friends. Frodo and Bilbo, for instance. Kristy, Stacey, Claudia and the gang (iykyk). Once, in the third grade, I wrote a teen murder mystery inspired by Christopher Pike. On solving my mystery in twelve pages, I decided I was a terrible writer and should never, ever do that again.

Fortunately, I didn't take my own advice.

I write romance for that feeling you get at the end, like you're standing on top of a mountain with a backpack full of hundred dollar bills. I write romcoms because is there anything better than banter and grand gestures? I write because I love to create and I love words. I love books, and I love stretching my imagination. I love love, and if you do too, bring your coffee and have a seat. I think we're gonna be friends.

www.stacihartnovels.com
staci@stacihartnovels.com